A Place
Between
Breaths

JENNIFER FROELICH

FOR CHRISTY

PROLOGUE

SAMANTHA KNEW she would die today. The thought no longer filled her with fear as it had when she was first taken. That was the first day she believed would be her last, but she had been wrong. She had been wrong for more than a year of days since – days so filled with horror, desperate prayers and aborted attempts at escape, her mind was now numb to the idea of death. She welcomed it even, if she could admit it, except when she thought about what it would mean to her mother.

At that thought, Samantha pushed scraped knuckles against her lips and forced down a hiccup of hysteria, determined to stay sane until the end. She lowered her head and repeated the silent prayer that had passed through her mind so often during the past 24 hours.

Lord, please give Mom peace with my death.

Samantha pushed her matted hair away from her face and stood. The ground tilted and the edges of the world began to blur. Grabbing a branch on the closest oak scrub, she took a deep breath and waited for the horizon to level. Looking east toward the brightening sky, she almost smiled, thinking of how her hair would shine in Heaven, cleaned by the presence of God.

Soon enough.

Samantha turned back to the trail.

Fifty paces farther, she stopped to catch her breath again, marking the spot with a torn piece of her dress. It was difficult work. Her head ached and her throat burned, but that was nothing compared to the pain in her battered hands. She tried not to think about what she had done to free herself from his ropes, but her stomach twisted, threatening revolt as it had two nights ago when he brought them to her cell.

Samantha had cried quietly while he tightened them in the darkness.

"I can't lose you," he said.

That was the night he dragged her into the canyon.

Samantha tried to remember what she saw along the trail in the moonlight – a wider path forking to the left, careful footing over scattered boulders. Two, three, four arroyos and so many switch-backs, she was left breathless and stumbling in his wake. One wrong step would drop her over the cliff toward dark death below.

Pine trees gave way to desert brush and cactus, then bamboo and tropical foliage as they descended. The temperature increased, leaving her damp and filthy by the time they reached the cave. Entering it had been a nightmare. Once they were inside, he lowered her into a pit and chained her to a stake. He left without saying a word.

Shaking in the darkness, she fought for focus, but her mind betrayed her, tilting and fuzzy with terror. Her memory of their route was hopelessly muddled.

But dawn's cool breeze sharpened Samantha's senses this morning. Or perhaps it was freedom. She forced herself forward again, guessing she had traveled at least eight miles since her escape last night, heading northeast from the cave and up toward the rim. Many trails had tempted her during the last hour, causing her heart to skip a beat as she searched feverishly for signs that this one would widen and lead to civilization. But they had all been coyote trails – narrow, unkempt, or – worse – dropping away to crumbling oblivion. She couldn't take such chances. Death she accepted. The possibility of winding back into the canyon and toward him, she could not.

Samantha had been planning her escape for months, mostly at night when the walls of the shack swayed in the wind, making her wonder if death would come not by the hands of her captor, but with a violent gust and a shard of weathered wood. Her best chance for flight should have been during one of his long absences, when only his shadow was left to tend to her food stocks and basic needs, as if she were a neglected pet.

But months passed. Indecision joined her enemy and her chances grew slimmer. Her body, once a source of pride, became an obstacle as her muscles weakened from inactivity. Still she plotted, waiting for the perfect moment.

It didn't come. Instead, she was forced to act against her best ideas. He set her timetables always. Even her escape.

"Why are we here?" she asked when they had reached the cave.

His pause was almost imperceptible, but his sideways glance doused her uncertainty. She could smell his anticipation – an instinct humans only develop when death has become their friend.

Samantha couldn't wait any longer. She escaped during the blackest part of night and was now entering her fifth hour of sweet freedom. Without food or water in almost two days, she fostered no illusions of reaching civilization in time to live. But it would not, at least, be the death he had chosen for her.

A pale smile touched her lips as she marked another spot and pushed forward, thinking about her theft – a furious impulse she acted on while leaving the cave. But would he notice? She imagined him returning to find her gone. Surely he would be too angry to see that one of his precious trophies was missing.

It wasn't the only clue she carried on her small body, but she prayed it was the most significant. Samantha had once longed for more than escape – a return to student life and her athletic scholarship. A career, her own family someday. Night after night, her mind had tumbled – grasping, praying, bargaining. But her thoughts had grown random and shallow since she abandoned her future. Bleak determination reigned now.

"Each of us serves a purpose in life," Samantha's mother once told her, brushing away her tears, "until his last day – his dying breath."

She had been talking about Samantha's grandfather – a gentle man who no longer recognized his family, his mind given over to dementia.

"This is his final job, darling. Teaching us to love better, to care more deeply."

Samantha had not understood. She did now. She thought about her dying purpose as she pushed up and around another jealous cliff. Dawn was still taking its first breath, but hers were numbered. Her throat was beginning to contract – her tongue was swelling and her vision clouded.

She stumbled and veered toward the edge, creating an avalanche of rocks as she bounced off bushes that pulled at her skirt and grated her legs. Pain shot through her hands as she steadied herself against a boulder. Her stomach recoiled and she threw up – nothing but bile. It was all she had left. She wiped her mouth and pressed on, grasping at anything she could hold, pulling herself upward, inch by inch. Her heart contracted as she finally crested the cliff and focused on the cleared trail in front of her.

She had found it, a path she remembered!

Samantha rested for only a moment before continuing her ascent. After marking her last branch, she turned to watch the sun crest the horizon. It was the first sunrise she had seen all year – the last she would ever see. Now even tilting her head brought reeling vertigo. She dropped to the ground and closed her eyes.

Not yet. I need to be stronger. I need to go farther.

She pushed her doubts aside. It didn't matter. She'd done enough. She was in God's hands now.

Samantha crawled toward the largest bush she could find. It would shade her from the sun. Surely death wouldn't wait much longer.

She closed her eyes and began to pray. A tear spilled down her cheek, but quickly dried. She prayed for her mother, that her mourning would not last long. She wished she could see her once more and tell her how much she loved her, to thank her for all the sacrifices she had made.

Her mind began to drift then, to the past, when her father was still alive. A lurching sob escaped at the thought of seeing him again – so much sooner than he would expect. But Samantha's last prayer was for the people who would discover her clues.

Let them catch him soon, she prayed.

Then she closed her eyes and fell asleep for the last time.

1

"CAN YOU TELL me about your last conversation with Samantha?"

Maureen Davidson drew a broken breath. When she spoke, her voice was damp against the microphone. "She called me on Friday night."

"Friday, May twelfth?" Agent Hughes asked.

"Yes, just last Friday." Her shoes scraped against the linoleum. "I always had Samantha call me on Friday evenings. Before she went out with her friends, just to check in. It felt good to know she would call. Better than calling her, and hearing the phone ring and wondering ..."

"So she called you on the twelfth?" Hughes prodded.

"Yes, she sounded happy. She'd passed an exam – algebra, I think. Not her favorite subject and she was glad it was over. I could hear Angela laughing in the background."

"Angela Rowland?"

"Yes, that's right. Her roommate. From Winslow, or somewhere up near the reservation."

"Yes, we've talked to Angela."

"Nice girl."

"Did Samantha mention anyone else? Someone whose name isn't on this list?" Hughes pushed a piece of paper across the table. Mrs. Davidson sniffed and the paper crackled in her hands.

"No. I've looked at this list before. Everyone I know of is on here – everyone who knew her. Angela would know better if she had other friends, someone new in her life. Girls don't tell their mothers everything, do they?"

For five seconds, the microphone picked up nothing but her breathing. "I worried about her going away to college," she finally said. "Then she called me after her first week. 'I met some new friends at church,' she told me. Church. She went to church without me telling her to."

"Mrs. Davidson—"

"But you know, she was always a good girl, even when she was little," she went on. "One year, she was Little Bo Peep for Halloween, and I spent hours sewing row after row of lace onto her dress and bloomers. Her father made her a long staff out of PVC pipe or something. It was his last year with us—"

"Mrs. Davidson—"

"She had the sweetest way of sleeping as a child, with the covers pulled tight around her ears. 'Monsters, Mommy,' she'd say. So I sprayed air freshener on the foot of her bed and told her it would keep them away." Her voice suddenly pitched, tightening. "She believed me. She trusted me."

Deep, shuddering hiccups blasted against the microphone.

"We are doing everything we can to find her, ma'am." Hughes's voice was gentle, meant to calm.

"No!" Her chair scraped back across the linoleum, tipping over with an ear-splitting crash. "No, that's not good enough. None of this is good enough. We need to do more. She's been missing for five days. Five days! She needs to be home now. Home with me!"

"Mrs. Davidson, please—"

SPECIAL AGENT Rachel Mueller paused the MP3 player in her lap and yanked out her ear buds. The recording of Mrs. Davidson's interview went on for another five minutes, but she couldn't listen to any more.

Pressing her fingertip to the bridge of her nose, Rachel stared out the window and waited for the knot in her throat to dissolve. Her plane would pass over Arizona's southern border soon. Somewhere below her, Agent Hughes had already arrived in Sierra Vista to give Mrs. Davidson the news – a body matching the description of her missing daughter was found early that morning near a Copper Canyon hiking trail in Chihuahua, Mexico.

Rachel had gotten to know Maureen Davidson well over the past year. She was a resilient woman, who had learned to shelve her fears and mount a campaign to keep her daughter's case viable. Rachel looked out the window again and wondered how she was taking it.

Hughes knows her well too, she reminded herself. *And he's good at handling grief.*

No, their supervisor had made the right decision – splitting them up to accomplish more in less time. But Rachel shouldn't have listened to the recording. Not so soon after hearing the news, not when she was traveling away from her own son.

What would I do if anything ever happened to Danny?

Don't go there, she told herself.

Compartmentalize, they taught at the academy. It's half the job.

Rachel pulled out a legal pad and added two more bullet points to her growing list —

1. *Follow up – Samantha in newspaper after competition.* Republic – Tribune – Herald? *Date? Fan mail?*

2. *Revisit Samantha's church in Tempe. Friends? Group activities?*

Rachel recapped her pen. She doubted it would garner anything new, but she would still reexamine every lead since Samantha's disappearance from an off-campus concert venue last year.

She remembered clearly the day she had interviewed Angela Rowe at Manzanita Hall – the same dorm Rachel had lived in during her freshman year at Arizona State. It was the week before finals and the dorm was unusually quiet while its residents studied for exams, trying not to think about their missing classmate or the TV news trucks blocking traffic on University Drive.

"Samantha would never stay out overnight – and definitely not without telling me." Angela twisted long brown hair around her fingertips. A psychology textbook looking too new for a semester's worth of use lay in her lap. "She's super disciplined. You know, her studies, her training."

She blinked, her eyes brimming. "I was glad she went to the concert. I thought it would be good for her, you know?"

"Any new boyfriends? Secret admirers?"

"No."

"How about unwanted advances?"

Angela shrugged. "A few guys who asked and she said no. I can give you some names, but I think they were pretty harmless."

Angela had been right. Not a single lead panned out in the hours, days and weeks following Samantha's disappearance. Flyers featuring Samantha's face faded, making her all but invisible. After relentless coverage on *FOX News*, *CNN* and every local station for months, concern about Samantha tapered off. Even Nancy Grace moved on.

Rachel and Hughes worked alongside local law enforcement for months – canvassing neighborhoods, creating profiles, interviewing friends – following every credible lead, hoping for a break. But there was always so much improbability to weed out. How many hours had they spent interviewing one lonely citizen after another with nothing more than a television and an active imagination? Finding victims alive like Elizabeth Smart was encouraging, but rare. It was most likely that Samantha Davidson had been killed within 24 hours of her disappearance, and they knew it.

But we were all wrong, Rachel thought.

Samantha had stayed alive for more than a year, living under who-knew-what-kind of conditions before dying early this morning, just a few miles from a secluded Copper Canyon hotel.

So how did she get there?

"As luck would have it, an American hiker found the body," Special Agent in Charge Sandra Devlin explained when she briefed the team at the Phoenix field office. "She called the local authorities, the U.S. Embassy and the FBI. Chihuahuan police called in their federal authorities. At the State Department's request, they have invited us to participate in a joint investigation."

A wave of low grumbling crossed the conference room. Rachel stood by the door and could only make out one comment that included a particularly foul word and the phrase, "…always make our job twice as hard."

Working with Mexican authorities could be tricky – every FBI agent knew that. An immutable reputation for rampant corruption had not been overcome by continual restructuring, which a decade earlier had resulted in the formation of *la Agencia Federal de Investigación*, ostensibly modeled on the FBI. But then the AFI's chief was assassinated. A few months later, his second in command was arrested for receiving bribes from the Sinaloa Cartel.

Rachel had heard varying figures about corruption, but modest estimates reported as many as one-fifth of agents in the field were under investigation – many of them suspected of working as enforcers for the cartels. Just a few years ago, the agency had been torn apart and restructured once again. Most American agents believed the newest incarnation – *la Policía Federal Ministerial* – was doomed to decay, just like all its predecessors.

SAC Devlin cleared her throat, quieting the room. "They have sealed off the crime scene and the body has been taken to the closest medical facility. A preliminary examination estimates time of death within the last 24 hours."

She turned to Rachel. "Agent Mueller, you will fly to Chihuahua to partner with PFM investigators, study the crime scene and recover the body. Agent Hughes, you'll direct investigations here at home."

Hughes wasn't happy about staying behind, but Devlin told them the Mexican attorney general had made his invitation clear.

"Only one of you can go. I was able to negotiate the additional assistance of our attaché to the embassy in Mexico City, which we regard as a concession." She eyed Rachel meaningfully. "I want you to have an ally who is already familiar with the ins and outs of the system. His name is Agent Kirk Trent and he'll meet you on site."

"Yes, ma'am."

Rachel reached for her assignment packet, suppressing a groan. It had to be Trent, didn't it? When Rachel worked with him at the FBI field office in Austin, he had been a cocky, morally-challenged weasel, but with a flight to catch in fewer than two hours, she didn't have time to wonder if life and circumstance had changed him.

She shouldered her laptop bag and headed toward the parking garage, dialing Craig as she walked. Catching him on his way to court, she explained her sudden travel plans.

Rachel considered it a stroke of good timing that their son was on spring break this week and visiting her sister in Cottonwood. Craig, however, never responded well to changed plans.

"I'm supposed to have Danny on Saturday. Do you expect me to drive up there and get him?"

"No, I don't." She took a deep breath. The divorce was new. Working with each other's schedules was going to take patience. "I just thought you should know I'll be out of the country for a few days. I plan to be back by the weekend, but if I'm not, Melissa will be happy to keep him for an extra day or two."

"Nice of you to cut into my time with Danny, Rach."

"You have my number if you need me." Rachel cut off the connection.

Same old Craig. He could turn any wrinkle into a burden and then play both sides. But why did she still let it bother her?

"Promise me something, Rachel," her sister said before saying goodbye on Sunday. "Pamper yourself a little this week. Get a pedicure, go shopping. Danny is going to be fine."

Melissa was right about Danny, even if Rachel wouldn't have time to follow her advice. He seemed happier within minutes of reaching Cottonwood. Melissa and her husband had a three-acre farm with horses, an old barn to explore, a tree house and easy access to a creek. Rachel's eyes stung when she saw the familiar look of worry disappear from Danny's face as he kissed her goodbye and ran off with his cousins. During her drive back to Phoenix, she had revisited every decision she had made since learning about Craig's affair. By the time she pulled into her driveway, her heart felt like crumpled paper.

But what else could she have done?

Rachel shifted toward the airplane window, wishing she had taken off her jacket. The flight was full and she was warm despite the direct blast of air from her overhead vent. Lately, she didn't feel comfortable anywhere – not even in her own skin. She couldn't remember the last time she'd looked in a mirror and felt good about the reflection staring back.

The captain's voice over the loudspeaker interrupted Rachel's dismal thoughts. They were passing over the border now. It would be another hour before they landed in Chihuahua, a city Rachel had never visited. She had only been to Mexico once, but that was a memory best left for another day. Today had enough sorrow of its own.

C8

"*VAMOS a aterrizar en 20 minutos.*"

Agent Johnny Cruces's voice crackled in Rachel's headset, telling her that Creel was only twenty minutes away. She nodded and turned her attention back to the scenery below. Their helicopter was passing over the plains that surrounded the city of Chihuahua and heading west toward the Sierra Tarahumara.

Agent Cruces had been waiting for her on the tarmac at Chihuahua International Airport. He wasted no time, ushering her through customs before they boarded a helicopter bound for Creel, a town he described as the gateway to the Copper Canyon.

Tall and slope shouldered, Cruces was deliberate in response to her questions and struck Rachel as deceptively sharp. While they were fastening their seatbelts and donning headphones, he briefly described the Copper Canyon, telling her that it was a series of six canyons rather than one, more than a mile deep in places and altogether larger than the Grand Canyon.

"I thought the Grand Canyon was the largest canyon in the world," Rachel said.

"It is bigger than any *one* of the six canyons in this system and the topography is quite different," Cruces said. "The Copper Canyon in whole, however, is about the size of Colorado."

"Wow. I had no idea."

Cruces nodded.

A few minutes later, the plains gave way to green meadows skirted by large rock formations and rolling hills dotted with pine trees.

When Creel came into view, Cruces pointed to a white statue of Jesus that stood on a hill overlooking the town. They landed near a hangar with *Viajes de la Barranca/Canyon Tours* painted in red letters on the roof.

Rachel pulled off her headset and unbuckled her seatbelt. "Can we visit the crime scene first?"

"It's a two-hour hike from the trail head," Cruces said. "We can't get there and back before sunset and the topography makes it impossible to reach by helicopter. But not to worry. We've stationed a guard overnight."

Rachel didn't want chopper winds anywhere near the crime scene. She nodded. "I understand."

"Agent Suarez is the lead investigator on this case," Agent Cruces said as they exited the helicopter. He pointed to a dark car parked by the hangar. "He will take us to the hospital."

"And Agent Trent?"

"*Sí.*" Cruces paused. "He is here as well."

One of the men getting out of the car was shorter than the other and wearing a gray suit with cowboy boots. He walked toward her with his hand outstretched.

"Agent Mueller. Long time, no see."

"Agent Trent." Rachel shook his hand, taking in his trimmed beard and neat auburn hair. He looked just as she remembered him. "I learned today that you were working down here."

"Two years now." He continued to smile and nod, squinting into the sun. "Your flight was good?"

"Fine," she answered. They walked toward the open car trunk where Trent stowed her bag and closed the lid before turning to the other agent.

"Agent Mueller, this is Agent Suarez," he said.

In a dark suit and darker sunglasses, Suarez looked like a typical GI man, but as he stepped around the car, Rachel faltered, finding his movements familiar. She stood fixed in place, her hand dangling in midair as Suarez lowered his sunglasses and studied her.

It's Marius Bazán, she thought. *But it can't be.*

When she finally found her voice, it sounded far away, part of the past where this man belonged. "Agent *Suarez*?"

Something that looked like disappointment darted across his features before he rearranged them into a cool smile. "Agent Mueller." He reached to shake her hand. "Welcome to Mexico."

2

THE RIDE TO the medical clinic was brief – a blur of small town scenery that Rachel was too stunned to notice. Agent Cruces talked about Creel's population and elevation, he pointed to the train station for *El Chepe* – the *Chihuahua al Pacifico Railroad* – and said tourism had overtaken logging as the town's top industry, but Rachel wasn't listening.

More than fifteen years had passed since Marius told her goodbye on an August afternoon in Arizona. It was monsoon season and they were standing under an awning on Mill Avenue in Tempe when rain tore through the clouds and began striking the hot sidewalks like grease on a skillet. It was loud enough to drown out much of the venom she spat at him – a torrent of pain that made the storm seem mild in comparison. She remembered little of what she said now. The things she could recall made her cheeks flush. He hadn't argued or defended himself. He hadn't fought for her. He just kissed her goodbye and walked away, leaving her trembling and broken.

Sitting next to him now in the backseat of a Mexican police car on a mild spring day made her feel like Alice down the rabbit hole. With Samantha – and even Danny and Craig –occupying her thoughts all day, the last person she ever dreamed of seeing again was now inches away. Countless questions flooded her mind, but an uncomfortable sense of the physical kept her from entertaining them. She tried not to look at him – or away from him. Since she couldn't sit still but hated the implication of fidgeting, she was resigned to a stiff position where tension fought numbness. Meanwhile, Marius adjusted his watchband, looking bored.

It didn't take more than a casual glance to assess the changes that fifteen years had made in Marius Bazán – Suarez (whatever his name was) – as well as those things that hadn't altered at all. He was tall, with black hair that had a tendency to curl and was too long by her father's standards. It was still long, she noticed, turning under his ears in soft curls. His eyes were as dark as chocolate, his nose a little too sharp, his jaw angular and shaved clean. His shoulders had broadened over the years and sparse flecks of gray at his temple and crinkles around his eyes were evidence of his age. Was he forty-one now?

When they first made eye contact at the heliport, something deep within his expression had looked both hard and human, making him seem older still. Rachel was the first to turn away.

"What happened to Bazán?"

The question came out of her mouth before she could check it, though quietly enough that Trent and Cruces had not heard her from the front seat. Marius turned away from the window and looked at her, his expression unreadable.

"Bazán is my mother's name," he finally said. He turned back to the window. "That, at least, was not a lie."

His words stung. Rachel swallowed and pressed her hands against her knees. She wished she had bitten her tongue.

Rachel had first met Marius as a freshman enrolled in his Spanish 101 class at Arizona State. A graduate student teacher, he had introduced himself to the class by explaining that his father wanted to name him Mario, after his grandfather. His mother, being half French and an ardent fan of Victor Hugo, chose to name him Marius instead.

"That was her idea of a compromise," he said.

The class had greeted this information with boredom, except for Rachel, whose hand shot up and back down again. By then, it was too late to check her impulse.

"You have a question, Miss…?"

"Bishop," she said, reddening. "I just wondered … was your grandfather upset?"

He frowned and shifted on the edge of his desk.

"It's just that Victor Hugo tried to stay the execution of Emperor Maximillian," she stammered. "He wrote to Benito Juarez. Some people thought he was interfering with Mexican independence."

Marius was silent, but his lips twitched. "A history major, Miss Bishop?" he finally asked.

"Yes."

"And what curriculum have you studied that gives you such an unaccountable knowledge of Mexican history?"

"Um. It's just something I read." She studied the top of her desk. "Not for school – just … from the library."

"Well, my grandfather may have been displeased, but I don't know." He walked around his desk, but not before Rachel saw his mouth tighten as if he had tasted something bitter. "My mother and I moved back to Spain when I was young. I never knew him."

After that, Rachel vowed to keep her mouth shut. It was a promise she didn't keep that semester. She clearly still hadn't mastered that lesson.

But why did it matter what this man said or thought so many years ago? She was here for a job, not a reunion. And it was only for a few days. She would treat him as a colleague and nothing more. She didn't know him. It seemed now that she never had.

Rachel reached into her bag and pulled out Samantha's file. She skimmed the information, though she knew it by heart. After a moment, Marius cleared his throat.

"Can you tell me what you have on this case?"

"Of course."

Rachel thumbed back to the front of the file and handed it to him, hoping he didn't notice that her hand shook.

"Samantha Davidson was reported missing from her dorm room at ASU on the thirteenth of May, last year. It was a Saturday."

"Manzanita," he murmured quietly. Rachel nodded, remembering the first night Marius had walked her to her dorm and waited until she was safely inside before turning to walk away.

"She was last seen at a concert venue on Apache. No altercations there or unhealthy relationships that we know of. She was on athletic scholarship – a gymnast and a good student. A standard missing persons report was filed with the police. There was no evidence of foul play. Only Samantha's purse and the clothes she was wearing were missing. Two days later, her jacket was found at a rest stop on I-10, about an hour east of Tucson. Trace amounts of blood were on it. That's when we got involved.

"A serial killer was at large in New Mexico at the time. We thought maybe she was one of his victims. Agents in Las Cruces ended up catching him three months later. He had a solid alibi, albeit one linking him with another crime. After that, the trail went cold."

"The blood?"

"DNA tests proved it was Samantha's."

Marius's jaw tightened as he turned to Samantha's photo. He studied it briefly before handing the file back to Rachel.

"I'm afraid you've found her," he said quietly. Minutes later, they pulled to a stop in front of the clinic.

೫

THE NONDESCRIPT medical clinic was nearly hidden behind two large oak trees and a Spanish-style church that faced the town plaza. The stucco façade was cracked, but freshly painted and fitted with modern glass doors. Without comment, the four agents walked into the building and down a short corridor painted a familiar shade of institutional green.

"Dr. Gutierrez," Agent Cruces called as a bald man with a thin mustache stepped through a doorway at the end of the hall. The doctor walked toward them and shook hands.

"Dr. Gutierrez is our medical examiner from Chihuahua," Cruces said. "These are agents Mueller and Trent with the FBI."

The doctor led them into an exam room where a draped body lay on a table. Rachel took a quick breath as the doctor pulled it back. This part of the job was never easy.

She stepped forward to look closely at the pale, scratched face. "This is Samantha," she said quietly. Despite the evidence of trauma, she looked peaceful, making Rachel wonder again what she had endured this past year. A wordless prayer passed through her thoughts.

"Have you estimated a time of death?"

"*Temprano ayer, por la mañana*," the doctor said.

"Yesterday morning," Rachel repeated. "But she was found today? Right on a trail?"

"Close to it," Agent Cruces said. "Mrs. Harcourt first noticed a torn piece of pink fabric tied to a bush. She found the victim perhaps five or six meters below. It looked like she had fallen. Thinking she might still be alive, she climbed down to reach her. She recognized her right away, she said, having followed American television coverage of her disappearance."

"Ms. Harcourt is still at her hotel?" Rachel asked.

"Yes. She's been most anxious to speak to the FBI," Marius said.

Agent Trent cleared his throat. "I have an official request from the U.S. State Department, asking that the body be returned to Arizona for a complete examination and autopsy."

"Will that pose any problems for your investigation?" Rachel asked Cruces.

"No. Nothing I foresee."

"We trust that all reports and findings of the American pathologists will be promptly shared with our team?" asked Marius.

"I'll make sure of it," Rachel said. "For now, perhaps Dr. Gutierrez can give us a preliminary report?"

"She died of dehydration," he said. "The post-mortem fractures on her collarbone are consistent with the fall she took from the trail. One bite mark too, from a tiger scorpion."

He walked around the body and gently lifted one of her wrists, revealing purple bruises. "She was tied up for long intervals – for many months. The marks are deep and repetitive."

"Signs of a struggle?"

He winced. "Yes, against restraints. Scraping marks and broken bones in her hands tell us she probably pulled herself free. It would have been excruciating. But there's no skin under the nails, no defensive marks to indicate a violent attack at the time of death."

"She looks malnourished," Rachel said. "And her loss of muscle tone could indicate a confined environment, right?"

"*Sí*. Something else," the doctor said. "Her body is covered in sand and debris not consistent with a tumble down the cliff. A cursory examination indicates that the same were deposited in her pockets and undergarments, along with some broken eggshells."

"Our guess is that she did it intentionally," Marius said.

Dr. Gutierrez handed Rachel an evidence bag containing several eggshell fragments and a small vial of rocks, which she held up to the light. "Are these from the canyon area?"

"We should be able to have them analyzed without delay," Cruces said. "The canyon's climate and geology are different from the rim to the floor. That means different plant and wildlife too. It might help us, it might not."

"This trinket was discovered tied to her wrist," Marius said. He held up another bag containing a silver medallion. Rachel leaned in for a closer look.

"Do you think it's large enough to lift a print?" she asked.

"We'll find out."

"We're also analyzing the fibers of her clothing," Agent Cruces said. "It looks like she was recently in water."

"There are rivers and ponds in the canyons?" Rachel assumed. "Something she may have passed through during an escape?"

"We hope so, yes."

Rachel moved to the other side of the table, noticing that the sheet was starting to slip from Samantha's broken collarbone.

"Smart girl." She replaced the sheet and took a deep breath. "She's trying to tell us where she's been. Who did this to her."

Rachel looked up to find Marius watching her closely.

"*¿Estás bien?*" he asked quietly.

"I'm fine. It's just a headache."

Her cell phone rang. It would be Melissa. "Excuse me." She walked toward the door, glad for a reason to leave the exam room. "I'll take this in the hall."

"Hello?"

"Mom?"

"Hi, Danny." Comfort flooded over Rachel at the sound of her son's voice. "How's everything going?"

"Good." There was a long pause and Rachel smiled, waiting. Danny didn't like talking on the phone.

"Are you having a good time?" she finally prodded.

"Yeah." Another long pause. "Mom?"

"Yes, Danny?"

"Are you in Mexico?"

"Yes, I am."

"When will you be home?"

"In a couple of days, I hope. I'm still planning on picking you up on Saturday, okay? Are you and Grandpa going to Oak Creek Canyon tomorrow?"

"I think so, but I wish you were here now."

"I know, sweetheart. Me too." He sounded homesick. Rachel swallowed past a familiar knot. "What else have you been doing?"

"Nathan got a *Wii U* for his birthday – did you know that?"

"That's what I heard. Are you having fun with it?"

"Yeah." His voice brightened. "He has a new Mario game and I got through two levels already."

"That's impressive." Rachel heard the door rattling behind her. "I need to get back to work, Danny, okay?"

"Okay, Mom. I miss you."

"I miss you too. Be good for Aunt Melissa."

"I will."

"Love you."

"Love you too, Mom."

Rachel slipped her phone into her pocket and turned to find the men coming out of the exam room. Marius was watching her again, making her wonder how green she looked. She didn't like being examined – especially by him. Forcing her attention toward Agent Cruces, Rachel asked when Samantha's body would be released for transport.

"Tomorrow afternoon or early Wednesday," he said.

Was it too much to hope her part of the investigation would be done by then?

She shouldn't think that way, but her flight instinct was pushing full tilt at the moment. Still, she knew her job had little to do with a calendar or clock. Marius's presence didn't change that. As they returned to the car and headed toward the hotel, Rachel forced her thoughts away from everything but the task at hand. Finding Samantha's killer was her priority. Her suspicions pointed toward someone who was not content with one victim. If she was right, it was only a matter of time before he chose his next target.

3

"HEY STRANGER, welcome back."

The receptionist was smiling at him. Caroline? Catherine? Her name escaped him, but he played along, redirecting his footsteps from the elevators and twisting his mouth into an expression that was sure to please. She rewarded him with a wider smile.

It was late afternoon and the lobby was spotless. Even bathed in sunlight, the floors gleamed, the windows shone. In America, everything looked clean. It surprised him whenever he returned.

He leaned on the marble desk between them. "Hi yourself."

The woman scooted toward the edge of her chair, causing the hem of her skirt to climb up her legs. She tugged it down, giggling and offering him a generous view of her cleavage.

Constance! He knew it would come to him.

"You're looking good, Constance." He bit his lip, overplaying it. She didn't notice. "How have you been?"

"Upset with you." She tried to pout, but failed to commit her eyes to the act. Few women were good actors, he had learned.

"Why?"

"You promised to meet me for drinks at Sam's sometime. Then you disappeared again."

Play the game, he told himself. Still, he felt out of practice.

"You were serious about that?" He wrinkled his brow. "I thought you were just ..."

"What?"

He shrugged. "Being nice, I guess. Why would a pretty girl like you be interested in an old guy like me?"

"You're not old!"

"Well then." He leaned closer and brushed her hand with his fingertips. "I'm going to be in town for a while. How about we get together for drinks this weekend? We can do something afterward. Dinner. Whatever."

"Okay," she breathed. All pretense of anger evaporated.

"Good. It's all settled then." He cut his eyes toward the elevators. "Now I have to get upstairs for a meeting with the big guy. You know how he is."

He winked and walked away. Constance was already forgotten, his mind refocused on the problem that had consumed him for the past 48 hours.

Samantha got away.

It was the refrain of his heartbeat, his breath in and out, intensifying the fury he felt when he first discovered that she was gone. He had spent all day searching for her, his blood simmering and he plotted a painful death for her along the trail. Her body would rot out in the open – a fitting punishment for spoiling his plans.

But when night came and he still hadn't found her, his anger turned to panic. What if the unthinkable happened? What if Samantha had stumbled across a hiker and was even now giving the police his description?

He didn't sleep, but waited out the sunrise not far from the Hotel Divisadero. His relief was palpable when he entered the lobby this morning and learned that a body was discovered on a nearby hiking trail.

"Someone said it might be that missing college student from Arizona," an eager Canadian told him. "You know the one I mean? Her picture was all over the news for months."

"Here in the Copper Canyon?" He looked over his shoulder. "Doesn't make you feel exactly safe, does it?"

Within hours he was gathering his things at the shack and leaving by his usual route, undetected as investigators began to swarm.

His mind raged during the flight home. He hated Samantha for escaping, but he also analyzed his mistakes. Disappointment eventually trumped his anger, tinged heavily with exhaustion. He wouldn't think of giving up, but choosing another candidate seemed insupportable at that moment.

Just waiting for another vision would be hard enough.

The dream that offered him Samantha was still clear in his mind – it had been so perfect. He was running, his feet striking the ground with even strokes as cool air passed in and out of his lungs. Rhythmic. Reassuring. A bird swooped into his path as if delivered by the gods. With a golden cap on her head and dark red feathers on her tail, she had teased him – darting in and out of trees, chirping a song. She returned to hover just inches from his grasp, then flitted away again, soaring high above, then so low that her wings brushed the earth.

He caught the bird in time. She struggled for a long time, but when her heartbeat finally stilled against his palm, he released her and watched, fascinated, as her spirit soared up into the sky. Soon, he was flying too.

The day after his dream, he saw Samantha for the first time, running laps at Sun Angel Stadium. She was so graceful, so strong. With her blond hair shining in the sun, he knew that she was the bird – that when he caught her and killed her, he would finally be free.

His plan was flawless. By the time Samantha grew wary, she was already his, leaving not so much as a gum wrapper behind.

He didn't want to keep her for so many months, but it couldn't be avoided. He couldn't dictate to the calendar. Everything had to be done at its appointed time. The perfect day had loomed for almost a year, circled in red.

Today.

He should be preparing her now, but she had never understood, no matter how many times he explained it. And now she was dead anyway.

What a waste.

The whole thing made him sick to his stomach. If only she had cooperated, he would be mere hours from freedom. Able to cast off this burden, to settle down and live the normal life in America he wanted.

But acceptance is part of this curse, he told himself.

It's not a curse, it's a blessing! hissed a familiar voice in his head.

He leaned against the elevator wall and closed his eyes.

"You're a special boy," the voice had told him long ago, "and marked by the gods. Someday you'll make your mark too, and earn your place among them."

The elevator chimed and he opened his eyes, putting his game face back in place as he walked toward the corner office. He smiled and greeted his co-workers, returning their insipid banter while he steeled his resolve.

Samantha must not have been as pure as she seemed, but he wouldn't give up now. He had already come too far. Another dream would direct him toward a better candidate. This time he would listen carefully. This time, his offering would be flawless.

4

THIS WAS a bad idea, thought Marius, not for the first time tonight.

His eyes darted from the dim cantina doorway to the clock hanging above the bar. It was five minutes past eleven. Aside from a group of young Americans sitting in the corner, Marius was alone in the bar. Overhearing their raucous laughter and loud conversation, he knew they were here to hike the canyon.

Marius wished they would keep it down, but felt old for it. He was dog tired. Wakened at dawn by news of Samantha's discovery, he was on his way to the canyon by nine and hiking down toward the body by ten. Sealing the crime scene, waiting on his forensics team and trying to gather evidence in increasingly windy weather, he felt as if he had already worked a full day by the time he was following the body bag up the trail and preparing to deal with the intrusion of two FBI agents – one all too familiar and the other a complete stranger.

Or so I thought.

Marius sipped his lukewarm decaf and glanced at the clock again. He would wait ten minutes longer and then go to bed, trying to forget he had ever acted on this foolish impulse.

He wasn't surprised when Rachel declined Trent's invitation to join them for dinner tonight. The headache she pleaded was real, he figured – the tension she revealed all afternoon could hardly have resulted in anything less.

But why couldn't he leave her alone with her thoughts – at least for tonight? Instead, he had sent her a brief note, inviting her to this late-night meeting.

He spent the rest of the evening second guessing his logic.

Marius was stunned when he first recognized Rachel this afternoon. It was her hair that had caused him to take a closer look – those familiar curls pulled in every direction by the wind. The color of honey, he used to tell her, wrapping a strand around his finger. But the changes he saw in her face had stirred up something altogether unsettling along with a raw burst of regret.

Her new last name and the gold band to match were hardly surprising. Whenever Marius thought of Rachel, he imagined her married with children, living that all-American dream.

"You have a history with her?" Johnny Cruces asked him earlier that afternoon. He had clearly noticed Rachel's reaction to Marius, though Agent Trent seemed oblivious. Johnny had good reason to be suspicious of any American agent, but his question irritated Marius nonetheless. He barely nodded his reply.

"Is it going to cause a problem?" Johnny persisted, his tone low. "Are you on good terms?"

"It's been more than fifteen years since I've seen her, *amigo*."

"But?"

"I don't know," Marius said.

It wasn't true. He was pretty sure she hated him.

He hadn't been ready to see his decade-old deception revealed today, that was certain. But what else could he do when Rachel asked him about his last name? After his confession – incomplete though it was – it seemed all she could do to keep from opening the car door and running in the opposite direction. He couldn't dismiss their final parting in Arizona all those years ago either, though Marius had often hoped time and perspective would soften her anger.

So much for that, he thought.

Rachel had not raised the subject for the rest of the day, but her obvious discomfort around him had outlasted his patience. Irritation followed. The possibility that she would let her feelings interfere with the investigation had prompted him to write his terse invitation – nothing else. He had no desire to reminisce, but he didn't think it was possible to sidestep the issue either. Maybe if he made a full confession tonight, they could put the past behind them and concentrate on the case.

With or without Rachel's involvement, a high-profile case like Samantha Davidson's couldn't have come at a worse time for Marius, though allowing that thought to surface made him wince.

When had he become so callous? It wasn't a good feeling.

A missing American woman found dead in Mexico was clearly significant enough to make headlines in the states, but Marius was struggling to make it his primary concern.

People are dying down here every day, he thought, considering a judge and police inspector who had been executed by drug lords in Zacatecas only last week. The entire local police force had refused to report for duty the next day, effectually giving over their town to the cartel.

Things were no better here in Chihuahua. They were worse in Juarez, where thousands were murdered each year, the innocent victims of drug wars that never ceased to rage. Families were moving away in droves, while others hid their children behind locked doors, afraid to openly celebrate a birthday or marriage for fear of being caught in the cartel's crossfire.

Before Marius's recent appointment to lead murder investigations in Chihuahua, his work smoking out corruption within *la agencia* in Mexico City had made him feel useful in the fight against complete capitulation to the cartels.

"You have to make a change – at least for a while," Johnny told him six months ago after the latest and most harrowing attempt on his life. "You're only one man."

"Maybe you're right," Marius said, feeling burned out and, for the first time, overwhelmed by the hopelessness of his self-made mission. When the agency was restructured, he asked for the transfer to Chihuahua. He was grateful that Johnny came with him, returning to his home state – a wild territory he both loved and missed.

Johnny had been Marius's mentor for many years, though circumstances beyond his control now made him his subordinate. Johnny didn't seem to mind. Marius preferred to think of them as partners. Their camaraderie and intuition followed similar lines – even those that now looked like they would drag them back into the very kind of investigation they had recently fled.

As soon as Agent Trent excused himself from dinner tonight, Johnny and Marius exchanged dark looks. The Bureau's presence in Chihuahua was complicating things – particularly Rachel's.

"The circumstances around this investigation are going to make progress difficult, even under the nose of the most obtuse FBI agent," Johnny said, staring into his drink.

"She's not incompetent, Johnny," Marius said sharply. "Hopefully she's still honest."

Rachel's integrity had once been above reproach, but circumstance could change a woman. Marius was painfully aware of that.

"Yeah, well honesty and loyalty don't always sit well together," Johnny said. "And Trent said they go way back."

Marius scowled. "It wouldn't be the first time he's exaggerated."

You're going to try to find out, though, right?" Johnny pushed his drink aside and lit a cigarette. "Kiss and make up, *amigo*. If Trent even catches a hint—"

"Johnny, enough. We can work this to our advantage."

Johnny ran a large hand over tired eyes.

"I hope you're right," he said.

Marius sighed. Looking at Johnny's weary expression was like peering into a mirror. "Many years have passed, Johnny. She's lived a lot of life in that time. She was always … headstrong."

Johnny nodded without comment and whacked Marius on the shoulder as he rose, leaving him to his unwanted memories.

With more than a decade of reflection, it was easy to see that Marius's romance with Rachel never should have begun in the first place. She had been naïve and stubborn – not to mention the daughter of a widowed businessman who saw all Hispanic men as dirty wetbacks. Marius had been sent to Arizona with an agenda based on deception, sanctioned though it might have been.

He had also been her teacher.

Marius's employment as an undercover DEA agent was arranged a few months after his graduation from the University of Madrid. Too weary to adapt to his mother's latest marriage, he had visited Mexico to reconnect with the father he barely knew. Warmly welcomed to the 11,000-acre Sonoran cattle ranch that had proved too lonely for his mother, Marius marveled that she gave her first marriage even two years.

Marius's father, Julian, had never remarried. Falling in love with the backup singer for a touring Spanish crooner had clearly been life altering for the quiet rancher's son. His joy at receiving her returned affection must have only been matched by his sorrow at her spiraling disillusionment when the excitement of an early pregnancy wore off.

Marius had a hard time imagining his mother on the ranch – so far from the society-driven life she enjoyed in Madrid. He figured that even if she had stuck with her vows, the luster that had so captivated his father would have eventually waned, bringing about the sad end of their marriage one way or another.

It didn't take Marius long to fall in love with the ranch. The quiet acceptance and peace of his father's world contrasted sharply with his life in Spain. But at twenty-two, he was still too young to accept his offered inheritance when immediate apprenticeship and isolation were part of the bargain.

"I want to see some of the world before I commit to this," he told his father, not understanding the specifics of his desires or the extent to which he was willing to offer them up.

Julian quietly agreed, wiser than he had been with Marius's mother and reluctant to strain the new bonds he and his son had begun to forge. He was well respected by then, no longer the shy ranch heir whose warm brown eyes had turned a showgirl's eye. He arranged a meeting between Marius and an old friend who was an official with the Federal Judicial Police, hoping he could offer Marius what he was looking for – without drawing him back to Europe and out of his life for good. Julian's friend had the unenviable job of recruiting fresh blood. Sometimes his recruits ended up working with the American Drug Enforcement Agency.

Looking back at the job he had accepted, Marius saw it as just one link in a chain of desperate attempts to counterbalance the drug trade problem between Mexico and America. *Vain attempts*, he reminded himself bitterly. After all these years, things had only gotten worse.

At the time he had eagerly signed up for the two-year assignment – on loan to the DEA – as one of several young agents placed in American and Mexican universities to investigate and report on drug trafficking efforts on campus. Feeling like the pay and opportunity to earn his master's degree at Arizona State far outweighed the threats he might face, he looked forward to his work.

What man his age wouldn't love the chance to become a spy?

Marius's Spanish citizenship, accent and European childhood provided the perfect cover for any suspected association with the Mexican government. He agreed to drop his father's name as part of the cover and to omit his recent time spent in Mexico when describing his background. After several months of training, he had reported for work in Arizona, confident – maybe even disappointed – that his assignment held little potential for danger. He didn't have much more to do than keep his eyes and ears open and report back to a handler once a week.

Romance had not been part of his plan. Loving Rachel defied logic and even will, but it had been too strong a force to ignore. Bitterness reigned for many years when he looked back on the rise and fall of their relationship. But in his heart, he never truly regretted it. His memories of the time he spent with Rachel had become more sweet than bitter over the years. He had hoped she was somewhere out there feeling the same way.

Maybe the disappointment of that simple wish was what bothered him most as he sat waiting in the cantina, determined yet unhappy about creating a new memory here that would surely replace all others in her mind.

Rachel walked through the doorway at that moment and paused as her eyes adjusted to the dim lighting. She wore a long, gray cardigan over a t-shirt and jeans and her hair was tied back at her neck, making her pale face appear both severe and youthful. She looked tired and somehow beaten, with dark circles under her eyes and a crease across the middle of her forehead that didn't speak of the apple-pie life he had imagined for her. She was no heavier than she had been all those years ago, but he couldn't help noticing that her body reflected the subtle changes of age and possibly childbirth, though he was reluctant to raise that subject.

She walked unsmiling toward him while he struggled to reconcile this reality with his memories.

"Thank you for coming," he said.

"What's this about, Marius?" She sat down across from him and wrapped her arms around her shoulders.

"It's nice to see you again too, *Raquel*," he said softly.

"Don't call me that." Her cheeks darkened. Marius felt a jolt, as if something warm had burst open in his chest.

"Do you want a drink?"

She sighed. "No. I want to go to sleep."

"You're not a night owl anymore?"

"Don't do this."

"Do what?"

"Pretend you know me. That I know you."

Marius frowned. "Hate me if you must, Rachel, but we have to work together."

"And this helps? Sending me notes? Meeting late at night?"

"I thought it might help, yes," he said. "If there are things you need to ask me to get past this, I wanted to give you that opportunity. Privately."

Rachel uncrossed her arms and laced her fingers on the table. Her voice was flat. "I imagined you in Spain."

"I imagined you … well, anywhere except with the FBI."

An uncomfortable silence followed. Marius twisted his coffee cup on the table while Rachel twisted in her seat.

"Bazán is your mother's last name, then," she asked, "and your father's…?"

"Suarez."

"He's here in Mexico? The son of your grandfather, Mario?" she asked.

"Yes," Marius said. "That's all true."

"And you were working undercover in Arizona?"

"Yes."

"Investigating…?"

"Drugs," Marius said. "Someone was suspected of dealing through a Spanish department vendor – the company that maintained audio equipment for the language laboratories. DEA officials had been tipped that there was a strong link to the Sinaloa Cartel. Similar trafficking patterns were discovered in other American and Mexican universities. Agents were placed there as well."

"The DEA recruited you?"

"Through the Mexican Judicial Police, yes."

"How long had you been doing undercover work before going to Arizona?"

"It was my first assignment."

"But you never told me," she said.

"No."

Rachel stared at her fingers for a moment. "You had a confidentiality agreement."

"Yes."

Rachel sat silently, her cheeks flushed and her jaw tight. The American hikers were making a commotion, happily drawing their attention away, if only for a moment. At least one in the party had consumed too much liquor and Marius knew he'd pay for it tomorrow. Cheap Mexican tequila meant harsher hangovers. He hoped, for their sakes, that they were on the end of their journey and not the beginning.

He turned away first and refocused on his coffee, now too cold to drink, but something to handle during Rachel's interrogation.

He had imagined this going differently.

"How much undercover work did you do after that?" Rachel began again. "Before coming to the PFM?"

"A bit." Marius shifted in his seat.

"And were there others like me?"

"¿Qué significas?"

"Other women," she said. "Diversions. Side plays."

"Rachel—"

"Was it exciting? Part of your spy games? Targeting women too young and naïve to see past your lies?"

"There were no others like you, Rachel." Marius was stunned and unable to keep the anger out of his voice. "And sarcasm doesn't suit you."

"You invited me here to ask questions," she said coldly. "I can't help it if you don't like the questions I ask."

Marius sat back and ran a hand through his hair. He had always heard that the confession of long-held wrongs brought sweet release from guilt, but he wasn't feeling it. Instead, he felt as if he was tearing open a wound that had merely been patched inadequately with time and distance.

"It was all such a long time ago, Rachel," he said wearily. He looked at her wedding band, which had found a way to sparkle under the dim cantina lighting. "You're married now, right? Happily?"

Her eyes shifted toward the bar. "Ever After," she said.

"Can we call a truce, then?" Marius swallowed hard. "We only have to work together for a few more days. After that, you can go on hating me."

Rachel nodded wordlessly. She had lost her will to fight. Silence hung between them, leaving Marius struggling for something else to say. He wondered if he should try to explain his motivation for taking the undercover job in the first place. Should he confess the guilt he felt? The strain he knew his deception had placed on their relationship?

He shook his head. Dragging them both back through the details was pointless. They had just been two kids, really, whose chance encounter had created a beautiful, if all-too-short bond.

It was so long ago, Marius thought again.

"Rachel, I *am* sorry." He was surprised by how much he meant it, how he had wanted to say it for years.

"Don't be. As you said, it was a long time ago."

"If there's anything—"

"Listen, I need to get some sleep," she interrupted. Standing, she tightened her grip on her sweater. "Good night, Marius."

5

RACHEL CLOSED her hotel room door and latched it quietly. The clock by her bed glowed, warning her it was already tomorrow, but for a moment she didn't move, didn't think. Numbness was good, she thought, especially tonight. But too many thoughts were pushing toward freedom. Rachel pushed back.

A hot shower, then sleep. Those were the only thoughts that mattered.

Peeling off her clothes, she crossed the small room and turned on the bathroom light and the shower. While the water warmed, she rummaged through her luggage for pajamas and her tooth brush, setting aside the package that had been delivered by the local outfitter. In a few hours, she would be hiking down to the crime scene with Agent Cruces.

Away from Marius for the better part of a day.

Her reflection in the mirror challenged her relief.

Coward, it said.

She turned away and stepped under the shower head. It shouldn't matter where he was or what he did. In a few days, she would leave and try hard to forget about him again.

But Marius and his apology were now fighting for control of her thoughts, more sincere than she was willing to remember.

"Focus on the case," she mumbled, "only the case."

After leaving the medical clinic this afternoon, Rachel had interviewed Mrs. Harcourt and then spent the rest of the day at the PFM command center, set up in a banquet room at the hotel, where agents had papered the walls with area maps and covered battered tables with computers. A copier, ancient fax machine and coffee maker crowded the raised hearth of an unlit fireplace at one end of the room, close to the rickety surface Rachel had been assigned as a "desk." She stared dubiously at the electrical outlet that fed all three and considered the possibility of a circuit breaker overload, plunging them all into darkness.

Agent Cruces assisted her with a Wi-Fi connection, phone service and in setting up a private room for conducting interviews. Agents were already transcribing statements and lining up witnesses for the following day among the locals and tourists. Marius had made a master list of hotel registries so they could seek out those who had slipped through their nets, some of whom were likely hiking the canyon today. Railroad tours often stopped only briefly in Creel and Divisadero, which was fifty kilometers to the southwest, but their passenger manifests had been gathered as well.

Not until Rachel saw a map of the canyon system and learned of its countless trails had she begun to appreciate the enormous probability of losing their killer. Up until that point, she had been naively optimistic about Samantha's pebbles and the silver medallion. Still, determined to focus on actionable items instead of drowning in the unknown, she shared her to-do list with the others, checked in with SAC Devlin and drafted a priority sheet for the following day.

While she and Agent Cruces hiked down to the crime scene in the morning, Agent Trent would interview more witnesses with PFM agents Gonzales and Castillo. Marius would manage the command center, direct junior field agents and explore the technical front, obtaining security footage from local banks, hotels and the railway in search of Samantha sightings.

As soon as the necessary red tape was completed, Samantha's body would be transported back to Arizona – possibly by tomorrow afternoon. Rachel's early hope of taking the same flight home had diminished as the evening approached and her to-do list lengthened.

"I'll take her back," Agent Trent said soberly. "Your knowledge of the case makes you much more valuable here."

Rachel nodded, noticing that across the room, Marius had stilled at Trent's words.

"Take a photograph of the medallion," she told Trent. "Make sure you ask Mrs. Davidson if it belonged to Samantha."

Rachel knew it was premature to pin her hopes on such a small clue, but she fostered them, nonetheless. If the medallion wasn't Samantha's, it might have belonged to another missing person in Rachel's files.

Samantha's kidnapping wasn't an isolated incident. Rachel knew it. The lack of evidence meant it had been carefully planned – probably by someone who had done this before. Rachel had a stack of lesser-known cases that she believed were related, but SAC Devlin hadn't been convinced that Rachel's hunch was backed with enough evidence to assign more resources.

"I'll keep an open mind if more comes of your theory," she said. It had been her only concession.

Rachel stepped out of the shower and began to towel dry her hair. Was it too much to hope that Samantha had finally given her the evidence she needed? Picturing Samantha's lifeless body, her eyes stung at the thought.

Pulling on her pajamas and flipping off the bathroom light, Rachel got into bed and stared bleary-eyed at the small stucco fireplace that had been lit in her absence by one of the quiet hotel employees. Only a few embers glowed now, but she appreciated its warmth.

She was almost too tired to sleep. Her room service had been cleared from the table, but the smell of roasted chicken and rice still lingered. She had been more than surprised by the note delivered with it. She picked it up from her night table now, remembering how the familiar black scrawl had made her heart lurch, and how the meal itself reminded her of one she and Marius shared long ago on a beach near Rocky Point. A storm had ruined their plans for the day, forcing them to spend the afternoon huddled together under the leaky tin awning of a beach-front dive.

"You never eat," Marius had said, trying to tempt her with another bite. She laughed, pushing his hand away and earning another stern look from the dour restaurant owner hovering nearby. How could she have explained that food, sleep – even air –seemed frivolous when they were together?

How quickly things change. From her failed romance with Marius to her failed marriage with Craig, the same thought applied, even grimmer in its meaning.

She stared at her wedding ring – the gold band she couldn't make herself take off, though the ink on her divorce papers had been dry for two weeks now. Rachel hadn't told Marius she was divorced, but then, she hadn't admitted it to anyone at the Bureau either. Instead, she hid the truth behind her ring. But why?

Rachel had always been a private person, but was that reason enough? Maybe nothing but pride kept her quiet. How much worse was Craig's infidelity when combined with the pity of her colleagues – or Marius…

I shouldn't think that way, she reminded herself. *Craig's betrayal wasn't about my failings, but his.* She had repeated this over and over during the past few months, but something in her reflection each night doubted that truth, leaving her feeling hopeless again.

"It's natural for things to feel unsettled for a while," Melissa said. "Give yourself a break."

But Rachel didn't know if she could. How do you let yourself fall apart when you have a disillusioned child to take care of, not to mention a demanding job that has become even more important to keep? Rachel's strength was something Craig admired in their early years together, before resentment set in. But she didn't feel strong now, she felt used and discarded.

When darkness finally claimed the fading fire embers, Rachel's alarm clock glowed that much brighter, admonishing her to sleep. Instead, she lay back against her pillow and thought about the road she had traveled from naïve school girl to FBI agent. It had been paved with patriotism, hard work and a certain amount of rebellion, but she hadn't been willing to explain any of that to Marius tonight. It would be too easy for him to tie it back to their failed relationship and she didn't want him assuming blame or credit.

But what did it say, she wondered, that they had gone their separate ways but made identical career choices?

6

RACHEL STOPPED, catching her breath, and peered over the edge of the trail. Vertigo threatened and she leveled her eyes, focusing on the vista beyond. In every direction, emerald cliffs rose from the misty canyon floor, rippling in soft velvet waves toward the horizon.

It was tragically beautiful – she couldn't see it any other way. At her feet, a small red flag marked the place where Samantha died.

Agent Cruces dismissed the officers left to guard the area overnight and leaned against a boulder, sipping from his canteen. Juan, their Tarahumara guide, squatted on the trail next to him. Rachel took a long drink from her own hydration pack and imagined Samantha's thirst.

That morning, Cruces had shown her a topographical map for the area, which was at the southern edge of Tararecua Canyon. Formed by the San Ignacio River, Tararecua was smaller than its mighty southern neighbor, *Barranca del Cobre*, but one of the most difficult areas to navigate.

"Hiking magazines don't send families from Albuquerque to hike the Tararecua," he said. He nodded at her worn-in Merrell hiking shoes. "What's your trail experience?"

"My husband and I hiked the Grand Canyon last spring, to Havasupai Falls."

It was beginning to feel strange to refer to Craig in those terms, she realized. Her mind seemed to be pushing to finally let go of all pretense.

Rachel knew that trails in the Copper Canyon would not be marked or maintained like those in the Grand Canyon. Cruces told her there were too many trails to keep track of – some were used only by the Tarahumara and barely passable. Others had been created by miners long ago and were now left to coyotes and ever-encroaching nature.

Their trailhead had been near Lake Arareco along the road to Batopilas, a town on the canyon floor that was only recently connected to civilization by a paved road. The topography around the lake was rocky, to say the least. Boulders larger than houses skirted thick pine tree copses or threatened to topple into the water.

It had taken them two hours to hike to this spot, which was about halfway between the rim and floor. The last mile of their descent had been particularly unforgiving. Sharp switch backs had frequently crumbled at the edges, keeping Rachel focused on each step.

"You can see where Samantha marked her way." Cruces pointed out torn scraps of pink fabric tied to trees and shrubbery along the trail below. Rachel easily reached the same conclusion he had – Samantha had been climbing out of the canyon, not escaping into it.

Carefully picking her way along the trail, she examined other flags the forensic team had used to mark Samantha's movements. It didn't take long for her to notice something that wasn't marked – a bright red feather resting at the foot of a bush with flame-colored thistles. Familiar pink threads were wrapped around the feather's shaft and the barbs looked worn, as if handled frequently, or perhaps crushed and concealed in a palm.

"Agent Cruces?" she called, pulling out her camera to snap several shots before donning a glove and carefully lifting the feather. "This looks tropical to me. Could it be from a local bird?"

Cruces's face reddened as he examined the feather. It was an amazing find a full day after the PFM team had sealed off the scene and searched it for clues.

"We'll have it analyzed, of course." He cleared his throat. "But I do know that some tropical birds live on the canyon floor."

Rachel sealed the feather inside an evidence bag and tucked it in her pack. She rose and again looked at the majestic canyon, knowing that what she saw was only a small piece of it.

"We need to go in deeper, don't we?"

"Yes. But without other leads, we could wander for weeks and never find anything."

"So Samantha's evidence – the feather, pebbles, egg shells – isn't likely to differentiate one bit of the canyon from another?"

"No. It tells us she was down there. *Nada más.*"

"But this trail gives us a starting place. We also think she may have passed through water."

Agent Cruces only nodded, clearly unconvinced.

Still, finding the feather stimulated Rachel's appetite for evidence. She insisted they spend the next hour scouring the crime scene for other missed clues. When they found none, she turned to follow Cruces and Juan back up the trail, hoping the investigation in Creel was yielding better results.

Cruces was quiet during their ascent, which suited Rachel fine. She was tired. Focusing on the trail took most of her concentration, though her thoughts wandered to the night before more than she would have liked.

"Marius is here," she told Melissa when she called to check on Danny.

"*Your* Marius?"

"He's not *my* Marius. Anyway, how many men named Marius do I know?"

Rachel described their reunion at the heliport and his position with the Mexican authorities. She left out the part about his past deception.

"This is bad," Melissa said. "You don't need this now."

Rachel shifted in her chair, regretting her impulse to share. Why couldn't her sister just listen for once, without offering advice?

"It's not a big deal, Melissa. I'll be home in a few days and never see him again."

"It's an unresolved relationship and you're in a foreign country," Melissa persisted. "That's a bad combination."

"Have you taken a good look at me lately? I doubt I offer much of a temptation."

"Don't do that," Melissa said. "You've gone through a stressful situation and maybe it shows a little, but it's nothing a little time and pampering won't fix."

Rachel had no response. It bothered her to think Marius's opinion still mattered, but somehow it did. Whether it was pride or simple vanity at work, she was angry that he was seeing her now, when the full count of 36 years was evident to anyone looking, from the dullness of her skin to the shadows under her eyes. She would rather be remembered as she once was – young and hopeful, if a little naïve and obstinate – with time to soften even those memories.

"You've been reading too much pop psychology and I need to go – I have another call." Rachel was glad for any excuse to end the conversation. "We'll talk tomorrow."

She switched calls, smiling when she saw Victor Katseli's face on her display.

"Hey, Vic. Are you back from your trip?"

"Just got in yesterday. Are you in town or can I presume that you're in Mexico?"

Rachel frowned, for once not finding the cocky edge to Victor's voice even slightly endearing.

"You talked to Craig?"

"No, but the buzz in the newsroom is that Samantha Davidson's body has been discovered in Chihuahua…"

"Would that be official buzz? As in sanctioned-by-a-release-from-the-Bureau buzz?"

"Uh, no. But without it, the rumor will still find its way to the front page and you know it."

"Vic, I answered the phone as your friend, not your source."

"Come on, don't be like that," he whined. "Off the record, I swear."

"You won't get the byline," she said. "I can tell you one thing about where I am – there isn't a soccer stadium within a hundred miles."

"Ouch!"

Rachel knew Victor wanted to move away from the sports section. But forgoing the travel perks of covering *fútbol* for *Soccer America* and *The Arizona Republic* was not yet worth the increase in status or pay. Still, whenever Rachel was working on something high profile, he would stick his nose in and become wistful, reminding her that his journalistic dream was breaking the big stories.

"Come on," he persisted. "Just one little morsel that won't hit until the release – I swear I'll protect my source."

Rachel laughed. "Yeah, as if that would work."

Victor groaned. "Well, at least let me take you and Danny out when you get back in town." He paused. "I miss you – both."

Rachel's answer was noncommittal and she said goodnight, promising to be in touch within a few days. She appreciated Victor's loyalty – she hadn't expected it after the divorce. He had been Craig's friend first, after all. Still, she wasn't sure where their friendship stood now that the divorce was final.

Victor had been openly appalled by Craig's betrayal – something she witnessed in all its glory on the night Craig moved out. He arrived just as Craig was loading boxes into his trunk and his censure had quickly escalated into an ugly argument. The things he said had been so scathing and brimmed with contempt, they shocked even Rachel. Craig had paled – stunned into silence – and Rachel saw guilt in his expression for the first time. Losing Vic's good opinion, it seemed, hurt him more than losing her.

Craig had abandoned the rest of his belongings and left. His only response to Victor's attack was an angry squeal of tires as he sped out of the driveway. Rachel burst into tears after he left, one thought foremost in her mind – she was glad Danny had not been home.

Victor walked her inside, brought her a glass of water and held her for almost an hour while she cried stupidly, feeling lonely and grateful, angry and confused all at once. When her tears stopped, he dried her eyes with his shirtsleeve and offered to help her get even with Craig in the wickedest way possible.

Rachel had laughed aloud. Such an audacious proposal was both flattering and non-threatening coming from Vic. A few moments later, he was kissing her forehead, saying goodnight and once again treating her like a favorite sister.

Since then, Victor made a point of spending time with Rachel and Danny – coming to YMCA basketball games and taking them to the zoo or movies. He usually timed his visits with forethought – when Craig bailed on Danny, for example, to spend more time with his girlfriend, whom Victor called, "Trixie, the cocktail waitress."

"Her name is Trisha and she's a paralegal," Rachel reminded him. Vic would only shake his head, refusing to acknowledge anything above the stereotype.

Rachel had refused to take his flirtation seriously until recently, when he had been unusually quiet. She was glad when he left on this latest trip – was it Puerto Rico, this time? – hoping that by the time he returned, he would have snapped out of it.

Their conversation last night had not put her mind at ease.

Rachel's legs began to burn from the climb, bringing her thoughts back to the present. She slowed her pace, noticing that Agent Cruces followed suit. Juan did not, lengthening his distance to fifteen meters ahead.

"Don't let him push you to overdo it," Cruces said. "I know I won't."

"Tell me about him," Rachel asked, guessing that Juan was around sixteen years old.

"It's hard to know his age for sure – Tarahumara don't typically keep track of such things."

"He moves fast," Rachel said.

"They call themselves *Rarámuri* – it means 'light feet' – and are known locally for their running prowess. Some American runner wrote a book about them a few years back, gaining them a lot of attention." He shook his head. "But I've heard stories about their hunting practices since childhood – how they can chase a deer for days until it falls over from sheer exhaustion."

Rachel raised her eyebrows, but didn't comment. They were drawing near the trailhead and her energy was running out. Cruces seemed unaffected, however, and kept talking, telling her that many of the Tarahumara still lived in caves and rustic homesteads scattered throughout the canyons.

When they reached their Jeep by the lake, Rachel saw several Tarahumara women along the shore, dressed in bright colors and carrying stacks of hand-woven baskets.

"They sell them to tourists," Cruces said.

It was nearly two o'clock by the time they got back to the hotel. Rachel excused herself and headed for her room, wanting nothing more than a shower, food and a few minutes to call Danny.

As she peeled off her dusty clothes, she couldn't shake her disappointment. Their hike to the crime scene was meant to give her a solid sense of direction on the case. Instead, she had more questions than the day before.

Rachel stepped under the shower head and tried to wash away her doubts, but Samantha's feather admonished her.

Find him, it said.

7

WHEN RACHEL REACHED the command center that afternoon, she found Agent Trent and Marius in the middle of an argument.

"We made it clear that her body might not be released until tomorrow," Marius was saying.

"Her family is waiting." Trent's hands were on his hips. Despite the afternoon heat, his tie was tightly knotted. "They want to bury her, Suarez, and put this behind them. News of her death has already been leaked to the media."

"Your media, not ours. Perhaps the Bureau should keep a tighter lid on its investigations."

"It wouldn't matter if there wasn't so much red tape to cut through down here," Trent said. "There's no reason the body should not be released to me now."

"You are criticizing my government for red tape? Last time I checked–"

"What's this about?"

Both men stopped, turning toward the door at the sound of Rachel's voice. Marius offered her a curt nod and glared out the window while Trent let out an exasperated sigh.

"Samantha's body won't be released until tomorrow – and I've already told her mother I would bring her home tonight."

"Why did you do that?" Rachel asked. "You knew it might take one more day."

"But there's no good reason for the delay," Trent insisted. "Now I'll have to change my flight and disappoint Mrs. Davidson," he turned and glared at Marius, "who has waited long enough, I think."

"Perhaps you have another appointment you're worried about missing as well?" Marius asked softly.

Rachel frowned, but decided to let that comment go.

"What is the nature of the delay?"

Marius reached for a sheet of paper on the fax machine and handed it to her. "The medical examiner has completed her report and signed the release, but the Agency of Disease Control must also clear the body for travel. Their testing cannot be rushed."

"Needless red tape, as I said," said Trent.

"Trent, just change your flight." Rachel rubbed her forehead. Was it too late to go back to her room and take a nap? "Call Mrs. Davidson and apologize for the confusion – and don't you dare pass the blame onto Mexico. You know very well this is standard procedure. You shouldn't have made a promise you couldn't keep."

Trent cast another dark glance toward Marius and left the room, grumbling under his breath.

"Please tell me you two have accomplished more than this today," Rachel said.

A smile tugged at the corner of Marius's mouth as he reached for a manila folder. "I'll share my day if you share yours."

"Okay." Rachel pulled the feather from her bag. "Your team missed this at the crime scene. Samantha left us another clue."

Marius grimaced and took the evidence bag, examined it, and handed it back to her. "It doesn't tell us much."

"No. It just solidifies our belief that she was held somewhere on the canyon floor. So what do you have?"

"According to Agent Trent, none of his interviews produced any leads. My contacts within the DEA had nothing to share either, though they're beating the bushes to see if Samantha had a run in with any mules or growers in the area."

"The DEA operates here?"

"Did you expect their absence anywhere in Chihuahua?" He shook his head. "The canyon system has many good places for marijuana crops – places that are hard to reach by authorities, though we do try. Hikers occasionally stumble across them. The consequences are not pleasant."

He pointed to a map on the wall. "These places highlighted in orange are the hottest drug areas in the region – in Sinforosa Canyon and certain places near Batopilas. The cartels also have been pressing young Tarahumara into service in recent years, capitalizing on their running skills. I doubt Samantha's captor was a drug lord, but we don't want to leave that rock unturned."

"How about surveillance tapes?" Rachel asked. "Did anything show up?"

"No. There's not much sophisticated surveillance around Creel, but we did hear a curious story from a young man named Chu who, coincidentally, is a cousin to your trail guide."

"Relevant?"

"I think so. It is our best lead anyway. Chu thinks he can identify the kidnapper."

"Really?" Rachel sat on a rickety chair and crossed her arms. "I'm all ears."

"Be prepared." Marius smiled. "His story begins with a *bruja*."

"A witch?"

Marius nodded and leaned against the table behind him. "She lived in the canyon many years ago. She was a Tarahumara woman, but an outcast from her family, living in a ruin next to an abandoned mining camp. She had a daughter, but no one knew the identity of the girl's father. They speculated that he was a devil or phantom, because the daughter grew up to be even more mysterious than her mother."

"Mysterious?"

Marius shrugged. "Chu was vague. He was anxious to tell his story, but nervous about the details."

"Sounds like something he's making up."

"I don't think so," Marius said. "I'm learning that the Tarahumara are superstitious. Most claim to be Catholic, but clearly their beliefs mix with something more ancient – animist even. Cruces tells me that many practice magic – laying curses on each other during sporting events, eating peyote, sharing stories about mythical creatures that swim in *el Rio Urique* – things like this. But this *bruja* and her daughter crossed the line in a way I don't understand."

"Did Chu name either of the women?"

"Not the mother. The daughter's name was Yala. She must have been lonely – Chu said she tried to ingratiate herself with others in the area and was somewhat successful with the men. Evidently she was quite beautiful. She ended up pregnant, of course, and gave birth to a son, though no man would claim him.

"As the boy grew, it became clear that he wasn't typical either. Cut off as they are, the Tarahumara don't know much about mental illness, birth defects, or disabilities, so I can't speculate about his neurology. But with three generations of trouble evident in the family, some locals feared the worst. They asked them to leave – and left little room for refusal. Chu said they went to Chihuahua City and lived in one of the *colonias* there for many years. After some time, the old woman returned with the boy and settled back into her old home."

"And Yala?"

"Chu says no one saw her again. The boy grew up, but kept to himself. The Tarahumara avoided him as well, fearful that his condition could be caught like a contagious disease – or more like a curse, the way Chu tells it. He is seen from time to time – near the old mine, or further in the canyon. They think he lives mostly in a cave."

"What is his name?"

"Chu didn't know."

"How old would he be now?"

Marius shook his head. "With their cultural indifference to age, Chu couldn't say. We only know that he's a grown man, but not old."

"And the location of the cave?"

"Somewhere Chu said was cursed and avoided."

Rachel shifted in her seat. "So we have this poor outcast who probably just needs some medical attention and now he's the first person we should suspect? Why did Chu link him to Samantha?"

"He said he and some friends stumbled across the old *bruja's* shack one night when returning from a *tesquinada*…"

"A what?"

"*Tesquinada*. It's a ceremonial drinking party that usually lasts two or three days during which vast amounts of *tesquino* – beer made from corn – is consumed."

"Got it. Drunken teenage boys come across old 'haunted' shack and see – what? Samantha tied up in chains?"

"They saw nothing," Marius said. "But Chu says he heard a woman crying."

"Did they investigate?"

Marius shook his head, his face grave. "Like you said, they were thoroughly drunk. Maybe even high on peyote. Chu thinks he heard the grandson's voice as well. He said it sounded as if he was trying to pacify the woman – as if she was pleading with him."

Rachel rubbed her arms. Despite her doubts, goose bumps were rising on her skin. "Did they understand what she said? Was it in Spanish? English?"

"I don't know. Chu only said that they believed the man had conjured up the spirit of his dead grandmother. The air was thick with smoke – something that is apparently high on their superstitions list. They didn't linger. Chu said he forgot about it until Samantha's death became the news of the plaza."

"We need to find this shack – and that cave."

"Agent Cruces is talking to an old friend as we speak. They will try to convince Chu and his friends to help us."

"They are reluctant?"

Marius smiled. "Still afraid of the ghost *bruja* and her hexes."

Rachel stood up and walked toward the map on the wall. Even if Agent Cruces was only able to come away with a general area, she wanted to be prepared to go into the canyon again first thing in the morning. Her finger touched the place where Samantha was discovered, then moved in circles around it. Would it take three days? Four?

It's looking less likely that I will be picking up Danny on Saturday, she thought.

"You're anxious to get home."

Marius's voice broke into her thoughts. She turned and looked at him. Had she spoken aloud?

"Yes." She paused. "My son is staying with Melissa this week in Cottonwood. I was set to pick him up on Saturday. Of course, that was before we received the call about Samantha."

"How old is he?"

"Eight," she said.

Her eyes flickered to his, where something sparked a memory from years ago. He was kissing her ankle on a beach as they lay watching a toddler weave toward the shoreline. His father had chased after him, swooping in to carry him back to his mother.

That will be us someday, Marius had said.

"Your husband can pick him up, then? If you're delayed?"

Rachel nodded and then wondered if it counted as a lie.

"It won't change my focus," she assured him. "Wanting to get home to Danny, I mean." She thought of Mrs. Davidson, whose child would never be safe again. "I'll stay as long as necessary – to find whoever took Samantha."

೫

THE NEXT MORNING, Rachel crouched by the Jeep, examining her pack under a dim street lamp while she waited for Agent Cruces. She had slept hard and waking was difficult. Her muscles were tight after yesterday's hike, but she was anxious to hit the trail again.

The sound of boot tread on gravel announced his arrival, but when Rachel straightened to greet him, she saw Marius, not Cruces, emerge from the shadows.

She searched the darkness beyond him, desperate for expectation to contradict what she saw – boots, gear, a backpack – all on the wrong agent. Finally, she lifted her eyes to his.

Marius managed to look apologetic.

"I'm afraid you're stuck with me for the next couple of days," he said.

8

SHE'S NOT going to like this.

When Marius approached the Jeep in the predawn gloom and saw Rachel bent over her pack, her hair was already fighting to work free of the knot she'd tied at the back of her head. Another knot was tightening in his gut.

"Where is Agent Cruces?" she asked, looking past him.

Marius lowered his pack to the ground.

"He is ill." He shifted his feet. "Suffering from an uncomfortable condition as a result of last night's meeting with old friends."

"He's hung over?" Rachel's voice went up an octave.

"No." Marius tried not to smile at her outrage. "Something worse, I'm afraid – along the lines of what you Americans call Montezuma's Revenge. Good manners dictated that he partake in tesquino last night, as well as some kind of stew. The combination did not agree with him." He shook his head. "My room is next to his. Trust me, he isn't in any shape for hiking this morning."

Rachel winced. "I'm sorry for him. But was his visit a success? Did he learn the location of the old woman's shack?"

"No. Unfortunately, his contacts could not agree on that. Still, Chu and Juan insist that it is within a day's walk of the cave where the bruja's son lived. That's the direction we're headed first."

Her eyes searched the darkness again. "Where are they? Will they act as our guides?"

"Yes. Two of their friends will try to find the mine from a different route. Agents Gonzales and Castillo will go with them. This way, we cover more area in less time."

Rachel frowned and Marius suspected she was trying to figure out a way to go with one party while he went with another. He zipped up his jacket against the morning chill and waited in silence until her brow cleared. He figured her resignation was the best he could hope for.

Juan and Chu emerged from the direction of the plaza then, both looking ill prepared for the coming trek, just as Johnny said they would.

"They'll wear sandals – don't bother trying to talk them into hiking boots," he told Marius this morning. His face was ashen and he clung to his hotel room door with hands that shook. "Watch your food stocks too – I've heard of guides who eat a week's worth of provisions in the first two days of a hike."

He tried to give more instructions, but Marius sent him back to bed and started packing. He considered asking Agent Trent to take his place on the trail, but quickly dismissed the idea. Trent didn't seem like an outdoorsman and Marius couldn't afford to inhibit his return to the U.S. Rachel was just going to have to overcome her disappointment.

"Have everything we need?" he asked.

Rachel was folding a checklist that looked well gone over. She smiled tightly and handed him her pack. "I think so."

Marius frowned. Johnny said Rachel was experienced, hiking the Grand Canyon in a recent trip with her husband. Still, her pack felt too heavy.

"What does this thing weigh?" he asked, hoisting it in the back of the Jeep.

She made a face. "What it should – somewhere less than a third of my body weight. Let's just leave it at that."

Marius's eyes darted over her trim figure. He cleared his throat and closed the hatch. "Good enough."

છ

THEY TALKED very little along the trail, hiking single file with Juan and Chu in the lead. By noon, they reached the canyon floor and stopped to eat next to the San Ignacio River. Rachel refilled her hydration pack, adding purification tablets before stretching out on a boulder shaded by tall blades of tropical grass. Juan and Chu ate on the roots of a large tree some distance down the river – a practice of separation Marius was beginning to expect. After following them to ask about the next leg of their journey, he returned to lean against Rachel's rock.

"Can you tell me something?" he asked.

She set down her sandwich.

"Your reaction to Samantha's silver medallion yesterday caught my attention. What was that about?"

Rachel shifted toward him, her freckled nose wrinkling against the dappled sunlight. "I have a theory about Samantha's killer that involves a few other unsolved missing persons cases. If the medallion belonged to one of them, it could go a long way toward proving I'm right."

"Can you give me details?"

"Yes. But I should warn you – my theory has been dismissed by my superiors."

"Perhaps I am more open-minded?" he suggested.

"Okay. Over the past six years, two other young women and one young man have gone missing in Arizona, all matching a profile similar to one I created for Samantha."

"What kind of profile?"

She frowned. "An unconventional one. They all had different economic backgrounds, habits and professions. If we include Samantha in the list, two were white and two were Hispanic. Two of the cases were investigated as possible foul play, but the others were not. One had a history of drug use, childhood abuse—"

"People likely to have just wandered away from life?" Marius asked.

"Yes, that is more plausible, statistically."

"Did you use these details to try to convince your colleagues, or to dissuade them?" he asked dryly.

"Marius—"

"Sorry. So what's the connection?"

"A time pattern for one. The abductions were each separated by about eight months."

Marius shifted against the boulder. "That's odd, but hardly astonishing."

"Yes, I know," Rachel said impatiently. "But here's another thing – all of them were remarkably petite for adults – even the young man. Samantha was the tallest at 5 foot 2. And all of them were..." she paused, searching the air for words, "let's say beautiful. Maybe even perfect. Physically fit, remarkably good looking."

"What else?"

"The way they were all just gone without a trace. The absence of evidence – the neatness of these crimes..." Her voice tapered off. After a minute, she shook her head and began to pack up the remnants of her lunch.

"I won't deny that it's a gut feeling." Her eyes settled briefly on Marius's face before turning to the river. "When I look at their cases – their photographs – their eyes stare back at me with innocence. Loss. I feel a connection. As if they are trying to tell me something, just like Samantha tried to speak to us with her pebbles and egg shells."

Marius felt the flesh along his neck prickle. He didn't want to think about Rachel's sense of connection with these victims.

He cleared his throat. "Rachel, you're a sensitive person—"

"Please don't patronize me, Marius." Her eyes flashed, her cheeks warmed more by passion than by the sun. "I know I'm sensitive. I don't happen to see that as a fault."

He held up his hands defensively. "Neither do I. Can I see what you have on these other victims when we get back to Creel?"

Rachel nodded, her voice softer. "Yes. Thank you."

Marius glanced down the river. "Are you ready to continue?"

Rachel stood and stretched. "Yes. Whenever you are."

Marius started walking toward Juan and Chu.

"Marius?"

He stopped, turning back. "Yes?"

"I never even considered that Samantha could have been taken out of the States." She looked past him, her eyes panning the landscape. "It makes me wonder..."

"What?"

"If the others were brought here too." She refocused on his face. "And how did he do it? Bringing four young people across the border without anyone seeing – anything."

"I don't know," Marius said. "But I will help you find out."

He meant it.

9

THE WALLS SHOOK when he slammed his front door. He didn't notice – his priority was the remote control. It took him only seconds to find the local news broadcast. The camera crew filmed from a distance as Samantha's coffin was transferred from the airplane to a dark hearse. Mrs. Davidson stood to one side, her back bent with grief. He watched her stillness, holding his breath. When she turned away, he did too.

What a waste.

Samantha had been a warrior, a worthy sacrifice. He nodded, still convinced. The dream had been clear and he had followed the pattern, just like with the others.

What, then, had gone wrong?

With a few strides, he was in the bathroom, splashing tepid water on his face, staring at his reflection.

"Let your dreams be your mirror, child. They will guide you."

The voice was a memory, but still present, reverberating from the walls. It thrilled and frightened him, as it always had – the voice of his grandmother, the only person who truly understood him. The voice that set him on this path.

"Why can't I have the real mirror?" he had asked her, more than once.

"You have everything you need right here," she would say, grasping his head with gnarled fingers and giving it a gentle shake. Her eyes were like obsidian – fierce and passionate, always measuring him from the inside out. Her scrutiny inevitably overwhelmed him, forcing him to look away. The memory of his cowardice brought shame to him still. He had been so young. But what was age to a child of destiny?

He blinked at his reflection, examining the differences between image and reality, wondering how well he had mastered his craft.

His cell phone rang and he plucked it from his pocket, frowning at the display. Constance again? He was tired of this part of the game. Tired of vapid women with perfect nails who wore Juicy and frequented tanning beds. He pushed the unanswered phone back into his pocket and considered his reflection again. He still wanted the real mirror, the one his grandmother had spoken of so reverently.

Closing his eyes, he saw her little room in *la colonia*, the fire burning in the grate and the low mattress pulled close. She was never warm enough. It was his favorite place in the evenings, after he had grown tired of playing in the streets and filled his belly with supper.

"Tell me the story again, Grandmother," he would say, his voice sleepy as he curled up against her knee. Her wavering tone gave immediate comfort, compelling him to close his eyes and listen with relish as she repeated words that were becoming part of his very makeup.

"Mother and Father Earth created our world long ago," she began, "and they had four sons together – a child created to be god of each direction – north, south, east and west. Tezcatlipoca was the god of the north. He was clever and handsome, but he and his naughty brothers fought constantly instead of obeying their parents and living in harmony."

"What happened, Grandmother?"

"The world was destroyed as they struggled. Again and again it was reborn and each time one brother would find a way to defeat another and kill him, only to destroy the world again."

"How could their fights end the world?"

"Everything is a balance, my darling, like a scale that must not tip too far in any direction. The brothers were selfish though, taking too much for themselves without considering the consequences, upsetting the scales over and over."

"Tell me about the twins."

"Tezcatlipoca and Quetzalcoatl were their names. They were the two most powerful brothers – and also the biggest troublemakers. Tezcatlipoca became the god of the ancient Toltecs in the time of the Maya. They grew stronger and stronger, conquering those tribes that worshipped their brothers. With each victory, Tezacatlipoca became more powerful, taking over his brothers' powers one by one. The great Aztec Empire was born out of his leadership, and soon all of his brothers became his allies. In their weakened state, they could do little else.

"But as rulers often do, Tezcatlipoca became too proud. He never expected the children of his brothers to rebel against him, but they did. With their support, Quetzalcoatl was able to depose him. But when he saw that he would never be as strong a ruler as his brother had been, Quetzalcoatl was overcome with jealousy. He refused to spare his brother's life and threw Tezcatlipoca into the sea."

"But he didn't die?"

"Tezcatlipoca can never be killed," she said sharply. "He came back stronger, as a jaguar. He used his magic smoking mirror to show everyone Quetzalcoatl's true image – the feathered serpent – thus shaming him into exile in the underworld."

"And Tezcatlipoca ruled the Aztecs?" he asked, ever hopeful that the answer would be different.

"No child." Her voice grew sad. "You remember that these boys were naughty brothers, who should help each other, and not fight. But Tezcatlipoca did not remember. He wanted to take revenge on the Aztecs. He took the form of a powerful man and convinced our ancestors that Conquistador Hernando Cortez was Quetzalcoatl, returning from the underworld to rule them as before. When Cortez destroyed the Aztec Empire, Tezcatlipoca's revenge was complete."

"What happened next, Grandmother?"

"Tezcatlipoca could not see past his anger – that the man he had invited in was a strong opponent. By the time Cortez was slaughtering our people, Tezcatlipoca could do nothing to stop him. In shame and remorse, he exiled himself alongside his twin. He has waited there in the underworld for centuries, biding his time until atonement can be offered for his schemes."

"And he was punished for disobeying his parents?" A shiver of dread ran down his small spine.

"Yes." Grandmother's voice was kind again, indulgent. "He learned to love his brother, Quetzalcoatl, and to take care of him, as a stronger brother must always care for a weaker one. But the Earth Mother, Tlaltecuhtli, was harsh to Tezcatlipoca, tearing off a piece of his foot to punish him and remind him of his shame."

He had always scooted closer to Grandmother during that part of the story, fearing the Earth Mother.

"And has Tezcatlipoca come again?"

Grandmother reached under his blanket and stroked his left foot with her gnarled fingers, never flinching away from the place where three toes had never formed.

"Yes, child. Tezcatlipoca has come again."

He breathed in deeply, letting the memory of Grandmother's words strengthen him. Whatever had gone wrong with Samantha, he would not let it undo him now. It would not alter his final plan.

Perhaps it was a test of strength. Of will. It didn't matter. Grandmother had always said atonement was possible – that with redemption would come the release of his obligation. Sweet freedom would follow. Opening his eyes to stare into the bathroom mirror, he smiled, no longer seeing the man staring back at him. In his place, eyes gleaming, stood the jaguar.

10

"*NO VAMOS a ir más lejos.*"

Juan crossed his arms and planted his feet in the sand, refusing to take another step toward the narrow side canyon. Chu squatted by his side, looking toward the river indifferently as Marius once again tried to convince them that they would not be hexed when they reached the cave.

"Marius, give up," Rachel said. "We've been standing here for ten minutes. Clearly they never had any intention of leading us all the way in."

"Something they might have told us before accepting the job as guides," he answered darkly, pushing off his cap to run fingers through his hair.

It was the second day of their hike and they were all dusty and tired, but there was no way Rachel was stopping now that they were finally within hours of their destination. It was clear that Marius felt the same.

"If you won't go farther, then you can make camp," Rachel told Juan and Chu. "Take our supplies back to that wide stretch of beach by the mouth of the spring. We'll camp there tonight. Agent Suarez and I will continue into the canyon by ourselves and meet you before dusk."

Juan and Chu turned to walk back across the creek as if the preceding stalemate had little to do with them. Marius stood at her side, his jaw tightening as he worked to check his anger.

"*Idiotas supersticiosos,*" he said under his breath.

Rachel turned away to hide her smile. They had made good progress today, the trail sometimes leading them up and away from the river, over arroyos and grassy plains, or running alongside stretches of beach. It was during the last leg of the trip that the trail had started to turn to the south and descend into a deeper section of the canyon. They stood now at the entrance to a side canyon that was almost obscured by thick trees, rocks and tropical grasses. This was the avenue, Chu and Juan said, which led to the cursed cave.

"We'll make better progress without them," Rachel said, standing up. Marius responded with little more than a growl before following her around the bend.

The temperature dropped immediately, the trees shading their path and providing a refreshing change for Rachel, who had shed her camp shirt after lunch and since soaked through her green tank top. She felt filthy with sweat and grime and knew that her face was red and shining with exertion, but she pushed the unattractive image to the back of her mind. They hiked for ten minutes without conversation before coming to a large rock pile, which they were forced to climb over. As she pulled herself to the top, Rachel looked upward with trepidation, wondering about the likeliness of another rockslide. There was very little they could do to protect themselves if boulders started to rain on their heads.

They had replenished their water supply at the spring by the beach and as Rachel took another sip from her hydration pack, she hoped that Juan and Chu were accurate in their prediction that it would take no more than an hour to reach the cave.

They were not. It took them two hours to reach a dead end.

"Could that have been it?" Rachel asked again, pointing back at a wide indentation in the canyon wall that they had dismissed after only a short inspection.

"No, Rachel," Marius said with measured patience. "Clearly, that's not it."

Rachel bit back a caustic reply, but disappointment outweighed her annoyance. The idea that they had traveled to this place only to find nothing at all carried with it the double-edged sword of lost investigation time and a literal dead end. She returned to examine the spot again while Marius paced along the place where their route had ended abruptly, giving way to soaring cliffs and RV-sized boulders. After several moments, his laughter broke the silence.

"What is it?" She walked toward him.

He flashed a smile. "A way through."

Rachel frowned, looking over his shoulder but seeing nothing. "Where?"

"Right here."

He bent over and pushed aside a sorry-looking crop of tropical grass that grew in front of the boulders. Rachel now understood why they looked so trampled – they had been. There was a gap – low to the ground where the touching boulders curved away from each other to create a tunnel. She could see light shining through from the other side.

"We'll have to crawl," she said.

Marius's smile was shameless. "Ladies first."

Shooting him a dark glance, Rachel shrugged off her pack and thrust it at him before lowering herself to hands and knees. She wished there was a more dignified way to proceed through the opening, but was too relieved by its existence to let that stop her. The tunnel was short, widening on the other side before claustrophobia set in. As she crawled out, her hand brushed something soft on the ground. She turned to examine it, cocking her head to let the sunlight pass.

"Marius, look." She scrambled to one side, letting him through and pointing at a familiar scrap of pink fabric. "Samantha was here."

Rachel pulled out her camera and took several shots while Marius waited. Her hands shook when she placed the scrap inside an evidence bag, exhilarated to find proof that they were on the right track.

"Ready?" he asked.

She nodded and turned to follow him deeper into the canyon. Fifteen minutes later, they came to a stop again, facing more boulders that seemed to block their path. Not deterred, they found a narrow opening mostly obscured by thick lichen and overgrown plants.

"I'll go first this time," Marius said.

"You mean now that we can pass through on foot."

He grinned and then disappeared through the natural gate, leaving Rachel to follow. The ground sloped sharply downward on the other side, forcing her to take it at a run to keep from falling.

"¡Cuidado!" Marius steadied her by the arm.

"This place is like a maze." Rachel brushed a fresh layer of dust from her pants. "How many more—"

"Shh." Marius put a finger to her lips. "Do you hear that?"

Rachel stepped back, frowning. Then she heard it too.

"Water."

They moved around the next turn, pushing foliage away from their faces until they reached a sandy clearing. What they saw there made them both stop short.

"*¡Cielos!*"

Rachel blinked with wonder. A waterfall cascading from a cliff ledge thirty meters overhead emptied into a lagoon with water as green as any Tahitian paradise, spreading from one steep cliff side to the other. Trees and other tropical plant life grew around the jagged rocks overhead, creating a lush canopy.

Marius walked toward the north wall of the canyon along the curve of the water, which settled peacefully against a narrow strip of sand, but was otherwise skirted by more enormous boulders. Finally able to think beyond the beauty of the place, Rachel began to search in the other direction. After several minutes spent peering over boulders and squatting to look beneath them, she gave up. She looked back at Marius, who was standing in one place now, staring at the waterfall.

"What do you see?" she asked.

"Have you ever heard of the waterfall in Chiapas called Miso-Ha?"

"No."

"It's a big tourist attraction near Palenque, passing over the cliffs in a way that allows people to walk underneath and see it from the backside," he said.

"You think the cave is back there?" she asked, squinting toward the falls.

"It would explain how Samantha's clothes got wet."

Rachel walked past him to the north canyon wall. She focused on the waterfall as she traced his steps, looking for a dark place behind the ribbons of water, but saw nothing. Meanwhile, Marius found a low boulder to sit on and was taking off his boots and unzipping the legs of his cargo pants, converting them into shorts. Rachel's eyes widened.

"You're going in?"

Marius nodded.

Looking back at the water, she instinctively licked her lips, thirsty again and remembering that her hydration pack was nearly empty. Her hair had become more disheveled than usual during the day's hike and now several thick curls were stuck to the back of her neck, creating paths for the sweat that continued to travel down her back. She wiped her brow and tried not to think of how cool the water would feel against her skin.

"You just want to get in that water," she said. "Admit it."

Marius smiled. "If that were true, would you blame me?"

"Yes, I think I would." She crossed her arms.

Marius shrugged, peeling off his T-shirt as he headed toward the water.

"Feel free to join me," he said over his shoulder.

Rachel looked at her watch, annoyed. It was getting late. Even if they did find the cave, their daylight hours were dwindling. She sat down on the rock and kicked away his boots, trying not to watch as he waded out into the water. Instead, she looked at the waterfall and wondered how thunderous it would appear during the rainy season. Her eyes narrowed as she focused on a dark place above the falls. Could the cave be up there? She circled the shoreline again, looking up. After a few minutes, she gave up the idea and sat back down. If a cave was there, she saw no way of reaching it.

Marius was treading water now at the base of the waterfall. Without a backward glance, he took a deep breath and disappeared, leaving the lagoon to swallow him up and lap in peaceful oblivion at the edges of the beach. Rachel silently began counting in her head. How long could he hold his breath?

Thirty seconds passed.

Her pulse quickened. The lagoon remained still but for the rippling effects of the waterfall. Her heart beat out the passing seconds. Thirty more. It seemed much longer.

Where was he?

Rachel stood up. "Marius!"

Nothing. And now it was two minutes.

Rachel's throat constricted. What if he had gotten trapped below the surface and was now struggling for his last breath? She yanked on her boot laces, fumbling over a knot with shaking fingers, finally tugging herself free. Her pants were lightweight, but still felt heavy as she splashed into the water, her fantasies of a refreshing swim forgotten as she struck out toward the waterfall.

"Marius!" she called again.

Her voice echoed back to her, shrill with panic. She wasn't a strong swimmer herself, and the thought that both of them would drown here today passed through her mind. How quickly would their indifferent guides react to their absence?

Rachel shook her head and began to tread water. She couldn't let herself get distracted. She took a deep breath.

Marius burst to the surface, just inches from her face.

Relief lit up Rachel's nervous system like a double shot of espresso. She threw her arms around him.

"You're okay!"

Together, they dipped below the water. Rachel quickly pulled away, leaving Marius to sputter to the surface again, coughing.

"Are you trying to kill me?" he asked, gasping.

"I'm sorry." Her cheeks colored and she swam backward, giving him space. "I'm just relieved to see you. I thought you had gotten stuck."

Marius shot her a look of exasperation and swam toward the shore. Rachel followed and soon they were crawling onto the sand, breathing hard and pushing dripping hair from their faces.

"Do you have a dry sack with you?" he asked.

"Yes."

"Will it hold your camera, flashlight, evidence bags?"

"Yes."

"How long can you hold your breath?"

"I don't know – long enough, I think. Marius, what did you find? What happened down there?"

He shook his head, his face pale and wet. "It would be better if I show you."

11

RACHEL DUG through her backpack, searching for shorts.

"It will just take me a minute to change," she promised Marius before racing back up through the natural gate for privacy. Now she wasn't sure she had told the truth – just pulling off her wet khakis was proving tricky. She shivered as she fumbled with the zipper – whether from the cold water or adrenalin, she couldn't say. Her cheeks stayed warm, however, when she thought about the way she had thrown her arms around Marius. The memory of his wet skin under her hands and the way his arms had momentarily closed around her made her heart lurch uncomfortably.

Snap out of it, she told herself, flinging her wet pants over a rock to dry. She finished dressing and hurried back down the hill in bare feet, impatient to see what was hidden in the depths of the lagoon.

Marius was waiting ankle-deep in the water with his hands on his hips.

"Are you ready?"

She nodded, avoiding his eyes as she double-checked the contents of her bag, sealed it and strapped it to her waist. Her hair was becoming a problem, still tangled up at the back of her head with an elastic band, but escaping in large ringlets that kept falling in her face.

"Give me half a sec," she said, struggling to pull the band free with shaking fingers.

"I don't know how you manage that every day," Marius said impatiently. He moved behind her and tugged at the band.

"Ouch."

"Hold still. There. Now, it's out." He handed it to her and watched her tie it back again in a simple ponytail.

"Okay, I'm ready."

"When we get to the waterfall, take a deep breath and follow me," Marius said.

"The entrance to the cave is behind the waterfall?" she asked.

"Yes, but underwater, which I didn't account for. We have to swim through a short underground tunnel and up through the cave floor."

Rachel shuddered. "How narrow is the tunnel?"

He smiled, his eyes passing over her. "I made it through. You won't have any trouble."

He turned and swam toward the waterfall. Rachel followed.

"Ready?"

"I'll be right behind you."

Marius disappeared beneath the water and, taking a deep breath, Rachel dove in after him. Her eyes adjusted easily to the water, clear and green down below just as it was above. She swam hard to keep up, quickly spotting a dark place ahead that must be the cave entrance. It looked too small to fit inside at first, but as they got closer she watched Marius effortlessly disappear into it – and none too soon since her lungs were about to burst. She kicked harder and swooped down toward the hole, cringing with claustrophobia as she swam through, desperate to reach the air Marius promised was waiting inside. The tunnel was short and turned upward at the end. Finally, she broke to the surface in the dark, gasping for air.

"Marius?" she sputtered.

"I'm here." He reached toward her, taking hold of her arm to help her up. She scrambled over the ledge and turned to sit beside him, her feet dangling in the water as she caught her breath and began squeezing water from her hair.

"How did you see anything in here before?" She shifted and pulled a flashlight from her pouch.

"The light comes from there." Marius tilted his head back and pointed up. Rachel had to lean back on her elbows to see the cave's ceiling, which sloped upward to where a small opening to the sky was visible.

"It's just above the waterfall isn't it?" she asked. "Do you think it's accessible?"

"Probably from the top of the cliff, with ropes."

"A drier route, if it's passable. But Samantha escaped through water…"

"Which means she passed the way we came." Marius's voice was grim. "Come on." He stood and reached down to help Rachel to her feet. "It's getting darker by the minute. We'll have to move quickly."

"Wait a minute." A puddle was forming at their feet. "We're too wet."

Using her palms, she began wiping water from her skin. Any needless contact or careless touch could contaminate evidence or lead to the loss of vital information.

"We'll keep to the edge of the cave wherever possible." Marius copied her actions with some impatience. "But dripping is unavoidable. We don't have time to air dry."

"Fine. Here." She handed him the flashlight. He aimed the beam at the floor, sweeping carefully from left to right as they inched their way along a narrow passageway.

"Watch your footing."

The floor sloped unevenly upward as they passed into a wider cavern. Rachel assessed the space, gauging the dimensions as similar to a large bedroom. The dark corners invited her interest, but Marius was quick to draw her attention toward the opposite wall, about five meters in from them.

"This is what I wanted you to see."

A larger than life figure was painted on the wall, flitting across the space as if dancing in the wavering flashlight beam.

"Something that glitters is mixed in with the paint," Marius said.

"Mica or obsidian, maybe?" Rachel moved closer. The figure shifted with her, and her throat constricted.

It's just the flashlight, she told herself.

Still, for a moment she was almost convinced that Juan and Chu had not been so foolish in their superstitions. The figure was ominous in stature and design – and so meticulously created that she imagined the artist spending hours here, working in the faint light to create something he meant to share only with his victims. She stepped back, as if she could escape her imagination, but it didn't work. Instead, it felt like the evil of Samantha's imprisonment had seeped into the pores of the stone and polluted the air.

"Is there more?" Her voice sounded impressively even.

Marius nodded. "This way."

Rachel glanced frequently at the ground to maintain her footing. A small spring of water trickled down the wall on her left and then across the ground. A fresh helping of disquiet filled her as she imagined it swollen with rain and pouring in to fill the cave, trapping them within. She took a deep breath and kept moving. The wall of the cave was curving again, creating another alcove that opened before them in the wide beam of the flashlight.

"Can you see it all?" Marius's words were soft but crisp as they echoed against the walls.

"Yes."

The flashlight beam traveled with her as she approached the place where three objects hung on railroad nails hammered directly into the cave wall. Above each nail, a different symbol was painted in familiar glittering black paint, none of them recognizable to Rachel. Her eyes darted over the collection, taking in the obvious – there were three objects, but four nails. Something was missing.

"Jewelry," Marius said. Rachel nodded.

"It looks like a cross pattern." Two of the nails were positioned vertically in a line, while the other two were set wider, spaced horizontally.

"Perhaps a compass rose," Marius ventured.

"I think you're right."

She dug for her camera and then silently catalogued the bracelet, locket and gold chain that hung from what she now assumed were the western, eastern and southern points. She stared at the empty northern nail for a moment. "The sand-dollar necklace must have been here."

"Yes." He stepped aside to make room for her wide-angle shot.

Rachel took several, making sure the empty peg and each of the four symbols were captured as well.

"Do you understand these symbols?"

Marius shook his head. "No, but I would guess they're Aztec."

Rachel took a step toward a corner that looked darker than the rest and then yelped as the ground disappeared beneath her.

Marius grabbed her arm, pulling her back from the edge of a hole. The camera, strapped to her neck, swung wide and then bounced painfully against her chest as he held her in place. When the camera stilled, her heart kept pounding.

"Thank you." Her voice threaded through the darkness and Marius let go and stepped around her, pointing the flashlight over the edge.

The hole was deep. Something at the bottom caught the light's beam as it swept past and Marius refocused, finding another railroad nail, this one hammered into the ground and attached to a chain and shackles.

Rachel's hand shook as she once again aimed her camera, taking several shots of the place where Samantha had clearly been chained like an animal.

"Samantha was not the only victim he kept here," Marius said.

Rachel nodded. Their fate, she imagined, couldn't have been better than Samantha's.

"We need to take the jewelry with us." She put the camera away and pulled on gloves.

"Yes, but we're losing light," Marius said. "Make it quick."

He was right, but she hesitated. There were dark stains on the shackles that looked like blood.

"Marius—"

"We will send a team back tomorrow," he assured her. "They can lower equipment from the ceiling entrance, take brighter shots, collect samples and dust for fingerprints." He turned his head, squinting into the gloom. "We need to make sure there are no graves in here."

Rachel nodded and turned toward the trophy wall where she removed each piece of jewelry, sealed them in evidence bags and labeled them – west, east and south. Tucking them in her submergible pack, she followed Marius back toward the water tunnel.

Marius lowered himself into the water and held onto the edge while Rachel sat and scooted forward, adjusting her pack. Her feet dangled in the water, stirring green circles that reflected against their faces.

"Ready?" he asked.

"Almost. But, Marius. This place – these trophies. They were put here by someone with a degree of intelligence that does not match the description we've been given of the *bruja's* son. He's methodical and clever. A sociopath with an inner directive."

"I agree," he said. "But Chu's story led us here, to the place where Samantha was imprisoned. Some connection must exist, and now we're one step closer to finding it."

12

MARIUS AND RACHEL reached the campsite just after dark. Juan and Chu had laid a small campfire, but sat at a distance on a flat boulder upstream, eyeing them for signs of the witch's hex.

Hungry and tired, Marius ignored their stares and low murmurs – they spoke in *Raramuri,* which would be meaningless to him even if they were closer – and sat down next to Rachel to eat. Their meal consisted of pouched tuna, crackers and dried fruit, leaving Marius unsatisfied when he had finished, though he was too weary to dig through his pack for more. The night air was muggy, leading him to doubt his damp clothes would dry anytime soon, even with the aid of the fire. Still, he made no move to change. Instead, he stretched out on the ground, using his backpack as a pillow, and watched Rachel through half-closed eyes.

She ate slowly, fatigue sharpening her features in the firelight. Since their awkward reunion on Monday, he had frequently seen something flicker in her eyes that hinted at indefinable fragility. Today, she had shown more stamina than he expected, but still he wondered.

When Rachel packed away the remnants of her meal, she dug through her backpack, pulling out dry clothing and laying a green iPod on top of her pack. She stood and focused the beam of her flashlight on the cliff behind them.

"I'll be back in a few minutes," she said.

Twenty paces north of their campsite was the mouth of a creek that ran through a narrow arroyo. Marius assumed it would be her destination for fresh water and privacy. He nodded and reached for her iPod.

"Do you mind?" he asked.

Rachel shook her head. "Just don't make fun of my musical tastes, okay?"

He waited until she was out of sight before turning it on and scrolling through her playlists. He recognized a few songs that he knew were old favorites of hers, but most of the music was more current, spanning genres and languages – the eclectic tastes of a stranger. For a minute he listened to a Spanish love song that spoke of estrangement, false hope and self-delusion, but he soon pulled off the headphones, unsettled by a murky feeling in his gut. He shouldn't have his hearing compromised anyway, he told himself, while she was out of sight.

The following half hour passed slowly. Juan and Chu moved several meters farther down the beach to tuck in for the night, claiming to know of a ridge where the grass made thick beds. Marius checked the campsite for scorpions and hoped Rachel was being watchful.

She's from Arizona, he told himself. *She knows how to take care of herself.*

When she finally emerged through the tall grass, he sat back down and fiddled with his pack, acknowledging her return with only a curt nod.

Rachel sat down and began methodically repacking her bag. Marius watched her pull out plastic storage bags, roll them free of air as she resealed them, then carefully layer them back inside.

"Are you almost done?" he asked after several minutes. He lay back and closed his eyes again. "Just watching you wears me out."

"It won't fit if I just shove it all in."

"Then you over packed." Through veiled lids, he saw her make a face at him. He tried not to smile.

"Here," she said, tossing him a film canister.

He caught it, then rattled it in the air. "Why are you giving me this?"

"It makes sense, I think, to pack it separately – I'll keep the evidence bags, you keep the film."

Marius shook his head, but dutifully shoved the canister into his backpack. It was too bad they couldn't switch to digital cameras like the rest of the world, but when it came to evidence, real film was still much harder to tamper with.

Eventually Rachel ran out of things to reorganize. She zipped her pack and stood up, stretching as she walked past him to stand close to the river. For several minutes she stood watching the water while absently running her fingers through her damp hair.

She cleared her throat. "Marius?"

"Yes?"

"The letters you wrote me during our summers apart in college – they were all postmarked in Spain." She didn't look at him. "Were you really there?"

The question surprised him. He rose and walked toward the river's edge where they stood side by side, looking out to where a three-quarter moon shone on the water.

"Most of the time," he finally said. "But I wrote a few letters from Mexico. Those I saved and mailed when I reached my mother's house."

"So that I wouldn't know," she said.

Marius turned to look at her.

"Would it have been so bad for me to know?"

"Rachel, I'm sorry."

"I saved them for a long time," she said. "But after you left – the last time – I threw them all away."

"I hardly blame you."

She turned to face him, but didn't look angry as she had in the cantina. Maybe the shock of his deception was wearing off. Or maybe the saying was true – a woman only has trouble forgiving those whom she loves.

"Was your operation successful?"

"Hmm? What operation?"

"In Arizona. Your undercover work to catch drug dealers. Was it successful? Did you catch them?"

"We prosecuted some." He looked at the river again. "Fighting the cartels – it has always been like cutting the tail off a salamander."

Rachel nodded and turned back toward the campfire. Marius thought about the letters she had written him. They were probably still in a box somewhere at his father's ranch.

"I'm going to walk downstream a bit," he said. "I'll be back in a few minutes."

Following the curve of the cliff until he could no longer hear the fire crackle, Marius found what he was looking for – a fat boulder they had passed earlier in the day. He climbed up and sat down, staring out at the river with a strange feeling in his gut. Maybe he had eaten too fast.

He closed his eyes and took a deep breath, trying to clear his mind. Instead, he saw Rachel refilling her backpack. It was not a memory from today, but from her first year at ASU.

It was Halloween. Marius was standing behind a column in the subterranean courtyard of Hayden Library. Directly across from him, in the elevator alcove, a kid in a Billabong hoodie was selling drugs. Marius had begged his DEA handler to let him call campus police, but was ordered not to interfere.

"We have bigger fish to fry," Agent Johnson said.

"He's targeting freshmen," Marius said. "Pretty ones. Lonely ones."

"If you'll just keep your eyes open and your mouth shut, Bazán, he's going to be our bait."

Marius watched him make three transactions with female students over the next hour, but nothing suggested he would lead them to bigger fish. When the boy abruptly abandoned his storefront to follow a passing student up the staircase, Marius followed.

Another customer, he thought. But when he recognized Rachel Bishop from his Spanish class, he knew he must be mistaken. If Rachel was the dealer's target, she was an unwilling one – Marius would bet his life on it. He had only been teaching her for a few months, but just couldn't imagine that she was the type to waste her future.

It was a quiet night on that part of campus. Only three people walked north along Hayden Mall – Rachel, pursued by the dealer, and Marius bringing up the tail, trying to keep an eye on both of them without being seen. As the misaligned trio drew closer to University Drive, the sounds of multiple Halloween parties filled the air. Rachel had turned and looked pointedly at the frat boy at least twice, but so far she had not seen Marius. Each time, she increased her pace. Marius wondered what game the dealer was playing. Was he taunting her? Pursuing her? Or was he just high himself?

When the dealer suddenly broke away at University, Marius felt tension he hadn't even known he was carrying fall from his shoulders. Rachel stopped to watch him break into a sprint along the sidewalk before haphazardly cutting through traffic to cross the street. She took a quick step backward when it looked like one of the speeding cars would surely hit him, but then turned toward the footbridge that spanned the busy road and led to several dormitories on the other side of the street. Marius continued to follow her. He would feel more comfortable once she was safely inside her dorm, he told himself.

When something hit the back of Rachel's head with a dull splat Marius was close enough to recognize it as an egg, but not quick enough to see which car it had been thrown from. Rachel dropped her backpack on impact and reached up to the back of her head, ignoring her books as they broke through the weak zipper and scattered across the sidewalk. Marius ran toward her.

"Are you okay?" he asked.

She jumped and turned to face him with eyes dilated with confusion and fear.

"Mr. Bazán?"

He was reaching into his pocket for a handkerchief and holding it to the back of her head. "It was an egg," he said. "Are you hurt?"

Rachel shook her head. She reached up to replace his hand with her own. Pulling back her fingers, now wet with yolk, she examined them in the streetlight. Marius saw her stiffen.

"Let me help you—"

"No," she interrupted. Dropping to her knees, she began gathering her books. "I'm okay. Thank you."

Marius stepped back and watched her refill her backpack with shaking hands, her spine stiff, her movements mechanical. He wanted to reassure her – to tell her it was just a random prank that had nothing to do with her, but he checked his impulse. What could he say that wouldn't sound obvious or condescending? It would probably only add to her embarrassment.

"I'll walk you home," he said quietly, reaching for her damaged bag and putting it firmly over his shoulder. She hesitated for a moment, but then relented.

"Thanks."

They walked across the footbridge and to the door of Manzanita, where he waited until she was safely inside. He tugged on both doors to make sure they were locked before turning to walk home.

Marius had wondered then how someone could look so fragile and strong, so naïve and mature in the same moment. He wondered it again, sitting by the river, some sixteen years later. For the life of him, he couldn't understand why he kept seeing the same vulnerability in Rachel now.

13

"RACHEL, WAKE UP."

Rachel stirred, but didn't open her eyes, despite the flashlight shining in her face.

Marius shook her again. "It's raining. You need to wake up."

Rachel squinted and put her hand up to block the light. Rainwater was dripping from the brim of Marius's cap, but otherwise she was still dry, having placed her sleeping bag under the curve of the cliff.

"I'll scoot over." Her words were heavy, slurred. "You can sleep next to me."

Marius grabbed her hands and pulled her into a sitting position. "Sounds nice, *querida*, but we need to move. The rain is coming from the north and the river can swell quickly. This beach will be underwater in a matter of minutes."

"Cruces said it's not the rainy season," she said stubbornly.

"It's not. Now, put on your boots and get your pack."

He seized her sleeping bag and rolled it. Rachel struggled to her feet.

"Where are Juan and Chu?" she asked.

"Gone. Out-of-season rain must be more than enough proof of a curse for them. Are you ready?"

"Can we go up by way of the stream?" Rachel asked, jerking her chin toward the arroyo she had visited earlier.

Marius shook his head. "Flood waters are just as likely to come that way. We need to get up higher."

Rachel nodded and focused the beam of her flashlight, finally awake. Marius let her pass, then followed her down the beach, expecting at any moment to hear a rush of water behind them. Two nylon ropes were clipped to his belt loop. He knew they would need them.

He felt like an idiot. Falling asleep less than an hour ago, he had vague memories of lightning flashing in the distant sky. He had noticed the wind picking up in the trees, but didn't make the connection then that should have spurred them to higher ground.

"There." Rachel pointed at a path that zigzagged up the cliff. Marius passed his flashlight beam across it in sweeping arcs. It was narrow and steep, but would have to make due. There was no time to search for another route.

"Hurry."

Rachel began to climb with Marius close behind her. He gauged the ascent at about ten vertical meters before it curved away from the edge and flattened into a ridge where they might safely wait out the storm. The rain was roaring now, making it impossible for them to listen for the sound of floodwaters. He turned frequently to look north as they climbed up the slippery switchback, hand over hand in many places as the soil and rocks dropped around them.

They had climbed almost a third of the way up when Rachel slipped and fell. It happened in the blink of an eye, her cry of surprise barely registering with Marius in the torrent. He watched in horror as she tumbled past him, just out of the reach of his fingertips, rolling and bouncing against the cliff before landing on the beach below to lie silent and still amid a small avalanche of rocks and dirt.

"Rachel!" he shouted.

She didn't move.

Marius's heart hammered against his chest as he began to climb back down. Realizing that part of his path had been wiped out by Rachel's fall, he stopped and held on to the slippery rock, searching for another route. Seconds ticked by and his fear festered. There was nothing – not one way to reach her.

Lightning flashed closer than ever and Marius spotted a tree growing from the cliff about three meters to the north. There was a ledge there, not much wider than a man's shoulders, jutting out of the sheer vertical face.

Looking back down at Rachel's still body and again to the north – black with deadly water or merciful space – he began to climb, inching his way toward the tree.

Thirty seconds passed before Marius reached the trunk. It felt like hours since Rachel fell. With another frantic glance to the north, he hoisted his backpack onto one of the sturdier limbs and tied his ropes to the tree. With shaking fingers, he gathered them both and pushed off the ledge, rappelling down to the canyon floor.

"Rachel," he said sharply. She did not respond. Working quickly, he removed her backpack and secured the rope to her waist. He tried to ignore the possible damage he could be doing if her injuries were spinal. They didn't have the luxury of time.

Rachel groaned. Her eyes opened and she winced in pain.

"My wrist," she said weakly.

"It's okay." Marius was so relieved to see her lift her head and move her legs, he smiled. "I'm going to get you out of here."

Then the first wave hit.

The water was cold, moving across them in a broad stroke that immediately filled the riverbed, wall to wall, with two feet of water. Rachel gasped. Marius lifted her into his arms and fought the current as he waded back toward the cliff, his smile gone and his fears dark.

"We need to climb." He adjusted the rope to fit snugly under her hips. "Can you plant your feet on the wall and pull yourself up?"

Rachel tried, but couldn't grip the rope with her right hand.

"It might be broken," she said.

Another wave crashed against them, carrying them along until the rope caught on the tree above, jerking them back. Marius grabbed Rachel just in time. Her backpack shot past them, down the swollen river and for a second Marius thought ridiculously of her iPod.

"Marius," Rachel said against his chest. "The water is only going to get higher."

His jaw tightened. "I know."

"I once read about a storm that flooded a canyon in Utah. It came in waves like this. It carried away cars, boulders."

"I'm going to get us up the cliff, Rachel."

"I know. But you're going to have to leave me down here to do it."

Lightning flashed again, lighting up Rachel's face. He knew she was right. The only way to get her up the cliff was to climb it first and then lift her as well.

If he was strong enough. If their ropes held.

He nodded, unable to speak.

"I trust you," she said.

For a moment, Marius forgot all the years that had passed. He kissed her forehead. "We'll wait for the next swell together," he said.

They didn't have to wait long. The water came at them like a plow, furiously pushing them downstream. By now, branches and uprooted bushes were hurtling by. Marius turned them this way and that, trying to avoid the larger pieces until the water settled again at their knees. He quickly secured Rachel's rope around her left hand and let go.

"I'll be fast!" he yelled.

The rain pelted his face as he fought for traction against the cliff with wet hands and shoes. He felt like he was losing a meter for every two he gained, all the time fighting the urge to abandon their plan and return to Rachel.

What if her rope snapped? What if she wasn't strong enough to hold herself steady with one hand? What if the next swell was the biggest yet?

It was her reminder of boulders and trees that kept him going. She would die down there if he didn't succeed. He thought of Danny and his grip tightened.

An eternity passed before he gained hold of the tree. His chest burning from exertion, he secured his position by shortening one rope and turned to pull Rachel upward with the other. She rose inch by inch, able to do little but hang on, her face lifted upward, taut with fear.

She turned suddenly, looking north.

"Marius."

Her voice was sharp, rising above the rain. He understood without looking.

The water was returning with a roar – a solid wall, much higher than the previous wave – maybe even high enough to rip him off his perch and carry them both downstream.

He didn't turn, instead he pulled faster, willing his muscles to function, fighting the pain of rope scoring his palms.

Finally, Rachel was within reach.

"Grab my arm!"

She squeezed his wrist. With a final pull, he dragged her on top of him as the wave rolled over them both.

The water crushed them against the cliff face, stealing his breath before twisting them back toward the edge. Marius tightened his grip on Rachel, praying his rope would hold, that the tree's roots were stubborn and strong. Seconds ticked by and the water kept coming while his overtaxed lungs threatened to betray him. Rachel tightened her fingers around his arm and he willed himself to keep holding his breath.

It was just enough. The swell pulled back and the water leveled out, leaving them sputtering on the edge of their narrow perch. As Rachel predicted, uprooted trees and even boulders were hurtling past – some crashing against each other before careening off in different directions downstream.

Marius pulled his eyes from the swollen river and looked up, searching the canyon walls for another crevice or ledge. The water level was too close. He wasn't sure they could survive another wave.

There's nowhere else to go.

Rachel turned to him and he realized he had spoken out loud.

"We could climb the tree," she said.

Marius shook his head.

"It's more precarious than the ledge." He pointed to yet another tree that passed in the torrent, its roots visible and still clumped with soil. He scooted back toward the cliff wall, pulling Rachel with him. There still wasn't enough clearance between them and the edge. He tried not to think about more logs and boulders – how they could easily lurch in their direction, crushing them, or dragging them under.

"At least here, we're on solid rock," he said. He wasn't sure if he was trying to reassure Rachel or himself.

"But we're still tied to the tree," she said wearily, and Marius realized she was right.

"We'll secure ourselves as best we can," he said with forced conviction, "and ride it out. How's your head?"

"Fine." She waved him off as he tried to see if her eyes were evenly dilated. They were both bleeding from cuts and scratches, but nothing looked serious.

The rain had lessened considerably during the past minute, but Marius didn't dare to hope. Instead, he tightened their ropes, then turned north and waited for the next wave.

CB

"MARIUS."

Rachel whispered his name and he opened his eyes. When had he closed them? The sky was clear and the moon was bright, reaching for the western horizon.

"What is it?"

"The water is going down," she said.

Then he remembered – the next wave had never come, though he had waited for an hour, his jaw clenched with anticipation.

He shifted, rubbing his forehead. "Sorry I fell asleep." It was amazing they hadn't both tumbled over the edge.

"You needed the rest."

"Did you sleep?"

"Yes, some. But my wrist is throbbing and I'm numb all over."

Marius shifted to give her more room. He tried to ignore his aching muscles while he carefully examined her wrist in the moonlight. It was bruised and swollen.

"I'm sorry," he said. "I should have done something with this earlier."

"Like what? Make a cast with leaves and tree sap?"

Marius laughed. Rachel joined him and, for a few moments, neither of them could stop.

"It might just be a bad sprain," she said.

Marius looked up at his backpack, hanging precariously in the tree above them. "I have Advil in there somewhere," he said.

Rachel's smile faded. "Marius, we lost the evidence bags in my backpack."

Marius turned and looked south, watching the river continue to roll, though the water was clearly going down. "At least you insisted on giving me the film," he said.

For a while, neither of them had anything to say. Marius felt sore and cold, but not tired.

"You're shivering," he said to Rachel.

"I'd love a blanket," she admitted.

"Here." Marius shifted. "Turn around – carefully."

Rachel complied, moving her feet away from him and turning so that her head was on his shoulder and his arm was around her back.

"Any warmer?" he asked after a minute, trying not to think about how familiar it felt to have his arms around her.

"Some," she said. "You're still really wet, you know?"

Marius smiled, but was pleased when she stopped shivering.

"I don't suppose we could untie these ropes."

"Uh, no."

"Didn't think you'd let me get away with that."

"I don't want to fish you out of the river again."

Rachel turned and looked at him. "I'm never going to hear the end of that, am I?"

For a minute, they just smiled at each other. Then confusion and guilt flickered in Rachel's eyes and her smile disappeared. Marius looked away and cleared his throat.

It was the exhilaration of survival that was making them act as they once had quite naturally. For a moment, they had both forgotten that their present circumstances were just that. That their future was not intertwined.

"Can you sleep again?" he ventured.

"I don't think so," she said. "Can we talk?"

"About?" he asked warily.

"I don't care." Rachel's voice was raw. "Tell me something I don't know. Are you married? Do you have kids?"

She was in more pain than she was letting on and clearly looking for nothing more than a distraction. Still, he wished she had asked something else.

"Not anymore," he said.

He stared out at the moon, wondering if he could leave it there. But she was waiting quietly and hurting. So he told her about Carmen – just the high points at first – how they had met when he was working in Oaxaca and she was a bank teller. He didn't tell her how vivacious Carmen was, how she laughed all the time, was often daring to the point of inviting trouble, or how he had found her dark beauty a welcome antidote to the memories of the naïve American he had once loved.

Marius had forgotten Rachel was a good listener – she did not judge, interject or murmur unnecessarily. She gave him her full attention, but was still and soft as the night, disappearing for a time into the darkness and becoming only a safe place for him to leave his story.

So he kept talking, finding that the more he said, the more he had to say. He told her how he and Carmen had married a year after they met and about the pregnancy that came four years later, a blessing that delighted and surprised them both after several miscarriages. Then he told her about his son's birth – and how he had never opened his eyes and died within the hour.

"He was beautiful," he said, his soul heavy. "You couldn't tell that anything was wrong by looking at him."

"Marius, I'm so sorry." She squeezed his hand. "What was his name?"

"Xavier."

For several minutes they sat in silence.

It was difficult," he said finally. "And before Carmen had finished mourning our son, her younger sister died in a car accident, leaving her husband to raise his three children alone.

"Carmen began caring for her nieces and nephews right after the funeral. For a time, I thought it was a good thing. Perhaps it was. She was happier with them than she was at home. After a while, she began leaving the house earlier each morning, coming home later at night."

Marius shifted and Rachel sat up. He watched her carefully draw her knees up to her chest, laying her hurt wrist across the top of them.

"One night she didn't come home," he said. "She called the next day and told me they needed her more than I did. That he needed her more too."

Several minutes passed silently.

"How long ago was it?" Rachel asked.

"My son would have been nine in February."

Together they turned back toward the river to stare at the images he had painted as they hovered over the water and floated away with all the other debris.

14

RACHEL WOKE to the sound of helicopter blades slicing through a cloud-free sky. She sat up carefully, pushing herself off Marius's leg with a brief apology and trying to shake off sleep. Her efforts were hardly effective. She felt drugged. Memories of the preceding night darted through her mind, cloaked in a surreal haze.

The sun was already high in the sky and the air was thick and hot, pressing in on her parched throat like an invisible turtleneck. Her head and swollen wrist were throbbing with competing rhythms of pain and the rest of her body felt like one big bruise, reminding her of their precarious bed and the fall she had taken the night before.

I won't think about how I look, she thought.

She straightened her damp shirt, which was already beginning to smell sour and cleared her throat.

"Where is it?" She stared at the sky.

Marius was tilting his head back and had one hand over his eyes. "I don't see it. Probably to the northeast." He held his flashlight lens at an angle, catching the reflection of the sun to aid their rescuers.

"Do you know what time it is?"

"Late morning." He turned to face her. "I didn't expect them to find us this soon."

Clearly he had not slept since last night. His eyes were bloodshot and dark underneath, his lips were chapped and his face was shadowed by morning stubble. Rachel felt an insane desire to run her thumb along his chin and over his rough lips. She rubbed the back of her neck instead.

The river below them was still swollen but relatively peaceful. It was difficult to connect its muddy depths with the life-threatening torrent of only a few hours ago. It looked more like chocolate milk being mixed by the wind.

"I'm sorry for all of this." Marius eyes were deep with guilt. "I saw the lightning last night. I should have known what it meant."

Rachel tilted her head. "Sorry? Marius, you saved my life."

"Still—"

"Still nothing, Marius." She reached for his hand. "Thank you."

Marius looked down at their hands and his thumb shifted, a feather against her palm.

Rachel swallowed hard. The space between them was suddenly charged and her lightheadedness returned. Marius's jaw tightened in some unknown struggle while her heart began to strike at her ribcage. For a moment she could imagine nothing but that it felt at home, finding a familiar echo in his, its long lost twin.

His head dipped toward her.

"*Raquel…*"

The helicopter burst into view overhead, making Rachel jump.

"Steady." His arms held her firmly in place. "It's almost over now."

The rescue team spotted them moments later. A full hour passed before they were onboard and riding back toward Creel.

"We left at dawn and found Chu and Juan on the west rim." Cruces shook his head. "They figured you for dead. Seemed to take it in stride. I suppose you were hexed?"

"Apparently." Marius drained the last bit of water from a Dasani bottle. "If you'll hand me that map, I'll mark the location of the cave. It needs to be thoroughly searched."

"Down river?" Cruces squinted out the window. "It will be impassable now."

"No, the elevation was higher at the cave, wasn't it?" Rachel said. "And there was a skylight entrance from the cliff above."

The helicopter swooped eastward, making her feel queasy. Perhaps she'd emptied her own water bottle too quickly.

Marius studied her, frowning. "Don't worry. They'll find it and post a guard until the water recedes."

Rachel closed her eyes. "My backpack. You probably won't find it, but keep a lookout. The evidence…"

Marius's voice faded in her ear.

"Rest, Rachel. *Todo es bien.*"

Rachel dozed until the helicopter landed and yet still struggled to keep her eyes open as they drove the short distance to the medical clinic.

"You both need fluids," the doctor told them, but his frown deepened when he looked at Rachel. "We'll get some medicine for your pain," he told her.

"First, she needs a telephone," Marius said. Rachel looked at him gratefully and spent the next few minutes talking to Melissa and then Danny, glossing over the details of their ordeal and infusing enough normalcy into her voice to alleviate their worries.

"I need to go now," she told Danny as the doctor returned for her. "I'll call you again this evening, okay?"

She followed him into a small exam room and sat on the edge of a creaky bed while he gently prodded her wrist and looked for signs of a concussion. She answered his questions mechanically, wanting nothing more than to return to her hotel room to shower and sleep.

"We have no X-ray facilities in Creel," the doctor said apologetically. "But I think it's just a bad sprain. Of course, you can fly to *la ciudad* to rule out a fracture."

Rachel shook her head. "No, just splint it, *por favor.*"

When the doctor left, Rachel lay back against the pillows and closed her eyes. She opened them a few minutes later and found Marius at the foot of her bed, looking no worse than tired.

"Don't get up," he said, but Rachel was already pushing her legs over the edge of her bed and struggling to ignore the swimming room.

"How are you?" she asked.

"Tired." He rubbed his hand over the back of his neck. "*Y tú?*"

"I'll be fine." She looked down at her wrinkled clothes. "I'm ready to get cleaned up. Do you think they'll let us go back to the hotel?"

He frowned. "You must have a concussion. Your fall…"

"The doctor doesn't know, but he told me what to watch for. He said what I need most is rest." She shifted back and forth, causing the bed to shudder underneath her. "I'm not going to sleep here as well as I would back at the hotel."

Marius considered her for a moment and then turned toward the door. "I'll see what I can do."

Rachel heard his voice blending with the doctor's in the hallway. Finally the doctor came back in, carrying a small package.

"Demerol for your pain," he said. "Agent Suarez has promised me that you will go straight to your hotel room and rest – and to check on you as well. *Mañana, no trabajo.* Agreed?"

"No work. I understand."

Rachel fought to stay upright as they drove back to the hotel, but as soon as she had closed her door and taken two pain pills, she collapsed on top of her bed, no longer caring how dirty she was. She fell asleep at once and did not wake until dinnertime.

Still weaving from the medicine and wincing from her aching muscles, she took a shower – difficult with only one good hand – and came out feeling clean but spent. Her mind wandered as she pulled on sweats and began to finger-dry her hair. In the bottom of her suitcase she spied her worn copy of *Jane Eyre* and pulled it out, running her hand along its brittle spine. She wished she could bury herself in its comforting pages. Instead, she carried it to her bedside table and sat, staring at it.

Without considering her grades or corresponding growth in knowledge – and she hadn't – Rachel viewed her freshman year at Arizona State as a miserable failure. She had made few friends and was finding campus life too vibrant for her introspective personality. Paired with a roommate unknown to her until her first day on campus, Rachel quickly became disillusioned with dorm life, visions of instant bonding and sisterhood disappearing behind a web of torn fishnet stockings.

Her roommate, Debbie, was a monochromatic film major who layered their room with black clothing and smelled of antiseptic – necessary to treat the infected piercings she continued to add to her body. Debbie hung with a crowd of similarly macabre girls living on the same floor. Rachel came to understand that their affinity for vampire novels and *The Cure* was not an unshakeable attribute of their collective character – they were college students, after all, and every last one of them enrolled on Daddy's dime – but rather their preferred method for identifying themselves as an impenetrable unit. Being the only unpaired member had made Debbie the most vulnerable sister in their club, so she had found a healthy outlet for her feelings – channeling them into overdone annoyance with Rachel's horrid normalness.

Rachel thought about trying to change roommates, or even moving into a single, but decided against it. Her father – who was paying for her education as well – had only reluctantly agreed to her enrollment at ASU. She wasn't going to reassure him by revealing Debbie's odd practices or – more recently – her boyfriend, Chad. He should have been pre-med, Rachel thought, given the degree of time and attention he paid to Debbie's anatomy.

"Do you think you can make yourself scarce tonight?" Debbie asked Rachel in the Memorial Union one Friday afternoon. Rachel was standing with her back to a large and unnecessary fireplace flanked by cushioned benches. Her backpack was heavy and she was impatient to find a corner to unload and study. "Chad's coming over. It would be good if you stayed out late. Or all night."

"No problem," Rachel answered flatly. She wondered if she would end up sleeping on the couch in the common room again. Debbie rolled her eyes and slouched away, apparently not even pleased when Rachel behaved like a doormat.

"You're welcome," she called to Debbie's back, confident the crowd would swallow her voice. Turning around, she found a seat between the fireplace and a man in the corner buried behind a newspaper. She lowered her pack and retrieved her tattered copy of *Jane Eyre* from its depths. These moments were made for escape.

"Lit class?"

Rachel looked up. The man with the paper was her Spanish teacher, Marius Bazán. She blushed, fingering her bookmark. He had been too close to miss her conversation with Debbie. If he didn't think she was a complete loser the night she was egged, he certainly would now.

"It's a good book." Marius nodded toward her paperback. "Are you enjoying it?"

Rachel frowned, skeptical. "You've read *Jane Eyre*?"

"Yes, honestly!" He smiled. "Though I will admit, it wasn't by choice. My mother and I moved often when I was young. Two years before I was to enter university, we moved to Madrid. My new literature teacher had just assigned everyone a different classic novel to read." He shrugged. "I was stuck with *Jane Eyre* because everything else was already taken."

Rachel smiled. "That happened to me once. My junior year, we each had to choose a book title out of a hat. I was stuck with *Moby Dick*." She made a face. "Did you know there are entire chapters in that book devoted to the bone structure of whales?"

"So you have a happier assignment now, then?" Marius asked.

"It's not actually from a class," Rachel said. She turned the book over in her hands. "It's my favorite. I reread it often."

Marius watched her for a moment. "You surprise me, Miss Bishop. You have time to read for pleasure in the weeks before finals?"

"I make time, I guess." She tilted her head. "And why do you still call me Miss Bishop? The other students notice."

He smiled. "You call me Señor Bazán, though everyone else has learned to call me Marius. I just assumed you prefer things to remain … more formal."

Rachel didn't know what to say, so she stood and tucked her book under one arm. "I should go."

"I'm sorry. I didn't mean to make you uncomfortable. Stay and read – I won't disturb you."

"No, you didn't." She zipped her backpack, pushing it onto her shoulder. "It's just – college is so different from what I expected. I'm not sure I'm…" She stopped. "I don't think I will ever get used to calling you by your first name."

He nodded. Rachel turned to leave.

"Miss Bishop?"

She turned around.

He hesitated, looking pained. "If you ever need somewhere to go to… accommodate your roommate, please be careful. Some place well lit. And if you ever need an escort home—"

"Thank you." She looked at her feet. "I'll keep that in mind."

Rachel had never taken Marius up on his offer, though she had spent many nights away from her room – until Chad became a Gap-wearing party boy and threw Debbie off for a cheerleader. Now as she reached for *Jane Eyre*, she remembered spending the rest of that particular evening cloistered behind the fourth floor stacks in the library, reading about Jane's agony over leaving Mr. Rochester. It all happened so long ago, yet here was the same book in her hands.

She didn't open it. Instead, she thought about Marius's lost child and the wife who had left him for someone else. She had hurt with him while listening to his story, feeling sure he had not said it all out loud before. At some point before falling asleep on his knee, Rachel had considered telling him about her own divorce. Something stopped her. It wasn't the right time, she decided. Their situations were different, after all. His son had died.

Still, she would have to tell him soon. Things had changed last night. It no longer felt like discretion to keep silent, more like deception.

But what would be implied in such a confession?

She tried to script the words in her head but cringed with each revision, unable to make it come out right. It seemed like a plea for pity at best. And at worst? Rachel's cheeks reddened and she was back on the ledge with Marius bending toward her.

Had she only imagined that he was about to kiss her?

She put the book down and shifted on her bed, aching all over. It was hard to know what Marius was going to do, she decided. She had been exhausted and dehydrated. But his expression had taken her back to a time when she knew what it was to anticipate his kiss, to yearn for it with a heat that was almost painful.

One thing she understood – almost losing their lives together in the flood had rekindled her connection to him. Her anger about his deceit had been all but washed away in the swollen river and, with it, her defense against confusing feelings. But she couldn't get around the fact that Marius thought she was still married and she had done nothing to correct him. It felt like a lie to keep silent and like an invitation to come clean.

Melissa had warned her to be careful. Was this what she was afraid of? That proximity would turn to caring? That caring would lead to more?

Rachel had no easy answers. She looked down at her wedding band, now battered and misshapen, the gold nicked and dented from her fall. For the first time, it felt like a shackle to her failed marriage. She began to twist it, working it off. A knock on the door made her jump. Pushing her ring back in place, she rose and opened it.

Agent Trent was leaning against the doorway, smiling like the Cheshire cat.

"I shouldn't have left you alone down here." He shook his head. "This is a dangerous country, Mueller. What were you thinking, going into the canyon with the natives? Not your best idea."

"We found the kidnapper's hiding place," Rachel said. Her voice was tight, her arms crossed.

Trent shrugged and walked past her to sit uninvited in one of the chairs by the window. Flicking the curtain, he looked out at the darkening sky. "I have contacts here that could have been at your disposal. All you had to do was ask. Putting yourself at risk was completely unnecessary."

"We hit pay dirt in that cave, Trent. And I would have liked to see your contacts prevent a flash flood."

Trent laughed. "That's good. I like your attitude. Might as well keep your sense of humor."

Rachel pressed her lips together and silently counted to ten. Had this man not changed at all since Texas? She stared pointedly at the open door, hoping he wouldn't stay long.

"I'm glad you had Suarez with you at least," Trent said soberly. He settled back against his chair and stretched out his legs. "He's former Internal Affairs down here. Did you know?"

Rachel sat down on the corner of her bed. "No, I didn't."

"Tough as nails. He's been fighting the cartels' influence from within the federal police for years – one of the few to survive the job. A losing battle, though. Last year a car bomb got too close and he finally gave it up."

"But you're not his biggest fan," Rachel said.

Trent looked at her blankly.

"The argument I interrupted the other day?" she prodded. "It didn't seem exactly – fresh."

"Oh that." Trent made a dismissive noise. "Well, he isn't a big fan of Americans either, is he? But you see that. Now, Agent Cruces is another story. He's from Chihuahua originally."

"Yes, he told me."

Trent leaned forward, lowering his voice. "Listen, Cruces strikes me as a decent-enough man, and Agent Suarez certainly trusts him, but some DEA buddies of mine told me they were sorry to see him working up here again. They don't trust him."

"Why?"

"Some hushed up thing from a long time ago," Trent said. "I don't know the details, but something about a woman getting killed. Cruces' accounting of how things went down was questionable at best."

"Sounds like idle gossip."

"Yeah, well. Who's to say?" Trent shrugged. "But there's something off about him. I hope he's not involved in anything underhanded. He didn't look exactly pleased to see me when I arrived today."

I'm never exactly pleased to see you either, Rachel thought.

"You got back from Arizona quickly," she said, changing the subject. "How did it go with Mrs. Davidson?"

"Well as can be expected, I suppose."

"Did you show her the sand dollar necklace?"

"Yeah, she wasn't sure where it came from."

"But was it Samantha's?" Rachel pressed.

"Well whose would it be if it wasn't hers?"

"Agent Trent," Rachel no longer tried to hide her exasperation, "were you even listening to me when I asked you to show her the necklace? We need to know if it belonged to Samantha at all. If it didn't, it may have belonged to another victim."

"Another victim? You really want this case to be a big deal, don't you?" Trent smiled widely. "Nothing but a captured serial killer to be added to your file. Good for you. But I think you're off track. This guy we're tracking doesn't seem the type."

"I'm *not* building my career, and the evidence in the cave supports..." Rachel stopped. "Wait. Do you have new intel on the suspect?"

"Of course. You didn't think we were sitting on our thumbs yesterday while you were in the canyon, did you?" Trent asked. "No, just minutes after I returned, one of those boys from the plaza came rushing in to tell us they found the old homestead belonging to the suspect's grandmother."

"And?"

"It's not too far from town. A short drive. The road is terrible though. I have a toothache just thinking about it. We have it under surveillance, hoping he returns soon so we can nab him."

"I hope he didn't find his way back to the cave," Rachel said. "Do you know if Cruces was successful in securing it today?"

Trent shook his head. "You'll have to ask him – or Suarez. I suppose you're good friends now. Sounds like things got dicey down there."

"Yes," she said. "He saved my life."

"Well, he's not like most agents down here, I'll tell you that. It must come from the IA job, or because he was raised in Europe. Who knows? But left to themselves, Mexicans can never keep the cartels from placing their own people in the agency. It's just a different way of thinking down here. Different rules have to be applied."

Trent leaned forward, his grin so wide, she could see his molars. "When I was in Phoenix, I spoke to SAC Devlin about it – asked her if she would approve an extra allowance for bribes."

"Wallowing in the mire, Trent?"

"Oh, get off your high horse, Mueller." It looked like she had finally hit a nerve. "You know it's sometimes necessary – the ugly side of covert operations. No use taking it all so seriously."

"I seriously hope you're kidding," Rachel said darkly. "And besides, there can be no covert element to this investigation – not if we plan on presenting evidence that will stand up in court."

"You think any of this is going to an American court?" he asked skeptically.

"That's why I'm here, Trent. To bring this killer to justice."

"There's more than one kind of justice," he said. "And the Mexican mindset is just different. Don't you read the news? Down here, justice is meted out quite swiftly. Trust me. I know."

"Mexican justice being…?"

"You read about what happened in Acapulco." He made a cutting gesture with his hand. "Heads will roll."

"So Mexican citizens and the cartels are one and the same now, is that it?" Rachel asked. "Has it ever occurred to you that most people here just want to live their lives in peace?"

Trent shook his head. "You can grandstand all you want, but I live here, and let me tell you – Mexicans just don't think as rationally as—"

"Excuse me. Am I interrupting?"

Marius stood in the open doorway, his eyes dark as stone. Rachel remembered the expression from long ago when he had overheard a similar dismissive of Mexican values from her father. Family loyalty kept Rachel from doing more than side step her father's attitudes then, horrifying as they were. Looking back, she wondered if that had been the beginning of the end for them.

"How are you, Agent Suarez?" she asked softly.

"I'm well, thank you." Marius handed her a bag without comment. It smelled like food, but Rachel kept her eyes on him. He looked anything but well, making her wonder if he had rested at all today.

Trent stood up and shamelessly stuck his hand out to Marius.

"Thanks for keeping our girl safe," he said.

Rachel groaned.

Undaunted, Trent went on – praising Marius for his heroism in the canyon and cursing his own absence, hinting that he could have prevented Rachel's fall – and perhaps even escaped the flood altogether – if he had been there.

Rachel couldn't listen to any more.

"Thanks for dropping by." She avoided Marius's face as she stood up and prodded Trent toward the door. "I'm afraid I'm a little spent."

"Yes, of course," Trent said. "We'll go then." He turned to Marius. "Care to join me for a drink in the cantina?"

Marius nodded curtly. "Yes. I'll join you in a few minutes."

Trent waved cheerfully and walked out the door while Rachel set the bag on the table and sat down again.

"Thank you for this." She glanced up at him and then focused on the bag again. "I never know whether to laugh or scream at that man."

Marius said nothing, but stood by the open doorway. He didn't look angry anymore, just tired.

"Will you sit down?" The food smelled good, but Rachel's stomach was unsettled.

"No, I can't stay." His mouth twisted. "I've just committed myself, haven't I?"

"Yes you have. But why?"

"I have my reasons. Anyway, I came to deliver a message." He handed her a folded slip of paper. Rachel opened it and read it silently, her heart suddenly out of rhythm.

Your husband called. 5 p.m. Call back A.S.A.P.

It was Marius's handwriting.

"Craig?" she asked stupidly.

Marius nodded. "Perhaps your cell phone is off?"

"Yes. I think it is," she said. "Marius, there's something—"

"Another time," he interrupted. "When you've had more rest."

He looked out at the darkness, his jaw tight. "I shouldn't keep Trent waiting. Goodnight, Rachel."

15

SOMEONE WAS BANGING on the door. Marius opened his eyes and blinked into the blackness of his hotel room before rolling over to read the digital clock. It was seven in the morning.

"Un momento!"

Marius staggered toward the door, his head heavy and his mouth thick. He didn't bother with a shirt. He knew whom to expect.

"Agent Suarez."

"Give me fifteen minutes."

Agent Castillo nodded and walked away. Marius headed for the shower. Twenty minutes later, he walked into the command center, nodding tersely at Gonzalez and Castillo before reaching for the coffee pot. Agent Cruces joined him.

"You look worse than you did yesterday," Johnny said.

Tell me something I don't know, Marius thought. He had seen the cuts and bruises in the mirror. But they weren't as bad as the dark circles under his eyes – or the way every subtle movement brought a fresh wave of aching muscles.

"¿Tienes Advil?"

"Let me go look."

Johnny returned with a bottle and stood waiting while Marius tapped two tablets into his hand.

"Who is on the cave this morning?"

"Barreto. We'll be able to go in today."

"*Bueno*. Take Gonzalez and Fuerte along. I'll keep Castillo here."

Johnny nodded. Marius walked to the wall map and studied it, struggling to ignore his swimming mind. He had to make up for lost time. A night and morning sacrificed to the flood incident may have been unavoidable, but allowing Craig Mueller's brief phone call yesterday to destroy his focus was inexcusable.

"Good morning, Agent Mueller," he heard Johnny say behind him. "How are you feeling?"

Marius swallowed another sip of coffee and continued to study the map, though he heard Rachel's quiet response. She joined him after several minutes with a steaming Styrofoam cup in her hand.

"How is your wrist?" he asked.

"Better." She paused. "Trent told me they found the *bruja's* shack yesterday."

"Unfortunately, he was mistaken."

She turned toward him, frowning.

He glanced at her. "It was only the *ranchito* where the *tesguinada* was likely held."

"That's – disappointing."

"Perhaps. But we'll find it today." He felt confident of that at least. "If we're lucky, we'll find Samantha's kidnapper too.

"This is the cave." He pointed to the map. "And up here is the *ranchito* – owned by Señor Montéz – northeast of Tararecua Canyon, above these foothills."

"And when Chu and Juan passed the shack, where were they headed?" Rachel asked.

"To Juan's mother's home – over here." Marius spread his fingers and tapped them on the map. "So the shack must be in this area. It should help that it was near an abandoned mine. Many are marked on our maps."

"Will they be easy to spot by air?"

"I don't know. It's a large area. I'll start searching from the helicopter and see what I find."

"When do we leave?"

Marius studied Rachel. She looked tired but better than she had yesterday, despite the cuts and bruises on her face and arms. Still, his mind shot back to how she had looked lying at the foot of the cliff with flood waters approaching. Wet, pale, still. He suppressed a shudder and took a sip of his coffee.

He didn't want her to come along, but could hardly tell her that. She would ask why, and neither truth – that he didn't want to risk being alone with her or that he simply couldn't endure the idea of putting her in danger again – was something he dare admit. She was an FBI agent, after all, and had proven her toughness over the past forty-eight hours. She was also married. What she was not, he kept reminding himself, was a naïve school girl in need of his protection – their shared night in the canyon notwithstanding.

"I want in on this, whatever it is," Agent Trent said loudly as he walked into the room and headed toward them.

For once, Marius was glad to see him.

"We leave within the hour," he said.

C3

"I THINK that might be it."

"It looks uninhabitable."

Rachel lowered her binoculars and stared at Agent Trent. "That's why we keep using the word 'shack.'"

She turned to Marius. "What do you think? Could Juan and Chu have passed by here when they left Mr. Montéz's house?"

Marius looked up from his map. "It's possible. We need to get closer."

They had already spent more than an hour that morning searching by air, eliminating every other mine marked on his map. This last one drew them to the eastern rim of Tararecua, where the canyon walls jogged inland into a deep slot hidden from view by dense tree coverage. Their only option had been to land in a nearby cow pasture and hike in. An abandoned *ranchito* built on an adjacent bluff had to be investigated first, but they found nothing of interest inside, just some broken pottery and what seemed like about five-years-worth of trash. From there, they set out on foot, heading northeast while swatting away an annoying abundance of flies and stepping carefully to avoid cow chips.

Trent had not shut up since they climbed out of the chopper, offering a running commentary on every hiccup along their path, incessantly whining about their progress, and criticizing everything from his shoes to the Chihuahua government and their dismal failure at trail maintenance.

But whenever they drew near the rim, amazing canyon views managed to silence even Trent – soaring to jagged peaks and plunging to a floor so far below, the river that had almost killed them could not be seen. In the distance, the mountains near El Tejabán were draped in endless folds of emerald velvet lichen, glistening in the sunlight, making Marius wish he was visiting under better circumstances.

Moments ago, when they had been forced to retreat from a path that ended at the rim, Rachel spotted the shack just a stone's throw from what looked like the dark opening of a mine shaft. A direct route seemed unlikely – the terrain below was jagged and impassable. Luckily, the map showed the canyon narrowing into a dry arroyo about two kilometers to the east.

"We'll head that way," Marius said.

Trent's scowl deepened. "Is this really necessary? I guarantee, no one lives in that pile of rotting wood. We'll find it abandoned, just like that *ranchito*," he waved vaguely behind his head, "mark my words."

"You want to wait here?" Rachel asked.

Marius frowned. "No, he doesn't. *Vamanos*."

They turned back and found a path that gradually curved northeast along the cliff. But when it also ended abruptly – pitching itself over the edge in what was surely an impassable trail, even to the most dexterous Tarahumara – they detoured to the south. Cutting across a sloping meadow, they circled a high mesa, climbed through a rocky arroyo, and finally turned eastward again. Ten minutes later, they emerged in a field fringed with large boulders. In the distance, they could see the place they had stood when they first spotted the shack.

"The helicopter could have dropped us here," Trent whined.

"Let's keep going," Rachel said.

Beyond the boulders, they followed a trail that wound back toward the mine under a dense canopy of trees. The shack was no more than fifty meters in front of them when Marius ducked behind a tree and signaled Rachel and Trent to follow suit.

He nodded toward the north. "Someone is there."

From a distance, they watched the man work his way toward the shack. He looked at ease, Marius thought, as if he were out for a stroll. He made no furtive movements – no glances over his shoulder, change in direction or variation in speed. His features were indistinct from this distance, but he walked with a rolling gait, his shoulders sloped forward and his hands held steady by his sides. Still, his destination made him suspect. As soon as he disappeared inside the small building, Marius drew his firearm and turned to the others.

"Trent, you take the north side, I'll take the east. We'll circle toward the door on the west – agreed?"

Trent nodded.

Marius turned to Rachel and looked pointedly at her braced wrist. "Can you cover us from the mine?"

Rachel nodded and pulled her Glock from its holster, following them along the trail. They reached the mine quickly, where she detached and found cover behind a tree. Marius and Trent soundlessly approached the shack.

Marius's heart drummed against his chest. They had cornered the suspect so easily – it made him feel more cautious than confident. Edging his way around the small building, he winced at its crumbling foundation, a small avalanche with every step. He stopped, listening. Had he been heard? He imagined the worst – a veritable armory inside, their suspect setting booby traps. Marius crouched under a window, boarded up with newer wood, fresh nails. Was it to keep someone inside? His fingers tightened around the grip of his gun and he inched forward.

Just as he cleared the window, the wall next to him shuddered with a heavy thump, spraying him with decades of dust. For a moment, there was silence and then an animalistic shout arose from the other side. Abandoning stealth, Marius rounded the corner to see Trent staggering out the doorway. Their suspect was a blur as he knocked past him and disappeared around the west side of the building.

Trent moved quickly, scrambling to the balls of his feet. "I got it!" He tore after him.

Marius went the way he came, running. He didn't know where the suspect was heading – back along the path he had followed this morning? Into the canyon? Toward Rachel at the mine?

Rachel.

Marius heard her shout just as he cleared the corner.

"Stop!"

A gunshot rang out, stilling his heart as he tore through the trees. Rachel was standing on the trail in front of the mine with her gun drawn. Her face had drained of blood, but her stance and aim were steady. Trent stood closer to the shack, his gun still smoking from the bullet that had ripped through the suspect's back. The man whimpered and dropped a rifle before slumping to the ground. The weight of his body carried him down the trail, where he rolled, coming to rest at Rachel's feet.

Trent turned to Marius, his eyes wide. "He might have killed her," he said.

Marius nodded wordlessly and watched Rachel holster her gun and kneel beside the suspect, feeling needlessly for a pulse.

16

WITHIN AN HOUR, the shack, mine and surrounding area were swarming with law enforcement. Every federal agent in the vicinity had been called in, along with local police and a few Tarahumara elders who stood on the fringe, looking bewildered.

Marius had radioed the helicopter pilot while gun smoke still hung in the air, trapped with the acrid smell of death under the canopy of trees. He ordered him back to Creel to recall the rest of the team. They came in three groups, landing in the nearby meadow and reporting to Marius, who had set up a perimeter around the scene.

The rest of the day passed in a blur of function for Rachel. She focused on her assigned task – helping Cruces catalogue evidence – and nothing more. Her wrist throbbed in protest, but she fought to ignore it. When memories of the suspect's dying expression intruded, she forced them away too.

It was late afternoon when Cruces sent her to the makeshift command post set up at the edge of the meadow. Agent Trent and Marius were waiting.

"I want you to return to Creel with the body," Marius told them. "Write your statements while everything is fresh in your minds."

Rachel nodded, but said nothing. She had been mentally preparing her statement for the past hour, defending Trent's decision from a standpoint of logic and procedure. Like a mantra she had repeated it in her head – the suspect was carrying a rifle, he was headed toward her. He was warned to stop and did not obey.

"Shouldn't one member of the FBI stay here?" Trent asked.

Marius looked weary rather than annoyed. "Jurisdiction," he said flatly. "Write a thorough report. It's the best help you can give."

Trent didn't argue. He walked toward the helicopter while Rachel handed Marius her clipboard. "Evidence bag inventory," she said.

Marius took the clipboard without looking at it. "How's the wrist?" he asked.

"It hurts."

"Get some rest after you've written your statement. You can leave it on my desk."

⚃

RACHEL SAW three men running from the shack. One of them should have been a stranger, but he wasn't. He raised his rifle and brought her into his sights. Rachel's chest filled with the weight of his betrayal. It felt like he had already pulled the trigger. She drew her gun.

"Stop!" she shouted. He didn't. Instead his eyes widened in confusion. Trent's shot echoed through the trees, scattering birds and making her flinch as if she had been hit. Then she was running – through miles of quicksand – and turning over his body. It wasn't the man from the canyon. It was Victor.

"*No*. No, no!"

"Rachel." The pounding was urgent. "Rachel, *abra la puerta*!"

She opened her eyes, sobbing, struggling through the darkness toward the door. Everything would be okay when she opened it. She fumbled with the lock. And then the door was open and Marius was there with steady arms, murmuring against her temple.

"Everything is alright, Rachel." He closed the door and guided her to the corner of the bed. "It was just a bad dream."

Reality was bleeding through, staining the edges of her mind. It wasn't Victor who was killed on the canyon rim, but it had been his dead face in her dream. Today's killing and his unanswered phone message must have fused in her subconscious thought, a twisted and cruel trick of the mind.

"It wasn't just a dream. That man—"

"Shh," Marius said. "He can't hurt you now."

Rachel shook her head. "You don't understand. You didn't see his face." Her words were thick and muffled by tears. She couldn't get the image out of her head – the dead man who was probably now lying on the same table that had held Samantha's body only a few days ago. "He was terrified, Marius. He didn't...he couldn't..."

Her words wouldn't form.

Marius pulled her against his chest. "Shh. *Todo está bien.*"

Rachel wasn't sure. She had forced the man's dying expression from her thoughts all day and focused on her job, just as her training required. But now it pushed itself relentlessly forward, filling her with sorrow and a terrifying sense of loss.

The man had burst around the edge of the shack like a one-man stampede, but his round jaw had been slack and soft, his eyes confused and full of fear. From her vantage, his movements looked awkward and childlike, and his grip on the rifle had been clumsy – with outstretched fingers that did not touch the trigger, much less take aim. In the instant before Trent fired his gun, she had taken all of it in.

This couldn't be Samantha's kidnapper. This was a child trapped in a man's body.

And so she had commanded him to stop. It should have been enough. He should have dropped the gun and raised his hands. But it was too late. Trent had already fired his fatal blow.

Marius turned on a lamp and hunted down a box of tissues while Rachel brought her emotions under control.

"He was terrified," she repeated hopelessly. "I saw it in his face, Marius. Mentally, he was just a boy."

Marius rubbed his hands across his chin. For a minute, he said nothing, but his face looked grave.

"Trent couldn't see that," he said after a minute. "Not from where he stood. He had to follow protocol."

"I know," she said miserably. Still, she hated Trent for killing him.

"Did you include all of this in your report?"

Rachel nodded. "It will be taken as a footnote by the Bureau. If not for my injury, Trent might have trusted me to take the shot. Then I could have disarmed the man instead of—"

"Don't do that to yourself. Second guessing is always a mistake. You must know that. The autopsy may tell us more about his neurology, but Rachel," She looked up from her wrinkled tissue, "Samantha's wallet was in the shack."

She paused, letting this sink in.

"Well then there was someone else," she reasoned.

"We'll examine everything carefully. There may be fingerprints, other DNA. But…"

"What?"

"An accomplice isn't likely, is it? It doesn't match your profile."

Rachel stood up and threw her tissue away.

"That dead man doesn't match it either, Marius. And could you really call him an accomplice? If his mental capacity was as I imagine, he could have simply been in the wrong place at the wrong time – or a victim himself, pressed into working for the real kidnapper."

She paced, her sorrow burning off in anger.

"Intelligent, creative, with means of travel. Attractive, charismatic, a man who has positioned himself in or close to law enforcement – that's the man we're looking for."

Marius nodded, but he was placating her, not agreeing.

"My profile is sound." She crossed her arms over her chest. "The trophies in the cave back it up."

"Yes, they do." Marius sounded tired. "But they're gone – we only have photos to go on. Cruces and his team brought back other evidence today – DNA samples that need to be analyzed. But you need to be prepared. If forensic evidence doesn't indicate another suspect, my agency will consider this case solved."

"Even though we have no motive?"

Marius nodded.

"Or a valid theory for how he might have smuggled her across the border?"

"I understand your frustration, Rachel, but you know as well as I that many cases get filed without satisfactory answers to every detail."

"Those are pretty big details, Marius."

"I agree. I'll do what I can, but can you honestly tell me the Bureau is going to want you pursuing this?"

She thought about Agent Trent, wrapping up his report, already planning to be back at his consulate desk in Mexico City by Monday morning. She lowered herself to the floor and leaned against the edge of the bed, feeling defeated.

Marius walked toward the door. "I'll let you rest."

Rachel looked at the clock. It was seven thirty. Her nap would mean another sleepless night.

"Wait," she said.

Marius turned around.

"Would you sit with me for a minute?" She knew she sounded needy and pathetic, but she didn't care. She just didn't want to be alone yet.

Marius hesitated, but turned back, lowering himself next to her on the floor. They sat side by side, silently staring at the unlit fireplace. After a few minutes, she shifted, raising her knees, rubbing her wrist.

"Are you in pain?" he asked quietly.

"No." She lowered her arm.

"Can I order you something to eat?"

Rachel smiled. "What is it with you and food? Do you realize that in the time we've been in Creel, you've ordered more meals for me than I've ordered for myself?"

He looked embarrassed. "That's an exaggeration."

"Not much of one."

"Food is comforting," he said, looking at the floor between his feet. "And it's tangible. Something I can do."

"Well, I'm not hungry," she said.

"You're never hungry." He grinned, reminding Rachel of when they sat together on the floor of another Mexican motel room, a nearly untouched feast spread out on a blanket in front of them while they watched *Casablanca* on TV. He had laughed at her attempts to understand the Spanish overdubbing while she made fun of the voices reading for Humphrey Bogart and Ingrid Bergman.

"He sounds all wrong," she said, giggling. "Maybe if Bogart had a cold – and a bag of marbles in his mouth."

But they had both stopped laughing long enough to watch Nick and Ilsa say goodbye on the wet airport tarmac. For Rachel's part, she had been happy to cry only for their sorrow, resting her head against Marius's shoulder and thinking, *I'm so glad that will never be me.*

Rachel cleared her throat. "Why did you come tonight?"

"You didn't look well earlier," Marius said, "after the shooting. I just wanted to see if you were all right."

"Thank you."

She was leaning over to kiss his cheek before the impulse could be considered and suppressed. It was an action conceived in gratitude, but sometime after the command left her brain, its innocence shifted, heating the space between them. When she pulled away, she saw a raw flicker in Marius's eyes that connected to her own shortness of breath.

"Marius, I didn't mean…"

But he was standing up and backing toward the door. "Please, Rachel," he said. "I need to go."

Rachel stood, feeling a wash of guilt flood her cheeks. She looked down at her hands. "Craig and I are…" She stopped. *Divorced.* Why couldn't she say it?

"What?" Marius asked, his brow knit together. "Not happy anymore? Is that what this is about?"

"No." Rachel's flush deepened. "Yes. I mean, that's not what I was going to say—"

"I don't need to hear this." Marius shook his head, his jaw tightening. "Your work is all but done here, Rachel. And in the flood, after almost losing…"

He swallowed hard and looked at her again, his eyes burning. "You have a son," he finally said, jerking the door open. "Go home and raise him. And for his sake, Rachel, whatever your troubles are with your husband, work them out."

17

FRIDAY DAWNED, too beautiful for autopsies and DNA analysis. Marius hardly noticed, feeling sleep-deprived and wishing everything could be considered done instead of being the bulk of the day ahead. He had left his bed before the birds began to sing this morning and walked briskly from the hotel, past the plaza, across the railroad track and into the woods. There, he blindly trusted the trails while his mind circled from Rachel to Trent to Cruces to Samantha to the dead suspect and back around again.

Rachel. Just the memory of her disheveled blond curls, wet eyes and red nose last night was enough to twist his insides into knots. She would be gone soon, though.

And good riddance, he thought, lengthening his stride.

He had done the right thing last night, but hardly felt honorable for it. Fighting feelings he shouldn't have entertained in the first place wasn't noble. During the night, he had become convinced that, for her part at least, those feelings had been nothing more than symptoms of a heart heavy with marital woes and confusion by his reentry into her life. Not to mention their shared life-threatening experience in the canyon.

Which makes me all the more a fool, he thought bitterly.

So he had pounded his pillow and then pounded the trail, trying not to think about what it would have felt like to kiss her again. His thoughts had been accommodative – and not – pushing him so far from yesterday that, before he realized it, he was thinking about their first kiss instead, the one that had doomed them from the beginning.

Rachel became Marius's favorite student even before he had seen her safely to her dorm on Halloween night. In a sea of bored freshmen, she progressed quickly – grasping conjugation, memorizing vocabulary and pronouncing words like a native. At the time, his duplicitous careers were weighing heavily on him, and since he could do nothing right in the eyes of his DEA handler, he worked harder at his cover job. Rachel's thirst for knowledge made it easy. Soon he began to see his successes and failures mostly through her responses to his instruction.

He didn't realize other students were taking notice.

The week before finals, Marius overheard two of her classmates make a suggestive leap about the extent of his favoritism. The remark surprised him, but he didn't challenge it. When the semester ended, he turned his mind to more pressing matters – working for the DEA and gearing up for his master's course studies for the coming semester.

But Marius couldn't deny the pleasure he felt at seeing Rachel's name on the roster for his spring Spanish 102 class. This time, he told himself, he would make a stronger effort to treat her like any other student. That became even more challenging when she joined the Spanish club – the management of which Marius had been urged to undertake by both his department head and his DEA handler.

Things were getting worse between Marius and Agent Johnson, who gave him no leeway to act on his own instincts, but continued to criticize his lack of results.

"But what should I expect when we outsource to Mexico?" Johnson asked.

Marius learned to bite back his instinctive response – a trick which became invaluable years later when his job was tracking corrupt agents. Looking back, he realized he matured in America, learning that the best answer to prejudice was the dispassionate contradiction of its assumptions. On the other hand, his opinion of the U.S. had suffered. Perhaps experiencing America for the first time while employed to examine her darkest habits was not the best way to convince a young man of her merits. With time and maturity – both of which allowed him to see the same kind of prejudices at work in Mexico – Marius recognized that Agent Johnson, rather than his country, was accountable for those negative feelings.

But that spring, Marius was struggling. He had envisioned his undercover work so differently – producing results, earning him praise, crippling crime. Maybe that was why his thoughts so often turned to Rachel. She was all innocence, conviction and honesty – the antithesis of the criminals he was trying to catch. While she was reciting subjunctive verbs or getting on her soapbox about American exacerbation of the Mexican stereotype, he found his attention drifting to the way she carried herself, wrinkled her freckled nose or twisted her hair around her pencil.

His schedule was crazy and he was hardly sleeping, but he began to look forward to Spanish club events, finding purpose and attainable results in fundraising, volunteer work and cultural outreach, even if that meant nothing more than selling T-shirts at Sun Devil Stadium, reading to ESL students at a Tempe elementary school or serving churros at a *Cinco de Mayo* party. Marius and Rachel came to gravitate toward each other during these events. As time passed, Rachel overcame her reserve, always greeting him with a warm smile and often with some bit of news about one of her classes, or an opinion about a book or article in the *State Press*.

The Spanish club met for the last time that semester on a warm evening toward the end of April. Only a handful of members bothered to attend, with finals just around the corner and the heady smell of orange blossoms permeating the air all over campus. They met in a small study room on the third floor of Hayden Library, and Marius, busy with his own coursework, had kept the subject light by talking about the attributes of several of Mexico's most popular vacation destinations, none of which he had ever visited.

Rachel and a few others passed around brochures. One student was familiar with Puerto Peñasco and had a lot to say about the way it had changed over the years, which street vendors could be trusted and where to buy the best Chinese food – a detail Marius found amusing. Another had been on a cruise to the Yúcatan and had strong opinions about which cruise lines should be avoided.

When the meeting ended, Marius stayed behind to gather up the brochures. A few minutes passed and then Rachel reappeared to retrieve her forgotten backpack.

"How are you?" he asked, realizing that they hadn't spoken outside of class or meetings since spring break. "I heard a student disrupted the governor's visit to a sociology lecture last week – asking about aliens and a government cover-up?" Marius shook his head, smiling. "Was that your class?"

Rachel nodded. "Yes. It was bizarre." She turned to go.

"Wait a minute, is something wrong? Are you sick?"

"No, I'm not sick." She blinked and looked away, but not before Marius saw a trace of tears in her eyes.

"Are you having trouble with your roommate again?"

She shook her head. "I'm all right." She tried to laugh. It came out as a choking sob.

Marius touched her shoulder and felt it quiver. He was not a stranger to feminine tears – his mother's had been frequent, if theatrical – but they had never made him feel this raw sense of helplessness.

"Tell me," he said softy, guiding her back to the table. Rachel took a steadying breath and said her father had dismissed their housekeeper – a woman who had worked for her family many years, filling the void left with her mother's death and her sister's marriage.

"Dad said he didn't need her anymore. He had been thinking about it since I left for school, but never told me. When I went back for spring break, she was just gone." She shook her head. "I didn't get to say goodbye. I keep thinking, if I hadn't gone away to school – or maybe if I had gone to school in Flagstaff, and been home every weekend..."

She dug into her backpack and pulled out a small packet of tissues.

"Do you know where she is? Can you visit her?"

Rachel shook her head. "She went back to Mexico. I tried to get an address, but couldn't find one. Her family lives near Los Mochis. When we started talking about vacation destinations tonight, I kept picturing her working at one of those hotels.

"It's stupid, I know." She paused to blow her nose. "It would probably be a good job – better than most. But Alma was always there when I went home. It's so hard to picture it without her."

Marius touched her hand and felt warm blood flood his heart when she turned his over and squeezed it. Her simple story said so much. The isolation she felt as a kid spilling over into her college experience, her desire to master Spanish – he was willing to bet Alma had taught her some at the kitchen table – even the animosity she sometimes revealed toward her father. So he swallowed the knot in his throat and began to talk about his childhood in Spain, the way he and his mother had moved every few years, and how he had just begun to form an attachment to Stepfather Number Two when another divorce sent him away.

They sat silently for several minutes after that. Rachel's tears were spent and Marius felt strangely relieved by unburdening revelations he had never shared with anyone.

"Thank you, Marius." She let go of his hand and stood. Together, they walked to the door.

Marius would never be able to distance himself from that moment long enough to understand how he came to be kissing her – whether the gradual building of a friendship, the sharing of personal loss, the way he had been denying a growing attraction to her all year or, perhaps, just finally hearing his name pass through her lips had been the thing that propelled them toward each other in that quiet instant. Maybe it would never have happened if they had not been meeting in a secluded corner of the library, or if Rachel had not stopped and turned back in the doorway just as Marius was there himself, turning out the lights and leaning forward to listen for her quiet goodbye.

She kissed him back. He knew that. He felt her soft responsive lips in memory long afterward, along with the fingers she had traced along his jaw and her heart beating against his chest.

She was the first to pull away. Her eyes met his. "I need to go," she said.

Marius backed against the door, the dread of his mistake beginning to cloud the beauty of the moment. "I'm sorry," he said. It was ridiculously inadequate.

Rachel tightened her grip on her backpack and walked away, leaving Marius feeling like the embodiment of a torrid Police lyric. He knew then that what he had done was inexcusable, but not how far-reaching the fallout would be.

Today, he wondered if he ever would.

Marius was breathing hard by the time he stepped out of the trees and into a meadow that delivered a clear view of Jesus, captured in stone and watching over the waking town of Creel like the Gentle Shepherd he was. He looked away. He had never felt compelled to pray to a statue, but the figure reminded him, nonetheless, of his sins. For a rare and metaphysical moment, he wondered about atonement, temptation and forgiveness. He thought of Rachel as she had been then and again last night, vulnerable and hurting.

I did the right thing, he told himself again. Turning, he headed back toward town.

CB

"Where were you?"

"Walking."

Marius followed Johnny out of the command center, trying not to slosh hot coffee on his hand. "What's the latest?"

"No I.D. on the suspect, but his fingerprints are on Samantha Davidson's wallet – even on her driver's license. His prints are all over the shack – it was clearly his residence. Chu and Juan are bringing some of their clan to town today – they knew the *bruja* and her grandson. They should be able to tell us if it's him."

Johnny led Marius past the cantina, through the lobby and out into a small courtyard as he talked, looking from right to left until he found what he was looking for – a secluded alcove, screened by thick vines climbing over a metal trellis. A small fountain sputtered nearby to camouflage their conversation.

"Do you think we'll ever get a name?"

Johnny shrugged, lighting a cigarette. "Probably nothing official. Most Tarahumara don't have birth records. They keep to themselves and avoid things like school, immunization, bureaucracy of any kind."

"Maybe if we tracked down the daughter in Chihuahua—"

He smiled. "The mysterious Yala."

"We can put out feelers in the *colonias*. See if anyone knows what happened to her."

"It's not a lot to go on and we have a bigger issue looming."

Marius crossed his arms and glanced around again. "Our other project? What can you tell me?"

"Trent took the bait."

"Good. That gives us more time." Marius was thinking about Rachel, safely home and away from all this.

"Yes, but we need to tread carefully. That DEA agent – Trent's friend – is getting suspicious."

"Based on what?"

"They don't do their jobs successfully without having a bit of intuition, amigo. His concerns are primarily about my involvement."

"Don't go there, Johnny. I know you wanted to stay out of this one, but I need you."

"I know." Johnny looked grim, dragging on his cigarette. "I just wish we had more control over the chain of information."

Marius nodded. "Can our man inside do anything about it?"

"He's already done enough. The dates, GPS – Marius do you realize how big this shipment is?"

"Yes."

"How much money we're talking about?"

Marius looked over Johnny's head, feeling deflated. "Yes, Johnny. It's a king's ransom."

"Do you ever imagine—"

"*No. Nunca.*"

Johnny stared at him hard for a moment. "She's getting to you, isn't she?"

"What? Who?"

Johnny jerked his head back toward the hotel.

"I've been tired of this game for a long time, Johnny. You know that. Agent Mueller doesn't have anything to do with it."

"Does she know about Anna?"

Marius took a step forward, speaking low to control his anger. "Nothing is going on with Anna and nothing is going on with Rachel, either. Tread carefully, Johnny. I'm in no mood for your games."

The foliage behind Johnny rustled, startling them both. Johnny whipped around while Marius gazed hard at the tangled mass of vines, realizing that it was thicker than he had first imagined. A bird emerged from the top and flew over their heads into the gray sky.

Johnny threw his cigarette butt on the ground and stomped on it. "A lot of noise for a little bird," he said.

"I'm going to tell her."

"What?"

Marius nodded, sure it was the right thing to do. "Rachel is no friend of Trent's, Johnny. She's leaving soon. I don't like the idea of her learning about it afterward through Bureau gossip."

"It's a bad idea, Marius."

"No, it's not. Maybe she can help."

"In what way?"

"Accountability."

Marius whacked Johnny on the shoulder and walked away. He glanced at his watch as he headed toward the command center. It was already nine thirty and the day was vanishing in a sea of activity that he had yet to embrace. A few agents were still working on their computers. One was using the fax machine. Everyone else was dismantling the room, rolling up the wall maps, filling banker's boxes with files and supplies.

Rachel wasn't there.

He had to stop and speak to Agent Castillo about the autopsy report, then Agent Barretto needed his signature on an inventory list. A few minutes passed and he was free again, retracing his steps to the corridor, then taking the familiar path toward Rachel's room.

He heard her voice before he reached the door, which was unaccountably open. She was across the room with her back to him, her cell phone against one ear, her finger pressed to the other. Marius frowned and started to back away when her angry words began to register, stopping him.

"Our divorce was final two weeks ago, Craig, or have you forgotten? I don't really care to hear your girlfriend's opinion on Danny – or my career. His stability was shattered the day you decided to cheat."

Rachel turned then and saw Marius standing in the doorway. Her face was pinched and drained of color. She didn't look away, but her voice lost its edge. "I have nothing else to tell you, Craig. You can pick Danny up Sunday evening." She tapped her phone.

For a moment they just stared at each other.

"You're divorced," Marius said.

"Yes." Her eyes were dark with pain. "Yes, I am."

18

TEN MINUTES EARLIER, Rachel had been walking back to her room, her heart knocking angrily against her ribcage as she tried to understand what she overheard in the courtyard. She recognized the distinctive ring of her cell phone as she was turning the key in the lock and crossed the room to answer it without bothering to close the door.

Of course, it was Craig.

"Finally you answer. Where have you been?"

"I left two messages for you yesterday," she said. "What's going on?"

"Danny's near hysterical and you're still traipsing around Mexico. Why aren't you home yet?"

Rachel frowned. "I spoke to Danny just two hours ago. I've spoken to him several times since I got your message – he sounds fine."

Craig snorted. "Well he called me two days ago, upset, wanting me to fly down to Mexico and rescue you after you tumbled down some hill. What's that about?"

Rachel opened her mouth and closed it again, wanting to hang up that instant and talk to her son again. Poor Danny. It hadn't occurred to her that he would mask his concerns for her safety, only to take them to his dad.

"I'm sorry," she said. "I didn't know it upset him so much. I'm fine, Craig, it's just a sprained wrist, and I'll be home tonight. As I said, he seems alright whenever I talk to him. Were you able to calm him down?"

"I tried! I told him about our plans for Monday night – that I bought tickets for the Suns game. He barely listened. How do you think that made me feel?"

Rachel was silent, more concerned about Danny's feelings than Craig's. She had spent years cajoling her husband when he was upset, admitting fault when she felt little – placating, reasoning. Twisting herself into a pretzel, trying to make him happy. Look where it had gotten her.

"Are you listening to me, Rachel?"

"Craig, why are you calling?"

Craig's bone-rattling sigh was as familiar as the bile churning in her stomach.

"Because I'm sick of it," he said. He paused and covered the phone, his muffled voice combining with a woman's in the background. After a moment he came back on the line.

"I think it's time you gave up the FBI, Rachel. Danny is high strung and getting to be a little bit whiny, if you want the truth. What he needs is stability – you at home, working in a safe environment – not trying to find meaning in your life by proving how tough you are."

Rachel was struck momentarily mute with anger. She could have reminded him of the truth – that she had wanted to leave her job after Danny was born, when she knew he would be the only child she could safely carry. It was Craig who had urged her to take advantage of the bureau's part-time program instead, and Craig who had asked her to go back to full-time when Danny entered preschool. He had wanted to buy the showy house on South Mountain that only two incomes could afford. Now who was stuck living in it? Rachel mentioned none of these things. They had been down that road together before and it had gotten them nowhere.

But the very idea that Trish was standing at his elbow, coaching him through this diatribe pushed her over the edge.

"Our divorce was final two weeks ago, Craig, or have you forgotten?" she said. "And I don't really care to hear your girlfriend's opinion of Danny – or my career. His stability was shattered the day you decided to cheat."

"You asked me to leave, Rachel. Don't act as if I don't have a say in this. He's my son too."

Rachel had turned then to see Marius standing in the doorway. Her body went numb while her mind began to flood, swirling in a vortex of conclusions she had accepted about Craig and those she still refused to draw about Marius, whom she had just begun to trust again. It was too much hurt and betrayal to digest.

"I have nothing else to tell you, Craig. You can pick Danny up Sunday evening, as planned."

She disconnected the call and looked down at her ring, regretting that she had not taken it off two nights ago when the urge had first struck her.

"You're divorced," Marius said.

"Yes, I am."

Rachel set down her cell phone on the edge of the bed, next to her battered copy of *Jane Eyre*. She needed to pack. And figure out how she was getting back to the airport. But her stomach wouldn't stop churning and no matter where her thoughts carried her, they came back to the dark look in Marius's eyes.

When she stumbled away from the backside of the vine-enclosed courtyard where he and Cruces had been talking just a short time ago, her stomach had dropped, just as it did whenever she missed a bottom step and her foot fumbled in empty space. The feeling had only grown worse, aggravated by Craig's insults.

Rachel had gotten up late this morning. The pain medication she swallowed after Marius's humiliating departure last night had mercifully rendered her unconscious for nine hours straight. Showering, dressing and reporting to the command center only to find it dismantled and nearly empty, she had wandered through the hotel, unsure where her attention should be focused. She had come across the little metal bench that backed up to the courtyard and sat down for no specific reason, her mind drawn back to Marius's parting words. A familiar cycle of guilt kept her thoughts engaged until she heard voices from the other side of the vines. By the time she recognized them, their meaning held her arrested, daring not to move – hardly to breath – for trying to find a way of denying their meaning.

She had listened until a woman named Anna was mentioned, then she could hear no more. Rachel did not even know that a bird had covered her escape.

It's not what it sounded like, she kept telling herself.

But now that Rachel stood face to face with Marius, a sense of fatal clarity overcame her. Anger and betrayal sat on her shoulders, crowding her thoughts.

"Tell me I misunderstood what I just overheard." She hoped he did not notice her shaking voice or her pleading tone.

Marius looked confused. "What *you* overhead?"

"Yes."

"I just overheard you say you're divorced." That muscle was tightening along his jaw again. "Why didn't you tell me?"

"I tried. Twice."

"No, you said you were happy," he said evenly. "The first night, in the cantina."

"I didn't trust you," she said. "I haven't even told the people I work with about this. I tried to tell you later, it just never felt like the right time."

"How about when I was pouring my guts out over my own divorce?"

"I was supposed to break in? Diminish your suffering with my own sob story?"

"I thought you were married!" he said hoarsely. He took two steps forward before stopping abruptly. He pushed his fingers through his hair. "Do you realize…"

"What?"

He shook his head and looked away. "I knew you couldn't trust me. But I can only apologize so many times for what happened sixteen years ago, Rachel."

"What about ten minutes ago, in the courtyard." She drew in a shaky breath. Marius stilled at her words and was now watching her carefully.

"You were in the courtyard?"

"On a bench. Behind the vines."

"And what is it that you *think* you overheard?"

"Please don't do it, Marius." Rachel felt a sweeping sense of panic wash over her. "Please. I heard about the shipment, the money. Whatever part you are playing, surely you can get out of it? The cartels will never be your friends in the long run."

"You think I'm planning a drug deal." Marius looked slightly sick. He laughed, but there was no humor in it.

"Agent Trent told me something was going on with Cruces, but I thought it was just gossip." Rachel paced at the foot of the bed. "He told me the DEA are watching him. If they are watching him, they'll be watching you too, Marius."

"Rachel." Marius reached for her arms, stopping her, turning her to face him. "You suddenly trust Trent? You trust him more than you trust me?"

Rachel turned her head, refusing to face him. Hot tears were burning her throat and escaping down her cheeks. "Sometimes even an untrustworthy person will stumble across the truth."

"And sometimes a person you trust with your life will betray you," he said softly. "But who are we talking about, *querida*?"

Rachel pushed away from him and walked toward the fireplace. "Please don't try to confuse me. I overheard everything you said – about your mole, a plan to bait Trent and his DEA contact away from the location – all of it."

"And this is what you think of me?" he asked quietly.

"I don't know what I think. But whatever it is, Marius – call it off. Please."

Marius stood silently beside the bed. After a moment he reached down and picked up *Jane Eyre*. He turned it over and put it back down. When he looked up, his eyes were dark and wet.

"It's too late, Rachel. Some decisions can't be undone. Not with a lifetime of wishing."

19

AN EVENING BREEZE passed through the mesquite trees and over Rachel's patio, carrying the fragrance of orange blossoms for the first time this year. She inhaled deeply, wishing it would last.

Nothing lasts, she thought grimly.

Danny was with Craig tonight and, finding the house too lonely and full of memories, Rachel had come outside to stare at the Phoenix skyline and wish away her dark mood. Instead, the heady fragrance had made it worse, reminding her of Marius and the night he had first kissed her. She had walked back to her dorm in the sweetly-infused air, numb on the surface but alive at the core of her being.

She felt numb again – had felt numb ever since Saturday when she packed her bags and flew home from Mexico. Now she wondered, was the feeling inseparable from life-changing moments, whether a first kiss or a final goodbye?

"From Agent Suarez," Cruces said as he shook her hand on the heliport's tarmac. He handed her a manila envelope with her name scrawled across its flap. His eyes said more, but Rachel had been in no mood to interpret.

She did not open the envelope on the helicopter, but waited until her plane crossed the American border, feeling bolstered to face whatever it might contain with Purple Mountain's Majesty below her. Inside was a dog-eared file folder with a brief note scrawled in Marius's handwriting clipped to its cover.

Consider your actions carefully. —M

The folder sat on the glass table beside her, sprinkled with bougainvillea blossoms from a nearby bush, its cover fluttering in the warm evening air like the blood-splattered wing of a wounded bird. It was too dark to read now, but it didn't matter. Rachel had the file almost memorized, having punished herself with its blatant truths at least half a dozen times since first reading it Saturday afternoon.

No more action needed to be taken, officially speaking. Not yet, at least. She had dutifully presented a copy to SAC Devlin this morning, along with her completed report on the Davidson case. As Marius suggested, the FBI was not interested in pursuing another perpetrator unless the dead man's DNA failed to match samples taken from Samantha's fingernails.

"Of course, follow up any leads you come across, providing they don't interfere with your regular case load," Devlin said. Her smile was brief and grim and, like Rachel, her thoughts clearly focused on Marius's report.

Devlin had scanned the contents of the folder, focusing through bifocals, her platinum bob swinging gently against her cheeks. She picked up the phone to call Assistant Director Foster, but when it rang to his voice mail, she hung up and looked briefly at Rachel before rising to close her office door. When she returned to her desk, she tapped the file with her fingertips.

"How credible do you find this?"

"Very." Rachel's throat felt thick with shame. "I believe you can trust its veracity without reservation."

"What makes you so sure?"

"Agent Trent told me of his suspicions about Agent Cruces' activities and of contacts within the DEA who were the source of these rumors. He gave no specifics." Rachel rubbed her hands across her knees. "As to Agent Suarez, Trent spoke highly of him, praising his reputation within the PFM and his dedication as an internal affairs investigator fighting corruption—"

"Agent Mueller, you're being too careful," Devlin interrupted. "Speak candidly, please. If this report is valid, Agent Trent's expressed opinions about these agents are easily interpreted. I need your forthright evaluation."

Rachel nodded. "Agent Cruces was courteous and accommodative, but I sensed a measure of distrust in him that I could not account for. It would be consistent with Trent's accounting of things, but also with the assertions of this file, which I now find more credible. As for Agent

Suarez, he saved my life, putting his own at considerable risk. He was consistently professional and honest. He gave us this information, which shows a depth of courtesy I frankly don't think would be returned by most within the Bureau. If I had handled this differently – if I had taken this to Trent instead of you – it would have ruined Agent Suarez's investigation, perhaps put his life at risk." She shook her head and spoke more quietly. "He would have been thoroughly justified to leave us in the dark."

"Did you discuss this information with Agent Suarez?"

"No. I read it for the first time on the plane returning from Chihuahua."

Devlin frowned. "I wonder why he didn't tell you about it in person."

Rachel's cheeks reddened. "I think he planned to. I… overheard him discussing some of this with Agent Cruces. I misunderstood, initially seeing things through the bias of Agent Trent's duplicity."

"I see." Devlin swiveled toward the window, giving Rachel only her profile to analyze. She sighed deeply. "We don't need this. It's a PR nightmare."

After a moment of silence, she swiveled back. "Do you remember those convictions a few years ago – fifteen American law enforcement officers and even a judge mixed up in this kind of corruption?"

"Yes, I do," Rachel said. "But we can turn it to our advantage. Their investigation has been going on without us for some time. Agent Suarez is giving us a gift. Can't you just see the press release – the FBI and DEA standing shoulder to shoulder with Mexican officials to weed out corruption?"

"Even with Suarez's generous offer, we're still looking at fallout. Corruption in Mexican officials is hardly newsworthy, but when an FBI agent is involved? And a DEA officer?" Devlin's well-plucked eyebrows disappeared behind her bangs. "We send $40 million a year to Mexico just to fight the drug trade and, from what I hear, the president is getting ready to sign a bill authorizing a significant increase. No, we're paying for it, one way or another."

"I understand that," Rachel said. "But that money isn't an altruistic gift. If Americans weren't buying their products, the drug cartels would be out of business. Not to mention that our border security problems make it possible for the cartels to get most of their guns from the U.S. No, we're covering our own culpability as much as theirs."

Devlin nodded and turned back to the folder. "I think we are left with little choice but to let the exchange play out and not get involved. The

Mexican government will have jurisdiction as far as I'm concerned. I think Agent Suarez was counting on that. Smart man. The only thing left for us to do is prepare our statements."

"Yes, ma'am."

"Of course, I'll have to present this to AD Foster. He may have a different position – he still harbors resentment over being dragged into the ATF's Fast and Furious debacle."

Rachel shook her head. It was always something.

"And the DEA will have to be notified," Devlin continued. "They'll try to change Suarez's mind, if given the opportunity."

Rachel frowned, inching forward in her seat. "Can that communication be delayed? Agents Suarez and Cruces, not to mention their contact within the DEA, could be placed in more danger if the wrong person is put on guard."

Devlin nodded. "I understand your concern, and will proceed cautiously. But I can't sit on information like this. You know that."

"Yes, of course," Rachel said. "But I have concerns about their DEA contact – that he would provide intelligence to Mexican agents, but not disclose to someone within the agency?"

"I see your point," Devlin said. "But perhaps he has and it is the DEA withholding information from us. It wouldn't be the first time."

"No, ma'am."

"So," Devlin tapped her pen on her desk calendar, "if everything goes according to their plan, this will all be over in forty-eight hours. I assume their communication with the Bureau will be swift and through traditional channels – unless you think Agent Suarez will contact you directly."

Rachel looked out the window. "No. I don't think I will hear from Agent Suarez again."

Some decisions can't be undone, not with a lifetime of wishing.

Rachel couldn't displace Marius's prophetic words from her mind. She tried to blame the circumstances – it had been hard to focus on a legitimate explanation for his conversation with Cruces when she was fighting with Craig and worrying about Danny. Even thirty minutes between the two conflicts might have given her more clarity, but she hadn't had it. So she responded in fear, jumping to a conclusion that illustrated most horrifically just what kind of a poor judge of character she had become.

After work, she wanted to come home and go straight to bed, but her mind wouldn't rest. Her thoughts turned to her pain pills, the last of which she had taken the night before. The black folds of unconsciousness they provided would have been welcome with Danny away, though she recognized the irony of her longing. Her prescription had offered the same kind of opiatic stupor provided by the drug traffickers whom Agent Trent was now helping.

"When will it end?" Devlin had asked as Rachel stood to leave her office this morning. "Just when kids began to understand the consequences of heroin and cocaine, meth came along—"

"And was even more addictive and destructive."

Devlin nodded. "My nephew got mixed up with Meth. Up in Michigan. He and his girlfriend robbed their parents, ran away, lived on the streets – were in and out of jail all the time." She shook her head. "I tried to help, but it did no good. She had four babies in six years. All of them were taken away by Child Protective Services. Now, my sister is raising two of them. The others were adopted. Last winter, the girlfriend died of exposure under a freeway overpass."

Rachel's eyes stung. "And your nephew?"

"He's been in jail for about a year now." Her voice was hollow. "He was arrested after trying to prostitute himself to an undercover cop."

Rachel looked away. The truth was ugly.

As she sat on the patio that night, she prayed fervently that Marius's plan to stop Trent and his cohorts would be successful, even if it meant keeping just one more kid off the streets. She rubbed her hands over her arms, suddenly chilled. She'd feel better when she saw Danny after school tomorrow. Coming home after a week away only to turn around and hand him over to Craig had been miserable. He had seemed fine, at least, when she picked him up in Cottonwood Saturday night – hugging her briefly before racing back outside to help his cousin feed the dog. He had given her braced wrist only a quick glance.

Craig had exaggerated Danny's fears, then. *How typical*, she thought. He was a master of manipulation – she had seen it in the courtroom many times – how he could draw out self-doubt in his target before making his accusations, putting them in a tail spin. After twelve years of marriage, why wasn't she on guard against it?

"Because he's good at it," Melissa had said. "Craig has no qualms about putting his own needs first every time. You can't win a fight against someone who makes his own rules."

Rachel nodded silently, still feeling like a fool.

"Will you stay the night?" Melissa asked. "Maybe go to church with us in the morning before heading back? I'll ask Dad to join us for lunch."

Rachel agreed, to Danny's delight, but lay sleepless in the creaky guest bed that night, still fixated on Marius's report. His conversation with Cruces had been easy to understand once she read the file, but it was too late to take back her accusations – too late to give him the benefit of the doubt. The hours clicked by and she continued to toss and turn under the cool country air passing through her open window. Her regrets circled back to Danny, sleeping across the hall with his cousins, and eventually settled on her failed marriage.

On Sunday morning when she was dressing for church, she could hardly look at her reflection in the mirror. The truth was there beyond the dark circles – she hadn't believed Marius because she was too bruised and broken to trust anyone anymore.

Danny didn't want to leave Cottonwood after lunch, though Rachel was anxious to get home. As expected, her father had dominated the conversation at lunch with his favorite arguments about politics and religion. Melissa had rolled her eyes and taken it in stride as always. Rachel didn't know why he still had the power to make her so angry.

"Mom, do you ever think about living in Cottonwood again?" Danny asked as they drove home.

"Not really," she answered. "My job is in Phoenix."

He was silent for several moments. "Do you ever think about getting a different job?"

Rachel had not answered him. How could she explain to her eight-year-old son that she didn't think about much of anything these days except getting through the next moment?

An alarm sounding from inside the house pulled Rachel from her memories. She stumbled through the dark kitchen and found the annoyance – a spy watch Danny's grandmother had bought him for his birthday. It had secret compartments and a red laser light and told him what time it was in Moscow and Sydney. But it also had an alarm that sounded at odd hours of the night, alerting him to exciting missions, no doubt, but also earning itself a place far from their bedrooms, under the sandwich bags in a kitchen drawer.

Rachel pushed the button that shut off the noise, then walked around her quiet house, closing the sliding door, putting a mug in the sink. When she finally lay down on her pillow, her thoughts returned to Marius. Regret overwhelmed her, overflowing in tears that wet her pillow. After everything they had been through, both in the past and in the past week, their time together in Mexico had offered them nothing more than a second chance to say goodbye.

20

"*¡VIVA MÉXICO!*"

The man popped out of the cantina's doorway like a cork, slurring his patriotic exclamation as he stumbled onto the crowded sidewalk and collided with Marius.

"*¡Sí! Pero no tome nada más esta noche.*"

With some difficulty, Marius set the man on his feet and turned the corner, cursing the foolish thinking that had brought him to Juárez on Mexico's Independence Day. It was just after dusk and the muggy September air was becoming as saturated with the smell of spirits as it was with the Ranchera music he despised. Assembly workers released early from the closest maquiladoras had been at their drinking for several hours and were now spilling out into the streets, singing along with the music, flirting with the young women who passed in giggling clusters and pretending that tomorrow would never come.

This is a night for trouble, he thought, his eyes narrowing at the young women who passed, unseeing, by a pink cross painted on a telephone pole. He worried for them – that one of them would not make it home tonight, instead meeting the kind of serial tragedy that had overtaken hundreds of women in the city over the past twenty years.

But which one should I worry for? he asked himself.

"*¡Las muertas! ¡Las feminicidios!*" cried a sad drunk clinging to the pole, not consoled by the joy around her and eerily echoing his thoughts. *Las muertas del Juárez* were largely unsolved, though city leaders tried to push the brutal murders under the carpet. There were newer threats to focus on – kidnappings and murder in the streets that were driving people to leave the city in droves. The cartels were taking over, but Marius couldn't help seeing the missing women as Juarez's greatest tragedy. Singers lamented the dead in song, mothers painted pink crosses on telephone poles and journalists received death threats for their exposés – but where was justice?

And why are you still focused on one solved murder, when so many go unsolved?

Marius tried to ignore the question that echoed his steps, but felt familiar fingers of hopelessness gripping his shoulders. Unsettled, he crossed the street and entered a dark avenue that passed into one of the city's oldest and most dilapidated *colonias*. He found it even more filth-ridden than the last time he visited. Skirting a man roasting nuts over a barrel fire, he ducked out of the way when the wet cardboard walls of one house began to tear away and fall into the street. His mood darkened still – something Johnny would not have thought possible if he had been invited along.

"Your vacation did you no good," he said this morning as Marius pocketed his keys. "Why are you doing this? It's a dead end, *amigo*. A waste of time."

"You're like an old grandmother," Marius said, heading out the door. He knew the lead was shaky at best, but he was determined to follow it. He didn't need Johnny constantly unfolding the odds in front of him like a street map.

The day before, Marius had been interviewing a retired schoolteacher in Lomas del Santuario about a recent murder. He listened patiently as she lamented the girl's death, just in case she might recall some detail she had failed to report to the police. But she knew nothing, it seemed. It was dark and she really had been asleep in front of the television.

"The neighborhood isn't safe anymore," Señora DeSalvo said. "I should have left years ago with Yala. 'They have good jobs in Juarez,' she said. But I didn't go."

"Yala?" Marius asked. "Was that a friend of yours?"

"Yes." Her brow creased. "Why?"

"Was she Tarahumara? Did she have a son?"

Her frown deepened. She crossed her arms over her ample chest and said nothing.

"I only ask," Marius said more gently, "because this spring I was searching for a woman of that name. It's unusual, yes? Her son was killed in the canyon and we had to bury him without a name."

She shook her head. "No, Yala took her son with her, though for a while he lived with his grandmother next door. She visited them once a month, but never stayed. The boy wasn't always right in the head, though sometimes, he could be quite clever and charming."

"What was her last name?"

"Torres."

"Do you know what happened to her mother?"

"She packed up in the middle of the night and left. Someone said she returned to the canyon. You would know that if you were there," she added suspiciously.

"I was told she died years ago," he said.

"Ah, well that's likely, isn't it? Yala always said they were unkind to her."

"Do you know anything about the boy's father?"

Señora DeSalvo shrugged. "Yala once said he was a tourist. From somewhere overseas. Greece, maybe? Another time, she said he was American. I don't know. I'm not sure she knew for sure. Yala had a way with men."

"What about her son? What was his name?"

"They called him Manny."

"Do you know where she was working in Juarez?"

"One of the maquiladoras in Anapra. I wrote once or twice, but never heard from her again."

"Do you still have that address?"

She hesitated.

Marius smiled. "*Por favor*. We need to find out if it was her son who died in the canyon this spring."

Finally she nodded.

"*Gracias, Señora*. You have been a great help."

A spark of adrenalin quickened Marius's step as he headed back to his office, determined to visit Juárez as soon as possible to track down Yala Torres. It was an unfamiliar feeling after many months of grinding through his work days, pushing for results he could not feel, ignoring both the small victories and defeats that had once made his job meaningful.

"Don't even think about it," Johnny told him gruffly Monday morning when he returned from his father's ranch and spoke of retiring.

So much had changed since his last visit. He had been shocked by the signs of age settling across his father's hips and shoulders – the way his step sometimes faltered and his mind wandered. It was the first time Marius had seriously considered his repeated invitation – "Come home, *Mijo*. The ranch is yours, just as soon as you're ready."

Driving back from Sonora, Marius had let himself imagine it. Perhaps his decision to transfer from internal affairs was not a big enough change after all.

But Johnny disagreed. "Leaving the agency now will only make you feel worse," he said. "It will haunt you."

They didn't talk about the main cause of Marius's restlessness – had not spoken Agent Trent's name out loud since they saw him smiling broadly for the cameras after his acquittal, descending the courthouse steps with his Mexican wife clinging to his arm as if he were a pardoned Maximilian.

"He won't work for the Bureau again," Johnny had said, striking a match as they turned away. Marius tried to take comfort in that, but it didn't stick to his ribs. He knew the bust this spring had taken a few *passadores* and gatekeepers out of play. It had prevented a supply of more than 3,000 kilos from hitting the American streets, but had it made permanent changes? Had it hit the *patrones* running the syndicates?

"You aim too high," Johnny said.

And he had come close to hitting his target, he thought, remembering the car bomb that nearly killed him last year. But it had not been enough to put Trent away. The failure pushed Marius into months of compulsion, constantly revisiting the facts, hoping to convince himself again that he had done all he could.

More than three years had passed since Agent Cruces interrogated a smart young *passadore* working for the Tijuana Cartel. The kid was just a street pusher, but had planned ahead, understanding that he was an easy target for arrest and expendable to his superiors. He had used their belief in his insignificance to his advantage, memorizing tidbits of information he overheard to create a fairly detailed picture of the organization's mid-level practices.

"They have a new *chota* – someone high up in *la policía*," he told Cruces. Then he gave a few specifics and asked for a deal.

His information proved accurate – especially those concerning shipments passing through a particular plaza along the ninety-mile border of Arizona's Tohono O'odham Reservation. It was heavily monitored by Federal Police and DEA during those months, though the cartel's runners were evading interference with a talent near clairvoyance.

"He's telling the truth. Someone on the inside is covering their tracks," Marius told Cruces one day as they poured over maps and a list of possible leaks. He started to dig deep, using weekly intel passed along from Cruces's informant. Just days before the car bombing, he narrowed his list to a group of American bureaucrats working in Mexico City.

Agent Trent had been an attaché to the American Embassy in Mexico City for two years, earning a reputation worthy of amused derision from some and watchful consideration from others. He married a local woman, set up house and started spending money with little discretion. It put him on their short list, but wasn't enough for accusations. The investigation was still active when Marius relinquished his IA badge. He left the case file in the hands of his replacement and moved on to homicide in Chihuahua. He had only been there for a few weeks when a missing piece to the same puzzle landed in his lap.

Tom Finnigan, an old DEA acquaintance, called Marius one day when cardboard boxes still cluttered his office. He asked to meet him at the Plaza del Sol in Chihuahua's *Periferico de la Juventud* district.

"We'll catch up," Tom said.

Marius was surprised by Tom's appearance when they met two nights later. He had grown older and heavy since Marius last saw him ten years ago. With dark hair gone gray, a wheezing cough that projected from his oversized torso like the bark of a sick sea lion and a red complexion that Marius hoped could be attributed to rosacea rather than a high consumption of alcohol, Tom bore little resemblance to the quick-moving young man he once knew.

"How have you been?" Marius asked, pulling up a chair across from Tom, who was finishing off the last of a Cinnabon. They sat in the food court of the dazzlingly white mall, which looked both modern and dated, reminding Marius of a mall in Phoenix where he had often met Agent Johnson years ago.

"Better," Tom said, pushing his sticky paper plate away with regret. Without preamble, he told Marius that his current DEA supervisor – "a cocky young punk named Edward Lewis" – was tipping off one of the cartels to their patrol routes along certain plazas bordering Arizona and New Mexico.

"You're sure?"

"I don't have proof."

Marius frowned. "Why tell me? There are agency procedures in place when ethical questions arise."

Tom shook his head. "Because I'm a drunk, Suarez."

Marius sat back in his chair. "Is that the PC term they're using these days?"

Tom smiled weakly. "Don't get me wrong, I'm sober – have been for thirteen months – but back when I wasn't thinking clearly, I let some rookie get the best of me. I mouthed off, made accusations that weren't founded and ended up looking like an idiot."

"And now you're the boy who cried wolf."

Tom nodded, his red-rimmed eyes murky. "I'm just lucky I'm not the boy who lost his pension."

"What can I do?"

"I don't know. Someone else is involved. Probably the guy who's handling the money."

"Do you know which cartel? Tijuana? Sinaloa?"

Tom didn't. Marius tapped his fingers on the table, wondering if it would be a stretch to tie this information to the case he had handed off in Mexico City. He asked Tom to pass on anything else that came his way, including all he could uncover about Lewis's history and education.

Tom agreed, communicating mostly through a G-mail account he set up cloak-and-dagger style at a library across town from his office. When he told Marius that Edward Lewis and Kirk Trent worked a case together in Corpus Christi, Marius began to tighten his net.

Details of that connection, communications between Marius and the new IA investigator in Mexico City and evidence of their case were all included in the file Cruces handed to Rachel seven months ago. What they did not have was definitive proof.

It had been risky to bait Trent when he returned to Arizona with Samantha Davidson's body, but Marius saw it as an opportunity to exploit his distraction and arrogance. The plan relied heavily on Cruces's *passadore*, who posed as a cartel courier and passed false information to Trent. If the communication link worked and the money trail followed, they would have proof of Trent and Edward's involvement.

The plan had worked – or so they thought. Trent had taken their bait and the PFM and DEA had been ready and waiting when the shipment truck – an animal caravan loaded with cattle – ambled across the border.

Twelve arrests were made, including Trent and Lewis, both of whom plead not guilty.

Marius knew they had been careful. He knew the evidence – large bank deposits, timely exchanges between Trent's and Lewis's accounts, travel and phone logs – all supported the indictments. He had run it all through his mind again and again, like a gerbil on a wheel, refusing to believe Johnny's simple explanation.

"The jury just didn't believe the *passadore*, amigo. They didn't believe me either."

Johnny accepted their defeat and moved on. Marius couldn't. And as he found the street he was looking for in Juárez, he wondered again about the purity of his lasting resentment, if the failure would have tasted so sour if it had not been for Rachel.

He had seen it in her eyes when he left her hotel room – the way she would remember it all later – that he had been gracious about her mistake, forgiving her before she even knew she was in the wrong. In truth, his kindness was born of shock more than anything. When time had passed, his feelings were far from forgiving. Later still, it bothered him to have her thinking him noble, far above the crimes she had so easily assigned to him. He bitterly imagined telling her the things he had done – the deceptions and lies, the allowing of lesser crimes in hopes of trapping greater criminals.

The hypocrisy of it all burned in his stomach like the pain of their first goodbye. Sometimes it woke him before dawn, festering in the dark until he shoved back the covers and trampled it under his running shoes or pummeled it on his speed bag. Eventually, it always struck back, reminding him of how broken she was, how altered and fragile. Then he would forgive her all over again until the next time he forgot.

If you didn't forgive her, you wouldn't be here now, he told himself.

He had reached the address Señora DeSalvo gave him and knocked on the door, waiting patiently until a tiny woman opened it.

"Señora Guzman?" He held up his badge. "Agent Suarez, *con la Policía Federal Ministerial*."

Her eyes turned fearful. The crack in her door narrowed. "Yes?"

"You have nothing to fear, *Señora*. I'm looking for Yala Torres. A neighbor of hers in Chihuahua gave me your address and said she once lived here. May I come in?"

Mrs. Guzman hesitated for a moment before stepping aside and pointing toward two buckling chairs. She had overcome her initial fear, it seemed, and now smiled as she sat across from him, her apple cheeks rising to underline merry eyes.

"Yes, I rented a room to her. But that was years ago. Fifteen, maybe more."

"Do you know where she went?"

"America. She was determined to go from the moment she moved in." She leaned forward, whispering. "I told her about a coyote I knew of, but she wouldn't hear of it. 'We're not going just to be sent back,' she said.

"She always talked about a better life for her son. She taught him English for hours each night, correcting his accent, punishing him when he didn't study enough." She shook her head in disapproval. "She hired a lawyer and paid him well – more than money, I'm afraid – to get them into Texas legally. It took many years, but she did it. I was glad for her. She had a horrible mother. *Una mujer loca.*"

"So her son lived with her here?" he asked.

There was the briefest pause. "Yes," she said.

"Because my contact in Chihuahua said the boy stayed with his grandmother for months at a time, while Yala only visited periodically."

Mrs. Guzman didn't seem troubled by the contradiction. She crossed her hands in her lap and looked past him, cocking her head to one side. "I imagine them in America sometimes and wonder if they have a nice home. Perhaps a car. I bet Yala sent him to a good school."

"Señora Guzman, I'm sorry to tell you this, but Yala's son is dead. He was killed several months ago in the Copper Canyon. That's why I'm looking for her."

The woman's eyes flickered sadness for a moment, but she said nothing.

"Señora, I think you know something," Marius pressed. "*Dígame, por favor.*"

Her eyes flickered, considering. Picking up a ball of yellow yarn from her side table, she began wrapping a strand around her finger. Finally she leaned forward and whispered. "Yala never knew I figured it out."

Marius leaned forward too. "What was that?" he asked softly.

"She went back to Chihuahua once a month or so, just as you said, and always took Manny with her. He was so little at first, I didn't notice anything was the matter with him. But then, after a while, I began to see it."

Marius leaned back, disappointed. "Yes, we believe he was mentally deficient in some way."

"Yes. But you see, he wasn't always that way."

"Did something happen to him? An injury or accident?"

She shook her head. "No he was born that way, I'm sure. That's not what I meant. It took me a while to notice the pattern. By the end, I could see the difference. They were starting to change and grow. Yala was busy with her plans by then. In her excitement, she was not so careful."

Marius's heart stilled. "They?" he asked.

Her face spread into a cat-like grin and he could almost imagine canary feathers drifting from her lips.

"Manny wasn't one little boy," she said. "He was two."

21

THE JAGUAR PROWLED his dark home, clothed in nothing, smeared with ash from temple to temple. He moved sightlessly, finding a path among the clutter, relishing his discomfort.

The house was closing in around him, becoming a cage. Unwashed linens were strewn along the hallway, unopened mail covered dusty tables and piles of newspapers toppled in every corner. Sticky food containers were abandoned on the coffee table and countless bags of overflowing trash crowded the kitchen floor. The air had grown stagnant, a fetid stew of neglect, pervading his house like death.

Only his laundry room remained spotless – the place where he meticulously washed and pressed his clothes before emerging from the house each day, mask intact. He could not mourn in public. Beyond these walls he was forced to wear ill-fitting normalcy as a second skin. Underneath, his soul trembled, twisted with the loss of his half self.

Manny.

He had been so innocent. When the bullet pierced his heart, his twin had felt it across the miles, his dark blood gushing in phantom pain. He staggered, clutching his chest, startled to see nothing but air pass through his fingers. It was his brother's death he felt. He knew it instantly.

Acting normal in the middle of his workday had been torture – acute and terrifying. He had wanted to run from his false life, to find Manny's killer and rip his heart from his chest. Instead, he held the pain inside. Once home, he went straight to the kitchen. Fumbling in the dark for a knife, he cut parallel marks along his arm, one after the other, until they numbered the years he and Manny had lived.

The release he felt was too brief. The cuts were too shallow. His blood splashed to the floor in a pathetic drip, drip, drip, mocking him.

He fantasized about deepening his cuts until his blood flowed across the floor like his brother's across the soil. *I could end it all*, he told himself, imagining a reunion with Manny and his mother in the underworld. Maybe she would forgive him. Then they could wait together for another opportunity to ascend.

But Grandmother's voice stilled his knife, reminding him of the victories he had already won. He had come so close to completing his task. Giving up now would be unforgiveable.

He dropped the knife and wailed, dragging blood-stained fingertips across his walls, marking his house as a place of mourning. When he was spent and dizzy, he sunk to the floor and wept.

The next day, he covered his cuts with fresh bandages and hid them under a carefully-pressed shirt. He wore a convincing smile and explained away the shadows beneath his red-rimmed eyes by hinting at a night of debauchery. In the weeks and months that followed, he hid his grief and let his wounds heal. But at night he shed his clothes, smeared ash across his eyes and prowled in the filth of remorse, revisiting the paths that had led him here.

He and his brother had shared the same name through childhood, though it had never really been his. The second to leave his mother's womb, he was a malformed, sickly child and never expected to survive long enough for a name of his own. But he had been stronger than any illness, growing to show a sharp intellect that set him apart from his sturdy twin, who, though beautiful, stared vacantly into space and laughed and cried when he should not.

He always thought of his brother as the real Manny, a distinction confirmed when he was renamed at the U.S. border. And though he seldom spent time with his brother – just one day a month when Mother would exchange them at Grandmother's house – he had shared his spaces, the echo of his spirit always beside him.

"You have one sound mind and one sound body between you," Grandmother once said. "Our people always saw me as nothing but a witch. They distrusted your mother too and, I fear, would have seen you and your brother as all the evidence they needed to run us off for good."

"Do you want to go home to the canyon, Grandmother?" He only remembered it in scattered, blurred images.

"Yes." Her eyes misted. "It is a place of power and redemption. You will see that for yourself one day. And you will need your brother then, more than you can imagine now. Depend on each other and you'll never feel lost."

It was only after many months living north of the border that Manny's echo started to fade and his twin first began to feel the tear in their connection, to consider the truth in Grandmother's words. He had never minded his limp. Comparing it to his brother's simplicity had always made him feel the more blessed of the two. But being bullied by bigger kids in his American school had changed his opinion. Manny would have come in handy as a protector.

"Why couldn't he come with us?" he asked his mother.

"It's the way it has to be." Her jaw was set firm. "Don't ask me again."

They had scrambled to make a life for themselves in America, spending six horrible months in an El Paso barrio before heading north again and embracing the second false identity she created. There, she again plied a trade that brought many men through their door. For years he tried to avoid their sidelong leers, their groping hands and bruising fists. "Such a pretty boy," one said. He lost weight and began to fail in school.

But he should have known his mother would have bigger plans. They moved again and she made him memorize another false history. Within a few months, she used her pretty smile and accomplished accent to charm a wealthy man. For him, she became something she was not.

"You make yourself believe it first, son, and then whatever you say becomes truth. It's what we do to survive."

Shortly before his thirteenth birthday, his mother and new stepfather made an announcement. "You're going to be a brother," she said.

Part of him wanted to blurt out the truth, bringing all her deceptions to light – especially her abandonment of Manny. *I already* am *a brother!* His mouth watered, and he wondered what it would taste like to wipe abject happiness off his stepfather's face.

But when he saw fear erupt in his mother's eyes, their relationship suddenly shifted.

Don't. Please, she silently pleaded.

The power she handed him with that one look flooded over him, so warm and pleasant that his priorities changed in an instant and he gladly held his tongue.

"Great," he said. His contrived accent fused with his new-found power to give the illusion of real happiness. "Will I have a brother or a sister?"

As things turned out, he would have neither. His mother miscarried five weeks later. The day after she returned from the hospital, she lay crumpled on the bathroom floor, keening and pulling at her son as if he could offer absolution.

"I thought I could forget," she said. "I told myself he would be fine without me – that he hardly knew me. But, Manny! I want Manny – and now I'm being punished."

"Mother, stop. It will be all right—"

"No." She shook her head wildly. "I don't get to be a mother again. Not ever. It's punishment. Punishment I deserve!"

An unfamiliar buzz filled his head as he watched her cry. He didn't care about the baby. But would this regret mean confession? Would she bring Manny to join them? Recently, he had forgotten to miss his twin – forgotten that he once hoped for a chance like this to beg for his return from exile. His thoughts swirled. He wasn't sure what he wanted.

He pulled on her hand. "Mother, get up. You should be in bed."

She stayed on the floor.

"You're both in here, you know." Her voice was weak, but she struck her chest with a force that made him flinch. "You and Manny live in my heart, but it hurts. It's tearing and bleeding. I can't stand the pain!"

The buzz returned, louder this time. He dropped her hand, backing away in horror.

"Tlaltecuhtli," he whispered.

She looked up. "What did you say?"

He did not answer. His mind was now filled with an image his Grandmother had described – the earth monster, Tlaltecuhtli, whose heart had been torn in two by her twin sons, Quetzalcoatl and Tezcatlipoca.

My mother.

Pushing away his disgust, he ran to the phone. His stepfather rushed home from work and took his new wife to the doctor for antidepressants.

They didn't work. The next day, she swallowed a triple dose along with several of her husband's blood pressure pills and a fifth of whiskey. Her son found her still, blue body on his bedroom floor when he got home from school. Nudging her with the toe of his sneaker, he laughed – horror mixed with fascination.

His stepfather turned out to be a truly decent man after all. He buried his pretty bride and then adopted her son. Within a few months, he consulted a podiatrist who fitted him with a special prosthetic that took away his limp. The bullying stopped as soon as he grew in girth and height and began catching the attention of lovesick school girls. Two years later, his stepfather married again, choosing a wife, like himself, who chose to see only goodness in others. She cried the first time he called her Mom.

But as much as he appeared to excel in American life, he never truly shed his former self. Manny called to him more and more after his mother's death. He felt him acutely during the day, but painfully at night. His mother began calling to him too, her keening voice twisted and horrible as she emerged in his dreams through broken earth, holding her torn heart in her hands as she begged him to make things right.

He tried to remember all of Grandmother's stories – especially those of the earth monster and the twins, Tezcatlipoca and Quetzalcoatl – but the edges were hazy, the details distorted. He began to search the school library, then the city library, then the university library. Gradually he began to fill in the blanks. He studied the legends voraciously until they began to shift toward reality.

When his stepfather's notice and commendations – "You're really attacking this history project with enthusiasm. Good for you." – began to display an edge of concern – "Don't overwork yourself, son. Why not spread your net a little – read some Greek Mythology?"— he dispelled his fears with plenty of outdoor activity and trips to the theater with classmates.

They were not his friends.

He had long ago stopped trying to feel the benefit of American life, or of real companionship. Grandmother's stories had altered his path forever, connecting him to his lost brother, his dead mother, and to his destiny more surely than football, girls or parties ever could.

No one knew. He was good at playing the part – honing his deceptive skills and perfecting his role. Through high school and college, he mastered it, studying enough to graduate and please his adoptive parents, while engaging in just enough bad behavior to make them believe he was just like any other red-blooded American male.

He had learned to fool them all.

When he finally returned to Mexico, he found Manny in the canyon without difficulty – the way a dog can find its way home – and they had laughed and cried, staring at each other the way a man looks at his reflection in a funhouse mirror. He took care of him from that day forward – setting up his home, supplying him with food, clothing and work.

"Brothers help each other. The stronger helps the weaker," Grandmother had said. "Sometimes, the weak can help the strong."

He helped Manny have a better life, and after many years, he asked for his help in return – but nothing Manny couldn't handle. Yes, he often became too attached to the prisoners he cared for. Sometimes he even begged his brother to let them go. But he could be taught reason. Ultimately, he followed orders.

Manny always cried when his brother told Grandmother's story. He knew his mother was dead and it hurt to be reminded, but his twin was relentless. He had to make him understand.

"Long ago, Tezcatlipoca and Quetzalcoatl entered the body of the earth monster, Tlaltecuhtli. They met in her heart and somehow tore it in two. They didn't mean to hurt her," he said, his voice gentle. "But it angered her, just the same.

"She's waiting in the underworld, comforted by our brother who was conceived but never born – Huitzilopochtli. I was wrong to hate him – wrong to hate her. She's waiting for our tribute – innocent blood, the purest of hearts. It's the only way to please her – the only way she'll leave me alone."

Manny's simple mind could not understand the importance of the sacrifices, but then it had never been tormented by the dreams either. Sometimes his twin had to use more force than he liked. Fear could be a useful tool, he reminded himself, and though Quetzalcoatl and Tezcatlipoca were sometimes allies, they were opponents as well.

Most of all, though, we were brothers.

He had needed Manny. Offering his sacrifices while maintaining his cover life would have been impossible without him. The rage he felt over his twin's death had shaken him to the core, but as he looked around his fetid house, he realized he had mourned long enough. He had to go on and complete the cycle. Grandmother foretold it. His mother demanded it.

The Jaguar lowered his head.

How will I complete the next sacrifice without him?

22

RACHEL BLEW on her hands and stared at the white-dappled field in front of her, thinking about Christmas, just three weeks away. Mist hung low on the horizon, skirting the Estrella Mountains and mirroring her breath, visible in white puffs against the gray dawn. She closed her eyes and imagined it was snow spread across the field, but the illusion wouldn't stick. It wasn't snow, it was cotton – twenty acres of it, ready for harvest.

An errant wisp, dirty with mud, blew across the road and tangled itself around the heel of her shoe. Rachel tried to kick it loose, but failed. She gave up and glanced sideways at Gloria, a young Maricopa woman who reminded her of a Chihuahua – shaking with adrenalin and likely to run and hide.

It was that last tendency that had Rachel worried.

With most informants, Rachel would be pushing harder by now – throwing around words like "accessory" or "obstruction of justice," but with Gloria, she waited. The woman had called the tip line, returned Rachel's phone call and agreed to meet her under the power lines at the edge of the Gila River Reservation, five miles from the casino where she was soon due to start her shift. Clearly she wanted to help.

But Rachel couldn't wait any longer. "Tell me what you saw, Gloria. You didn't meet me here to waste my time."

Gloria continued to shake from head to toe, her large eyes swollen with tears. "I didn't agree to testify. He's gone. There isn't nothin' gonna bring him back."

"When you say gone, you mean dead, right?" Rachel squinted into the rising sun. "Hank killed him, didn't he?"

Gloria nodded. She played with her keys and took a timid step back toward her ancient Monte Carlo. If she tried to run now, Rachel would have to stop her, arrest her if necessary.

"Were you there, Gloria?" Rachel's voice was soft. "Did you see Hank kill him?"

Again, a small nod. "Now he's gonna kill me for telling."

"We're not going to abandon you," Rachel said. "I can call the Bureau's victim specialist right now. Her name is Pamela. She's a friend of mine and very nice. Together, we can make sure you're safe. We can make sure that doesn't happen again." Rachel glanced meaningfully at Gloria's upper lip, which was cut and swollen under a thick coat of makeup.

"He didn't mean it," she responded tonelessly. Rachel knew it was just a reflexive comment, but still she marveled. Gloria was afraid her boyfriend would kill her – just like he had killed Douglas Angel – but was still unwilling to admit he was truly violent.

"Where's Douglas's body, Gloria?"

She shifted her feet. "I can show you. Not now, though, I'm late for work."

Rachel nodded. "Yes, you can show me. But I can't let you go until you at least give me an idea of where to search. Why don't you let us take it from here? Get this burden off your shoulders."

Gloria pushed a bitter laugh through her lips and dragged in another shaky breath. "He isn't going nowhere."

Rachel picked up a map from the hood of her car. It was already neatly pressed open to the casino and its vicinity – the last place Douglas Angel had been seen. He was an eighteen-year-old man missing since July and was last seen after arguing with Gloria's boyfriend, Hank Souch. Sadly, his story had not gotten the same news play as Samantha Davidson's.

"Missing white girls are more newsworthy to the average American," Victor said.

"Sensationalism," Rachel answered. Newsworthy or not, she was determined to solve the case. Today was going to be the day.

She handed the map to Gloria.

"Show me," she said.

☙

IT WAS five-thirty on Friday evening by the time Rachel was driving home from the crime scene. Douglas Angel's decaying body had been unearthed in a shallow grave right where Gloria said it would be and Hank Souch had been apprehended – halfway to drunk at *The Copper Stallion* – and arrested.

"Good work, agent," SAC Devlin had said when she visited the scene.

"Thank you, Ma'am."

It felt good to be noticed for results. During the nine months since her trip to Mexico, Rachel had accomplished little more than annoying her superior with her relentless belief that Samantha's true killer was still at large. Marius's unsettling call in September had only added credence to that belief. SAC Devlin remained skeptical.

"Agent Mueller," she said, holding up her hand to stop another barrage of evidence. "Even if what Agent Suarez learned is true – that the man killed in Chihuahua had an undocumented twin – nothing ties that twin to the murder. What some woman in a Mexican barrio believes is far from supportable evidence."

Rachel was given no leeway to add resources to the investigation, which left her no option but to study it late at night when Danny was sleeping. Her study walls were virtually papered with her findings – those relating to Samantha and the other missing women on her list as well as pictures from the Copper Canyon cave she had developed from the film canister Marius had saved from the flood. She had enlargements made of each trophy, as well as the symbols and strange figure painted on the wall. Stacks of library books on Mesoamerican mythology, hieroglyphs and history littered her desk, shelves and chairs, fighting with her endless notes for space. The more she studied, the darker became her profile of the man responsible.

"It's not good for you to spend all your free time locked up in there," Victor told her once when she caught him rattling her office door. She admitted she kept it locked not only to hide the mess, but because she was afraid one glimpse would give Danny nightmares.

"And I don't want to run my new housekeeper off in frustration," she told him.

"How's she working out?"

"Good." She left out the part about how expensive she was. "She's certified for child care as well. Once she and Danny get to know each other a little better, I may extend her hours."

As Rachel pulled into her driveway and walked to her neighbor's house in the fading twilight, she wondered if Danny's bonding period with Juanita might have to be rushed. A text from Wanda told her Danny and his best friend, Jonathan, had been fighting again.

"Hi Rachel." Wanda answered the door with her one-year-old daughter on her hip. "Come on in."

"I got your message." Rachel offered the baby her finger. "Have they been better this afternoon?"

Wanda looked weary. "I bribed them with cookies and sent them out in the yard. At least when they're outside, I can't hear them bickering." Wanda slid open the glass door and shouted into the backyard. "Danny, your mom is here!"

"I'm sorry, Wanda," Rachel said. "They used to play so well together—"

"I know, Rachel. It's never been a burden to have Danny here," Wanda said. "It kept Jonathan occupied and gave me time to get a few things done." She glanced toward a half-folded stack of laundry on the couch.

"There's a 'but' in there."

Wanda's eyes pooled with sympathy. "I know what you've been through this year, but the divorce has changed Danny. He's more aggressive, he shows less respect…"

"I know." Rachel's cheeks reddened. It was the same story she heard from his third grade teacher and his guidance counselor. "I've been trying to work on it with him."

"Maybe the boys need a break from each other." Wanda shifted the baby. "You've been generous with me and I'm building up quite a vacation fund with the babysitting money. But, what do you think? Do you have someone else who can watch him for a couple of weeks? Maybe we can try again after the New Year."

Rachel walked Danny back home at a clipped pace. Concern, embarrassment and anger competed with each other for dominance in her thoughts.

"What are we going to do about this problem between you and Jonathan, Danny?" she asked as she pushed open the front door and guided him to the kitchen, jabbing her finger toward a chair. Her son dropped his backpack on the floor and slumped in his seat with a sour expression. Rachel silently counted to ten. She had not expected behavior like this – at least not until he hit adolescence. She crossed her arms over her chest and stared at him. "Well?"

"I told you, I want to be called Dan, not Danny. I'm not a baby."

"You're acting like a baby. Fighting with Jonathan over Legos? The *Wii*?" Rachel turned and opened the pantry door, looking for something easy to fix for dinner. "You've lost the privilege of going over to Jonathan's because of this. Doesn't that bother you?"

"Fine with me," he said, kicking the chair leg. "He's lame anyway."

Rachel shut the door a little too firmly, making Danny jump. "Everything's lame, isn't it Danny? School, friends – the movies we've gone to see, the zoo? It's your favorite word lately." Although he had used worse language last week, shocking her enough to call his father.

"Lighten up, will you, Rachel?" Craig's answer had been. "We hardly live in a *Brady Bunch* world. You can't expect the kid to set himself completely apart from his peers by sticking to your outdated moral code."

"I wasn't aware, before this past year, of course, that you and I had a different moral code," Rachel said hotly. "Of course, when he tells me that 'Trisha says it all the time' I shouldn't be surprised. Do you think you can rein in your girlfriend?"

Craig made a dismissive hissing noise. "He's growing up, Rachel. Whether you like it or not. Why do you make such a big deal about everything?"

"Can I go play video games?" Danny asked, breaking into Rachel's thoughts.

"No." She opened the fridge and peered hopelessly inside. "No video games for a week. That should give you plenty of time to think about how to treat your friends."

"Whatever," Danny said. "I'll just wait until this weekend. Dad's *Playstation* is way cooler than *Wii*."

That was it. Rachel opened her mouth, intent on grounding the attitude right out of him when the doorbell rang. "This discussion is not over. Get started on your homework." She walked toward the front door, hating the feeling of helplessness that was threatening to overwhelm her.

"I have *Carolina's*," Victor said loudly from outside. Rachel opened the door and he stepped through, carrying a greasy bag that smelled of *carnitas*, beans and freshly made tortillas. "And a kid's meal for Danny," he added.

"Thank you! You're a lifesaver." Rachel led the way back toward the kitchen. "But my surly child isn't answering to Danny today. It's 'Dan' now."

"I'm too old to be Danny anymore," he said with a decided whine.

"Too cool for us, huh?" Victor asked, bumping Danny playfully with his hip and almost losing his balance in the process. Danny tried to maintain his rebellious expression, but couldn't keep from laughing as Victor overacted his near fall. He grabbed for the kid's meal, which Victor swung over his head like a pendulum.

"I understand," he said, sitting next to Danny, finally plunking the bright sack on top of his notebook. "You're the man of the house, right?"

Rachel set plates on the table. "Well, he needs to change his attitude at home, school *and* his friend's house before he gets that kind of promotion from me."

"Watch out," Victor said, leaning toward Danny. "I think she means it."

Danny shot her a scathing look, but his face transformed when he found the toy in the bottom of his bag. "Look, Batman!"

Half an hour later, Rachel put the last of their dirty dishes in the dishwasher and motioned Victor toward the living room.

"Mom?" Danny squirmed in his seat. "Can I be excused?"

Rachel frowned. "Finish your spelling, then come see me. Okay?"

She shook her head and sat across from Victor on the couch. "I don't know what's going on with him."

"Sure you do," he said. "You just wish you didn't. Try not to worry. He'll work himself out of it. You're doing a great job, by the way."

"Well thank you for that. And for the food," Rachel said. "But what brings you here tonight? Isn't there a soccer game you should be covering somewhere?"

Victor tapped his fingers on the arm of his chair. "The New Year's Eve Gala is just a few weeks away, Rachel. A night of dancing at South Mountain Resort..."

"Oh, Victor, I don't know..."

He held up his hands. "I have no dark ulterior motives. Scout's honor. I just want to see you dressed up and having a good time – not worrying about Danny or that oh-so-secret case you're obsessing about."

"Don't start with me."

He grinned. "I don't want to ask anyone else. Things with my former dates have always gotten complicated after the New Year."

"Maybe that's because you never call them again."

He grimaced. "Will you think about it at least? You'd be doing me a real favor. And it's for the kids. You know how important it is to me."

Rachel groaned. Victor's father ran a charity that supported Latin American orphanages and international adoptions. Their biggest fundraiser of the year was this New Year's Eve gala. "Make me feel like a heel, why don't you? You know I've always done what I can to help."

Victor looked at his watch and stood up. "I need to get going. Just think about it, okay?"

Rachel nodded and walked him to the door.

"Goodnight, *Dan*," Victor called into the kitchen.

"Night Vic," Danny called back.

An hour later, Rachel flipped on Danny's nightlight and turned out his bedroom light. "Good night, honey. Love you."

"Mom?"

"Yes?"

"What about nightmares?"

She walked back into his room and knelt by his bedside again. "We prayed 'no bad dreams.' Remember?"

He nodded, but still looked unsure. Rachel's heart melted.

He's so young, she reminded herself, *a little boy who doesn't know how to deal with what's happening in his life.* She stroked his head.

"What else can we do?" he asked.

"You want the song?" She twisted her face into a silly grimace. Danny smiled and nodded.

It had been a long time. Rachel cleared her throat. "*Well, I'd like to visit the moon...*"

It took another fifteen minutes for Danny to settle down. After another trip to the bathroom, a second cup of water and a sleepy request that they move to Cottonwood, she tucked him in for the last time and whispered goodnight.

Rachel had her toothbrush in her mouth and was pulling on her nightshirt when the phone rang.

"I saw the news tonight about the body found on the reservation," Melissa said. "Was that your case?"

"Yeah, my boss was happy – for once." Rachel rinsed her toothbrush and flopped on the bed before giving her sister a summary of her day.

"What's this gala that Victor invited you to?"

"A fancy New Year's Eve party to raise money for *Ayuda del Norte*. It's a charity that benefits Mexican and Central American adoptions by American families. His father started it years ago."

"Hmm. Seems like I heard something about them on the news."

"There was a segment last year – some activists were upset about Americans adopting Mexican kids," Rachel said. "The Mexican government has a strict policy about in-country placement whenever possible, but critics said *Ayuda del Norte* was bending rules."

"Were they?"

Rachel shrugged. "Vic said it was political – another agency raising a fuss after being denied accreditation by the Mexican Central Authority."

"Are you going to go to the gala?"

"I don't have anything to wear. I'm leaning toward not."

"Good idea."

Rachel laughed. "You don't trust Victor, do you?"

"I've never met him." Melissa sounded defensive. "But I can't say I fully understand his motives. Do you?"

"No," Rachel admitted. "Usually I think he's just trying to be a friend. Other times, I wonder."

"Remind me again how you and Craig met him?"

"He met Craig at a golf tournament about a year ago," Rachel said. "I've never known Craig to hit it off with someone so quickly – in hindsight, it's probably because Vic showed so much interest in Craig. He's a good listener. Anyway, that was right about the time Samantha Davidson went missing and I was working a lot – Craig and Vic spent a lot of time together golfing or going to D-backs games. He invited him for dinner one night and Victor was so funny and so good with Danny. That was that, I guess."

"Don't get me wrong," Melissa said. "I appreciate his loyalty to you over Craig."

"He'd win you over if you met him, 'Liss," Rachel said. "He's a real charmer – you should see the attention he gets whenever we're out. That's one of the reasons I don't think he's really interested in me. He could have any woman he wanted."

"What if he wants you?" Melissa asked. "Don't sell yourself short."

Rachel changed the subject. "Danny asked me about moving to Cottonwood again."

"And?"

"You know the answer."

Melissa sighed. "I can dream can't I? Did you talk to the realtor yet?"

"Yes, but my mortgage is severely upside down." Rachel stared at the ceiling. "Why did I agree to buy this house? Even with Craig and I working together, the payments were difficult. And now…"

"You were trying to be supportive of his dreams," Melissa reminded her. "Unselfish, accommodative."

"Look what it got me."

"You could always give Danny's request some serious thought," Melissa said. "Move in with us for a while. Rent out your house."

Rachel shook her head, frustrated to be traveling this road with her sister again. "We would be stepping on each other's toes within two weeks. And my job is here, 'Liss."

"For how long? Seriously, are you going to be running around, chasing criminals forever?"

"My work is important." Rachel swung her legs to the floor. "I'm proud of what I do. It makes a difference – think about the killer we captured today."

"I know," Melissa said. "But there's going to be a point when you've grown past it – when you realize your priorities are different. Like it or not, your divorce has changed your reality."

"It's made keeping a job that much more critical, don't you think?" Rachel ran her hands through her hair. "Listen, I'm tired and need to get to bed."

"I'm sorry, Rachel," Melissa said. "You know I love you."

"I know. I love you too. Good night."

Rachel walked through the dark house, checking the garage door and locks before climbing back into bed, feeling wearier than she should. Melissa's attitude frustrated her. She married her high school sweetheart and had been a stay-at-home mom ever since. Yes, she did without to make it happen – older cars, clothes, furniture, appliances, but she lived with a sense of peace that Rachel rarely felt. "Everything will work out," Melissa always said.

Rachel had never been that optimistic. Since her divorce from Craig, it was harder than ever to see life in those terms. It was too simplistic to believe she could just drop her whole life and move back home. And just the thought of living in the same town as her dad made Rachel cringe. Their relationship had never been close, but things were worse since the divorce. Of course he had thought highly of Craig – unlike Marius. When she told him about the affair, he had defended his son-in-law.

"Men stray sometimes, Rachel," he said. "You don't have to take it personally. Just stick it out. He'll tire of her soon enough and come back – as long as he has a home to return to."

Rachel lay down again and stared at the dark ceiling, her mind jumping from betrayal to betrayal.

Don't go there, she told herself. But bitterness had an aftertaste.

A lump started to grow against her throat and two thick, hot tears worked their way down her cheek. She rolled onto her side, her mind wandering to the role her father had played in her break-up with Marius. How unfair that he would have her chase away a good man, then cling to a snake – all because of geography and skin color.

Rachel had spent most of the summer after her freshman year trying not to think about Marius or his kiss in the library. When the memory only grew stronger, she took on a new strategy for forgetting and began to date a fellow undergraduate she knew from high school. They started out their sophomore year at ASU together, but it didn't take long for Rachel to realize they had little in common. Peter had been different in Cottonwood – perhaps because her father had hired him to work the rental counter at his dealership and much of their time had been spent in his presence. As soon as they got back to Tempe, Peter wanted to fully embrace the party scene and saw Rachel's restraint as a flaw in her character – just like the cautious tempo she set for their physical relationship.

"Come on, Rachel," Peter said one night, having her all but pinned against her dorm bed. He traced his thumb along her collarbone. "We're away from Daddy now. You can make your own choices – embrace your freedom." His thumb moved lower until her breath caught and her skin crawled. She pushed him away and sat up.

"My choices or yours, Peter?"

They argued until Peter called her an "ice queen" and stormed out of the room, leaving Rachel feeling weary but relieved. He wasted no time in moving on and Rachel was content to focus on her studies. Her Spanish classes were going well. Her new teacher was tough and efficient, if a little lacking in personality. But Rachel worked hard not to think about those differences, no matter how often she saw Marius on campus in the distance, walking to class, reading a paper in the MU or jogging along Palm Walk in the early morning.

One Saturday afternoon she was scanning the used CDs at *Zia's* Record Exchange when she looked up to see Marius watching her from the other side of the rack.

"Hi." He smiled.

"Hi."

After an awkward silence, he shuffled his feet and nodded toward the CDs in her hands. "What are you looking at?"

She wrinkled her nose and reluctantly held them up.

"*American Pie* and *Teaser and the Firecat?*" he read.

"Not exactly cutting edge stuff," Rachel admitted.

"No." The corners of his mouth twitched.

"You're laughing at me," she said.

"I am not. Well, maybe a little bit."

"Thanks."

He walked around the rack and held out his hand. Rachel handed him the CDs and watched him turn them over, reading the playlists.

"I found those on vinyl this summer in the back of a closet. I think they belonged to my mom. My dad doesn't listen to music – except maybe a bit of country on the radio. Anyway, he doesn't have a turntable, so I had no way of listening to them. I just wanted to hear what she liked." Her voice trailed away. She was rambling.

Marius handed the CDs back. "How old were you when she died?"

"Seven. She was an ER nurse. She died in a car accident on her way home from a late shift."

"I'm sorry."

Rachel shrugged and then wished she hadn't. "My memories of her are faded."

For a moment they were both silent, then she snatched the CD he was holding.

"*Rage Against the Machine*?"

"Now who's laughing?" he asked.

"Do you have anger issues?" she teased, handing it back to him.

He just shook his head. Rachel smiled and backed away. "Nice seeing you."

For the rest of the fall semester, whenever they saw each other on campus, they would stop and chat – mostly about their classes and professors. One night, she ran into him at a late-night showing of *Like Water for Chocolate* at the Mill Avenue Art Theater. It was almost completely empty and Marius sat down right next to her, smiling.

"Are you following me?" he asked.

She stole a piece of his popcorn. "Who's following who?"

The lights fell and they watched the movie together in silence. Rachel tried not to rely on the subtitles, but still struggled with the speed of the spoken Spanish. As the story progressed, she forgot her intention, caught up in the younger sister's fight for love. When the movie was over and Rachel was trying to dry her eyes without Marius noticing, he surprised her by squeezing her hand and standing up.

"Come on," he said. "That made me hungry for chocolate."

They crossed the street to the Coffee Plantation, where Marius bought two cups of coffee and a huge chocolate brownie, which he split down the middle with a plastic knife. They ate and drank slowly, discussing the movie mostly, though Marius had other Spanish films and books to recommend.

"Still rooming with Goth Girl?" he asked when they walked back toward campus.

"Hardly. No, I'm on my own this semester."

"And Spanish class?"

"It's going well." She was sorry he asked. For a while, she had forgotten that he was once her teacher. She stopped under a Palo Verde tree and wrapped her arms over her chest. The wind was picking up, rustling the branches overhead, which dropped yellow petals on their shoulders. "I'm going that way," she said, turning. "Thanks for…"

Marius took her hand, stopping her. "Rachel. I'm not your teacher anymore."

He kissed her and his lips tasted like chocolate. Rachel's heart tilted toward him and her body followed, leaning into his chest as his arms encircled her.

"*Querida*," he whispered, his lips moving to her temple.

Rachel could still hear his voice, almost two decades later. It was the kind of memory that never let go. She rolled over in bed. Time had not erased the pain either. Eventually, she fell into an uneasy sleep, waking through the night to wrestle with her covers and her dreams. In them, she searched for Marius, wandering through meandering gardens overgrown with dying flowers and into dim houses where his scent lingered and his voice echoed. Then she was running through lamp-lit suburban streets, calling his name while sirens screamed in the distance, drawing closer and more insistent. She stirred and picked up her cell phone, jabbing at buttons. The sirens stopped.

"Hello?"

"Rachel." It was Marius. Had she found him, then? "Rachel, are you awake?"

She sat up, finally awake.

"Marius?" She could feel his tension across the miles. "What is it? What's wrong?"

"We've uncovered another body, Rachel. I think she might be one of your missing women."

23

MARIUS WAS WAITING at the customs gate when Rachel landed at the Chihuahua airport on Monday morning. Their greeting was brief and conversation impossible as he shouldered her bag and navigated a path through the swollen holiday crowd. His pace was clipped, but Rachel hardly noticed. It matched the tempo she had maintained all weekend, gaining travel approval from SAC Devlin, booking her flight and worrying over Danny's care in her absence.

"I don't know what to do," she told Melissa on the phone. "Craig's leaving today for a two-week ski trip and Danny's winter break doesn't begin until next week. I can't ask Wanda."

"I'll come down tomorrow night and stay the week with him," Melissa said. "I can get some holiday shopping done while Danny's in school. If you're not back by the end of the week, I'll bring him home with me and you can join us in Cottonwood for Christmas."

"I can't ask you to do that, Liss. What about your kids?"

"They are old enough to fend for themselves after school until Rich gets home. They'll order pizza or eat frozen dinners – stay up late and watch too much television. They'll love it."

"What would I do without u?"

"We'll never know. But Rachel, be careful."

Rachel hadn't slept well Sunday night. Danny was delighted to have his Aunt Melissa visiting and had been on his best behavior. Rachel packed all the research she could fit in her luggage, but still worried over what she might have missed. And then there was Marius, whom she would see the next day. He still deserved an apology.

But if Marius had been nursing a grudge over the past several months, Rachel couldn't see it from several paces behind, weaving through travelers, luggage and brightly-wrapped packages, passing through sliding doors and dodging cars until they reached his Jeep in the parking lot. She thought about stopping him then and stumbling through her apology, but when he turned to look at her, his eyes were flat and unreadable. Rachel let the moment pass.

"Agent Cruces went ahead of us to the morgue." He checked his watch. "He'll try to hold up the medical examiner. We should still catch them if we hurry."

"Thank you." Rachel climbed in the Jeep and watched the sky darken as they weaved out of the parking lot and headed away from the airport. It started to rain.

"Do you think we'll make it to the crime scene today?" she asked.

Marius looked at the sky. "I think so, if the weather clears. It's in a small valley on the eastern end of Tararecua – fewer than two kilometers from the skylight entrance to the cave we found. Luckily, there's a plateau of sorts not far away, perfect for the helicopter to set down. It's only a short hike from there."

"I'm still confused about how it was discovered."

His smile was brief. "I didn't explain it clearly on the phone. A group of students from Quebec found the grave about two weeks ago." He shook his head. "I think at least one of them thought he was Indiana Jones uncovering a hidden tomb. He was quite – territorial."

"They were digging in the area?"

"No, just hiking. They likely would not have noticed it at all if not for our flash flood this spring." Marius glanced at her. "The water must have shifted the rocks covering the grave. The students were camping nearby and one of them started grabbing rocks to make a fire ring. Not far into the pile, he came across her remains. He and his friends started snapping pictures and moving more rocks. Eventually one of them had the sense to realize the bones were not ancient."

Rachel winced. "Was anything at the scene preserved?"

"Perhaps the grave itself. Little else." He shrugged. "We won't get footprints. That was unlikely anyway, with a crime this cold, but our team has been thoroughly over the site. I've left it guarded, cordoned off and canopied. Snow fell last night, so it's probably slushy up there today, but it's the best we could do."

They stopped at a red light.

"When the students got back to Creel, they reported their find to the local police, who, in turn, took their time calling us," Marius said. "I don't think they appreciated our presence the last time we were there."

"I get that a lot on the reservations," Rachel said.

Marius turned back to the road. "It wasn't until I saw the remains that I thought of your cases. Her stature, signs of ritualism in the burial and the proximity to the cave sent me back to look at the notes you left me. I'm sorry it took so long."

"Don't be. Has the medical examiner assigned a cause of death?"

Marius turned right into a small lot and parked next to a drab gray building. "Let's go find out."

Agent Cruces greeted them at the door and escorted them through a maze of unadorned hallways until they reached the morgue. He was polite as usual, if perhaps a little more reserved than he had been in March.

"You remember Dr. Gutierrez, our medical examiner," Cruces said.

"Yes. Good to see you again." She shook his hand.

"And this is Dr. Delgado, a forensic anthropologist who consults from the university on such cases."

"*Mucho gusto.*" Rachel shook hands with a tall, striking woman in her forties. "I take it the body is in an advanced state of decay?"

"Yes. The remains are not much more than skeletal," Dr. Delgado said. "You've brought missing persons cases that may be a match?"

"Yes, I have four possible cases."

"*Bueno.* Let's see whom we might eliminate first."

They filed into an examination room where Rachel's attention was drawn to the form laid on an autopsy table. Draped in a thin white sheet, it was so small it looked like a child. Dr. Gutierrez removed the drape. Dr. Delgado's description had at least prepared her for what she now saw – little more than bones dressed in small patches of paper-thin soft tissue. The way they had been placed in anatomical order gave Rachel the impression of a marionette. Her eyes passed down the skeleton, stopping when they reached the shin bones, which were both cut just above the ankles.

"Her feet were severed." Marius came to stand beside her. "They were buried in the grave with the rest of her body, but positioned underneath her head."

Rachel turned to Dr. Gutierrez. "Is this how she died?"

"It's possible," he said.

"But we suspect her feet were severed post mortem," Dr. Delgado added.

"Why?"

"The tibia and fibula of each leg were cut through with a single stroke of the weapon – likely a sharpened axe, each in equal distance from the ankle bones." She pursed her lips. "There's no sign that she moved her legs during either attack. If the assailant was struggling to keep her in place, we might see a second strike mark – a crushing of the bones, or even a less exact angle in the cut. Of course, if more tissue was still present, we might see rope or shackle marks to take away some of the guess work."

Rachel worked her hand into a fist and then released it. "You don't know for certain, then, how she died?" she asked.

"It is clearly homicide," Cruces said.

"But it can be difficult to determine cause of death with skeletal remains," Dr. Delgado said. "We are fortunate, at least, to have the entire body rather than individual bones to examine. There are other clues as well – enough for me to make an educated guess."

"Which is?"

"I believe she was killed by transaction of the carotid arteries. The killer used an extremely sharp blade in a single motion, cutting her across the throat while holding her from behind."

Rachel circled the table and watched Dr. Delgado point to the neck bones. "Here on the cervical vertebrae you can see narrow cuts that angle diagonally, down from right to left. A cut that deep would have nearly severed the head."

"The killer was not tentative in his attack," Marius said.

"He's left-handed?" Cruces asked.

"If my guess is correct, *sí*," said Dr. Delgado. "But those cuts are not the only evidence of a mortal wound." She pointed to the ribcage. "Here on the right side of the sternum, several ribs have been cut through. The cuts are narrow, like those on the vertebrae. He probably used the same weapon, but held it differently – overhand, with his fingers curved around the back of the handle."

"Would those cuts go through the heart?" Marius asked.

"Given the ritualistic tones of this murder, Dr. Delgado and I have another theory," said Dr. Gutierrez. "We think he killed her by slashing her throat – the carotid transaction – and then turned her over and cut out her heart. These cuts would give him access without having to remove other organs."

"Would that match your profile?" Cruces asked Rachel.

"Yes." She cleared her throat.

"Why would he do that?"

"Ingestion, burial, incineration, trophy keeping – there are many possibilities. I don't need to tell you that all of them put this killer in a category of extreme rarity and concern."

"We did have some luck at the grave site," Marius said. "A small chip of a metal or a metal-like substance was sifted from the dirt and rock. Dr. Delgado thinks it might be a piece of the murder weapon."

He handed Rachel a glass vial which she held up to the light. In it was a small triangle of dark blue.

"What is it?"

"The lab analysis will be on my desk by this afternoon," Dr. Delgado said. "But my guess is obsidian."

"Is it a common substance?"

"Its composition is too complex to be classified as a single metal or mineral, though it's mineral like," she said. "It's volcanic glass."

"Where does it come from? Can it be traced?"

"Obsidian flows are all over the place – Mexico and the Western U.S., Greece, Scotland. Our geologist should be able to regionalize it and find a source."

"I Googled obsidian while we were waiting for you," Cruces said, earning a small shake of the head from his partner. "I learned that it's known for its sharpness. The ancients used it to make arrowheads. Today, it's sometimes used to make surgical scalpels – it tends to create less noticeable scars."

"Could these cuts have been made with a scalpel?" Rachel asked.

Dr. Delgado shook her head. "The wounds indicate a wider weapon – and are consistent with the piece we found."

"Several dealers in handmade obsidian hunting knives came up on my Internet search," Cruces said. "We'll contact them and see what more we can learn about a source. At least we know that the weapon he used is missing a piece."

"I suppose no such weapon was recovered at the cave or the shack?" Rachel asked.

"We are double checking the catalog of items, but no," Marius said, "I don't think so."

"If we were lucky enough to find the weapon and match it to that chip…" Cruces said.

"The knife would be important to him," Rachel said. "Either he'll use the same weapon for all killings, or he'll need to find a similar – near perfect – replacement."

"Unfortunately," Marius said, "both your agency and mine are convinced that the killer has already been captured and killed."

"Making evidence to the contrary that much more vital." Rachel turned to Dr. Delgado. "Can you determine when she died?"

"Bones can be used to determine age, sex, weight, but pinning down the exact date of death is difficult. Chemical analysis shows high levels of nitrogen in the bones. That, combined with increased amounts of radioactive isotopes and considerable fluorescence under ultra-violet light rules out the possibility that they are ancient – part of some century-old sacrifice, as the Canadian students hoped, which narrows it down to the past fifty years."

She shifted down the table, pointing to the leg bones. "More specifically, though, is the presence of bits of the periosteum, tendon and ligament tags on the bones. You can see them here. That means decomposition began no more than five years ago."

"You keep saying 'she,'" Cruces said. "Are you sure?"

"Stature and bone thickness suggest a female," Dr. Delgado said. "Also, the pelvis is wide and has a broader sciatic notch." She circled back to the head of the table and pointed to the jaw bone. "Do you see the posterior ramus, or back branch of the mandible here? It's straight. In males, it tends to curve inward."

"That rules out one of my missing persons," Rachel said. "The only male – Jonas Flynn. What about her height and weight?"

"She was one and a half meters tall and weighed approximately thirty-eight kilograms at the time of death."

"That's — what, about four foot eleven, eighty-three pounds?"

"Approximately, *sí*."

"What about race?"

"Caucasoid. She could have been Caucasian or Hispanic."

"Can you tell how old she was?"

"The growth plates in her long bones and the sterna areas where the rib cage meets the breast bone tells me she was between twenty-three and twenty-five years of age."

"That rules out another case," Rachel said. She grabbed her briefcase from a chair near the door and thumbed through her files until she found two folders, which she handed to Dr. Delgado. "If this is really one of my missing persons, it is either Mary Ellen Potter or Libby Stuart."

"What can you tell us about them?" Cruces asked.

"Mary Ellen was twenty-three and Libby twenty-five. Mary Ellen disappeared about a year before Samantha Davidson from Tucson, where she worked as a records clerk for a trucking company. She lived alone. Her supervisor called the police when she failed to show up for work two days in a row.

"Libby disappeared two years earlier, in May, as reported by her husband. She was a waitress in Parker, Arizona."

Dr. Delgado flipped through the files. "No recorded broken bones or previous injuries to help us." She looked up. "Dr. Alvarez, our forensic odontologist, will be here this afternoon to consult on the dental X-rays. With any luck, he'll make a positive ID."

"What about DNA?" Marius asked.

"Dental work can be just as reliable – and less time consuming."

Rachel nodded absently, thinking about Libby and Mary Ellen. Which one of them had endured the horrors they just discussed so clinically? Experts often said proof of death could come as a relief to those who mourned, but Rachel knew it was more complicated than that. Libby's husband, for example, had waited two days before filing a MP report because he and his wife had recently argued and he thought she had gone home to her mother. And then there was Mary Ellen's grandmother, her only living relative, who now lived in a nursing home, waiting every day to hear about her safe return.

Rachel watched Dr. Gutierrez replace the surgical drape and wondered, how could learning this kind of truth be healing for anyone?

ᘓ

"IT DOESN'T SEEM large enough."

Marius crouched down across from Rachel, the grave between them. "No it doesn't. But of course, she was buried in a fetal position, with her feet under her head."

Rachel shifted her feet, letting the late afternoon sunlight shine on the grave. "I think I've seen something similar in my research – some ancient burial site. Aztec, Toltec," she shook her head, "I can't remember which, or where. But his ritualism is clearly critical."

"He's been following a careful plan, hasn't he?" Marius asked, his face screwed up against the cold wind. "I have to admit, this kind of murder is out of my league, Rachel. I learned about it in my training, yes, but my reality has been killers who have a solid reason for their crimes. Drugs and money. This is…"

"Yes," Rachel said. *Too horrible for words.*

The temperature was dropping, chasing the sun, carried along by wind that stung Rachel's cheeks and tugged at her hair. If any winter birds were perched in the trees nearby, she imagined that God had asked them to still their song. This was a place of sorrow. She rose to her feet and took a deep breath, but the crisp pine-scented air did little to freshen her perspective. Even Marius's face seemed blue as death, washed in the canopy's translucent light. She shivered and turned away to watch the sun disappear through the trees.

"You look cold. We should go."

"I'm fine."

Marius stepped around the grave and walked past her toward a clearing that afforded views of the southeast. Rachel gladly followed, wanting to expunge the decay that hung like a cloud over the entire scene.

"You questioned Indiana Jones and his friends, I presume?"

He smiled grimly. "Yes. I have copies of the transcripts back at the hotel. You're welcome to interview them yourself, of course."

"Did you get their film?"

"They were using digital – we downloaded the images from their flash drives and managed to scare them out of posting the images on Twitter."

"Have you had any media trouble?"

Marius shook his head. "There was a horrible murder up in Los Huertos last week. And a cartel attack east of Juarez – you've heard of it, I'm sure. Another missing American?"

"Yes. We have Bureau agents helping on that front too, I think."

He nodded. "Plenty of evil vying for media attention, although one reporter has named this killer. I heard it this morning on the radio."

"Let's have it."

"The Copper Canyon Killer."

Rachel made a face. "Alliterative." She crossed her arms, squinting at the darkening sky.

"You're cold," Marius said again.

Rachel shook her head. In truth, she was overwhelmed. She knew she should be connecting the dots, returning to her research, hiking the perimeter or marking topography on a map. She wanted more help from the Bureau, but knew it was not coming. And though she was beginning to formulate theories about the killer, she still didn't understand his targeting method, how – or even why – he chose American victims and brought them across the border, how she would go about proving he was still at large, or – most concerning of all – how long they had before he chose another victim.

"Do you need to see anything else before we lose daylight?" Marius asked.

She should have answered his question. Instead, she said what she had been trying to say for eight months in her head.

"Marius, I'm sorry. In the spring, I shouldn't have accused you. I should not have even suspected you…" She stopped. Nothing she could say was adequate.

Marius studied the horizon for a moment. "Forget about it," he finally said.

Rachel stared at his profile. "What does that mean?"

"Nothing." He shifted his feet. "It means don't worry about it. No harm done. Can we go?"

Rachel felt heat rise to her throat. "Because in recent years, whenever I hear 'forget about it,' it mostly means, 'I still hold a grudge, but don't want to deal with it right now.' Is that about right?"

"Rachel, I'm not…No, that's not right at all." Marius looked exasperated. He stared past her, as if the right words were among the tree branches. "I just want to forget. I wish it didn't bother me – what you thought I was capable of – but it does. And yet, I can't fault you, not after what I did. That's what I'd really like – for you to forget the lie I made you believe, that you went on believing for sixteen years."

Rachel turned up her collar and looked at her feet, her thoughts tumbling beyond their apologies to wrestle with more abstract truths – like the way things said by a naïve girl or a headstrong boy could leave marks that even a thoughtful woman or rational man could not overcome.

"We forgive, but we're not built for forgetting, are we?" she finally said.

"Rachel, I hold nothing against you." He took her hand and squeezed it. "You have my forgiveness, even if I haven't yet earned yours. Now, can we leave? We'll be lucky to make it back to the chopper before dark."

24

HE WOKE in pain, his muscles cramping. Sweat poured from his skin.
"No!"

He cried out, but there was no answer, just the echo of his voice against bare walls.

He focused on his breath – *in, out, in, out* – and then his house. Stark walls, polished floors, slick appliances, shining glass. Finally purged of mourning, it was once again a sterile space – vacuous ambiance that should calm his spirit.

Tonight, it didn't.

He began to pace, counting his steps. He paused in the kitchen to turn the lights on and off twice, then circled back to check the door, touch his keys and nudge his leather chair so that it made an exact right angle to the couch. Everything was in place tonight, but it didn't matter. It didn't help.

Returning to the kitchen, he flipped the light switch again, squinting against the brightness as he stumbled toward his wallet, next to his keys and phone. His hands shook as he withdrew the picture – the only picture he carried. The miniature face smiled up at him and he couldn't help smiling back, caressing the plastic covered image, admiring those eyes. Wishing, as he often had…

But then the dream returned with such force that he dropped the photo and his wallet. He slumped to the floor, shaking from head to toe.

"No. No," he said again.

Yes, the Earth Monster whispered. *And you know why.*

She beckoned and he followed, closing his eyes. Once again, he was in his childhood bedroom, looking down at his mother's still body. How long had he stood and stared? Long enough to be sure she was dead. Long enough to plan his endgame.

He executed it calmly – pulling the crumpled piece of paper from her hand and carrying it to the barbeque grate, where he burned it until nothing but ash remained. Only then did he call 9-1-1. His hands did not shake as he dialed. Why did they shake now?

He had left the page for her to find, knowing the words he wrote would push his fragile mother over the edge. He imagined his grandmother's approval as he crafted the note. She always said he was destined for greatness. It was fitting, then, that he should destroy the monster inside his mother with only his words.

For years afterward, he saw no sign of retribution. But then the dreams had come and he learned the awful truth. The earth monster's death would not go unpunished. He must make atonement.

But not this way. *Surely not!*

His lips trembled. Had Samantha Davidson been nothing but a test?

The stove clock caught his eye, innocently proclaiming the hour. It was twenty minutes past midnight. Sudden hope lurched in his heart.

Had he dreamed yesterday or today?

He scrambled to his feet and consulted the calendar, confirming what he already knew. At midnight, the *trecena* had changed. The days of *Mazatl* had passed and the days of *Xochitl* begun.

So had the dream, come from his own spirit – the spirit of Tezcatlipoca, whose voice echoes in the wilderness of his heart – calling him to the true hunt? Or had he dreamed under the spell of the trickster, the irreverent Old Coyote who would delight in such a joke and tear away his mask and carefully-laid plans – just for sport?

His doubt was enough. His heartbeat began to slow, reassuring him that he could wait for a surer sign. He could hope. Or...

At least while waiting, he could prepare for the possibility, however horrible, that the sacrifice he dreamed of was indeed necessary.

25

"LOOK AT this one."

"Have mercy, Rachel." Marius rubbed his eyes, feeling weary. "I told you, I can't tell them apart."

She pushed aside his half-eaten dinner and set the heavy book in front of him. "Look at the foot."

"I wasn't done with that."

"It's a circle with a handle," she persisted. "And look, there's another one on the back of his head. It's supposed to be a mirror."

Marius looked at the image, then reached for the enlarged photograph of the cave figure, comparing the two. She was right. One of the character's feet was round.

"That's a mirror?" he asked skeptically, tipping back in his chair.

"Yes. Like a hand mirror. He's called 'the god of the smoking mirror.'"

"I don't see how that's a mirror. Show me the other one again."

She leaned over him, forcing his chair back on four legs, and flipped a few pages back in the book.

"This one is Quetzalcoatl," she said, tapping the book. "See? A regular foot."

"And the smoking-mirror guy – what's his name?"

"Tezcatlipoca. It's him on the cave wall. I'm pretty sure."

He looked at the pictures again. "I think you're right."

"Still, Quetzalcoatl doesn't lose his significance," she said. "They were twin gods."

Marius raised his eyebrows. "That works nicely with Señora Guzman's story."

"Yes it does," she said. "And look at that paragraph to the right of the picture."

"He had an obsidian knife fetish?"

Rachel nodded. "He was left-handed too."

"Seriously?"

"Yes." She pulled the book out of his hands. "You finish eating. I'll keep reading."

Two hours had passed since their ride back from the canyon. Night had fallen – darker, somehow, because of the horrors they studied. They sat at the conference room's lone table, set up near the fireplace, which a quiet worker had lit when their food was delivered.

Marius was struggling to shrug off discomfort and irritability tonight. For some reason, he couldn't get one image out of his mind – Rachel standing next to the gravesite.

He tamped it down again, and flipped through his own files, pulling out a report that he turned for Rachel to read. "Lab analysis of the cave paintings turned up obsidian in the paint. It must be significant."

"Can you make sure the geologist who examines the obsidian chip also has access to this report?"

"Yes." Marius scribbled a note and turned back to the photo of the cave painting. "So if this is Tezcatlipoca, what does that tell us?"

"That his story influences the killer's rituals and identity," Rachel said. "He may be worshipping him, or he might identify with him on a more personal level. Maybe he believes he is channeling his spirit – or that he has become him in a reincarnated form."

The thought sickened Marius. He pushed the rest of his food out of reach.

"I know it's disturbing," Rachel said. "But knowing his methodology can help us anticipate his patterns of behavior, perhaps even how he selects his victims. It also reveals a certain kind of rigidity to his plans – perfectionism, 'Type A,' obsessive compulsive – take your pick."

She turned in her chair, studying the fire. "What happened with Samantha, for example? How did her escape affect his plans? We can only hope it sets him on his heels for a long time."

"But he won't be dissuaded," Marius said. "No setback is going to stop him from trying again."

"No. I don't think so," she said. "I think that's going to be up to us."

Marius's phone rang, making Rachel jump. He connected the call with the speaker phone.

"Agent Cruces? I'm here with Agent Mueller."

"Dr. Delgado called," Cruces said over the line. "She was able to match the dental records."

Rachel stilled. "Libby Stuart?" she asked.

"Yes."

She nodded. "I had a feeling."

Marius picked up the phone and finished the conversation while Rachel rose and moved closer to the fire, wrapping her sweater around her body. Finally she took in a deep breath and looked at her watch.

"I'll call Agent Hughes in the morning. He can drive out to Parker and give Mr. Stuart the news." She cleared her throat. "Will some of the paperwork be processed by then?"

"Yes," Marius said. "I'll have Cruces ready to fax the preliminary reports first thing tomorrow."

"Thank you."

Rachel picked up a folder and sat down again. For several minutes, they passed files back and forth without conversation. It reminded Marius of their college days together with books and notebooks scattered across the table between them. Those spring weeks following their kiss under the Palo Verde tree had been some of the happiest of his life. They had studied quietly just like this in Hayden Library, speaking only with their eyes or a nudge of the foot under the table. Other times their textbooks were pushed aside for CD cases and Chinese takeout boxes in Marius's one-room apartment. He had accomplished very little as he watched her bent over a textbook, jotting notes or pushing back her ever-encroaching curls.

"It's past midnight," he had said many times, pulling a book or pen from her hand. "Let me walk you home."

They would walk slowly toward her dorm, sometimes holding hands, though they never lingered at her doorway.

"You may not be my teacher anymore, but you still teach," Rachel said.

"Not next semester." He pulled her close, willfully forgetting that only an extended assignment from the DEA made it true. "I'll just be a student, like you, with another year to finish my thesis." He kissed her, his joy and relief genuine, even if his studies were – at that moment – far from his thoughts.

Rachel was not naturally suspicious. Whenever Marius was called unexpectedly to meet his DEA handler, she accepted his excuses with nothing more than disappointment. Her innocence only made Marius love her more deeply. The opposing pieces of his life, however, often crashed down on him in the dead of night as he lay awake, struggling to find the means by which he might tell her the truth. Instead, the impossibility of it all grew alongside their love.

He might have been tempted to abandon his work with the DEA altogether if it had continued along the same futile path, but intelligence he provided was finally yielding measurable results, leading to the arrest of a major dealer. Higher ups in the agency were pleased with his work and thought another year would increase their returns. His handler remained typically derisive, but Marius finally felt validated. It was the first time he considered making law enforcement a career.

Toward the end of spring semester, Rachel and Marius bought a pair of cheap student tickets to see *Les Misérables* from Gammage Auditorium's second balcony. Rachel had cried throughout.

"Now I know why your mother insisted on naming you Marius," she said as they ducked under Frank Lloyd Wright's delicate terra cotta arches and headed toward her dorm. "It's a beautiful story."

"But Marius wasn't exactly heroic, was he?" he asked. "He spent half of the story vacillating between his love for Cosette and his political loyalties – the other half unconscious, being carried through the sewers by a man twice his age."

"He got the girl in the end." She tugged on his arm. "He was blessed, I would say. In real life, I suppose, a choice between love and duty doesn't usually end in happily ever after."

Marius had always remembered those words.

Rachel shuffled her files, dropping one and snapping Marius back to the present. He cleared his throat.

"Maybe you could explain what you know about these characters." He tapped a book on Aztec deities. "I'm not making much headway reading."

"Sure." She shuffled through several folders. "Where are those notes?"

For the next half hour, Rachel read out loud to him.

"Tezcatlipoca was called the god of many things – the night, the north, beauty, royalty. War, sin, misery. He's associated with the planet Venus and Ursa Major. His animal form is a jaguar. He's a shape-shifter but usually appeared as a magician who carried a smoking mirror that killed his enemies."

"Hence the name."

"Yes. He was able to see all by looking in the mirror. It even had a name meaning the 'place from which he watches' – Itlachiayaque."

Marius smiled. "Can you say that again?"

"You try to do better!"

"Sorry. But why the mirror for a foot?"

Rachel turned several pages.

"Here it is. His foot was torn off by the earth monster during the fifth creation of the world."

"The fifth?"

"Yes. According to Toltec legend, the earth's viability as a planet is always precarious and only the gods are able to keep it alive. They consistently fail, which always leads to the death of every living thing and a need for a new creation."

"And the smoking mirror guy was involved in these creation stories?"

"Yes. Quetzalcoatl was there as well. Usually they were adversaries, but sometimes allies. Hang on." Rachel reached for another book and quickly found what she was looking for. "Okay, I'll try to summarize. Tezcatlipoca ruled a race of giants on the first earth until Quetzalcoatl overthrew him – literally. He threw him over his head and into the sea. He was reborn as a jaguar and managed to overthrow Quetzalcoatl, thus destroying the second creation. Two other gods ruled through the next two creations, which were destroyed by a great flood."

"Finally something familiar."

Rachel smiled. "Yes, the next time around, Tezcatlipoca and Quetzalcoatl worked together to restore creation. Now this is where it gets weird."

"*This* is where it gets weird?"

"Weirder. There are several versions of the fifth creation. One has the twin brothers transforming into trees to help bear up the sky." She paused, apparently enjoying Marius's reaction to each part of the tale.

"But two other versions involve the earth monster – named Tlaltecuhtli. In one story, the brothers meet inside her heart to help raise the heavens. In the other, they wrap themselves around her, breaking her in two. Her two halves became the heavens and the earth."

"That's more than weird," he said.

"Yes, but getting back to our purpose, it could be significant." Rachel lowered her voice, all playfulness gone. "It says here that Tlaltecuhtli was angered by this defilement. The brother gods tried to comfort her, but the stories say she would only be appeased by one thing."

"What?"

"The sacrifice of human hearts."

26

SUNLIGHT REFLECTED off snowy patches on the cliff, blinding Rachel as she and Marius stepped out of the helicopter the next morning. Rachel fumbled for her sunglasses and almost slipped on a patch of ice, but Marius steadied her before turning to give instructions to the pilot. She picked her way more carefully to a bare bit of earth, feeling grumpy and tired.

"So much for the snow melting," she said when he joined her.

"It was colder than expected last night," he said. "It will melt before noon. *Vamanos*."

Rachel followed Marius as he headed back down the trail toward the gravesite, glad, at least, that no more snow had fallen in the night to cover their tracks from the day before. Even though she had agreed to this early morning search before heading to bed last night, she wished now she had thought it through. More research at the edge of a roaring fire seemed like a gentler way to begin their day. She said as much to Marius.

"You're too tired to stay awake sitting down," he said. "And we lost our conference room today – didn't I tell you? The inn is hosting a Christmas party tonight."

"In that room? I hope they're not expecting a crowd."

"They're clearing it out as we speak. I carried your books back to my room for safe keeping. I didn't want to wake you any earlier than necessary. You're still not a morning person, are you?"

"Not if I can help it," she said darkly. Marius just smiled.

Rachel had always been a night owl during their college days, but had to admit that last night's study session was proving hard to overcome this morning. Still, she picked up her pace, determined not to feel old or hold up their progress along the trail.

It had been well past midnight when they pushed aside their suppositions about Tezcatlipoca and the Earth Monster.

"Can we look at the symbols painted on the cave wall again?" Marius ran his hands over tired eyes.

"They represented the four major directions – north, south, east and west." She pulled a folder from beneath her books. "But they were also year-bearing day signs on the Aztec agricultural calendar."

"Year bearing?"

"Yes. The calendar had 365 days, separated into eighteen twenty-day months. Each day had its own name – the last day of the year names the year. There were only four possibilities. *Tecpatl* for north, *Calli* for west, *Tochtli*, south and *Acatl*, east. They rotate in that order."

"And those are the symbols on the wall?"

"Yes, as you suspected, matching the compass positions," she said.

"What year is it now?"

"*Tochtli* or south." Rachel gathered several sleeved snapshots from her folder and passed one to Marius. "Here's the wall painting and here's a drawing of *Tochtli* – it's supposed to be a rabbit."

He squinted and held the picture closer to the light. "If you say so."

"Kind of fierce looking, isn't it? Here are the other symbols – House for west, reed for east and flint knife for north."

"Flint knife?"

"Yes. And I know what you're thinking. Listen to this: 'North – or *Tecpatl* – carries with it warnings that the mind and spirit must be sharpened like a glass blade to cut through to the core of truth.'"

"A glass blade – like obsidian."

"A recurring theme."

"Have you been able to identify the other pieces on the wall?"

"Unfortunately, no," she said. "As near as I can tell, they were all mass produced pieces. Certainly nothing that any family member could identify from a photo. Libby Stuart's husband said she did have a heart-shaped gold locket, but he wasn't sure it was the same as the one in the photo."

"Did he check her jewelry box?"

Rachel shook her head. "He had already given all her jewelry to various family members. I have a list of names, but haven't gotten further with it."

Marius dug through the stack of photos. "But if we were to assume that this necklace was Libby's..."

"Then it was on the western peg. That's the symbol for *Calli*."

Marius had pushed himself up from his chair and walked over to where a topographical map of Tararecua Canyon was laid open on the table. "Is this too easy a conclusion? What if the trophy wall with its directional pegs is like a map – an indication of where he buried them?"

"I thought of that too," Rachel said. "But, of course, with only one grave, we have no idea how far apart they are buried, even if we are right. It could be miles or meters."

"Libby's grave was here." He tapped the map. "We could search by helicopter – look for more grave mounds, using the compass directions to guide us."

Rachel rose and joined him. "It's unlikely we would see anything, isn't it? With ravines, streams, arroyos, tree coverage – it's rocky, too." She looked up from the map and met his eyes. "I hate to be cliché, but..."

He smiled. "Yes, a needle in a haystack. Still, it's a place to start."

They had headed out this morning with that idea in mind, but found that the remaining snow coverage made the search impossible by air.

"Let's go back to the gravesite on foot," Marius had said. "We can search the immediate area at least, and give the snow time to melt before taking to the skies again."

Twenty minutes later, they reached Libby's grave. Rachel stopped at its edge, breathing hard and wishing for more strong coffee. Marius seemed recharged by the morning air.

"Samantha was abducted last year, but her necklace was on this year's peg, suggesting his timeframe for killing her. If we assume the same pattern for the others, why do you suppose he kept them prisoner for a year before killing them?" he asked.

"Perhaps because Aztec sacrificial customs demanded that a victim was cared for in luxury for an entire year leading up to his or her death," Rachel said.

He looked up from the grave, disgust darkening his eyes. "I don't think chaining a woman to the floor of a cave could be described as pampering."

"Neither do I," Rachel agreed soberly. "But we should remember that even if our assumptions are correct and the killer is being guided by ancient traditions, he's going to be prevented by practicality from strict adherence."

"Do practicality and this kind of psychotic behavior function in the same mind?"

"I doubt he would admit to himself that such restrictions exist. He probably finds justification for any departure from the ancient pattern," she said. "He can't kill on a famous Aztec ruin, for example, without great risk of being caught. So he chose this location, perhaps for its remoteness. He is less likely to be disturbed, and I would imagine he looks no further than his personal history here to justify it."

"You're saying he just makes up the rules as he goes along."

"No. He may *hear* mental instructions – voices in his head, or his dreams. Or he may just interpret signs in ways that approve his choices. It makes sense in a sick way. Whether he thinks he's Tezcatlipoca incarnate or not – it's still just a form of self-worship we're talking about. Naturally, he can set his own standards."

"Self-worship comes in many forms – few include murder," Marius said. "And if he will override the myths wherever it suits him, then studying these Tezcat stories may be a waste of time."

"It still helps us establish his MO, don't you think?" Rachel asked. "If we even have a chance of anticipating his next move, I don't want to miss it."

"I would rather have hard proof that he's still out there," Marius said. "Without that—"

"I know, Marius."

They had already discussed the looming deadline for discovery on this case. As far as SAC Devlin was concerned, Rachel was here to identify and bring home the victim of a dead perpetrator. It was a report to file, a loose end to tie up. Rachel was needed back as soon as possible to handle her active caseload, which included a new human trafficking case, according to her last message from Devlin. Meanwhile, Marius was facing a growing barrage of kidnap for ransom cases in Chihuahua and had hinted that his staff of agents included several he suspected of working for the cartels.

"How bad is it?" Rachel had asked, wondering how he was adjusting to work outside of Internal Affairs while still trying to fight corruption within the agency.

"I'm shoveling snow in a blizzard," he said. "And I'm using a spoon."

They spent the next two hours scouring the gravesite, looking for evidence of another. The terrain was more uneven than Rachel remembered. Peaks, sharp ledges, arroyos and vegetation interrupting the path no matter which way they went. Marius checked his compass whenever they made headway, but nothing looked like a grave or aligned with the crime scene to create the pattern they hoped for. Eventually they gave up and headed back to the plateau where the helicopter was waiting. Another hour of searching by air yielded no better results.

"It was worth a try," Marius said.

Rachel stared out the window as they turned back toward Creel. The hours were ticking away and she had still found no viable evidence to share with Devlin.

Back in Creel, she and Marius walked from their hotel along the main drag to *Restaurant Veronica,* a pleasant little eating place filled with locals. They sat by the window at a table covered in a clean green and white checkered table cloth.

"¿Qué recomienda usted?" Rachel asked the quiet waitress, who suggested several items on the menu, most of which made Rachel's mouth water. Fifteen minutes after they ordered, their food was delivered on sizzling skillets.

"This is a lot of food," Rachel said, looking over mounds of tender steak, mushrooms, onions and green peppers, all sprinkled with cheese and avocado slices.

Marius looked up from his dish. "If you can't finish yours, I'll be happy to help."

For the next several minutes they ate quietly.

"Why do you suppose they do that?" Rachel asked, pointing out the window with her fork as another full-sized pickup cruised by, blasting Ranchera music through its open windows.

Marius shifted in his seat and watched the truck pass. "There's not much to entertain in a small town like this. Maybe he's showing off for a girl." Another truck passed and Marius watched it for a moment and then looked over his shoulder at the shy waitress as she delivered food to the table behind him.

"Did you see that?" His voice lowered conspiratorially.

Rachel nodded, smiling. The waitress's eyes had flickered toward the truck for only the briefest moment, but her cheeks colored.

"How does such a horrible murderer live among normal people like this?" Rachel asked. Her mind couldn't let go of the case – not even for lunch. "He could have eaten in this restaurant, driven by in a truck, talked to a pretty girl. Even though I know logically that serial killers are great deceivers, I can't help imagining that some obvious sign should be visible to the rest of us – like a flicker of evil in his eyes. Is that stupid?"

"No, just wishful. It's comforting to think human instinct can protect us from that kind of horror. Unfortunately, the facts don't support that idea. Take the BTK killer, for example – even his wife was fooled. Ted Bundy was charismatic. Others have been as well."

"Tezcatlipoca was said to be charming too," Rachel said. "In one story, he seduced a goddess away from her husband, all because she was a great beauty and he felt he deserved her."

"The mythology is interesting, but unless it predicts his next step…"

Rachel frowned. "Another Aztec calendar I read about served as a divination tool. I took it to be the equivalent of horoscopes or Chinese zodiac charts."

"They worked with two calendars?"

"Apparently one agricultural and one sacred," she said. "I haven't spent much time looking at the sacred calendar. Maybe it deserves another look."

They paid their bill and walked back toward the hotel in silence. Marius led the way to his room, where Rachel went immediately to the stack of books on a table by the window.

"Here it is," she said, pulling a book from the pile and flipping through its pages. "The Aztec sacred calendar is called the *tonalpohualli.* It's ripe with ritualism and superstition."

"Sounds like a logical source of guidance for him."

"Yes. Why didn't I consider it before? Its relationship with Aztec deities is stronger, though I admit, I found it hard to follow."

Marius sat on the edge of the bed and watched as she flipped from page to page, tilting the book toward the window for natural light. Finally she found one with a glossy picture of the round calendar.

Marius leaned in for a closer look. "Not the same one that people were losing their heads over in 2012, I presume?"

"No, that was Mayan, though they look similar and probably have a shared history."

"No matter the source or culture, I find those divination tools just vague enough to allow people to interpret them however they choose," he said. "Trying to figure out how he might interpret the signs could be an enormous waste of time."

"But it could be a clue. Somewhere to start—"

"No, it's just all we have," he said gently. "Don't confuse the two. You're looking here because there is no physical evidence to prove this killer is still at large. But none of this," he spread his fingers, taking in all her research, "will convince Devlin to keep you on the case."

"You're right." Rachel rubbed her eyes. Last night was catching up with her. "It's almost four o'clock, I'm leaving tomorrow and we've accomplished nothing."

"I wouldn't say *nothing*," Marius said. "Perhaps *close* to nothing."

"That's quite a distinction."

"Don't punish yourself, *querida*. Look at all the research you've done – the hours you've devoted. My mother used to say, '*No se ganó Zamora en una hora.*'"

Rachel smiled. "I suppose that's like 'Rome wasn't built in a day'?"

"Yes. Your work will not be for nothing, I promise. It all just needs to marinate. Now, come on." Marius reached for her hand.

"Where are we going?"

"You're going to your room," he said, propelling her out the door, "para una siesta. You need it, I think. I'll come get you at six-thirty, okay?"

"For what?"

"*La fiesta.*" He jerked his head back toward the conference room, which was now draped in colorful crepe paper. "I managed to get us an invitation."

27

RACHEL NAPPED only fitfully that afternoon after calling to check on Danny. He came to the phone briefly and answered her questions with monosyllables, eager to get back to his cousins and the gingerbread houses they were decorating. Rachel listened to their excited chatter in the background while she talked to her sister and felt a twinge of sadness for what she was missing. When she hung up, she lay down in the dark hotel room and imagined being there to help Danny frost his gingerbread roof. He would smile at her as he hadn't in weeks and she would know that they were going to be all right, in spite of everything.

I need to be there, not here, she thought.

But her mind soon snapped back to the case, to Samantha Davidson and her clues of sand, feathers, threads and pebbles. Samantha needed someone to keep searching – someone who would not stop until her kidnapper was captured. And while Rachel would be with Danny tomorrow, Mrs. Davidson would spend Christmas alone.

No, she thought. *I need to be here.*

The paradox created strange dreams she could not remember when she woke. Still, they left her unsettled – a feeling she pushed away as she headed for the shower. By the time she was drying her hair and applying fresh makeup, she was more focused on the present and wondering what she might find in her suitcase that would be appropriate for the party.

"I don't know about this," she had told Marius when she left the conference room after lunch. "When Agent Cruces attended a party in this area, it left him in a condition I shudder to consider."

Marius just smiled. "No *tesguinada* tonight. I promise."

Rachel finally settled on her black suit skirt paired with a black V-neck sweater.

"I look like I'm going to a funeral," she told her reflection.

It was getting close to six thirty and Rachel felt like she was waiting to be picked up for a date. Still, she had no Christmas memories with Marius to make the evening uncomfortable. They had never sipped eggnog together or kissed under mistletoe. She had gone home over the winter breaks and so had he. Marius had given her pearl earrings from Portugal one January when they returned to school – a gift that made her present to him – a book bag she had seen him admiring on Mill Avenue – seem embarrassingly impersonal.

"Women are easier to buy for," she complained.

"How do you figure?"

"You can't go wrong with jewelry." She touched her ears. "Perfume, flowers, theater tickets – we like everything."

"I like my bag." He scooted it out of her reach, as if she meant to take it back. "And you may be easy to please, but that's not true of everyone. My mother had many lovers – and many husbands. I saw her analyze every bouquet, each bauble, trying to read what each man expected or felt – and what power it gave her."

Rachel had kept the earrings, but she did not wear them anymore. Tonight, she wore diamond studs that Craig had bought her for their anniversary two years ago. They were her favorites, just sparkling enough through her curls. As she screwed them in place, she wondered about his expectations and how she had failed to meet them. Marius's knock at the door pulled her back to the present. She pushed her feet into heels and crossed the room to open the door.

"Hi."

"You look lovely," Marius said. He wore a black jacket over a midnight blue dress shirt, open at the neck. Rachel could have said the same to him.

Instead, she blushed and wrinkled her nose. "Thank you, but I'm afraid I'm slightly colorless for a party in Mexico."

Marius raised his eyebrow and Rachel's blush deepened.

"Oh. No, I meant my clothes," she said quickly. "Not my skin color."

He laughed. "You look elegant. We'll just tell people you're from New York."

Rachel smiled. "Yes – and they can tell their friends how nice I was, considering."

As she had expected, the party was crowded – the room too cramped to comfortably hold the fifty plus people in attendance. A trio of musicians was encamped elbow to elbow to the left of the fireplace, playing carols with a Ranchera flavor, each nearly indistinguishable from the last. Marius had already glanced their way with a pained expression, making Rachel wonder how long he would subject himself to their brand of entertainment.

The hotel manager and his wife waved from a place near the refreshment table, calling what she could only guess was, "*Feliz Navidad*!" Rachel waved back. A few minutes later, she nudged Marius with her elbow, discreetly pointing to their shy lunchtime waitress, who stood against a wall, blushing while the man from the truck leaned close, presumably roaring sweet nothings into her ear over the din. Marius grinned.

Though the doors and windows were open wide to the dry winter night, the air in the room was hot and Rachel's hair stuck to the back of her neck, reminding her why she usually wore it up.

The next time the song changed, the crowd shifted, creating a bare patch in the middle of the floor for dancing. The lights dimmed, all but for one, mounted high on the wall where it shined red against a disco ball that someone had hung from the ceiling with a wire coat hanger.

"Now that would have come in handy last night," Marius said.

"Funny."

He put his hand to her back. "Let's dance."

"Marius, no. There's no room to walk, much less dance. Not the way we dance."

His eyes softened, flashing surprise. "You remember?" he asked quietly.

"Of course."

"Come on. Please?" He squeezed her hand. Rachel nodded.

Rachel's first dance lesson was in Marius's one-room apartment above a garage on Ash Street, just west of campus. His landlord was working on his boat below and listening to music that carried through the thin floorboards, up to where Marius and Rachel were studying. Marius looked up from his book and closed his eyes, listening.

"I love that song."

"Nat King Cole?"

He opened his eyes. "You seem surprised."

"There's a wide gap between that," she pointed downstairs, "and that," she pointed at his stack of CDs.

Marius laughed. "Call it nostalgia. It reminds me of dancing lessons."

"You took dancing lessons?"

"Again with the surprise." He shook his head at her. "My mother was in show business, remember? When I was about twelve, we lived in Barcelona and she pulled some strings to get an old friend of hers a job choreographing a show. He repaid her by giving me dancing lessons. I wasn't given the option of turning them down."

"What kind of dancing?" Rachel was hoping for something more Fred Astaire and less Barishnikov.

"I had no theatrical bent," Marius said, following her thoughts. "My mother understood that right away. Monsieur Le Bricoleur taught me basic ballroom dancing. 'I will teach you to dance like a gentleman,' he said." Marius mimicked the French accent, drawing a grin from Rachel. "'Not zis ridiculous flailing of arms and shaking of bodies zat young people do today. Dance should be like a conversation between man and woman, not a grotesque pantomime of things done in the backseat of cars.'"

"Wow, that's a heavy commentary to lay on a twelve year old."

"Yes, he took himself quite seriously. I danced with his granddaughter to that song," he pointed below. "She was surprisingly agile for such a chubby little thing, 'zee grace of a swan!' he always said."

"Marius, stop!" Rachel couldn't stop laughing. "You're making this up."

"Okay, maybe that last part," he jumped up and pulled her to her feet, "but not the rest. I'll prove it."

And Marius taught her to dance – his hand at her waist, hers on his shoulder – just the way they did in old movies.

"A person could fit between us," Rachel said.

He raised one eyebrow. "I'll work on fixing that. But for now, you should be able to see my eyes. It will help – truly."

As Rachel learned to glide around the room on Marius's arm, avoiding the furniture and, eventually, his toes, she came to love it, secretly feeling like Cinderella at the ball.

"There it is," Marius said when she stopped watching her feet. He shook his head. "I can't believe it. Monsieur Le Bricoleur was right."

"Right about what?"

"The reason for dancing at all."

"Which is?"

His lip twisted mischievously. "It's a secret."

Under the disco ball in Mexico, it didn't take Rachel long to remember the way they had waltzed so long ago. Marius held her eyes as they turned in restricted circles, looking just like he had all those years ago.

The song ended and another began. More dancers crowded the floor.

"Marius, I'm warm," Rachel said. "Let's go outside."

He nodded and followed her as she wove through the small hotel and out into the courtyard. Tonight it was lit by tiny white Christmas lights and green and red streamers, but was otherwise deserted.

"Is this better?" he asked.

"Yes."

"Not too cold?"

"No, it feels wonderful." Rachel took a deep breath of the cold, pine-scented air. "I haven't danced since—" She stopped. She hadn't been thinking.

"Since?"

"Since my wedding."

Marius nodded slowly. He shoved his hands deep into his pockets and turned toward the arbor. "I'm sorry," he said quietly. "I didn't mean to cause painful memories."

She stared past him, focusing on the twinkling lights that had been thrown haphazardly across the foliage and trellis. She wanted to straighten them, make them hang right. She always wanted to fix things. Some things, she had learned, were beyond her reach.

"I knew it was over about a month after I learned about the affair," she told him. "I agreed to see a counselor with him, but it wasn't working." She crossed her arms. "Craig was good at charming people, adopting the repentant attitude – 'I'll do whatever it takes' – that kind of thing. But he resented accepting blame. He seemed to believe I owed him forgiveness more than he owed me fidelity in the first place."

Rachel kicked a pebble. "So I was angry, of course, and resentful. One day when I was taking out the trash, I looked down in the bag where egg shells and coffee grounds, worn razor blades and broken toy parts were all mixed together. And I saw our marriage – all the valuable things we once were – torn apart and mixed up. There was no way to piece it together again. Trying was agony. A slow painful death. I couldn't do anything but bag it up and throw it away." She was surprised to feel tears on her cheeks. "I'm afraid," she managed to say, "I wonder if I'm not broken too."

Pain flickered across his brow and he pulled her against his chest, wrapping his arms around her so completely that she could feel his heart beating against her ear. They stood that way for several minutes until a laughing trio of women passed by. Rachel pulled away.

"I'm tired, Marius." She shivered, not sure whether it was from the cold courtyard air against her damp skin, or the vulnerability she felt for oversharing. "Thanks for inviting me to the party, but I think I'll call it a night."

"Can I walk you to your room?"

Rachel nodded and they silently turned back through the lobby and followed the corridor to her room.

"Your fire went out," Marius said as she pushed open the door. Rachel kicked off her shoes and sat at the foot of the bed while Marius rebuilt the fire. When it was crackling on its own, she rose and moved closer.

"What you said in the courtyard," He put the fireplace poker back on the rack and adjusted the grate, "I understand. I was there myself, not long ago."

"I know, Marius." She moved even closer to the fireplace. Why couldn't she get warm? "It happens all the time, to people everywhere, but …"

"It's different when it happens to you."

She looked at him, but couldn't hold his eyes. "Yes. That's incredibly selfish, isn't it?"

"Just human." Marius took her hands. "Do you remember the dance instructor I told you about years ago?"

"Yes."

"He once told me that a man should have only one goal when dancing – to make a woman feel as beautiful as she looks."

"Was that the secret you wouldn't tell me?"

He smiled. "Yeah, I guess I did call it a secret. But I understood it for the first time when we danced that day. I saw it in your eyes. I already thought you were the most beautiful woman I had ever known, but when we danced, *you* felt beautiful. Your face lit up and I knew Monsieur Le Bricoleur was right.

Rachel looked down at their hands. "That was a long time ago."

"I saw it again tonight."

"No, Marius—"

"Look at me. Tell me I'm lying."

She looked in his eyes, liquid chocolate reflecting the firelight. He let go of her hands and was touching her cheek, his fingers electrifying as they traveled to her jaw, then the nape of her neck. Rachel trembled. He leaned forward and his lips touched hers briefly, achingly warm. He pulled back and searched her eyes, asking a question she could not keep from answering. She kissed him this time, wrapping her arms around his neck, finding safety in the breadth of his shoulders, as if without a firm grip, she would sink beneath the beautiful warm waves and be lost forever.

"*Querida*," he murmured moments later, his forehead pressed to hers. She closed her eyes, relishing the moment, begging time to stand still. The fire settled, crackling. She trembled again.

"You're still cold," Marius said.

"No." But she was stepping back, and already feeling colder outside his embrace. It would be so easy to step the other way, closer to his body, closer to the bed. "Marius…"

"I know, *Raquel*." He pulled her back into his arms and kissed her temple. "You'll heal, I promise. No matter how you feel now, you're not broken. You'll see it for yourself soon. Not everything in life breaks."

28

"DANNY!"

"Mom!"

Danny jumped off the porch swing and ran down the steps to meet her, unconcerned that his cousins were looking on. Rachel scooped him up in a smothering hug and kissed his head. He smelled of sweat and grass and had grown, it seemed, over the past four days.

"I missed you," she said.

"Me too. You're not going back to Mexico again, are you?"

"I don't know," she said. "Not for a while, at least."

They walked up Melissa's driveway together. "You've been having fun though, right?"

"Yeah. Wait 'til you see the tree!"

Rachel loved watching him walk. The way he twisted, kicked rocks and circled her, almost like a puppy. She reached forward to ruffle his hair, but he dodged her, ready for his independence again.

Melissa held the kitchen door open. "Hurry in. It's getting cold out there."

The house smelled of a busy day. Pot roast, fresh-baked bread and cookies, but Melissa still looked fresh and pretty, if a little tired.

"Now come and look, Mom." Danny pulled her toward the living room, where a Christmas tree twinkled in the corner, so covered with lights and homemade decorations, very little green was visible.

"Wow, Danny. Did you help with that?"

"Uh-huh. Look, we did the popcorn and cramberry string today." He held up his hands. "The cramberries made my hands turn red."

"Dinner will be ready in twenty minutes," Melissa called through the doorway.

"Can I help?"

"No, you and Danny get caught up. I'll let you help with the dishes afterward."

Danny showed her the stockings lined up on the fireplace mantel, then the ornaments he and his cousins had made out of construction paper and glitter, and finally, the gingerbread house he finished yesterday.

"It's kinda crooked." He twisted his head to straighten it out.

"Well, the north wind is pretty strong," she said.

"I beat Nathan at *Mario Kart*." Danny settled against her knee for a moment before darting off again. "And Megan keeps winning at *Go Fish*, but Aunt Melissa said that was just rotten luck and if I want to win, I have to keep playing, so..." He rolled his eyes.

"Have you been helping with the animals?"

"Yeah, I feed the chickens all the time."

"You've gotten so brave." He used to run from them, screaming.

"And Nathan and I climb to the top of the hill behind the barn every day." He pointed toward the back, though it was now too dark to see. "And I don't even get tired anymore. I can run the whole way."

The kitchen timer buzzed and Rachel heard her niece, nephew and brother-in-law stir in response downstairs.

"Let's go wash up. I'll bet you're starving."

His eyes widened in delight. "I am and Aunt Melissa always lets me have three rolls."

"Has he been doing as great as it seems?" Rachel asked Melissa after dinner. "In Phoenix he was 'Dan,' a premature adolescent who hated everyone and everything. Here, he's like his old self again."

Her sister nodded, reaching for a stack of dishes, which she plunged into a sink full of warm soapy water. "There have been a few problems, but nothing like what you've described with his classmates. He's been antsy all day today, but that's because he knew you were coming."

Rachel shook her head. "He certainly has needed whatever you've been providing."

Melissa looked at her. "Don't go down that road, Rachel. I know I've been hard on you, giving my opinions when nobody asked for them—"

"Apparently, you were right. At least about some things."

"You're a good mom," Melissa insisted. "There's no quick fix to divorce and what it does to kids – you know that. It's going to take time. It's not hard to figure out why Danny feels comfortable here. It hasn't changed when everything else has. Isn't that right in line with what the counselor said?"

"Yes." Rachel brought more dishes to the sink and unfolded a towel for drying. "But thank you – for making everything special – holiday crafts, baking, decorating…"

"Yeah, I'm a regular Martha Stewart." Melissa pointed with her elbow to her Hoosier cabinet, which was stacked to the toppling point with leftover craft supplies.

"You do it. That's what counts." Rachel kissed her on the cheek. "I don't know what I would do without you."

"I love you," Melissa said simply. "I'll do anything I can for you and Danny, you know that. Now tell me about your trip." Her eyes narrowed slightly. "You look…strangely content for a woman investigating grisly murders."

Rachel lowered her voice. "These murders are truly horrible, but you know I can't talk about it. I don't want to. It's Christmas time and I want to enjoy it with my family."

She and Melissa finished the dishes and headed down to the basement family room, where Rich and the kids were putting together a puzzle while watching *Home Alone* on TV. Rachel curled up on one end of the sofa and watched Danny, who came over to lean against her every few minutes. Within an hour, he was rubbing his eyes, and made no objection to having her send him off for pajamas and teeth brushing.

"Can I sleep in your bed?" he asked.

"Of course."

After all three kids and Rich had gone to bed, Rachel and Melissa pulled out the wrapping supplies and spread out across the dining room table.

"I always tell myself I'm going to tone it down, but then," Melissa spread her hands, "I still end up with piles of gifts to wrap."

"Where are we hiding them?" Rachel asked.

"Better be the barn loft this year. Nathan found a stash in the attic last Christmas."

"It's been a long time since he's believed in Santa Claus, I would think."

Melissa smiled. "I don't think he ever believed – even when he was Danny's age. He liked to play along, though."

"I appreciate him for hanging out with his little cousin all week. Not every twelve-year-old boy would be such a good sport."

"He's a good kid."

Rachel pulled out a bulging muslin sack of blocks and plunked it on the table, wondering how best to wrap it.

"You have a box this might fit in?"

Melissa dug through her stash and tossed her sister a large gift bag. "This is probably the best I can do. Where did those come from?"

Rachel opened the draw string and pulled out a handful of smooth wooden blocks. "Mexico," she said.

"These are cool." Melissa built a short tower, then handed them back. "I didn't know you made time for shopping."

"I didn't," Rachel said. "Marius bought them for Danny."

"So how was it?" she asked. "Seeing him again, I mean?"

Rachel paused. "It was good."

"Good? Oh, no."

"What?"

"The way your voice softened. What's going on?"

"Come on, Melissa. Give him a break."

"He broke your heart, remember?"

"I don't think I did his any good either," Rachel said.

"Well, I didn't have to see him crying himself to sleep night after night."

"That was way more than a decade ago, Lissa," Rachel said quietly. "And since then, he saved my life. Remember?"

"Well, yes." Melissa sounded only slightly contrite. "There is that."

For several minutes they wrapped in silence.

"I can't stand this," Melissa finally said. She put down her scissors and leaned on the table. "Tell me something – anything!"

Rachel shrugged. "We sat on the floor and talked. Almost all night."

"Talked?"

"Mostly."

Melissa groaned.

"No, seriously!" But Rachel was laughing. "He told me about his father's ranch. He wants Marius to retire early so he can take over its management. His foreman died last year, leaving behind a wife and young child."

"So he's quitting his job to become a rancher?"

"Eventually."

"What else?"

"Nothing."

Melissa crossed her arms, waiting.

"Okay, we kissed."

"I knew it! Rachel—"

"Nothing else happened. I promise. We talked about our jobs – Marius is an expert marksman. I didn't know that. I told him about working part time as a bureau analyst when Danny was a baby. You're imagining it all wrong."

Melissa picked up her scissors again. "Just be careful, okay?"

"I will."

Another long silence followed. Rachel added a tag to Marius's gift – *From Santa* – per his instructions. She pulled out another box, stifling a yawn.

"You look tired," Melissa said. "Why don't you go to bed?"

"In a minute."

"We expected you earlier today."

"I had to go into the office for a while after my plane landed."

Melissa shook her head. "I don't know how you do it."

"It was the best way to make sure I would have these holiday days free and clear." She rummaged for a bow. "You want me to take these out to the barn?"

"No, I have more to wrap, so I'll take them all at once."

"Still a night owl, even after a full-day of motherhood?" She smiled. "I don't know how *you* do it."

Melissa rose and hugged her. "Go get some rest."

"Good night."

Rachel headed downstairs to brush her teeth. Her reflection didn't lie about her fatigue. Her eyes were bloodshot and smudged with mascara. She uncapped her cleanser and went to work, her thoughts returning to her meeting with SAC Devlin that day. It had not been encouraging.

"Good work Mueller." Devlin flipped through Libby Stuart's file, which Rachel had updated during her flight home. "You were right about her."

Rachel tried to make the most of Devlin's praise. "Final autopsy results on the suspect killed in Mexico showed neurological damage consistent with my perception of his mental faculties," she said. "Yet you can see that the cave drawing and trophy wall, not to mention the skill involved in taking at least two American women south of the border without detection, indicate a vastly different profile. The perpetrator of these murders is intelligent, calculating and ostensibly motivated by Aztec lore, which he is likely mimicking with these killings. Our safest assumption is that he is still at large and will strike again."

"DNA evidence points to the killed John Doe," Devlin argued.

"And we have a witness who claims he was a twin."

"She didn't ID the body."

"But if they are identical, and if his surviving brother is the true culprit—"

"That's two 'ifs,' Agent Mueller. One more than I'll allow you on this." Devlin snapped the folder closed and handed it back to her. "Keep your eyes and ears open, by all means. More evidence could change my mind. And stay in touch with your PFM contacts – you are building a good rapport with them. That could be invaluable down the road."

"Yes, ma'am."

"But your caseload is already heavy and here's something new." She passed a folder across the desktop to Rachel. "Human trafficking. A Hispanic child who speaks no English – and little Spanish, for that matter – was found in an abandoned home near Show Low. He looks to be about twelve years old. We need to find out if he's tied to a larger trafficking ring."

"Where is he now?"

"With Child Protective Services. Can you swing through Show Low on your way home Tuesday to interview him? Look into Mexican missing children reports to see if we can work on an ID, but move quickly. Chances are he was sold."

"Yes, ma'am." Rachel wished Devlin a happy holiday as she hurried out of the office.

"Show Low's not exactly on the way home from Cottonwood," she muttered in the elevator. Craig was supposed to pick Danny up on Tuesday. How much grief would he give her if she asked him to meet her in Payson?

It bothered her to think of Danny as a burden that needed to be passed off so that she could focus on her job. It had never been that way before the divorce. Somehow she and Craig had always managed to make sure he was with people who truly loved him whenever they couldn't be with him themselves. She had always been rather proud, she now realized, thinking she had it so together – a career, motherhood and marriage all managed with grace and success.

What an idiot I've been.

Marius would tell her not to think that way.

She smiled, remembering his face when he handed over Danny's gift at the airport. He had looked slightly uncomfortable, as if a bag of blocks might overstep some invisible boundary.

"Thank you. You didn't have to do this."

He shrugged. "I knew this investigation would interrupt your shopping opportunities. I played with these when I was a boy. My father sent them to me in Spain. See?" He pointed to the bag where *HECHO EN MEXICO* was stamped.

"Not China, like every toy in America?"

"Lead free," he said. "I promise."

Rachel laughed. "Danny will love them."

Their goodbye had been brief. Marius squeezed her hand and kissed her cheek before turning back toward his Jeep. Nothing more was needed. There were no words to explain what was happening between them, though during her flight home and her drive up to Cottonwood, Rachel's thoughts had been occupied with little else. She imagined him rejoining Agent Cruces, his life, his work without her. But, somehow, she knew the case would lead them to each other again. The thought made her shudder.

29

"WHERE IS SHE?"

"I-4."

"An interrogation room?" Rachel scowled. "Why don't you just cuff her, Baldock?"

"Where would you put a nut job like that?"

Rachel ignored his question and flipped through her message log. Baldock was new, transferred from Seattle on the first of December and already she didn't like him. "Looks like she called for the first time a week ago, when I was in Mexico."

He crossed his arms. "Yeah, I took that call. She asked for the agent in charge of the Davidson case. She said the killer is still alive."

"Did she say anything else?"

"Yes. Something weird. She said she dreamed about a... cheetah? No, some other big cat."

The skin along Rachel's neck puckered. "A jaguar?"

"That's it! How did you know?"

She shook her head.

"Offer her some coffee. I'll be right there."

Nothing like hitting the ground running straight off of a holiday, Rachel thought. She hadn't even logged on to her computer yet. It was rare for someone to walk into the bureau field office and ask to speak with the agent in charge of a specific case – rarer still for that person to offer useful information. A quick background check showed no record of any kind for Hillary Crocker, a stay-at-home mom who had been screened and cleared two years ago through a well-known security service when she volunteered for a youth soccer organization.

Rachel grabbed a legal pad and pen and headed down the hall. She knocked and entered the room.

"Mrs. Crocker? Hi, I'm Special Agent Mueller." Rachel shook her hand and sat down across from her. "I was one of the lead investigators on the Davidson case. What can I do for you?"

Mrs. Crocker fingered her purse strap. She hadn't touched her coffee. When she spoke, her voice was strained. "I want to help," she said. "But I don't know what to do."

"What do you know about this case?"

"Only what I saw on the news," she said. "Last week, I saw the report about Libby Stuart. They said she was another victim of the man who kidnapped Samantha Davidson."

"Which news program?"

"Beverly Mendoza on Channel Twelve." Mrs. Crocker sniffed. "She said the killer had already been caught and killed last spring."

"A suspect was killed during the course of our investigation into Samantha Davidson's death," Rachel said carefully.

"Were you there?"

"Yes, I was." Rachel leaned forward. "Mrs. Crocker, do you know something else? Maybe someone who has made you suspicious?"

"I don't know anyone – or anything for sure." Her eyes glistened. "And, yet, I do. I know he's not dead – the man responsible for all of it. He's not dead and he's going to do it again."

"How do you know?"

"I dreamed it."

"How do you know it's him?"

She began to cry. "I dreamed about Samantha before she was taken. I didn't know it was her. I didn't understand until afterward. Until it was too late."

"What did you dream?'

"I was in Tempe, walking along the lake. There were thousands of gold flowers growing along the shore where, really, there's just grass. While I was admiring them, a huge black cat came out of nowhere and jumped into the flowers. He plucked one with his mouth and then leaped away. It scared me – actually, terrified me for some reason. I yelled at the cat, hoping he would drop the flower, but my feet wouldn't move and he didn't listen. I woke up in a sweat. My husband said I was screaming. He said I spoke her name. Samantha. I dreamed the same dream three nights in a row. I wanted to tell someone – call the police maybe. My husband talked me out of it. A month later, Samantha Davidson was kidnapped."

"Did you know her?"

"No."

"Do you know anyone named Samantha?"

"A few people. My cousin's daughter – I met her once at a family reunion. There's a girl named Samantha in my daughter's kindergarten class. They're both fine."

"Do you remember any other details from the dream?"

"The cat was huge, with markings on it. I think it was a black jaguar."

Rachel cleared her throat.

"Are you a medium?"

"No!" She sounded horrified. "Divination is a sin."

"I'm sorry. I didn't mean to offend you. Some people who provide such information prefer other names – clairvoyant, intuitive."

She shook her head. "I don't try to have these dreams. I wish I didn't."

"You've had others?"

She nodded. "Yes. For the past three nights."

"Was the jaguar in them?"

"Yes." She dug in her purse for a tissue.

"When you're ready, I would like to hear about them."

For a few minutes, Mrs. Crocker's narrow shoulders shook. Rachel gripped the table and her heart thumped, pushing for questions she knew could only be broached slowly. And the answers? She didn't know what she would do with them. Finally the tortured woman took a shaky breath and continued.

"The jaguar was stalking something through a field of white snow. It was noisy – like the sound of roaring water, but there was only ice, smooth as glass in the middle of the field. The noise grew louder and it scared me. Then I saw the jaguar lower himself on his haunches, ready to pounce."

"Did he attack?" Rachel asked. "Did he take something – like the flower from the other dream?"

Mrs. Crocker nodded. "He dug through the snow and picked up a seed with his mouth. It was ready to bud – so delicate. Then he leaped away just like in the other dream. The roaring continued and the snow – well, it shifted. I wanted to shout and warn them."

"Warn who? Was someone else there?"

She shook her head. "It was the snow. It was as if the snow wouldn't listen. But when I woke up, I knew I had to come talk to you. I can't do anything but dream, but you – you can stop this."

"Did you wake up like last time, saying a name?"

"I don't know. My husband went to visit his mother with the kids for a couple of days, so no one's there to hear me." She sniffed. "They'll be back tomorrow. If he was home, he would have talked me out of coming again. It makes him so uncomfortable, but I had to tell you – to warn you. I don't know how it could help – my dream about Samantha did no good. But how could I know?"

Rachel was at a loss. She had heard of many investigations that relied on information provided by clairvoyant citizens, but she had never been part of one. It made her uneasy. Part of her wanted to dismiss Mrs. Crocker as unbalanced, like Baldock had, but she couldn't. This was too important.

"I don't understand how your dreams work," she finally said, "or why you have them. But maybe if you had not dreamed about Samantha, you wouldn't be here now, trying to save another life."

Mrs. Crocker put her hand over her mouth. "I feel like I'm losing my mind. I keep thinking I must have done something wrong… to be this way."

Rachel thought about all the history she had read – secular and spiritual – that included stories of premonition or prophecy. She shook her head. "I don't believe that. You're a religious woman, right?"

Mrs. Crocker nodded.

"Maybe it's a gift from God." She stood up and handed Mrs. Crocker her business card. "And please call me if you remember any more details."

Rachel walked her through security and returned to her desk, where Agent Baldock was waiting with an audio file of the interview.

"Now, tell me that woman wasn't nuts," he said.

"She wasn't nuts." Rachel took the file and sat down.

"Is that your professional assessment?"

Rachel ignored the question. "Did you notice the way she was dressed?"

"She looked like an average soccer mom to me."

"What else?"

He shrugged.

"She was well-groomed – trimmed hair and nails, starched shirt, tasteful jewelry. That's not the MO for crazy."

He shrugged. "Maybe she's just looking for a little attention, then."

"Her shoes say no."

"I didn't notice her shoes."

"No, you wouldn't – they weren't vampy stilettos."

"How well you know me."

"They were loafers – the kind that were fashionable several years ago – and scuffed along the toe. Shoes like that speak of a normal mom – she hasn't given up on her appearance, but with uniforms and violin lessons, something has to slide on the priority list. It's usually the shoes."

"Whatever, Mueller. Prophetic dreams? Come on."

"It's not as if it's completely unheard of. Premonitions have gone hand in hand with almost every famous murder in American history – world history, even. Julius Caesar's wife dreamed about his death two days prior. Many Biblical figures predicted coming events through their dreams."

"The Bible?" He shook his head. "Your evidence is based on fairytales?"

"You don't believe in God, Baldock?"

He snorted. "Should I? A supernatural being who sets rules that just make people feel guilty? No thank you."

"Hmm."

"Hmm, what?"

"You reminded me of when my sister babysat me as a kid," Rachel said. "When she made a rule I didn't like, I just pretended she wasn't there."

~ ∝ ~

"I DON'T KNOW what to think of it," Rachel told Marius late that night. He had been calling almost every evening – a habit she was getting used to.

"I don't either. But it is something, poor woman."

"I'm going to talk to law enforcement in Northern Arizona – anywhere that might have snow this time of year," Rachel frowned, "though none of our lakes turn to ice. Maybe a pond, somewhere? Maybe in the White Mountains. We'll have three more months of snow in the high country, tops. I need to contact authorities in Utah and New Mexico too. "

"Don't be too literal in interpreting the dream, *querida*."

"Okay, well how about symbolism. First she dreamed about a flower, now it's a seed. What does that mean? Someone younger?"

He was silent for a moment. "Maybe. But it doesn't give us enough to change our focus."

"No. You're right. But I'm terrified, frankly. That I'll miss something and he's going to take someone else…"

"What we need are resources – something neither the Bureau nor *La Policía* are prepared to give us."

"I still think he's keeping an eye on us, Marius. Staying close to see what we uncover." She rubbed her eyes. "It's the one piece of his profile where I've gained no traction. I've been scanning news footage, looking through the crowds of bystanders for a familiar face."

"He won't show himself that easily, Rachel."

"No, he's too clever. So maybe I'm looking at this wrong – could he be working from inside one of our agencies? Or with the police?"

"I don't know."

"We need to check. Anyone related to the case, or someone working the case – even distantly – someone who travels back and forth over the border…"

"That could be a long list."

"It's like I can *feel* him. Hovering."

"Now who's having premonitions?"

Rachel adjusted her pillow and changed the subject. "Has Agent Cruces returned from New Mexico?"

"No. He won't get back until after the New Year. He hasn't found any new leads on Yala in America."

"I still don't know why he didn't let me know he was coming – I could have provided contacts for him in New Mexico."

"Johnny is a private man, Rachel. And he hasn't had the best interactions with American agencies. Let him do this his way, through channels he's already established."

Rachel opened her mouth to argue, but then closed it again. Marius's own history with the DEA hadn't been particularly pleasant either – something she knew nothing about until recently. It explained so much of the tension she had felt in the past whenever nationalism had been discussed.

Rachel had always been unabashedly patriotic. America wasn't perfect – how could it be? But she had always believed its liberties and opportunities far outweighed its faults. When they were younger, she had dreamed of a day when Marius would become a citizen and enjoy its freedoms with her. Marius had never shared her dream though, cynical and sure that his limited exposure told him all he needed to know.

She didn't know if time had softened his stubbornness – or if years of experience with Mexican life and politics had changed his perspective at all, but she was reluctant to tear into that old wound now.

"I've been trying to dig into more Aztec calendar lore," she told him. "But I haven't gotten far with this new case taking up my time."

"Has the child been able to tell you anything?"

"Not much. He knows he was in a Mexican orphanage, but doesn't know where, its name or whether it was state, church or privately operated. I have a friend who does a lot of charity work with a Hague-accredited adoption service. I'm going to see if he can help get me a list of Mexican facilities."

"I can contact the DIF for cross-reference, if you'd like."

"DIF?"

"*Sistema Nacional de Desarollo Integral de la Familia* – they oversee all family matters in Mexico, including adoption."

"Great. Thank you."

"Does he remember how he crossed the border?"

"All he will say is '*autobus*.'" Rachel shook her head. "It's not much to go on. Illegal immigrants come into the U.S. all the time by every means imaginable, but so many of them are caught. Which leads me back to this killer – why can't we figure out how he took his victims through going the other direction?"

"It's a large border," Marius said. "With varied terrain, roads, trails – nearby airstrips..."

"I've talked to colleagues with Border Patrol, but nothing pans out. If only I knew someone who looked at this from the other perspective – not how to secure the border, but how to break through it."

"You do, unfortunately," Marius said. "So do I. Maybe it's time for me to visit an old acquaintance in Mexico City."

30

HEAVY WINDS FORCED the cancellation of the New Year's Eve fireworks show advertised by the Wild Vista Casino, southeast of Phoenix. Not that it hurt them. Valley gamblers came in droves, fireworks or not, many of them ignoring the countdown and the crowds swelling around them as they fed coins to their idols.

At the stroke of midnight, he was not at the tables or among the throngs of drunkards who crisscrossed garish carpeting, belting out the wrong lyrics to *Auld Lang Syne*. Instead he was behind a potted palm tree, lock-lipped with a tipsy forty-something blonde whose dress was barely appropriate for a twenty year old.

This wasn't the way tonight was meant to end. He was supposed to be somewhere else – with someone else. Nonetheless, he led her to the elevators. Two hours later he stood in a shadowed hotel room, staring at her still figure on the bed.

A poor salve for rejection, he thought.

He imagined slitting her throat – offering her on this altar of Egyptian cotton and being free from his pledge. For a moment, imaginary liberty washed over him. What would it be like to have it all behind him?

What if you had never started this journey in the first place?

No. He couldn't think that way. It didn't matter anyway – this woman wasn't worthy of his blade. Hadn't his incessant dreams insisted on one more pure, even less defiled by the world than Samantha?

Over the past few weeks, he had come to accept what once made his skin crawl. But today, she had made him so mad, telling him no.

His nostrils flared. Maybe this woman should die anyway.

And how would that help? No, you need to walk away.

He did, pulling on his clothes in the darkness so as not to risk interrupting the sonorous rumbling from the bed. Still, just as he pushed open the door, a burst of laughter swept past him. Three revelers tripped by, their high-pitched braying undoing his discretion.

The blonde sat up in bed. "Hey! Where are you going?"

He ignored her, pulling the door closed and heading for the stairwell. The casino was still running full-bore downstairs, making it easy for him to blend in with the crowd. He wound through the slot machines and out a side door to the parking lot, where he found his car covered in dust from the passing storm.

"Divine whirlwind," he muttered.

The *tonalpohualli* had told him these were bad days to traffic with those on another path, good days for solitude, contemplation, self-discipline. These were his dead brother's days to rule.

So why had he ignored the signs?

"America will seduce you, if you let it," Grandmother had warned him. "She will offer many delights – a different jewel to tempt every man. You need to be stronger than that."

Was that why he felt guilty about the woman in the hotel room?

But it wasn't Grandmother's admonitions that tickled the back of his throat. It was someone who spoke of a different kind of honor.

He started his car and pulled out of the parking lot, speeding toward the city. If only he could outrun his tortured thoughts. It was a new year to those around him, a time for resolutions and self-discipline that would only last days for some, weeks for others. Few would stay committed to their goals. Most were doomed to fail and try again a year from now, repeating the pathetic routine until death took them in the end, much the same in vice as they ever were.

It's not too late for you to change course.

"No. I am not one of them," he told Grandmother, looking in the rearview mirror and seeing her dance behind the eyes of the jaguar.

He would not shed his responsibility. A night of setbacks could not deter him. This adopted home would mourn another one of its children in the New Year. He blinked back genuine tears at the thought of the coming sacrifice, one that would cost him so much. Perhaps everything he hoped for in this life.

But it will be pure, perfect, redemptive, he promised himself. *And I will be free.*

31

IT WAS a quarter to ten in the morning when Marius emerged from Mexico City's metro at the Polanco Station just north of Chapultepec Park and pulled up the lapel of his jacket. He squinted into the wind. It was unusually cool for January. Frost glistened on top of the grass and his breath was visible as he glanced back, his eyes drawn to the monolithic Torre Mayor building that towered over the city. He remembered a bomb being discovered in its parking garage not many months ago. It had been defused, and only consequential enough to have destroyed a few cars, even if detonated. Still, images of the Twin Towers on 9/11 never escaped his thoughts when he stood so near Latin America's tallest building. He turned his attention northward. A few blocks would take him to an appointment he couldn't help regarding as a necessary evil.

Better to get it over with, he thought.

Former FBI Agent Kirk Trent, who had just last spring shot Yala's son in the back on the rim of Tararecua Canyon and soon after been acquitted of drug trafficking charges, was enjoying his undeserved freedom, it would seem, within blocks of the U.S. Embassy where he had last seen legitimate employment.

"He's still working for the cartel," Marius told Rachel, "or has enough damaging information on them to barter for his own safety."

"Expensive safety," he muttered now as he turned onto the main avenue of Polanco, considered by many to be the Beverly Hills of Mexico City. He walked past Cartier, Louis Vuitton, Rolex and several upscale eateries before turning onto the street where Trent lived. His condominium was a modern glass and steel framed structure, bent in the middle to mirror the curve of the sidewalk. Marius handed his card to the doorman who ushered him into the gleaming lobby. He whistled in appreciation, and guessed even the smallest unit would cost upwards of $700,000 in U.S. money.

"Señor Trent is expecting you." The doorman pointed toward the elevator.

"*Gracias.*"

Marius rode to the fifth floor and turned down a hallway that forked to the right. Trent's wife was waiting for him at the door with a small dog perched high on her chest.

"*Ciao,* darling!" she called to her husband, kissing her adorned fingertips as she squeezed past Marius and out the door. Trent had come around the corner to watch her go, an indulgent smile on his face.

"Shopping again." He wore a casual white linen shirt over tan slacks, looking every bit the drug dealer, Marius thought, complete with gold bracelet and necklace. He wagged his finger at Marius. "I have you to thank for this. She'll spend the next three hours raiding my bank account – hair, nails, a new outfit for her *and* the dog, and something from Coach, even though I've asked her, 'If every other woman is carrying a Coach handbag, how can it be a status symbol?'" He shook his head. "Some things are meant to be a mystery to husbands, I'm convinced. Come in. Sit down."

They passed through a small entryway to an open living room with floor-to-ceiling windows and glossed concrete floors covered in a large geometric rug. The adjacent kitchen was open with maple cabinets, art deco pendant lighting and stainless steel appliances. Trent sat in a black leather arm chair framed in steel and pointed to its pair, which Marius took. Both were positioned to see either the large flat-panel TV or the view, which, through the trees, afforded a view of the Torre Mayor.

"You have a lovely home, Mr. Trent," Marius said politely. "I won't keep you long."

"Now see, I knew you would say something like that." Trent grinned so widely, Marius could see his fillings. "Always professional, but that grudge is still there, isn't it? I hold no animosity toward you, Agent Suarez. No ill will. It's just business, right?"

He laughed when Marius failed to respond. "And I would humbly suggest that my trade has kept *you* in business for the length of your career. Still, I know of some who would offer me more than just a pat on the back to learn the timing of your visit today."

Marius's eyes narrowed. "Is that a threat, Trent?"

"Of course not." He crossed his legs. "Merely an olive branch."

"I didn't come to revisit the past," Marius said smoothly. "But to ask for your advice – as a professional in the trade that…how did you say it? Has kept me in business for the length of my career?"

"Can you be more specific?"

"The Copper Canyon murder investigation."

"That?" He made a dismissive noise with his teeth. "I already killed the psycho responsible, what else do you want?"

Marius smiled thinly, his lips stretched only as far as his patience. "Indulge me if you will. I like things wrapped up neatly, as does Agent Mueller. We were hoping to gain an alternative perspective about entry points along the border – a plausible explanation for the killer's movements."

Trent didn't answer right away, but went to the kitchen, where he pulled a carton of orange juice from the refrigerator. He wagged it in the air toward Marius, who declined, and then poured himself a glass.

"You found another body, right? I read about it in *La Jornada*."

"Yes. Another victim from Agent Mueller's list."

"Really?" Trent carried his juice back to the living room. "I thought she was just gunning for a promotion. She was always a smart woman. Too smart for my tastes – or too strict. By the book, if you know what I mean." He looked toward the door, presumably a reflexive tracing of his wife's footsteps. Still he lowered his voice conspiratorially. "There might have been something there once, though, if I had pursued it. We worked together in Texas. Did she ever mention that?"

"She may have, yes," Marius said evenly.

"Don't tell me you and Mueller—"

"Can we get back to the point? I don't want to waste your time." Marius leaned forward. "We know routes exist in the desert – along the reservation, or adjacent to the Lukeville or Sasabe ports of entry—"

"That's the trouble with people like you and Mueller," Trent interrupted. "Let me guess, you poured over border maps and talked to patrol agents, DEA contacts? No wonder you haven't figured anything out. You're looking at it from the wrong side."

"As I said," Marius continued with barely veiled impatience. "That's why I'm here. Which routes are the *patrones* most partial to? Is there one that you know of that coyotes use consistently? Or perhaps a new tunnel that has not yet been discovered by the Americans?"

"Sharing information like that can get a man killed," he snapped his fingers, "just like that." For a moment, his smile faulted and Marius glimpsed the fear that he suspected never truly dissipated.

"Do you think I'm stupid?" Trent asked. "The man who talks too much ends up dead – within a week – no matter what kind of leverage he has."

"Such a man might do better to walk away, start fresh. Learn to rest peacefully each night," Marius said quietly.

Trent said nothing for a minute, then the haunted look passed and he smiled again.

"Actually, if such a man were to recruit another, one who knew the inside workings of a governmental machine on the verge of insignificance anyway – well, both of those men could live like kings." He spread his hands, offering up his home for consideration. "In such a way that would make this look like nothing."

Marius leaned forward and spoke with deadly calm. "Not on your life, Trent."

"It's something to think about."

"No, it's something to be ashamed of," Marius said, his voice growing warm. "Do you ever look out there, Trent? Past the borders of Polanco, this little peaceful neighborhood where you can pretend you're in America? Do you ever drive east, by Chalco or through any of the other *ciudades perdidas*?

"Why do you think people are pouring into the U.S. by the thousands, tens of thousands, only to send back most of what they earn to support the families they leave behind? You think that's what they dream of? Standing outside a Home Depot in Tucson, hoping someone will give them forty dollars for a day's work in the hot sun? They need work, but they need it here, at home. And you and your cartels," he shook his head with disgust, "you are a huge part of the problem. Corruption, tying up resources, putting a stranglehold on bureaucracy so that nothing happens, nothing improves.

"This is a beautiful country. Rich in tradition, pride, honor. The cartels make it like nothing to the Americans. A wasteland. A cesspool of poverty, depression, misery and danger. And you help them."

Trent blinked then drained his juice glass. "I've always liked you, Suarez, despite what you might think. But not everyone has what it takes to fight giants."

"Dig deep, Trent. It's there somewhere."

"It's a losing battle, my friend. You're tilting at windmills."

Marius said nothing.

"I don't know what to suggest about your killer's border crossing secret." Trent stood and walked toward the window. "I saw Mueller's profile on the guy. Intelligent. Crafty. Someone like that wouldn't drag his victim through the desert along coyote tracks. He would have a more sophisticated plan."

"Like what?"

"I don't know. But do you want to know which smugglers I always admired?" Trent asked, turning back to look at Marius. "The gutsy ones, their seat cushions full of weed, their fenders stuffed with coke. They are the ones who fill their cattle trucks with illegals gagging on the stench – twenty of them hiding in the middle of seven miserable cows. Those are the guys who make it work – the ones who slip in and out right under your noses – doing their business bold as brass in the light of day."

32

IT WAS eleven o'clock and considerably warmer by the time Marius left Polanco. He unbuttoned his jacket and walked to the park, where he sat on a bench angled perfectly for a postcard view of Chapultepec Castle – Emperor Maximilian's home during his illegitimate reign more than one hundred and fifty years ago.

He smiled, remembering how Rachel had caught him off guard with her knowledge of Mexican history that first day of Spanish class. He would like to bring her here, he thought. Someday, when this horrific investigation was over. They could tour the castle and take Danny to the zoo or, if he wasn't too scared, for a ride on the Russian Mountain roller coaster.

Marius sighed and rubbed the back of his neck. He had a tendency to get ahead of himself lately.

He was falling in love with her all over again, he realized. He couldn't wait to hear her voice every night, and wished more with each passing day that there was some way to write their future with a permanent marker, entwining their lives.

But our timing has always been horrible, he thought.

His mind faltered at the hurdles, past and present, that stood in their way. He didn't know if he ached more from wanting her like never before, or from the fear that by daring to try again, they were only doomed to follow the same destructive paths.

The summer after Rachel's sophomore year, she went home for two months and so did Marius – to Mexico, not Spain, where Rachel believed he was. Some days the simple process of rerouting his letters raised enough guilt for Marius to consider confessing all to Rachel. On the other hand, his extended assignment from the DEA was the only thing making it possible for him to go back to school in the fall – the only way he could be near her again.

He would tell her, he promised himself, when the time was right. And the confession of his duplicitous career would be a bridge they could cross together. It would only make them closer.

At the end of July, Marius was back in Tempe and packing a duffel bag for a Spanish club trip to Rocky Point, planned with Rachel and thirteen other club members. Two of them had decided to join the expedition at the last minute, overcrowding the rental van.

"Rachel and I can drive separately," Marius offered.

When Rachel arrived at his apartment, she was unusually quiet, her smile fleeting as she put her bag in his trunk.

"What is it? What's wrong?" he asked.

Rachel shook her head, but Marius wouldn't let it go. What if he had given something away in one of his letters? What if their time apart had given her enough perspective to start piecing together some of his discrepancies?

He took her hands, his nerves in full tilt. "Please, *querida*. Tell me. Did I do something?"

"No, Marius. Of course not. It's not you, it's my father." She pulled away from him and began searching through her purse, determined, he thought, to avoid his eyes. "We argued a lot this summer – he's just so...ugh! Where are my sunglasses?"

Rachel would not elaborate, but Marius had little doubt that her relationship with "that Mexican" was the focus of the disagreement. He might have pushed harder for details, but he had never seen Rachel this angry. It was the kind of fury that was almost visible – maybe even more so because of how hard she was trying to tamp it down.

Over the course of the five hour drive to the beach, Marius tried to pull her out of it – dramatizing stories from his childhood and singing along obnoxiously to the stereo, counting it a victory every time she smiled or laughed.

By the time they arrived at their beachside villa, Rachel's brow had cleared and she seemed much more like herself.

"Thank you," she said, kissing him.

"Anytime."

They changed into swimwear, hoping for at least a few of hours on the beach before a looming rainstorm arrived. When two hours had passed and the rains came but the van carrying their friends didn't, they began to worry. They ate dinner at the closest restaurant, sitting outside on the leaky patio so they could see the road from the north. They talked very little and tried not to imagine what might have gone wrong. Two more hours passed uneasily back at the villa until they saw the property manager hurry toward them.

Marius met him on the steps. "What is it?"

"Engine trouble, *Señor*." He held a damp message in his hand. Their friends had been stranded south of Yuma, forcing them to wait for a tow truck, exchange vans and postpone their departure until the following morning.

"At least they are okay!" Rachel said.

Marius thanked the manager and closed the door. Almost immediately, the villa seemed like a different place. Maybe it was simple relief over their friends' safety, or maybe it was the unexpected gift of privacy, but Marius felt almost intoxicated with happiness. He danced Rachel around the tile floor, making her laugh with more impressions of his dance instructor until neither one could catch their breath. They collapsed onto the couch. Marius pulled her into his arms and kissed her, realizing for the first time that he never wanted to see the last of nights like this one.

Even now, when he was swiftly approaching middle-age, Marius failed to completely understand the struggle within a man, the way natural desire fights chivalry for balance, either emotion able to make him feel less or more virile, depending on some formula outside his grasp. As a young man, his ability to separate and analyze those fighting forces had been considerably weaker, but it was still there.

He had let his relationship with Rachel develop slowly over the previous year for many reasons. Rachel had a strict religious upbringing for one, and although Marius did not, watching man after man parade in and out of his mother's life had taught him to crave something more lasting. Rachel's innocence, too, was not easy to dismiss. She had been raised without a mother and her father had clearly left all instruction to chance. Rachel's experience with men was more in keeping with a sheltered high school student than her collegiate peers.

None of that entered his mind that night in the villa. Not at first, when the rain and waves crashed against the world outside, enhancing the intimacy within. It had felt like a honeymoon suite, and for a while they both had been overcome with the life they imagined together – the beauty of how it could begin.

It was only when, in the flicker of candlelight, Marius saw absolute trust in Rachel's eyes that he was struck with an overwhelming sense of guilt. He pulled away.

"Marius?"

He didn't know how to explain himself, so he covered his feelings with action. Mindless of the rain, he pulled her to her feet and straight out into the surf where the cold waves knocked the edge off his passion.

"You're crazy, you know that?" She squealed as a wave nearly knocked her over.

"I'm crazy about you." He kissed her again while the ocean tugged at their feet.

Someday he would make love to her, he promised himself. At that moment, he couldn't imagine any other future than a life with her as his wife. But he couldn't do it like this. Not with his deceit between them.

When they returned to the villa and dried off, Marius turned on the television and found *Casa Blanca*, which he hoped would be an effective diversion from their truncated passion. They watched it from the floor, leaning against the foot of the bed. Rachel fell asleep with her head on his lap – a scene they had miraculously restaged just a few weeks ago in Creel.

Marius should have known that his antics that night had only diverted Rachel momentarily. She was innocent, but she was not gullible. His pulling away must have felt like rejection, but she hadn't challenged it. Instead she had pushed it down to reside in the same pit as her anger toward her father. There, it had festered.

Months later, when it all fell apart, he was able to look back on their trip to Mexico as a turning point – the end of happy days built on an unstable foundation of his own making.

It was easy to blame everyone else – Agent Johnson, who continued to feed him a weekly helping of bigotry, or Rachel's father, who, though not as present in his life, clearly judged him by the same standard. Never mind that Rachel was on Marius's side of that argument – there came a point where he refused to see. She didn't know he was being hit from two quarters. Unable to explain and unwilling to directly attack her father, Marius resorted to more general expressions of resentment – which always came out as wholly anti-American, hurting her more.

The culmination of all their resentment and misunderstandings was chemically disastrous – and the resulting explosion had been deep and mortal. Too afraid to confess the truth, too proud to see that the love they shared could never be replicated, Marius had walked away, telling himself that his dreams of marrying Rachel someday were nothing but delusions.

A coward, she had called him. And so he had been.

But there was no use reconstructing the past now – fixing decisions and conversations long left to the dusty, imperfect realm of memory. He told himself that, yet still his stomach churned. Perhaps it was just hunger, but the pain felt deeper – of echoing, unspoken words and the fear of hurting all over again.

He was terrified to love Rachel again, but he loved her just the same.

A young man sat down next to him and snapped open his newspaper. Marius pulled his thoughts back to the present and glanced at his watch.

"Banuelos."

"Suarez." Banuelos turned a page. *"Tiene alguna suerte?"*

"Sí." He switched to English. "We'll be lucky if the bug is not found within a week. If Trent has the kind of access we're hoping for, they'll do regular sweeps."

"I only hope he is reluctant to disclose your visit," Banuelos said. "It's worth a shot. You are sure Judge Alvarez is clean?"

Marius smiled. "If he wasn't, I would be dead by now."

Banuelos folded his paper. "How did you do this for so long?"

"One day at a time. Don't worry. I hear you're doing well." Marius stood up. "I have a plane to catch. Let me know if our bird sings."

He walked back to the metro station and boarded the orange train to the airport. As he passed familiar tunnels leading to the Zócalo and Zona Rosa where he and Carmen sometimes dined or shopped, he was surprised to find that his memories did not sting, touching him with sadness rather than pain.

He had tried to see his deception as a little thing with Rachel. With Carmen he had learned how vital truth is – even in all its pain. He didn't deserve another chance with Rachel. He had left her without a fight – all because he held guilt that was too big to ignore and too frightening to lay at her feet. Then she had moved on to be loved and hurt all over again by Craig Mueller, a man Marius would happily hate if doing so didn't make him feel like such a hypocrite.

Rachel was strong, but she had been broken. And though time was a great healer, Marius couldn't help feeling that it was not on their side.

33

"THAT'S ALL he said?"

"That's it."

Rachel stared at the dark ceiling. "I hope your bug catches something, otherwise it sounds like a wasted trip."

Marius's deep laugh resonated through the phone. "Trent's a scoundrel, Rachel, but he might be right."

"If the killer passed four times through a border gate with a woman hidden somewhere in his vehicle, then I would say his deity delusions received a serious boost by dumb luck."

"Or there's a border agent who has been paid to let him pass."

"A Mexican border agent *and* an American one? That's the only way it could account for his ease of travel."

"Seems unlikely when you put it that way. Still, I'm looking into it from my side, starting with the New Mexico entry points."

"Thank you. But, Marius, speaking of New Mexico," she bit her lip. "Have you heard from Agent Cruces?"

"No, but I expect him back in the office tomorrow. Why?"

"He's been in Arizona – out on the San Carlos Reservation. I got a call from the tribal sheriff who told me Cruces was asking suspicious questions in a bar east of Globe. He told them he was working with me, so I vouched for him."

"Are they holding him?" Marius asked.

"No, but they will keep an eye on him – and you can bet your last dime they will escort him to the New Mexico border. Apaches don't like strangers coming in among them, asking questions about their women.

"What trail is he following, Marius? If he thinks Yala ended up on tribal lands, it would have been best to tell me. I could have gotten him access – or gone looking for information myself, using contacts who owe me favors." She shook her head. "With this little fiasco, those favors are considered paid, I guarantee."

"I'm sorry," Marius said. "I'll ask him about it as soon as he gets back. Thank you for getting him out of there."

"Should I be worried?"

Marius was quiet for a minute. "I have a suspicion this isn't about the case, Rachel. It might be something more personal. I'll find out what's going on, I promise you."

Rachel wasn't sure. She thought about the story Agent Trent told her last spring about Cruces killing someone under questionable circumstances. Trent was a snake and a liar, but sometimes he wrapped his lies in bits of truth. She'd let Marius handle it for now, but she planned on keeping her eyes open.

"I've hit a dead end with the *tonalpohualli* dates," she said, changing the subject. "An anthropology professor at ASU has agreed to meet me on Friday. Hopefully she can make sense of them."

"Good. Our geologist submitted his findings about the obsidian we found with Libby Stuart's remains. It comes from a vein near Napa Valley, California. I'm waiting on word from a handful of American craftsmen who create knifes from that source."

"That's good news. When we have access to their records, we can narrow the list and question the buyers."

"How's your case load?"

"Still heavy. Most of it is typical grunt work – phone records, routine surveillance and security checks."

"And the boy from Mexico? Have you learned anything new?"

"No. Victor is compiling that list of orphanages. He thinks it's pretty complete for Baja, Sonora and Chihuahua – everything south of there is spotty. Still, I hope some image or name will be familiar to Flavio. It's the best we can hope for right now."

"Send me the list when you get it. I made contact with the DIF. If we strike out there, I'll contact the secretary for exterior relations."

"Thank you," she said. "I'll pass it along as soon as I get it."

She frowned, realizing that Victor had promised the list a week ago. She hoped he wasn't avoiding her – hurt because she ultimately turned down his invitation for New Year's Eve.

"I thought Craig was keeping Danny through the New Year," Victor said when he stopped by a few days after Christmas.

Rachel's smile was tight. "No. Evidently Trisha bought him tickets for that concert out at Wild Vista."

"So he ditched Danny for Trixie and a night at the casino?"

"Yes. And I can't get a sitter, Vic. I just can't." She squeezed his arm. "I'll send my donation, I promise. And I'll pledge my community service hours. But things have been going so well with Danny since Christmas – and he begged me to let him stay up late so we could watch the ball drop on TV together."

Victor scowled like a disappointed little boy. "I suppose dancing and champagne can't compete with microwave popcorn and a bunch of has-been celebrities behaving as if New York City is the center of the universe."

"You're a better sport than you pretend to be."

"Well, I wish I wasn't." He ran his hands through his hair and stood up. "Anyway, you know it's not you I'm mad at."

"I know."

He walked to the door and then stopped, his eyes narrowing. "Wait a minute. You're not just trying to avoid dancing with me are you?"

She put up her hands. "Guilty as charged. I'm afraid you'll step on my toes with those traditional Greek dance steps your father taught you."

"Ouch!" He looked at his watch. "You just reminded me – I need to pick him up at the Glendale Airport."

"Your father? Is he still flying?"

"He's crazy, if you ask me. Let's see: first class, major sucking up by pretty flight attendants, or trying to safely land a flying bus on your own. I'll take commercial flight any day of the week."

"He likes the adventure I guess."

"Maybe."

"I'm sorry about New Year's Eve, Vic."

He nodded, looking resigned. "I know. Danny's your priority."

Rachel said goodnight, still feeling guilty. Truthfully, she was relieved to have an excuse to miss the gala. Even though Danny was hurt by his dad's broken promise, she was happy to spend the evening with him. It had turned out just as she imagined – snuggled together under a blanket on the couch. Danny had been disappointed that a few illegal fireworks heard from a distance were the only evidence that the New Year had arrived in Arizona. He fell asleep on Rachel's shoulder as she carried him to bed, leaving her with an aching back and hopes that the coming year would be kinder to her son. That night she dreamed of dancing around a ballroom. Marius, not Victor, was her partner.

"Hey, are you still there?" Marius asked.

Rachel blushed. "I'm sorry. I guess I faded there for a minute."

"You're tired. I'll let you sleep."

"I'm okay. Danny's in bed and the house is quiet – it's one of my favorite times of day."

"How's he doing?"

"Good. He has been building roads, bridges and tunnels all over the house with the blocks you gave him. I keep tripping over them. 'Mom, you destroyed Sacramento!' he said today."

"He built Sacramento?"

She laughed. "Yep. Melissa gave him a book of states and capitals. I'm not trying to brag, but he's a pretty smart kid. Maybe he'll be an engineer someday – or an architect. Of course, he's also good at hide-and-seek. I don't know what kind of vocation that suggests."

"He could be a magician – one of those guys who squeezes himself into a box on stage and then appears at the back of the audience."

"Funny."

"Or he could be a Swiss banker."

"You're enjoying this, aren't you?"

"He could run the Witness Protection Program."

Rachel laughed. "Okay, I'm hanging up now."

"Rachel?"

"Yes?"

"Sleep well."

She tried but failed. Forty minutes later, she gave up. Flipping on the light switch, she scrolled down to Miles Davis on her docked iPod and then turned to face Craig's closet. It was full of storage boxes now – one which held memorabilia, old letters, birthday cards and drawings from Danny's preschool days. At the bottom, she found a shoe box of photos and carried it back to her bed.

It didn't take long to find the picture she was looking for – one an old classmate had handed her a few years ago at an ASU alumni event. It was a candid shot of Rachel and Marius by a bonfire. He had his arm around her and she was leaning against his shoulder. They were both laughing while the Baja surf crashed behind them.

"That was a fun trip, wasn't it?" she had asked Rachel. "After the broken-down-van debacle, that is. My family and I go to Rocky Point every year, but it's not the same. It's so overdeveloped now."

Rachel smiled and slid the photo into her purse. Craig was on his way back over with drinks and she didn't want to add fuel to the fight they had on the way to the party. It had been a time when Rachel learned to choose her words carefully, or not speak at all. The most innocuous thing could set Craig off, making her sick at her stomach for not knowing how to fix all that was falling apart between them. She had taken the photo home and stuffed it in a box. Her friend was right – the trip had gone well after everyone arrived, though Rachel's smile in the photo seemed a little forced. No, she didn't want to remember that trip at all – or the week leading up to it.

"You're not staying for church?" Melissa had asked Rachel early that Sunday morning as she shouldered her bag and headed out the back door. She had hoped to get out of the house undetected without any more painful distractions from her upcoming trip to Mexico, but Melissa's intuition had been acute those days, and her taste for confrontation high.

"And sit next to Dad?" Rachel jerked her thumb down the road toward her father's house. "The man who praises God with the same mouth he uses to spew venom?"

Melissa followed her outside. "He's not that bad."

"No? Last night I heard him tell Rich that the best they could hope for from my boyfriend was a little bit of quality yard work."

Melissa winced. "Well, don't come for him then, come for God. So Dad's being a jerk – he goes through these spells."

"And we all bite our tongues and walk away, acting like he's the one we gather to worship. He sent Alma packing without so much as a word to you or me – now he's threatening to pull me home from school because my boyfriend is Spanish? You can't defend that."

"He didn't say that."

"It was a veiled threat. Don't pretend otherwise."

"Rachel, please don't leave like this, okay?" Melissa blinked, close to tears. "I'm afraid every time you come home it's going to be the last time we see you. Please. Don't let Dad run you off for good."

Rachel rubbed her forehead, tired after a sleepless night. "Melissa, I wouldn't do that. Not to you."

"It's scary, you know. Watching you come into your own – becoming more woman and less girl. It's beautiful and necessary, but you need to be careful."

Rachel struggled not to roll her eyes. Melissa was seven years older and perhaps had a right to this kind of patronization, but Rachel couldn't help thinking her sister's struggle with infertility and the hormones she was taking were partly to blame. Since she couldn't have complete control over her own life, she was coping by mothering Rachel.

"You just need to trust me," Rachel said. "As for Dad, I'm not going to apologize for standing up to him."

"I'm not excusing him, Rachel. But you didn't just stand up to him last night, you were downright belligerent."

"Well maybe that's what he deserves." Rachel slammed her trunk closed. "All I know is that I'm too angry to pray and too angry to sit next to him in church thinking murderous thoughts. So I'm going on this trip. I'm having fun and I'm not going to even think about Dad."

"You really love Marius?"

"Yes, I do."

Melissa pulled her into a hug. "Then I'll pray for you both – and for Dad to adopt a better attitude. Just remember, our hearts can't always be trusted, Rachel. Don't leave your head out of it."

"I've been cautious all my life, Lissa," Rachel said. "Right now, I just want to be happy."

She got in her car and drove away.

But two hours later when she met Marius in Tempe, she was still brewing. It took several hours for him to coax her out of her funk, but she began to relax by his side, letting his warmth wash over her mile after mile until she felt numb to the outside world. By the time the storm rolled around that night, she was willing more than ready to engage in the deeper kind of comfort that fate offered them.

Marius's rejection did not immediately register the way it would with a more experienced woman. Instead it set a subtle yet nagging tone that echoed through the months that followed. He was holding himself back from her. He always had, she realized, when it was all over but the pain. What she hadn't known until this past spring was why.

Now as she sat in her bedroom, listening to *Recollections* and holding a picture from another place and time, she realized the pain was fading like a scar – passing from angry red to pink and finally, silver – more delicate than unmarred skin, but evidence of survival. So many of their arguments and misunderstandings were explained by Marius's undercover work. Even their agonizing goodbye seemed different when she plugged in his guilt. His lie revealed and regretted, it seemed, had more power for healing than years of suppressed anger ever could.

It had cost her so much to resent Marius. It had given her nothing. They had fought about family, country, culture – but the fight had always been the same. They were from two worlds, only meeting each other because of a contrived situation which should have only made the improbability of their relationship impossible instead.

But she had survived – crawling out of her misery, patching up her heart and even finding a career that gave her purpose. Eventually, she healed enough to love again and create a new family with Craig, leaving Marius banished to the dusty bottom of her heart where useless love lies dormant.

As painful as it had all been, Rachel could no longer regret it any more than she regretted her marriage to Craig. Love had come out of the first loss – broken, painful, soul-stretching, yes – but love, nonetheless. And love in the form of Danny was the result of the second.

So why did the dawn and death of both relationships seem bent on keeping her awake and uneasy tonight?

Maybe because being in touch with Marius again was somehow healing even more than the hurt between them. His nightly calls from Mexico were like a balm – administered at a safe distance. She wasn't just reconnecting with him, but with a part of herself she had lost along the way. And now, even when she thought of the most painful moment with Craig, the hurt would not stick like it once had. After each conversation with Marius, Rachel remembered more of why she fell in love with him in the first place.

She could feel it now, trying to resurface – to push past the scars, filled with hope. Rachel wrestled with twin desires – to let it fly or crush it once and for all. She hated to let fear lead her, but she wasn't a naïve girl anymore. Her mind held her back this time, telling her hope was premature, that all the obstacles that once proved insurmountable were still there, threatening.

Focus on the case, her organized mind begged her.

Rachel was happy to comply. She would take Marius's calls each night but she would not let her heart sing when his voice softened, reaching through the line to ask a question she could not answer. She had been too eager in the past – ready to give her whole heart to Marius, then ready to give all but its damaged tissue to Craig. She had learned her lesson. Her focus was rightly on Danny now, just as Victor said. Everything else – including what was growing in her heart for Marius – she must leave to time and providence.

34

"WHAT IS this?"

Rachel looked at the stack of papers in Melissa's hands, then glanced at Danny, who was coming through the back door.

"Water!" he croaked. He dropped his basketball on the floor. "It's hot out there!"

"There's a spring heat wave all over the state," Rachel said. Her eyes stayed on her sister as she grabbed him a bottle from the fridge. As soon as Danny left the room, she snatched the papers out of Melissa's hands.

"Don't look at me like that," Melissa said. "You told me to look for takeout menus in that drawer."

"I forgot. I put these in there yesterday when you and Danny got back from Cottonwood."

"El Paso, Rachel? Really?"

"It's just a possibility," Rachel said. She glanced at the relocation documents before turning them upside down on the countertop.

"Why?"

"You know I'm placed where I'm most needed – solely at the Bureau's discretion. I've been lucky to be in Phoenix for so long. In truth, my boss told the A.D. about the working relationship I've developed with Marius and Cruces in Chihuahua. They've been talking about creating a special task force. It would be an honor to be chosen – a promotion too."

"Couldn't they organize the task force here? I mean, Phoenix is a lot bigger than El Paso…"

"Phoenix is a possibility too – nothing has been decided." Rachel pushed her hair behind her ears. "But El Paso is a hotbed of trouble – you know that. The Juarez murders have been spilling across the border for some time. I'm just trying to be prepared. It might make more sense to run investigations from there."

"Maybe more sense to the FBI. But not for you – or Danny."

Rachel crossed her arms. She should have done a better job of hiding those papers. "No, he won't like moving – if it happens. But I'll cross that bridge when we get to it."

"Does Craig know?"

"Know what, Melissa? I already told you, nothing has happened yet. There's no need to get worked up over this until we know something more definite."

"You can't just wait. You need to have a plan."

"Melissa!" Rachel took a breath and then lowered her voice, thinking of Danny in the other room. "Have you ever – even once in your life – considered that I am a grown woman? That you could show me a little bit of respect and trust me to figure things out on my own?"

"But Rachel—"

"You act like I'll forget to consider what's best for my own son if you don't remind me!"

"Well, maybe you will," Melissa said stubbornly. "I've suspected for the past year that you are not thinking clearly – especially where Marius is concerned."

"I don't think you have ever been more insulting, Melissa."

"It's true, though, isn't it?" she pressed. "We might as well acknowledge it openly. If you move to El Paso, you'll be closer to him. Restarting that relationship will be easier – a lot sooner, I have to say, than you have any business getting involved with *any* man, let alone one who broke your heart."

"Melissa, enough!"

For a minute, they both glared at each other. They hadn't fought like this in years, despite Melissa's habit of mothering Rachel. But this time, she had touched a nerve.

Of course, Rachel had thought about what being closer to Marius would mean. How could she not? But she had tried not to dwell on it. Over the past few months, Marius had continued to call her regularly, but if she had once worried he would press for more from her, that had passed. For the time being, he seemed content with conversation.

"I'm sorry, but this whole situation worries me," Melissa said.

Rachel heard contrition in her sister's voice, but chose to ignore it. "What worries me is that you always jump to conclusions. That you can't seem to stop yourself from telling me what to do.

"No. Rachel, listen. I have so much respect for you—"

"So much that you question my integrity? My devotion to my son?"

"Of course not!"

"Don't insult me by backing down now. You have no idea what it's like to suddenly be on your own and responsible for everything. If the Bureau tells me to go, I'll go – I won't have a choice in the matter."

Melissa crossed her arms. "You have more choices than you're willing to acknowledge."

"Don't start that again, Melissa. My job is important – not just to the people I serve, but to me as well. If we do move, it may be providential. You know I can barely afford this house. I have almost nothing put away for the future – for Danny's education."

"Craig should be helping with those things."

"Well there are a lot of things Craig should do that he won't. I can't count on him – not for myself or for Danny. And I'm not rolling over like a damsel in distress either." Rachel leaned against the counter. "Do you understand that? I'm not running home to live with you or Dad. Danny needs to see that I'm strong, self-reliant."

"At what cost? His counselor said he needs you to keep emphasizing the stabilizing forces in his life."

"But he's been doing so much better!" Rachel said. "You've seen that yourself. He's learning to identify things that are within and outside of his control. Maybe he understands that better than you."

Rachel's phone rang. The sisters stared at each other for a moment and then, wordlessly, Melissa headed into the living room.

Rachel picked up her phone. "Hello?"

"Hey."

She smiled. "Victor. You're home."

"Just."

"How was – Puerto Rico, was it?"

"Yes. Good. But I'm so tired I'm ready to drop."

"So why don't you get some sleep instead of calling me?"

"I'm not calling for you," he said. "I'm calling for my man, Dan. Remember I promised him tickets to something fantastic when I got back?'

"It could have waited until tomorrow."

"Not if he wants Suns tickets – I'm looking at a ten minute window here, or they're gone."

"Okay, hang on." Rachel called Danny to the phone. After a few minutes of conversation with Victor, Danny lifted his head to the ceiling and let out an ear-shattering howl before handing Rachel the phone and running off.

"What on earth?" she asked Victor.

"I think he wants to see the Coyotes instead," he said.

"Ah. Is that doable?" she asked.

"Sure. I better get something soon, though. They made the playoffs, but I don't think they'll get too far. Any date restrictions?"

"No school nights. Just call me with the details. We'll work it out."

"Okay, goodnight."

"It's one in the afternoon, Vic."

"Is it? Okay. Goodnight."

Melissa walked back in the kitchen as Rachel hung up. "I'm sorry," she said. "I wish I could learn to hold back what I'm thinking."

"So do I." Still, she smiled.

"I would really miss you."

Rachel put her arm around Melissa's shoulders. "You would only miss bossing me around."

ങ

AFTER MELISSA LEFT, Rachel took the incriminating relocation papers to her office. As usual, one task gave way to another and soon she was sitting in front of her computer, plugging dates into a web-based *tonalpohualli* Professor Estefan had shared, once again hoping to find a combination that would point to the killer.

Rachel met Professor Estefan in Matthews Hall at ASU several weeks ago. A friendly woman in her mid-sixties, the professor had an office full of artifacts – each one with a story she wanted to share with

Rachel. It took some tactful sidestepping before Rachel was able to focus on what interested her most – a working *tonalpohualli* reproduction that dominated the professor's coffee table.

"The *tonalpohualli* is made up of two wheels," Professor Estefan said. "The inner wheel rotates inside the outer wheel like this, creating matches between the thirteen day signs, here," she pointed to the inner circle, "And the twenty *trecenas*, here," she pointed to the outer circle.

"*Trecenas*?"

"It's their 'week' of sorts, lasting thirteen days. Various gods rule over each day and each *trecena*."

"Which ones belong to Tezcatlipoca?"

"He is the ruler of the day called '*Acatl*' and also Lord of the Day for days with the number 10, which is "*mahtlactli*" in Nahuatl, the language of the Aztecs."

"Does he rule a *trecena* as well?"

"Not by that name. But *Mazatl*, meaning 'deer,' is ruled by Tepeyollotl, a variant of Tezcatlipoca. Tepeyollotl was called the Heart of the Mountain, the Jaguar of the Night – the lord of animals, darkened caves, echoes and earthquakes."

Rachel remembered his cave and suppressed a shudder. From Dr. Estefan she had also learned about Quetzalcoatl's *trecena*, called *Ocelotl*, which ironically meant 'jaguar.'

"We can't dismiss the connection between the two brothers," Dr. Estefan said. "Quetzalcoatl is often called the Precious Twin or even the White Tezcatlipoca – a contrast with his black-hearted brother."

"So days of significance to one brother would be critical to the other as well?"

"One way or another, yes. Like real brothers, sometimes they are shown working together, other times they are each other's fiercest enemy. But remember, all days and *trecenas* were important to the Aztecs, and their importance was often intertwined. For example, the *trecena* called *Acatl* is ruled by Chalchihuitlicue, the goddess of lakes, rivers and seas. It was known as a time that revealed what was in the heart – for introspection when a person could examine his motives for his life choices."

"That's quite a bit of self-analysis for the ancient world," Rachel said.

Dr. Estefan smiled. "Yes, well *Acatl* was also considered an excellent *trecena* for travel, so a person who held to these beliefs could be as introspective or superficial as he liked."

"If a person identified closely with Tezcatlipoca – is there a way to predict which days in the coming year might be key for him?"

"You might make an educated guess. If I had to guess which days are important to you, I might guess your son's birthday or your anniversary. So you might start with dates on the *tonalpohualli* that align Tezcatlipoca's day sign, number and *trecena*."

"And if they don't end up being significant?"

Dr. Estefan shrugged. "It gets more complicated then. One person might place great significance on the day her father died, for example. Another might identify strongly with something less obvious – the day he escaped abuse from a bully, the day she chose her college major, the day he lost the love of his life."

"If we use that kind of logic here…"

"Yes. The possibilities are as numerous as the days on the calendar."

Ever since their meeting, Rachel had been playing with the web-based *tonalpohualli* whenever she had a moment to spare, plugging in various combinations and hoping to identify a coming date of significance. But it wasn't until the night after her fight with Melissa that something finally clicked into place. She called Marius.

"What did you find?"

"We're on to something with this *tonalpohualli*," she said. "According to the online calculator, Samantha, Libby, Mary Ellen and Jonas were all abducted during the *trecena* of *Mazatl*."

"*Mazatl* – what is that?"

"It's a week of sorts. Thirteen days ruled by Tepeyollotl – an alias for Tezcatlipoca. It's eerie, Marius. The entire thirteen-day period is associated with hunting, or stalking prey. The website associates *Mazatl* with tracking and lying in wait. Camouflage, covering tracks and studying the routines of others."

"The calendar is 260 days, right?"

"Yes."

"Have you calculated when the next *Mazatl* comes around?"

"It runs June 22 through July 4. We can push for more vigilance during those weeks – heightened security on campuses, border checkpoints, highway patrol."

"Yes…'

"I know. It's not enough." Rachel swiveled in her office chair and stared out the window. "This man is obsessive about details – and losing

Samantha as a sacrifice has certainly thrown his plans off track – but how far off? Into a different pattern? One we can't predict?"

"And how have we changed it with our investigation? I don't think he'll return to the shack or the cave. My contacts in Creel have been keeping an eye open for suspicious activity – or more gravesites. They've seen nothing."

"So would he take another victim to the same region at all? Or has he abandoned this project altogether and gone searching for a new set of victims, a new place for killing them?"

Marius sighed. "We can't let those concerns paralyze us. We need to keep turning over rocks, and hope we uncover something before he does this again."

They stayed on the phone long into the night, planning. Rachel wanted to focus on more *tonalpohualli* dates. Marius was focused on ways to track the obsidian knife.

"We're spinning our wheels tonight, *Raquel*," he said when it was well after midnight. "Get some sleep or you'll be a zombie tomorrow. You're going to a movie with Danny, right?"

Rachel was touched by the tenderness in his voice. She had to stop herself from answering from the heart – *I wish you were coming too. Despite my resolve, I'm in love with you again and it scares me to death.*

"Yes," she said. "But no matter how tired I am, I go to bed and stare at the ceiling. Obsessing, I guess."

For a moment, the line was silent, heavy with things unspoken. Then Marius cleared his throat.

"Good night, *querida*," he said. "And if you can't sleep, you can always call me back. I'm right here. Anytime."

∞

THE DOORBELL RANG early the next morning, waking Rachel from a dream that was unmemorable but troubling. She hurried into a robe then peeked through the peephole before fumbling to unlock the door.

"Craig? What are you doing here?"

"May I come in?"

Rachel held open the door then followed him to the living room. "Did I miss something? It's six o'clock in the morning."

"Is it?" He looked confused and worse. His eyes were red, his face unshaven and his clothes were wrinkled. Many things Craig was, but he had always taken great care with his appearance.

"You look awful," she said. He nodded, but Rachel didn't think he heard her.

"Is Danny asleep?"

"Yes. I didn't expect you to pick him up until this afternoon."

Craig nodded again. Finally he sat down and stared past her at the city skyline.

"I always loved the view from this room," he said quietly, "especially at night. But it's great now too, when the air is clear and the buildings shine in the sunlight." He blinked rapidly, his eyes welling up.

Rachel frowned. "Craig, what is it? What's wrong?"

Finally he looked at her. "Rachel, I know I screwed it all up. I have no one to blame but myself. But I have to ask – I couldn't sleep last night for fear, but I have to ask anyway." He reached for her hand. "Take me back, Rachel. Forgive me, please. Let me come home."

35

MARIUS DIALED Rachel's phone and waited. When her voicemail engaged, he hung up. He had already left two messages, he wouldn't leave another. She was avoiding him, but he didn't know why.

He knew Rachel and Melissa had been arguing last week. Rachel wouldn't say why, though, which meant they had fought about him. He figured after all this time, her family was still able to sniff out and disapprove of his love – even before it was declared. Terrific.

Ever since, Marius had been trying to shrug off his concern, but couldn't – not until he talked to Rachel. With every unanswered message, his imagination took a darker turn.

When she finally answered the phone Tuesday evening, he hoped that just the sound of her voice would lay his fears to rest. Instead, his hope evaporated. Her voice had been bright, false. She said she had been busy and their conversation was stilted and brief. Almost a week passed before he was able to get a hold of her again.

"Sorry." She sounded out of breath. "I had my headphones on and didn't hear the phone."

Marius frowned. "Are you okay?"

"Fine."

There was an awkward pause. Marius thought of several work-related things to bring up, but stopped himself. If he told her Agent Cruces was following a promising lead on the obsidian knife, she might ask how he was doing, something Marius wasn't sure how to answer. He was reluctant to tell her which Sonoran orphanages he had heard back from too. What if she brought up her friend, Victor? It was a relationship he had never questioned out loud, but recently he couldn't help wondering if anything had happened there.

What kind of man hangs around a divorced woman and her kid, he wondered, if there's no hope that more will come of it? Suddenly he was irritable. All this tiptoeing around was not him. It wasn't her either.

"Rachel, what's going on?" he asked. He sounded whiny to his own ears, but knew from experience he probably sounded surly to her. "We haven't talked in days, which is glaringly obvious, and yet you clearly don't want to talk now. I can stick with the case, if that's what you want, but not with you avoiding my calls. And I would rather you were just straight with me."

When Rachel spoke, her voice was thick. "I'm sorry. You're right, I just…" She groaned. It was a hollow sound that made his stomach twist. "Something has come up that's – thrown me for a loop."

"What is it?"

She paused. "I want to talk about it, Marius, but I can't. Not yet."

"Rachel, you can talk to me about anything." He said it, even though he knew it wasn't true. There were things he didn't want to hear. *Dear Lord*, he prayed, *please don't let this be one of those things!*

"I'm sorry. Really sorry, Marius. Can you just trust me? Please? And give me a little time … to figure some things out?"

"Just tell me you're okay. That Danny's okay."

"We are," she said. "And I'm sorry – for being unavailable. Do you have something new on the case?"

"Not much," he admitted. He had been pouring over maps, trying to find a likely burial site for another grave, but coming up with nothing. He had also been reading about Aztec sacrificial customs and found a reference to a burial much like Libby's. But it wasn't much to go on – and wasn't something he needed to share now, when everything was so tense and awkward between them.

There was also a discrepancy in the list of orphanages Rachel had forwarded from Victor. It was probably just a clerical error, but he couldn't help adding it to the unknown man's annoying traits – lousy record keeping. He didn't mention that either, reluctant to sound as petty and jealous as he felt – and to admit that his digging had caught the attention of the Secretary for Exterior Relations. *Ayuda del Norte* was probably in for an accreditation audit.

Rachel promised they would talk again in a few days, and said goodnight. But a few days had passed and he still hadn't heard from her. Tonight his feelings ranged from vague alarm to ridiculous jealousy with each passing hour. He tried to sort out possible reasons for her sudden distance. They ranged from the plausible to the absurd.

The idea that Melissa, or even Rachel's father was responsible couldn't be dismissed, though Victor and Craig fought for prominence in his overtaxed mind – one who might have grown weary waiting for his opportunity, the other who was the source of all of Rachel's most far-reaching heartaches.

He tossed and turned, hating them both.

If only he could focus on work, but even there his mind turned to Rachel. Maybe his burial research was not critical enough to require her immediate attention – Victor's clerical error certainly wasn't – but he could honestly use her take on what was going on with Johnny lately. Marius had been keeping his eyes open after Johnny's vague excuses for being in Arizona. He thought he understood his reasons, but not why Johnny was growing more secretive every day. He used to confide in Marius.

So they are both keeping things from me, he thought. *Great.*

He had also been strangely unsettled ever since Rachel's visit from that intuitive woman. Her dreams about fields of snow, seeds and ice didn't make any sense to him, and yet, he couldn't shake this nagging sense that he was missing something.

He pushed back the covers and walked to his bedroom window. The city was still sprinkled with lights, but the edge of the black sky was lit with dawn.

Had he really been up all night?

He mentally reviewed his schedule for the day – shifting and reorganizing until he was satisfied it could all be changed. But not for a few hours. In the meantime, he would drag out his running shoes and pound away the night's worries. He pulled out his suitcase too, flopping it open on the edge of his bed. It had been years since he had visited Arizona. He had once vowed never to cross her border again.

Funny what love will do to a man, he thought.

36

RACHEL HUNG UP the phone. Marius was coming to see her. Tonight.

She looked up and caught her reflection in the window above her desk. She looked stunned and pale, like a ghost who just now understood she was dead. She had felt like a ghost for the past week, ever since Craig's early morning visit effectively shut down everything but her vital functions.

Agent Baldock rapped his fingers on her desk. "Mueller. Meeting."

"Coming." She collected her notes and headed to the conference room, hoping to stay focused enough to report coherently on her cases. An hour later, she emerged, unsure of her success. She dropped her files on her desk before continuing to the bathroom, where she gripped the edge of a sink and stared at her reflection in the mirror.

Why is this happening?

It was her go-to question this week. She had yet to find an answer. More than a year had passed since her divorce was final. More than a year since she met Marius again – hurting like an angry sunburn – raw and red, feeling ugly and misused. A few months before that, she would have been thrilled to hear Craig's Sunday morning speech. But he had been arrogant back then, belligerent – full of excuses. He had asked for forgiveness as soon as Rachel found out about the affair, but his eyes had been proud, his excuses self-serving – his plea phrased as if exoneration was his right. How she had wished to see even a flicker of real remorse in his face! For him to just once own up to his sins without the kind of phony victimization he used in the court room.

No wonder she felt so empty and worthless.

But during the past few months, she had begun to feel complete again. Romanticism might make her say Marius had filled the void Craig created, but that wasn't the truth. She knew it wasn't. It was her – Rachel. The woman who had gone missing for more years than she wished to count while her shell bent this way and that, giving and compromising to the point that she had almost ceased to exist altogether.

She didn't mean to dismiss the role Marius played. With him she had learned to be herself again – tentatively venturing out of that shell without embargo or sanction, feeling worthy of love and respect without conforming to a false standard. That simple knowledge had given her a starting place to heal. And even though he hadn't breathed a single word of renewed love to her, it had poured into her soul all the same – every time he laughed at her silly humor, sought her input on the case, praised her analysis of a problem, or even argued with her without an ounce of insecurity. With him, she had felt renewed, coming back to a sense of home within her own skin.

But Craig's visit last week had struck like a sledge hammer – crashing into the foundation of a new life she had not yet consciously embraced. And how he had that power – *still*, after all he had done to her – frustrated her to the point of distraction in which she now lived.

When he was grasping her hand and crying – with actual tears running down his face – Rachel had felt removed from the scene. Like that ghost, watching from above as paramedics tried to bring her back to life. She felt pity for him, but little else.

It almost made her marvel. His handsome features hadn't changed. She easily remembered how he had once been so hard to resist, especially when he smiled as if there was never a man so in love with his wife. But there was no getting around how her feelings had changed. The constant stretching and constricting of her heart for his sake had damaged it so entirely, affection was now a distant memory. The tears he shed might once have pushed her into his arms, but this time they bounced off like rain on a weatherproofed heart. She pulled her hand from his grasp and walked across the room.

"You need to pull yourself together," she said, adjusting her robe for modesty. "I don't want Danny to wake up and see you like this."

"Danny." He sniffed. "I've really screwed that up too, haven't I?"

"Yes, you have."

Craig talked for the next half hour, his voice low but emotional. Trisha had left him. They had been fighting a lot and Craig knew it wouldn't last, but his pride had pushed him blindly forward. He owned up to everything. His selfishness and jealousy – the way he had always punished Rachel for disagreeing with him, how he had often played both sides of an issue – fighting unfairly just so he would win. Rachel listened in silent surprise. He admitted to flaws she never realized he was aware of, though his honesty there only reminded her of the peace she enjoyed without him. Peace she had come to value more than all the divorce had cost her.

Except for what it did to Danny.

"Can we talk again?" Craig asked when she showed him to the door, insisting that he calm down before returning for Danny. "Is there any hope for us?"

"Yes, we can talk," she said tiredly. "But, no, Craig. I won't give you false reason for hope."

He nodded. "It's more than I deserve. More than I expected."

Despite Craig's parting words, Victor's call the next day made Rachel suspect her answer had not really been accepted.

"I just talked to Craig." Vic's voice was agitated. "Tell me you're not doing this. Tell me you're not even thinking of giving that..." He heaved a great sigh and lowered his voice. "Don't give him another chance Rachel. He'll break your heart again."

Rachel frowned. "When did you see him?"

"Today. He was at *Fuego*, picking over a Cuban sandwich."

She assured Victor she had no intention of welcoming Craig back into her heart or home and though he sounded mollified, he called her once a day for the next week, just to make sure.

"He's one of those guys who can't stand to be alone," Victor said. "You mark my words, if Trixie trotted her cute little tush back in the picture, we'd be seeing the same old Craig."

Rachel smiled weakly. "Is that supposed to make me feel better?"

But somehow, it did – at least for a few hours.

When her phone rang again late that night, it was Marius. Rachel knew she couldn't talk to him, but she didn't understand why. She let it pass to voicemail, then cried as she listened to his message. She picked up the phone and put it down again.

The days that followed were a blur. She worked. She cooked dinner for Danny and put out the trash. Craig came by more often, usually taking Danny to the park or out for ice cream. Sometimes he stayed and sat with his son, watching him build roads or play video games. He hadn't told Danny about Trisha moving out. Rachel understood, but wrestled with the twisted logic that meant the departure of such a woman would be unsettling to her son. She had little to say during Craig's visits, but he was surprisingly respectful of her distance. The questions he did ask, she answered honestly, pulling no punches about the painful issues of their marriage. He appeared to take it all in stride. He was still the image of the man she knew, but seemed truly changed.

She didn't trust how he seemed.

Still, stories of forgiveness bombarded her thoughts – Jo March forgiving Amy, Joseph, his brothers. King Arthur with Guinevere – Jesus and his murderers. She stayed up late every night, listening to music and brooding. Her moods shifted with each artist – Krauss, Krall, Groban, Matthews.

Marius called again and she picked up the phone, only to hear his hurt. She felt it acutely. He offered his ear and she bit her tongue, knowing that if she started, she wouldn't be able to stop. He would know it all – including the love she felt for him and how powerless she felt to fight it. She looked in the mirror and couldn't see who she was anymore. She told herself she forgave Craig, but wondered what that really meant. She fell asleep long after midnight, aching for Marius.

And tonight he was coming.

"I'm getting ready to board the plane," he told her, "so no arguments." His voice softened. "Some of what I've uncovered on this investigation needs to be discussed in person."

That's what he said, but she knew there was more to it. She agreed to a meeting place and hung up, wondering how they were ever going to focus on the case.

Rachel had spoken to Agent Cruces only a few times since his unauthorized foray into Arizona, but he had called her yesterday. His investigation into the obsidian knife had steered him toward an artisan living outside of Santa Fe whose record-keeping was as old-fashioned as his craft. Agent Hughes would meet Cruces at the artisan's studio. From there, they would travel to Albuquerque to follow a lead on Yala.

Cruces had given Rachel his travel itinerary, sounding more than slightly irritated that Agent Hughes would be shadowing his every move.

"He's a good man – a good agent," Rachel said.

"A babysitter—"

She sighed. "I was shadowed in Mexico. I see little difference."

"Things are different when we cross that border, Agent Mueller, like it or not. You should consider that when…"

She waited.

"When what?" she finally prodded.

"Cross border relationships – like the one you and Marius are toying with – they don't work."

Rachel frowned. "I don't—"

"He has retirement in a few years," he said. "And now that he's out of internal affairs, he might live to see it. His father wants him to take over the ranch – and Marius has promised to do it. It's a peaceful place – miraculously untouched by the drug war, all because it's too out of the way to be of any use to the cartels. And, of course, there's Anna to consider."

Rachel swallowed a knot. Anna was the woman Cruces mentioned last year. Marius said she was the widow of his father's foreman, but little else. Rachel had not asked.

"Her son was born six months after her husband was killed in a ranch accident. Nothing would please Marius's father more than to see that family whole again."

"And you think Marius is that eager to please his father?"

Cruces paused. "You get to be his age – or mine, for that matter – you start seeing things differently. Some things just make good sense."

"Freedom makes good sense," she said rather fiercely. "A young person might be easy to scare into family obligation, but Marius is a grown man. He can make his own decisions."

"I beg your pardon, Agent Mueller. But when he does – make his own decision, as you say – I hope you'll be gracious enough to stay out of the way."

It had taken Rachel all evening to calm down. Her indignation hadn't dissipated by the time she was again resisting her ringing phone – and resigning herself to another sleepless night.

And now he was coming to see her.

Her schedule had to be rearranged. Victor had called earlier this week to say he couldn't take Rachel and Danny to tonight's Coyotes game after all.

"My dad has the flu – and *Ayuda del Norte's* visitation program ends this weekend. Suddenly all my volunteers have vanished and somebody's got to get these kids home. The government is really strict about these 72-hour visas."

"It's okay, Vic. I can still take him."

"But I wanted to go with you." He whined like a grumpy teenager. "I wanted to see you too – to make sure you're doing okay."

"I told you, I'm fine."

"You don't sound fine." He sighed. "I'll leave your tickets at will-call. Just two of them – don't even think about inviting Craig to go with you."

Rachel sighed. "I won't. And thanks, Vic. We can catch a D-backs game this summer, okay? After school is out."

But with Marius coming tonight, she wouldn't be able to take Danny to the hockey game after all. He would be so disappointed if she cancelled – and that wasn't the best way to introduce him to Marius. Craig was the obvious answer, despite Victor's protest. Presumably, he had no other plans on a Friday night, being recently dumped. Still he faltered when she called to ask, checking himself, she figured, before he asked where she would be – and with whom. To his credit, he didn't, but arranged to pick up Danny half an hour before she was set to meet Marius.

The workday that followed would have been difficult if not for new activity on her trafficking case. A prostitute brought in for questioning in a local homicide investigation told detectives she had been sold as part of a child trafficking ring several years ago. Rachel was notified and her team responded swiftly, setting up surveillance in the seedy south Phoenix neighborhood where she had lived. Late Thursday they made an arrest. After questioning the suspect this morning, Rachel was convinced he was nothing but a thug – and certainly not the brains behind any complicated human trafficking scheme. For now he wasn't talking, but his loyalty would crack soon enough under the more pressing desire for freedom.

"Let him stew awhile," she told Baldock. "I bet before you go home tonight, he'll be ready to talk."

CB

THAT EVENING, Rachel paced her living room, ignoring the fiery sunset that bathed the city beyond her windows. She had changed her clothes and carefully reapplied her makeup as if she was going on a date, but her hand shook as she finger combed her curls. Could she call Marius and put this off? Prolong the moment when she must either lay her heart, soul and messy life bare to him or become a convincing liar?

Coward, she told her reflection.

Craig had been prompt picking up Danny, who nearly tore off his arm while he hopped up and down, howling like a coyote. "Let's go, Dad. Let's go!"

"You two look great," Rachel said. Danny had insisted they both wear white T-shirts. Craig seemed happy to comply.

"We don't want to ruin the White Out, right Danny?"

Rachel pulled her son into a hug, which he tolerated surprisingly well.

"Be good," she said, "and have fun. I love you."

"Love you too, Mom." Danny wiped her kiss off his cheek as he darted out the door.

"Thank you, Craig."

"Thank you." He held her gaze. "I threw too many of these chances away, Rach. One way or another, I'm going to show you that I'm a changed man."

"Don't show me, Craig. Show him."

He nodded and walked through the door. She watched them drive away, her stomach fluttering. In half an hour, she would see Marius again.

37

THE TIME HAD come, he had no doubt. He saw the change in the mirror. The jaguar was already starting to fade, his dappled coat giving way to rich plumage.

He had always been the Jaguar of the Night– the Heart of the Mountain. He felt safe stalking in those skins – called to the hunt by the echoing voice that drew him back to the canyon. His home. He had calculated everything carefully, following the same plan four times without detection. He understood the beating heart of his prey as much as his own.

And then Samantha's small victory had broken the cycle, sending him scraping through the brush to lick his wounds, temper his rage and alter plans.

But he never gave up.

And he never expected this – to shed his skin, reset his timetables – or choose such a special sacrifice. It was his punishment for losing Samantha. He accepted that now. But when he had first read the *tonalpohualli* signs, it had sickened him.

Don't. Walk away.

It was a voice he had heard before. He steeled his heart and ignored it again. Whatever he felt, he couldn't ignore the destiny his Grandmother had laid out for him – or the duty he owed the Earth Monster.

But he must tread carefully this time. Questions were finally being asked in the right places. Rachel was probing – she and the others keeping a watchful eye where they had once been blind. He had done what he could to cover his tracks, throw suspicion off his path and toward others – completing what his mother started so many years ago. Backtracking became a dance of deception. Now he must move with more care and yet ultimately take the greatest risk of all.

Excitement stirred his blood. The hunt was beginning again with a different prey, a new hunting ground – rules that must take into account the tenacious enemy.

This time I will succeed, he vowed. To his mother, yes, but to Manny as well.

He remembered his first visit to the lost city. He had returned to the canyon for the first time, looking for Manny – looking for himself among the ghosts of his past. He stood on the path where tourists gawked, reading the signs, feeling the tug of the old world swirling like a vortex. He was proud of his brother – a place like this, all in honor of him. And yet he knew that balance must be created. No white existed without black – no sacrifice to the Feathered Serpent without a similar tribute reflected in the Smoking Mirror. The place for such a monument had sought him out, revealing itself on the day he found Manny, confirming that the opposing forces he imagined were valid – that they should be fed, honored, worshipped.

And atonement was still needed, of course.

At night he could still hear his mother crying from the pain she suffered. He knew that only the sacrifice of blood would console her. But those he had already chosen meant nothing yet – not until the circle was complete. The purest sacrifice must be added to their number, if he was to lay Tlaltecuhtli to rest.

So what he once dreaded was actually a blessing – he had to keep reminding himself. He would don the plumage and make his sacrifice, appeasing the Earth Monster once and for all. That he could honor his dead brother and exact revenge against a long-hated enemy all at once made his hands shake with anticipation. Within 48 hours, Manny would be avenged, pure blood would atone and Tlaloc, whom he had kept close for so long, would finally be defeated.

"*¿A dónde vamos?*"

He startled, looking to the passenger seat, then grinned.

"Home," he said.

38

MARIUS AND RACHEL sat on the patio.   Paper lanterns swayed overhead as they watched the sun journey over the hill through a latticework of ficus branches. *Madam Woo's* had been remodeled and was filled with patrons – the Tempe dive Marius remembered from his days at ASU now happily situated near the new light rail station and within easy walking distance of the town lake.   The patio addition had once been nothing but the leaking roof of a Laundromat owned by Madam Woo's brother. Marius and Rachel had often brought their wash to Woo's on Saturday evenings, scraping money together for dinner while they waited for their jeans to dry. The Laundromat had since sold and been replaced with a Starbucks.

"My brother moved to Portland," Madam Woo said. Marius couldn't believe the tiny woman remembered them after all these years. Her face showed no special recognition as she led them upstairs, but Marius was almost sure he heard her say, "You stayed together. I win bet with my brother."

"What?"

She turned and smiled. "You'll like the patio – it's still quiet."

They both ordered the house special, twice-cooked chicken with steamed rice. When the waiter left, Marius watched Rachel play with her tea cup.   After so many months of only phone conversations, it felt strange to be sitting across from her again. He took in every detail of her face and was relieved to see her looking well.   But her eyes were troubled. They would only hold his for a few seconds before darting away, leaving him more convinced than ever that he had been right to come.

During his flight, Marius told himself he would skip any weak prelude and confront her directly. Immediately. Now that he sat across from her, his bravado failed him. So far they had talked about traffic and the weather. He had asked about Danny and learned that he was spending the evening with his father. Something in Rachel's expression changed when she mentioned Craig, but Marius wasn't sure how to interpret it. When their food came, it was as good as he remembered, though they both left it mostly uneaten. The waiter brought more tea and Rachel asked about the case.

Marius cleared his throat.

"Have you ever come across Paquime in your research?"

"Paquime," she repeated. "It sounds familiar."

"It was a thirteenth-century Pueblo city built in a remote part of Chihuahua."

"I remember now. It's an archaeology site, isn't it?"

Marius nodded. "When the Hohokam and Anasazi were disappearing up north and the Toltecs were giving way to the fledgling Aztecs, Paquime was somehow thriving in the middle of nowhere."

"The dig shows cultural advancement, right?"

"Yes. The city is fascinating, I gather. The structures were made of earth and some seven stories high in their day. They had a sophisticated potable water system that ran from canals, but also traditional ball courts and ceremonial mounds like the Aztecs."

"Ceremonial? As in sacrificial?"

"Exactly." He sipped his tea. "The most essential of which were shaped like a snake, a beheaded turkey and a cross."

"A cross?"

"Set up to indicate cardinal directions."

"Like a compass rose."

"Yes. And the snake-shaped mound was presumably dedicated to the Feathered Serpent deity."

"Quetzalcoatl. What about the turkey?"

Marius shook his head. "I don't know. But Paquime also had a T-shaped ball court used for religious ceremonies. Archaeologists have discovered graves at each end. Here's the point – the north grave entombed a woman whose feet were ritualistically severed."

Rachel stilled. "Like Libby's. Any association with Tezcatlipoca?"

"No. I thought your ASU resource might be able to help. What I did learn is that other artifacts suggest the Paquime venerated Quetzalcoatl more than any other god." He paused. "But another deity, Tlaloc, apparently was worshipped through the sacrifice of young people. They have found numerous graves dedicated to him holding the bones of adolescents."

Rachel put down her cup and dug out her phone.

"I'm texting Dr. Estefan with questions about Paquime, the turkey and Tlaloc," she said. "Maybe she'll know if there's a connection to Tezcat."

Marius paid the bill while Rachel finished her message. As they left, Madam Woo called, "Come again, okay?" Marius waved.

They turned and walked toward the lake.

"I was glad to see *Madam Woo's* is still open," he said.

"Well, reopened," Rachel said. "After they cleared up that health code violation."

"What?"

"Just kidding." She nudged him with her shoulder, grinning.

Marius smiled, relieved for a normal moment. He twisted the slip from his fortune cookie. It read: *Don't ask, don't say. Everything lies in silence.*

As they reached the water's edge, he decided to ignore the warning. He reached for Rachel's hand.

"Rachel, why am I here?"

Her eyes darted away, toward the black water where a reflection of the Mill Avenue Bridge pulsed against the wind. "To talk about the case."

"That's not it." He moved closer. "You know why, but I'm still in the dark. Something happened that you don't want to talk about."

"Marius, I'm fine. Really."

"You're not getting off that easy." He hooked his thumb back toward the restaurant. "I hardly know what I just ate. I don't know how much the bill was or which credit card I used to pay for it. I don't remember what we talked about. *Querida...* you have to talk to me."

"I'm sorry." Rachel's eyes met his, wet and sparkling under the park lights. She was beautiful as ever, but the stress of the past two weeks showed in the shadows under her eyes. It reminded him of their first reunion last year, when she was so changed by life and circumstance. Fear washed over him, deep and raw.

"Talk to me, Rachel," he said again, touching her hand. "Tell me what's happened."

She drew in a deep breath and let it out. Her voice was low. A gust of wind might have obscured it. Instead, Marius heard each word like a shard of glass.

"Craig has asked for reconciliation."

His heart twisted in his chest. Of all the scenarios that had run through his mind, he hadn't expected this. He cleared his throat, finding his voice. "And you're considering this?"

"I don't…"

Her pause was too long. Marius stepped back, the white heat of pain pulsing in his ears. "That's what this is about? You've spent two weeks trying to talk yourself into this?"

"Marius, that's not—"

"Rachel, think about this, please." He took her hands again. "Maybe you choose to forget, but I can't. When we met in Creel last spring, you seemed broken to me – a shadow of the woman you once were. But I was wrong. You were as strong as ever. Strong enough to drag yourself away from the wreckage—"

"Marius—"

"Now you're considering running back in? He broke your heart, Rachel—"

"So did you." She pulled her hands from his grasp. "How dare you … preach to me about wreckage? You left me behind all those years ago and never bothered looking back to see what kind of damage you had done."

"I never did what he did."

"No, you only lied to me about who you were." Rachel pointed south, toward campus. "Do you remember our last fight? Not a mile from here? I felt everything slipping away from us and begged you to move here permanently. I knew I was losing you."

Marius rubbed his temple.

"You accused me of trying to change you – to *Americanize* you." Her voice was thick with pain. "Do you know how I felt, watching you walk away without a fight?"

Marius nodded silently. He remembered the argument painfully well. That same morning his DEA handler had chewed him out for having no new leads, ignoring Marius's suspicion that dealers had gotten wind of their presence on campus and temporarily aborted all operations.

"Where's your work ethic?" Agent Johnson had asked. "I'm so sick of this lazy Mexican attitude that any job worth doing is worth doing slowly."

When it turned out that Marius was right, the investigation was cancelled, though he received no apology. Instead, the DEA pulled his visa and gave him 72 hours to leave the country.

Rachel couldn't have known that her innocent attempt at keeping him in Arizona would trigger his anger, too closely resembling – if only in his mind – the attitude of his handler. He wished he could explain all of this to her now, but decided to stop passing the blame. He had been young and headstrong, yes, but he shouldn't have been so simplistic as to lay the guilt of one bigot at her feet – or even at the feet of the country she loved. Instead, he cleared his throat and told her the part.of the story that was no less the truth.

"I knew we were losing each other," he said. "It felt inevitable. I picked a fight and walked away, convinced I was doing you a favor."

"How?"

"If you hated me, it would be easier to move on. I was a liar, Rachel. We both know it now – I knew it then. I told myself you would find someone else to love – an American, like you. Someone your family would love too."

Rachel's eyes widened. She stared at him for a moment. "Coward," she finally whispered. She turned to walk away.

Marius went after her, reaching for her hand. "Rachel, wait."

She shook him off, but turned around, her face flushed with pain. "So are you satisfied? Your plan worked. I found someone else, didn't I? Craig was exactly the kind of man you wished on me." She laughed, but it was an unhappy sound. "And my father loved him. How about that? He still does, in fact. No one would be happier if I took Craig back."

The torrent raging inside him instantly stilled.

"*If.* You mean…"

"I have no intention of reconciling with Craig, Marius." Rachel's voice was bitter. "But yes, I've struggled. For Danny's sake, but also for my own. I'm trying to understand what forgiveness really means – how long it takes, how total it should be, how I should feel afterward."

She blinked, but couldn't stop the tears. "Because I do forgive him, but it isn't enough. It isn't enough to make me love him again."

His heart twisted. "Why couldn't you tell me this?"

She shook her head. "I don't know. Maybe because I kept asking myself why it felt so different to forgive you, even when I was still hurt by your deception – when I was still afraid that the man I was falling in love with again was nothing but an illusion. A cover story."

"*Raquel.*" It was a whisper, a plea.

"I'm still afraid." She took a step backward. "I've tried to tell myself it's too late for us. I know it has to be over—"

"No, Rachel." His voice was hoarse. He pulled her toward him. "It's not over. I love you – it will never be over!"

He kissed her. His heart felt like it would burst from his ribcage, begging for contact with hers. His hands moved to the nape of her neck, his thumbs to her cheekbones, reveling in her beauty by touch, no longer jealous of his eyes. Rachel's face was wet with tears. He kissed them away and held her closer still, chasing away her fears, refusing to give heed to his own. It didn't matter now, he told himself. With Rachel in his arms, he knew he could leap over any border that separated them. Whatever obstacles might stand in their way would be eagerly forfeited.

Wind glanced off the lake and swirled around them, lifting her hair to create a cocoon – a small universe where only two existed. It lasted only a moment, but Marius willed it toward infinity. Life would never be the same.

"Marius," she murmured. Her cell phone rang and the wind stilled. She touched his face before stepping away to take her call. Cool lake air encircled him, chasing away her warmth.

"Mueller," Rachel said. After a moment, she frowned, looking up at Marius. "What? When? No. You were right. Keep him there. I'll call you back."

She lowered her phone.

"What is it?"

"Agent Cruces," she said slowly. "He was just arrested at the New Mexico border, trying to leave the country with a young woman hidden in his truck."

39

"TELL ME," Marius said. He squeezed her hand as they walked briskly back toward her car.

"I knew something was going on," she said. "I asked Agent Hughes to keep an eye on him."

Marius paused slightly between steps, but otherwise showed no displeasure.

"Where are we going?" he asked.

"I need to go home and grab some things from my office. And an overnight bag. We could drive or fly – I'll have to check with SAC Devlin." She stopped, checking her watch. "I need to ask Craig to keep Danny over the weekend. Maybe they'll be back before we leave so I can say goodbye."

"Rachel, wait." He squeezed her hand. Even as she tried to process shocking news, his touch sent a jolt of acute joy through her heart.

"What are you thinking?" Marius asked, his expression searching. "That Johnny is the Copper Canyon Killer?"

She stopped walking. "I think we have to consider it. Don't you?"

"Rachel—"

"We know the killer is from Chihuahua – so is Cruces. He has the ability to easily cross the border – something that is plausible for a man in law enforcement. His profile has always suggested a close interest in police matters."

Marius was shaking his head. "No. Rachel, he's been in Mexico City with me for years – not wandering around the Copper Canyon."

"You've watched him constantly? You're telling me he's never gone out of town?"

"Of course not," he said evenly. "But I know Johnny. This isn't him."

"We don't always know people like we think we do," Rachel said. "And there are stories about Cruces. The woman he killed—"

"Who told you about that?" he asked sharply.

Rachel wished she had held her tongue. "Trent," she admitted.

"That was a long time ago," Marius said quietly. "And since only a handful of people know the truth, I doubt Trent could have given you any accurate details."

"Of course not," she said. "I didn't put stock in it, Marius. I wouldn't have brought it up at all if not for this. You're sure it couldn't be related?"

"Absolutely."

"What about his visit to Arizona over the New Year?"

His frown deepened. "That also has nothing to do with the case."

She crossed her arms. "Are you going to explain any of this? Or is some kind of guy-pact involved that's more important than catching a killer?"

"I've tried to talk with you about it for a couple of weeks now, Rachel, but you weren't answering your phone, were you?"

She played with her keys. His frown gave way to a reluctant smile. Hooking his arm around her shoulders, he pulled her toward the car. "Come on. You drive. I'll call your Agent Hughes in New Mexico and see what else I can learn about the arrest. Then I'll tell you the whole story."

ᙍ

MARIUS STOOD in Rachel's living room, looking at Danny's photo on the fireplace mantel. He had grown, he noticed, looking older than the wallet-sized image Rachel had shown him last spring.

"Nice house," he said as Rachel returned to the room.

She made a face. "Thank you. But it's not exactly me, is it?"

248

"No." His eyes swept from left to right. "The furniture, maybe."

She sat down on the sofa. "That was the compromise. Craig loved the house, I picked the furniture. As it turned out, I ended up with both."

Marius sat down next to her, his thoughts briefly flickering to the day Carmen moved out. It felt like another lifetime – another man's dream that was lost. He took Rachel's hand, intent on changing her perspective soon.

"What did Hughes tell you?" she asked.

"Johnny tried to cross the border at Santa Teresa. When the border agent swept the truck with a flashlight and asked him to remove a tarp from the jump seat, Johnny became belligerent – 'throwing his position around,' according to Hughes. Eventually, they persuaded him to cooperate and that's when they found her."

Rachel winced. "Was she bound? Drugged?"

"No," Marius said. "She was hiding, *querida*, trying to cross the border without detection. She's his daughter."

"His daughter!"

"The woman Johnny killed – the one Trent told you about – that was her mother."

"Now I'm totally confused."

"Johnny has always seemed … untrusting to you, yes?"

"Yes." She frowned. "He was always polite, of course, but he doesn't generally like Americans, does he?"

Marius shook his head. "Johnny worked for the federal police in Chihuahua before he and I met. He was honest, but careful too when dealing with corruption. Being openly opposed to the drug cartel's influence is a death sentence – immediate and brutal. He chose his battles, but he let many go unchallenged and saw lives lost as a result. He tried to see the final picture, but it hardened him.

"When CIA operatives working covertly in the area became aware of his sympathies, he began sharing information with them, passing it through an undercover American agent who called herself Doris Vasquez. He didn't know her real name, but fell in love all the same. They carried on a secret affair for several years."

"What happened?"

"She wasn't what she pretended to be," Marius said. "She played games with him. They saw each other infrequently – often many months separated their meetings. They fought as often as anything else, I gather.

Johnny told me she was like an addiction. He knew she was bad for him, but he couldn't give her up.

"He saw things more clearly after her death. Evidence of her connection to the cartels was never in keeping with their investigations. She was working for them, it turned out, and the lover of *Patrone Orjuilla's* son. Johnny learned about one of their rendezvous and broke in on them. When Orjuilla reached for his weapon, Johnny was already firing his." Marius paused. "She must have loved Orjuilla – she jumped in front of him and ended up dying in Johnny's arms."

"How awful."

"The federal police covered up what they could – made it look like a lover's triangle and managed to scapegoat a *passadore* who was killed the same day. They protected Johnny so he could keep his job." Marius shook his head. "How Trent found out is beyond me."

"What about his daughter?"

"After Doris's death, he learned she was American Indian – not Hispanic as she claimed. When you told me about his visit to the Apache reservation, I suspected it had something to do with her, but when I asked him about it in January, he wouldn't talk. Just asked me to trust him. My guess is that he only recently learned of his daughter's existence and took the opportunity to do some digging."

"It's amazing to think he didn't know – all those years."

"I know." Marius nodded soberly. "Johnny has no family. He's often regretted being too old to start one. Heaven and Earth couldn't keep him away once he found out. She must be about seventeen years old."

"I'd like to know how he located her."

"So would I. Agent Hughes said he won't talk to them – he wants to talk to me instead. All he said is that she's been abused by her guardians and that, as his child, she is a legal Mexican citizen and has the right to return home with him."

"Does he have proof of paternity?"

"Johnny's nothing if not thorough. If he believes she's his daughter, there's proof somewhere."

"What has the girl said?"

"The same as Johnny. She wants to live with her father."

Rachel stared out the window for a minute. Finally she stood up. Marius took her hand.

"Where are you going?"

"We still need to make travel arrangements."

"Tomorrow." He pulled her down on his lap and brushed her hair from her face. "Johnny's not going anywhere. He can sit in the tank overnight for doing this the bull-headed way."

"Marius…"

"In the meantime." He kissed her jawbone. "I can think of a better way to occupy ourselves."

Several pleasant moments later, Rachel's cell phone rang. Marius groaned as she scooted out of reach and answered it on speakerphone.

"Professor Estefan?" she said.

"Yes, hello."

"I have Agent Suarez of the Federal Police with me here," she said.

"*Buenos noches*, Agent Suarez."

"Good evening."

"I got your message, Agent Mueller," the professor said. "I've never been to Paquime, but have read much about it, of course."

"What can you tell us about Tlaloc?"

"He was the god of rain, lightning, thunder and fertility. He was vengeful, using floods and droughts to punish humans."

"And subject to human sacrifice?" Marius said.

"Yes, of course, like most of their deities. But you asked about a connection to Tezcatlipoca."

"Yes. Is there one?" Rachel asked.

"Quite. If Tlaloc ever had an enemy, it was Tezcatlipoca. Tlaloc was once married to Xochiquetzal, the goddess of love, beauty, motherhood. But Tezcatlipoca seduced her away from him – or kidnapped her, depending on the stories."

"I remember that story now," Rachel said.

"I wonder if our Tezcatlipoca would have a negative association with Paquime, or a positive one," Marius mused.

"Either is possible," Dr. Estefan said. "That might be a question better asked of a psychologist, hmm? He might hate the place – seeing it as the antithesis of his existence – honor shown to all that he is not. Or he might covet it for himself."

"One of his victims was buried in a manner similar to a Paquime grave," Rachel said.

"Then there you go. Look for similar patterns and you may find more graves."

"Thank you for your time, Dr. Estefan," Rachel said, "especially on a Friday night."

"Oh, but we haven't talked about the turkey."

"That's right." Rachel looked at Marius, who was smiling at the doctor's affronted voice. "I had forgotten him. It doesn't seem like a very powerful symbol when compared with jaguars and fertility gods."

"No, I suppose our modern mind thinks little of a turkey, but you know it has been revered in many cultures. Even in America. Benjamin Franklin suggested it as a better symbol for our country than the bald eagle, calling the eagle 'a bird of bad moral character.'"

Marius laughed. Rachel shot him a grave look, but couldn't hide the amusement from her eyes.

"The turkey-shaped ceremonial mound at Paquime was beheaded, so to speak," Rachel continued. "Did I mention that?"

"Not a compliment to the turkey, then, is it?" Dr. Estefan asked. "It raises possibilities when considered alongside your *tonalpohualli* research. Since we know the Paquime venerated Quetzalcoatl, we should first note that he is the lord of nines on the sacred calendar. And on the ninth day, the turkey is considered volatile."

"Volatile?" Marius asked.

"A wild card. Inconstant, transient. He's a creature to watch warily because you can't predict what he'll do."

"Okay. What does that tell us?"

"Well – perhaps I should have mentioned this first – Tezcatlipoca has another *nagual* – or alias, as you like to call it…"

"Aside from Tepeyollotl?"

"Yes. The jeweled fowl – Chalchihuihtotolin."

"Say that again?"

Dr. Estefan said it slowly, then spelled it.

"This *nagual* is a sign of powerful sorcery. Tezcatlipoca is said to have the power to tempt people toward self-destruction. But as the jeweled fowl, he can help them make atonement, absolve them of guilt and overcome their fate."

"Does he rule a *trecena* on the calendar?"

"Oh, yes. He rules *Atl*, or water. I tried to use the online calendar to calculate when it occurs next, but the website is down for maintenance."

"Can you use the manual calendar?"

"I can try, but it will take time – and I can't guarantee my accuracy."

"Thank you for your help, Dr. Estefan. I'll check the on-line calendar again in the morning, see if it's back up."

"Happy to oblige, Agent Mueller."

Rachel hung up the phone and frowned. "I've been working under the assumption that the killer would stick to his MO and only abduct during *Mazatl* – the first week in July."

"And now you think perhaps he's donned this new unpronounceable alias and will change his course?"

"We have to consider it." She sat back. "I wish that website was working so we could know when *Atl* falls."

"Come here." Marius pulled her back into his arms. "You've already condemned and exonerated Agent Cruces tonight…"

"His own fault…" She rested her head against his shoulder.

"So the chances of catching any other killers before the day is out are pretty slim." He moved her hair, kissing her neck.

She closed her eyes. "Yes – I suppose that would be too much to expect."

"And I'm guessing the hockey game is almost over, meaning Danny and his father will be returning soon."

"Yes."

"And I should probably be gone by then."

She touched his jaw, searching his face. "Marius…"

"Do you think we'll get along?" he asked. "When the time is right to meet?"

She leaned up, kissing him. "He'll love you, like I do."

Her phone rang again five minutes later.

"Are you always this popular?" Marius asked.

Rachel rolled her eyes then picked up the phone.

"Craig? What is it? Is the game already over?"

40

"GIVE ME your car keys." Marius opened the passenger door, guiding her through it. "Sit down. You're shaking like a leaf."

Rachel's laugh was hollow. "I told you he's good at hide and seek. I didn't tell you he likes to play in public places."

Marius started the engine and backed out of the garage.

"He's done this before?"

She nodded. "At the zoo once. At church and the park. I thought he'd gotten over it."

"Wait a second."

He put the car in park and ran back in the house to grab Danny's picture from the fireplace mantel. He handed it to Rachel.

"We won't need it," he said.

Twenty-five minutes later, they exited the freeway in Glendale, just past the football stadium. Rachel pointed to the right. Marius stopped at the security checkpoint and showed their IDs to the police officer.

"This is Special Agent Rachel Mueller," he said.

The officer pointed toward the arena. "They're waiting for you at the barricade in front."

"They haven't found him yet," Rachel said as they pulled away.

Marius nodded, gripping the wheel, speeding through the parking lot. Somehow he still believed everything would be better once they reached the arena.

Rachel jumped from the car before he pulled to a complete stop.

"Agent Mueller." She flashed her badge at the nearest officer. "Have they found my son?"

"Not yet, ma'am." He led them through the barricades and briskly toward the front of the arena. Curious onlookers had been contained between two enormous water fountains, content to be on the fringe of real-life drama.

"How long has he been missing?" Marius asked.

"Forty-three minutes," the officer said. "A second sweep of the building should be complete within the next five minutes."

Inside the arena's main concourse a uniformed security manager and police sergeant were waiting to usher them into the arena's security suite – a large room filled with computers, phones and monitors. A quick glance told Marius arena employees were still searching seat by seat. He checked his watch.

"When were the police called?" He handed Danny's photo to the police sergeant.

"Ten minutes after Mr. Mueller reported him missing." Sergeant Kelly handed the photo to an assistant, who carried it over to a flatbed scanner.

A stocky man with sandy hair crossed the room toward Rachel.

"Who are you?" he asked Marius.

"Craig, this is Agent Suarez," Rachel said. "He's here with me." She turned back to Sergeant Kelly. "Tell me everything."

"A Code Adam was called at 10:22 when Mr. Mueller reported Danny missing. We followed procedure. Every employee from management to custodial began searching from the point of loss—"

"Which was?"

He pointed to an arena map on the wall. "A men's restroom – located here, adjacent to the team shop."

"An announcement was made?"

"Yes. But the game let out some fifteen minutes earlier." He glanced briefly toward Craig. "The concourse is a noisy place."

"And the exits?"

"All security and alternate exits were electronically closed and alarmed," said Coleman, the security manager. "Guards at the public exits were doubled up. We placed Mr. Mueller at the closest exit to watch for the boy."

"He just wasn't there," Craig said. "I still say he's in the building –hiding behind a garbage can, or a pallet of peanuts."

Sergeant Kelly's walkie-talkie squawked. The second sweep had concluded. "Still no sign of him," he said.

"Can you still broadcast throughout the arena?" Marius asked. "If Danny hears his mother's voice—"

"Good idea." Coleman led Rachel to a chair and handed her the microphone. "Press here," he said.

"Danny." Rachel swallowed. "Danny, it's Mom. I'm here at the arena and worried about you. Please come out onto the concourse and find a police officer... you're not in trouble." Her voice cracked. "We just want to take you home."

She stood and handed the microphone back to Coleman, who wagged his walkie-talkie. "We'll know immediately if he's found."

Rachel nodded. "What about the other Westgate buildings?"

"Code Adam was called throughout the shopping center as soon as our initial sweep came up empty," Sergeant Kelly said. "We have several officers and security guards sweeping from the arena north, through the restaurants and shops, toward the theaters. If he's still at Westgate, we'll find him."

If. Marius's stomach lurched at the weight of such a small word.

Rachel turned to Craig. "How did this happen?"

"Danny had to go to the bathroom late in the third period. I walked him to the stall. When I was done, I waited by the door. He couldn't have left without seeing me."

"Does the bathroom have two exits or one?" she asked the security manager.

"Two."

Craig ran his hands through his hair. "I didn't know that then. While I was waiting, Jack Gorman walked by – remember him? We chatted for a few minutes about this case we've been dealing with and before I knew it, the game was over. It was as if a floodgate had opened. I went back into the bathroom and called for Danny to hurry up, but the stall was empty. Then I went back out to the concourse and looked around. I asked the guy at the ice cream stand and the lady in the team shop. I even went back to our seats to see if he had gone that way." He shook his head. "He wasn't there. I came back to the bathroom and looked again. That's when I tracked down a security guard."

"How many minutes passed between the time you saw Danny go into the stall and when you reported him missing?"

He crossed his arms. "You don't have to sound indignant, Rachel. You know about his little games."

"Yes, but clearly this isn't hide-and-seek, and we don't have time for your hurt feelings. How long?"

"Probably twenty minutes."

Rachel pressed her lips together. "We need to trust the search," she said after a moment. "Two sweeps through the arena means Danny probably got out." She fumbled in her pocket for a business card, which she handed to the sergeant. "Add detail to the Westgate search. Call for back up if necessary. And call the Bureau's field office for standby readiness, should Danny not be found on site." She took a deep breath. "His data is already on file and ready for NCIC."

"Rachel..." Craig seemed ready to reach for her hand, but her expression stopped him.

She pointed to the monitors. "Craig and I will view video playback – we can spot him better than anyone. Split the feeds between us for better coverage. Can you have them set to start about 9:45?"

The security chief pointed toward two seats. "Sit here. Monica will start the playback whenever you're ready."

Rachel took the first chair and focused on the screen while Craig sat down next to her. When her cell phone rang, she handed it to Marius.

"Can you take care of this?" she asked.

Monica pressed play.

∾

"THERE! GO back ten – fifteen seconds on camera 37."

It was their second viewing of the video feed. Rachel had exchanged camera views with Craig just seconds before. Her heart lurched in her chest. "That's him. Walking out the north entrance."

Marius peered over her shoulder. "He's wearing a hockey mask!" He turned to the security officer. "Surely you don't let children pass through the doors with their faces covered like that."

He frowned. "Well, I—"

"We can't see his expression," Marius said. "For all we know he could have duct tape over his mouth!"

Craig squinted at the screen. "That can't be him – he doesn't have a hockey mask."

"It is – look," Rachel said. "That's the way he walks. He circles like a puppy. Those are his jeans, his shoes…" She turned to Monica. "What's the time stamp?"

"9:47," Monica said.

Rachel looked sharply at Craig. "That doesn't match what you said."

"What?"

"Code Adam was called at 10:22. You said he had been missing twenty minutes when you talked to security." She tapped the monitor. "That's Danny, Craig. He's leaving the building at 9:47!"

Marius turned to Sergeant Kelly. "Alert your searchers. Danny has been identified leaving the building at 9:47, thirty-five minutes before the Code Adam was called."

Craig stood up and pushed back his chair. "I…" He let out a deep breath. "I lost track of time I guess. Danny was mad, and I had to race after him just to keep up."

"What? Why was he mad?"

"I got on to him. He was fidgeting, trying to stand on his seat, asking for more snacks – he wouldn't even watch the game. When I caught him fiddling with my cell phone, I lost it a little. I told him to knock it off."

"Do you realize what a difference fifteen minutes can make?" Rachel asked. "He could be anywhere by now! Perimeters weren't even set up then."

"He's just hiding," Craig insisted.

Marius looked at Rachel. "You need to think about initiating an Amber Alert."

"That's for abduction cases," Rachel said.

"Are we still working under the assumption that Danny's movements are voluntary?" asked the sergeant.

Marius spoke softly. "The hockey mask, *querida*. Someone gave it to him."

Rachel blinked and looked away. Only fifteen minutes had passed since they reached the arena. It felt like hours. Marius squeezed her shoulder and shifted to look at the monitor.

"It looks like he's with the man to his right. See? He's looking up at him. Play it back again."

Monica rewound the recording and played it again.

"Yes. He's talking to him," Marius said.

Rachel leaned closer. "I can't see his face. He's wearing a ball cap low over his eyes."

Craig leaned in. "It looks like Victor,"

"No." Rachel shook her head. "Victor couldn't come tonight – that's why I called you. He had his charity thing."

Marius looked at her. "Does it look like him?"

"Maybe. But..." She turned to Craig. "Maybe Danny was calling him when he was fiddling with your phone."

"Why would he?"

"Because he was upset. Don't overthink the logic of a second grader, Craig. Maybe he called Victor to come get him." She was silent for a moment. "No, that doesn't make sense. He would have called me."

Marius handed Rachel her phone. She dialed Victor's number, but when it went straight to voicemail, she hung up.

Marius was still staring at the monitor. "With everyone wearing white, it's hard to tell one person from another."

Coleman nodded. "It's mayhem during playoffs. I understand the draw of a white-out, but I've got to say, it's not really smart from a security standpoint."

Rachel frowned. Something tugged at her memory as she imagined crowds of white-clad fans pouring through the concourse. Her heart began to pound.

"Well that's definitely Victor," Craig said. He tapped the monitor. "Look. He's limping as he passes through the door."

"Victor doesn't limp," Rachel said.

"He does when he's moving quickly," Craig insisted. "It's his foot – I saw it once in the gym locker room."

Rachel's ears began to buzz.

"Of course, when the fans are in their seats – it's amazing to see all that white," Coleman continued, undeterred by the changing conversation. "It's so loud – and the way everyone moves – it's like a snowstorm."

"A snowstorm?"

The room began to spin. Rachel felt like she was far away, but she remembered a woman's voice.

It was noisy – like the sound of roaring water, she had said. *And there was ice, smooth as glass in the middle of a field of snow.*

Marius grabbed Craig's shoulder. "What did you say about his foot?"

"It's disgusting." Craig made a face. "He's got a special orthotic to make up for it, but without it," he shook his head. "It looks as if someone took a huge bite out of his foot."

The world faded away. Rachel fell to her knees.

41

AN APB and Amber Alert were issued within minutes, effectively closing down the U.S.-Mexico border. Car-by-car searches caused mile-long backups at check points all across New Mexico, Arizona and California. Broadcast teams were dispatched, airing Danny's picture alongside speculation well past the evening news.

But it was all too late.

Victor crossed the border at Douglas just minutes before the alert went through, driving a van full of sleepy orphans. A border patrol agent admitted that their head count had been perfunctory. The numbers of kids matched the produced passports and visas. Familiar with Victor and his charity for their frequent passes through that checkpoint, they had seen nothing to arouse their suspicions. Within the hour, the van was found at an Agua Prieta orphanage. All children were accounted for but one – presumably one who was traded for Danny and sold somewhere in Arizona. Victor and Danny were gone and the orphanage director tightlipped about their time of departure, mode of transportation and direction of travel.

"Lock him up," Marius told his Sonoran counterpart by phone. "He's clearly involved – though probably only for the money changing hands."

He hung up and turned to Special Agent in Charge Devlin, who had arrived at the arena within half an hour of the APB. "I think we've ripped open your child-trafficking case," he said grimly. "That orphanage was the only one missing from Agent Mueller's list – supplied by Victor Katseli. I thought it was a clerical oversight."

"This is how he took victims across the border," Devlin said.

"And why he chose such petite ones – so they could be drugged with Ketamine and passed off as sleeping children."

"I'd still like to know how he reached the border within an hour and a half of Danny's disappearance from the arena," Devlin said.

"Time will tell. Right now, we need to find him."

"You think he's returned to the Copper Canyon?"

"Yes, I do." Marius tapped his foot impatiently. "But we need to check the vicinity of Paquime, to rule it out."

He walked away, dialing his phone with almost enough force to break the screen. He was furious – with border agents, Craig, Cruces – but mostly with himself. He glanced toward Rachel, sitting numb and still next to Craig, who was violently gripping her hand, his own eyes red-rimmed with shock.

"Agent Hughes," he said curtly into the phone. "Wake up Cruces. I need to speak to him."

He hung up five minutes later, his frustration mounting. Rachel caught his eye.

"What is it?"

Marius crouched in front of her. "Before Cruces was arrested, he tracked down that lead he was following on a woman matching Yala's description. She died a few years after moving to the states – suicide after a miscarriage." He took a deep breath. "Her son was adopted by her new husband. Erik Katseli."

"Victor's father." Rachel's eyes dilated, then darkened – reflecting her own private hell – swirling with distractions, lies and betrayal.

"He's taking him to the canyon," she said.

"Yes."

"When do we leave?"

SAC Devlin and Assistant Director Foster were adamantly against Rachel's involvement in the search.

"Emotions counteract judgments, waste time – are more likely to hurt our chances of a live recovery." Devlin's eyes were grave. "The first forty-eight hours—"

"Respectfully," Marius interrupted, "this is an exception. You haven't seen the canyon. It's over 25,000 square miles—"

"Our search will not cover the entire system, Agent Suarez."

He shook his head. "We spent days in just Tararecua Canyon, and only saw a fraction of it – with guides. It's rugged. Dangerous."

"Why would that make me want to put my distraught, distracted agent in the mix?"

"Because she's been there. These other agents are going in blind. Her experience shaves precious time off the search. She also knows this killer – how he thinks, how he's behaved in the past. She's the only one who can do that."

"She can share her information."

"An accurate debriefing would take days. We have hours at best."

Devlin relented, but insisted Rachel stay with Marius.

"Consider carefully – and objectively, agent, when or if you need to bench her. None of us – least of all Mueller – wants an emotional mistake costing us her boy's life."

Marius took the warning seriously. With FBI, PFM and local police involvement, they would have about two hundred members of law enforcement searching for Danny. It wasn't enough.

And they didn't have time to waste.

When Marius answered Rachel's cell phone at the arena, Professor Estefan was calling.

"I calculated Atl," she told Marius breathlessly. "It began last Thursday. Today is Atl-9, tomorrow Atl-10. Remember, nine belongs to Quetzalcoatl, ten to Tezcatlipoca—"

"Thanks – I'll call you back for details," Marius told her. "We're in the middle of a missing-child situation right now."

At that moment Marius had been sure, just like Craig, that Danny would be recovered soon, hiding nearby, his game gone sour and ending in fear of punishment. There would be plenty of time later to hear Professor Estefan's analysis of the Aztec calendar.

How could he have known the details he considered too trivial to mention then were now those he grasped at like a life line, desperate to stop the icy chills flurrying like snow in the pit of his stomach? He called Dr. Estefan back on the way to the airport, waking her from sleep, he presumed, well after midnight.

"Tell me more about *Atl*," he said. "About yesterday, today – anything that might be significant to Tezcatlipoca."

"*Atl* is ruled by Chalchihuihtotolin – Tezcatlipoca's turkey *nagual*," she reminded him. "It's regarded as a period of instability, accidents and coincidences. It's said to plunge and climb unexpectedly between all good and all bad – rapture and terror."

Marius swallowed a knot, instantly replaying the events of the day in his mind.

"During *Atl*, the priest warrior is advised to perfect the art of shapeshifting—"

"Like from jaguar to turkey?"

"Yes, and today – well yesterday, I guess – was the daysign *Ollin* – good for transmutation," she said. "The *tonalpohualli* warns believers to mimic the form of water during *Atl* to avoid becoming a target. It says a pure heart will cast no reflection in the smoking mirror."

"I have no idea what that means."

"Think about what it might mean to the killer, Agent Suarez, not to you."

He shook his head, too muddled to think clearly about anything right now. "Yesterday was *Ollin*, you said. What about today?"

"*Tecpatl* – the stone knife," she said gravely. "Today is especially auspicious. It is Chalchihuihtotolin's day *and trecena* – coinciding with Tezcatlipoca's day number – ten."

"Like a slot machine jackpot," Marius said grimly.

"A day of trials, tribulation. It tests one's character and stamina. Tecpatl warns that the mind and soul must be sharpened like a glass blade, cutting to the marrow of truth."

Marius's heart stilled.

"Glass blade?" he repeated numbly. "Like obsidian?"

"Yes, that's likely."

He didn't need to ask anything more. Cruces had learned something else in New Mexico – a detail Marius didn't share with Rachel. The knife craftsman knew where their glass chip had come from – it was a blade he sold several years ago to an enthusiastic young collector.

"I made another for him just last month," he said. "He wanted an exact replica, down to every detail. That's something I'm not likely to forget."

ଓ

MARIUS WAS SEATED seven rows behind Rachel and Craig on the plane bound for Chihuahua. If he shifted toward the aisle, he could see her better – but it didn't matter. She had barely moved during the flight. Her shoulders were rigid, tight with pain and fear. Craig's head leaned toward hers repeatedly, but as far as Marius could tell, she was not responding.

She's shutting down, he thought.

Maybe, for the moment, at least, that was a good thing.

But an hour into the flight, she moved – abandoning her seat so quickly, Marius didn't have time to push aside the canyon maps he had been studying before she reached him.

Her eyes searched his wildly. "I can't…I don't know what…Marius, what do I do?"

Her face crumbled and Marius was up and steadying her – holding her tight as he lowered her to the empty seat next to his.

She shook silently against his chest, great empty sobs reaching through the darkened plane for some measure of comfort. There was none to give.

He held her tighter. "We'll land soon," he said.

She leaned back against the seat, her lips moving in silent prayer. Marius willed himself to seem strong and able. Then he was praying too – for sharpness and strength to see them both through the day to come.

"Danny had to use an inhaler twice last winter." Her voice was low and tight. "Albuterol, for croup." She turned toward Marius. "What happens if he has breathing trouble in the canyon? What if he falls? Or if he's bitten by a snake? Would Victor leave him helpless?"

"Rachel, don't do this to yourself. It's not your fault."

She shook her head, either not hearing or refusing to agree. Marius pulled her against his shoulder and whispered into her hair, willing her strength for the hours to come. Eventually she stilled and Marius returned to his prayers. Even if she slept for only a few minutes, it would be a blessing. Marius knew he would not.

Still, when he closed his eyes his thoughts swam, settling unexpectedly on an image from his childhood – Michelangelo's *Pieta* in bloodless marble, a tribute to the aching pain of the mother who watched her guiltless Son's execution.

No.

He forced his eyes open. He wouldn't accept that.

The *tonalpohualli*'s message was clear. There would be no extended imprisonment this time. Victor Katseli planned to kill Danny within the next twenty-four hours.

Marius wasn't going to let that happen.

42

THE INCIDENT Command Center was teeming with agents by the time they reached Creel. Set up by the old lodge near Lake Arereco, it looked more like a military operation than a Search and Rescue base camp. Erected under canopies and managed by an FBI critical incident response group, the ICC was legally under the jurisdiction of the Mexican government. Unofficially, authority had been deferred to the Bureau. In an adjacent field, choppers rose and landed every few minutes, carrying searchers to various positions in the canyon where hasty searches were already underway.

The media had gotten wind of the search via reckless radio chatter, but were restricted to the Creel town plaza. Local police were working hard to maintain control and Bureau information officers were fielding questions, never veering from their official statement: The search for Victor Katseli and his captive, eight-year-old Danny Mueller, was a level one priority mission overseen by an international multi-agency task force.

Volunteer SAR workers from American and Mexican agencies were pouring in while local Tarahumara elders were supplying guides for every team. Luke Graham from the Houston FBI field office was acting as incident commander.

"Our theoretical search area is based on the suspect's last known position in Agua Prieta," Graham told Marius.

"New intel may broaden it," Marius said, handing over the report Agent Castillo had handed him as soon as they landed. "Katseli logged a flight plan at Glendale Municipal airport last night, lifting off in his father's Cessna at 10:15. He set down in Douglas forty-five minutes later."

"His father is a pilot," Rachel said. "Was he involved?"

"No, he was alone – and a licensed pilot himself. You didn't know?"

She shook her head numbly. "Danny was with him?"

Marius's throat knotted up. He squeezed Rachel's hand. "He appeared to be alone – but was carrying a travel golf bag."

Rachel moaned. Craig turned away, muttering expletives against a trembling fist.

"The plane is gone," Marius continued. "A car registered to the Agua Prieta orphanage was found at the Douglas airport. The director is telling Sonoran police that Katseli often borrowed his car – no questions asked – for a couple hundred dollars."

Marius turned to Graham. "There are landing strips nearby?"

Graham nodded. "A dirt strip outside El Tejabán, from what I hear. DEA tells me there are countless other spots drug runners use to take off and land that are well within our TSA. Helicopters are searching for signs of the plane, but this canyon..."

To his credit, Graham didn't let the canyon's size delay action. He handed out assignments as soon as hasty searchers returned, quickly sending his most skilled agents into areas around the gravesite, cave and mine shaft, asking for a seventy percent possibility of detection from each grid. Adjacent areas would also be heavily searched, with fewer teams working the perimeters – hoping for containment, if nothing else.

Marius and Rachel were teamed together per Devlin's instructions, and coded level three based on their lack of sleep and Rachel's personal stake. Still, Marius's marksmanship experience kept him at the perimeter of the hot zone. Their search grid was just east of the gravesite in an area plagued with steep arroyos, rocky peaks and plateaus.

Rachel moved to the front of the gathered agents and briefed them on Victor's profile. Her skin was ashen, but her voice was clear and strong, her words succinct, as if she weighed each second against their pressing need to be already in the canyon, searching.

As Rachel stepped back, Graham held up an eight-by-ten photo of Danny. "This is our motivation. This is why we will be observers, not merely searchers. This is why we will be smart and watchful. We will work quickly, but cautiously. We will stay free from injury. Stick to your search zones, work with your trackers and guides. Stay sharp and report findings quickly. Let's bring Danny home."

The agents dispersed, following their swift-footed Tarahumara guides toward the helipad and trails. Craig – asked to wait at base camp –pulled Rachel into a tight hug while Marius shouldered his pack and adjusted his rifle strap. He had already spoken to Graham about keeping Craig busy, for once feeling nothing but sympathy for him.

"*Vamanos,*" he said, turning to follow their guide. He was determined to find Danny within the hour, if only human will and fervent prayer would allow it.

ॐ

"IT'S TIME to check in."

"Five more minutes."

"No, we need to go now. We don't want them to stop looking for Danny and start looking for us. Let's go."

Rachel silently lowered her binoculars and followed him up the ridge. Marius kept his pace quick, offering her little to think about but keeping up. He had been task focused since they stepped off the helicopter, bordering on cruel for the past hour when the wild look in Rachel's eyes told him panic wasn't far off. They were already fifteen minutes late for their hourly check-in with base camp, which could only be accomplished by climbing to a high, bald patch of rock where the signal quality on his hand-held radio was strong enough to do the job. Even then, they were too many miles from base for direct communication and had to relay their message through a patrol.

Marius's heart hammered against his breast bone as they crested the hill. He unclipped the radio microphone from his shirt pocket and tried to steady his breath. His physical reaction had been similar at each check-in, his fear of hearing the death code overriding even his hope of better news. It was a detail he had kept from Rachel – any transmission including the phrase "red jacket" would mean all hope was lost – Danny had been found, but it was too late.

But this communication proved no different from the last. Marius received the same information he gave. Nothing had changed. It was four o'clock in the afternoon and no one had seen any trace of Danny or Victor.

Rachel's face was expressionless as she watched a chopper swing by in the distance, away and out of sight behind a ridge of pine trees. The constant drone of helicopters searching from the skies had provided a soundtrack to their day. It should have been comforting. Maybe it was the lateness of the hour that made it the opposite. It heightened Marius's sense of urgency, along with a desperate fear that their instincts had been wrong – that Victor had carried Danny to some unsearched jungle where he was free to do his worst without interference. When Marius saw Rachel's despondency, he knew she was following similar hellish circles. He steeled himself and pointed to a boulder.

"Sit and eat this." He handed her a protein bar. "We'll head back down in five minutes."

Marius turned away, hoping she wouldn't search his face. His thoughts kept settling on the clairvoyant woman's dream. Danny had been a seed, carried from the snow, then – what? Buried in a vast canyon, never to be found again? He shuddered, trying to shake off the image.

"I must have known on some level that it was Victor," Rachel told him as they descended from the cliff top, following their silent guide into a narrow slip canyon.

"How could you know?" The hollowness of her voice twisted his heart.

"I dreamed of him," she said. "After Trent shot Manny by the mining shack, I dreamed he shot Victor instead."

Marius remembered waking her from the nightmare – remembered her white face and shaking limbs. His jaw tightened. "You couldn't have known. I've compared the photos – they didn't look very much alike."

"They were identical twins."

"They were raised separately – one on a third world diet and no dental care, living on his own in this wilderness, exposed to the sun and elements – not to mention the changes mental deficiency can lend to a man's appearance."

"I must have seen something familiar," she insisted.

"Rachel—"

"If I had stopped then and thought about what it meant—"

"Stop." His tone was brusque. He picked up his speed. "Torturing yourself won't change things now. You need to focus on the trail."

They turned, dropping down into a place where the narrow canyon walls seemed to hem them in, weighed down by the shroud of late afternoon shadows.

Just another turn, Marius told himself. *One more ridge and we'll see Danny*.

43

"THERE. LOOK!"

Marius shifted his binoculars to the ridge above them, focusing on a place where the yucca and sycamores parted to reveal an old Tarahumara man waving his hand at them.

"José! Quickly!"

Their guide wasted no time scrambling toward him. Marius and Rachel quickened their pace, but couldn't keep up. By the time they reached the top of the trail, José was coming back.

"He saw a white child," he said.

"Danny!" Rachel gripped Marius's arm. "Where?"

"There." He pointed to the cliff wall on the other side of a deep ravine. "With a man – *el nieto de la bruja.*"

Marius's heart began to pound.

"Let's go."

Rachel was already picking her way along the trail, her eyes feverishly on the tree line to the west. Marius pulled out his map and studied it. Looking back at the cliff where the old man had stood, he suddenly realized where they were.

"Rachel, look at that peak – beyond the ridge." He pointed. "That's just southwest of Libby's grave."

Rachel lifted her binoculars. "We need to find a way over."

"Yes." Marius reached for his handheld. "And we need to call it in – let the searchers in that grid know he's coming their way."

But Marius couldn't raise a signal. "All the trees are interfering," he said.

José urged them forward. "There's the path."

A few minutes later, they emerged from the trees and the western ridge came into view again. While Marius studied the trail – narrowing ten meters farther along before plunging through several sharp switchbacks below – Rachel scanned the skyline.

Her intake of breath was sharp, audible.

"Danny!" Hope and fear echoed with his name.

Marius focused his binoculars on the neighboring ridge. His own breath caught. He saw Danny too, stumbling along a trail that ran parallel to the cliff. Prodding him along was a man who must be Victor, though his staccato appearance between trees made the hair stand up on Marius's neck. He was naked except for a loin covering, with dark paint streaked along his arms and face. His gait was quick, though – barefoot – he walked with a decided limp.

Marius reached out to steady Rachel. "He's alive," he said. His relief was quickly smothered by fresh fear. How would they reach him in time?

Rachel handed him the map, never taking her eyes off her son. Marius studied it quickly.

"He's not heading toward the gravesite," he said. "Unless this topo is wrong, there are no routes off the north side of that ridge. It's a dead end."

José pointed toward the north end of the ridge, which jutted out at a harsh angle. There, just beyond a thinning circle of pines, was a flat rock so perfectly level to the sky, it looked manmade.

"*Una mesa de los dioses.*" José's voice was tinged with awe and disgust.

A table of the gods.

"Marius." Rachel's voice was a tremulous plea, hovering between hysteria and paralysis.

He tried his radio again, but there was still no signal. Desperately, he looked at the trail below before scanning the other cliff. There it was – a narrow path leading up the side.

"It will take him at least fifteen minutes to reach the altar." Marius stepped back toward the trail. "If we head down now—"

"No." Rachel gripped his arm, pulling him back.

What was she doing?

"We can make it, *querida*. We just need to move!"

"That trail could lead to nothing." Her face was ashen. Her lips stumbled quickly over her words. "Boulders hemming us in, water blocking… a trail that falls to pieces. We might not get there in time."

Marius knew Rachel's fears were legitimate. Still, he shook his head.

"It's our only hope. We have to try. And we have to leave now!"

But Rachel wasn't listening. She was looking north along the cliff they had just climbed, which ran parallel to the opposite ridge until it turned, widening the gap. She lifted her binoculars, focused on a place in the distance and then reached for the map, studying it with trembling hands.

"What is it? Another way down?" He glanced at the topo, but saw nothing – only dark overlapping lines to suggest sharp, unyielding cliffs.

"No, here." She tapped the map. "You need to go here while I follow José down the trail."

"Rachel, no—"

"Your rifle, Marius." Her eyes filled with tears. She tried to blink them away. "You'll be in range."

"No. Rachel, I can't. Look at me." He held up a shaking hand. "I'm like a leaf in the wind."

"You can." She grasped his hands, pleading. "You have to. There's a good chance I won't make it in time – you know that."

"I could hit Danny." His voice was hoarse.

"You won't. Please." Her eyes were tortured. In them he saw the hell she imagined – arriving at the clearing too late, Danny cold and still, Victor's knife wet with innocent blood. He resisted the image, but it wouldn't let go.

"Please," she repeated. She whispered against his cheek. "Please, Marius. Don't let him do this to my son."

"*Raquel…*"

She pulled away. "You saved my life in this canyon. You can save his too." She turned and disappeared down the trail with José close behind.

Marius fought every instinct in his body by not following her. Instead, he obeyed her instincts, turning north along a trail that passed through thick groupings of trees and boulders, heavily shadowed in the pale light of approaching dusk.

Please, God, don't let this be a mistake!

But he worried with each step. What if Rachel moved too quickly down the switchback? She could lose her footing on the trail, plummeting to the rocky canyon below. But he had not prevented her fall last spring, even though he had been right by her side. Worse still, he knew she cared nothing for her own life right now beyond its usefulness in stopping Victor.

It took almost ten minutes to reach the spot Rachel had pointed out on the map. When Marius emerged from the trees, he immediately trained his binoculars on the western ridge. Victor and Danny were nowhere in sight. Looking at the canyon below only frustrated him. He couldn't see the trail Rachel had descended or the one she would climb on the opposite cliff.

He couldn't worry about that now. He needed to find a flat piece of ground with a clear view of the altar. A few paces to the west, he found it. Dropping his pack to the ground, he tried not to think about the last marksmanship practice he had – or how sandbags, nonliving targets and a trainer standing over his shoulder made that experience in no way comparable to this one. Still he quickly got to work, brushing the ground free of rocks and brush.

Marius lifted his binoculars and focused on the altar, gauging it to be about 600 meters away. His hands shook as he lowered them.

He took a deep breath in and out. Then he made himself do it again, four times.

You've done it before, he told himself.

He took a few seconds, gauging the wind. Pulling the AR15 off his shoulder, he pulled the protective cap off the scope and went through a quick visual check, longing for a night-vision sight in the quickening twilight. This wouldn't work if the sun dipped much lower behind the ridge. He pushed that thought away.

Empty your mind, he told himself. *Don't think about it, just prepare.*

He lowered himself to the ground and lay flat on his stomach, his feet pointing out, shoulder width apart as he positioned his rifle and leaned his left arm against his backpack – a poor substitute for sandbags. He checked his line of sight and bullet path and adjusted the rifle, placing the butt against his firing shoulder and grasping the pistol grip as he lowered his right elbow to the ground. Scooting slightly backward, he brought his shoulders level with his feet and adjusted his forearms to a vertical position so they wouldn't shake. Peering through the scope again, he adjusted his position again until the altar was naturally just below his crosshairs.

Then he went through the whole process again, checking his feet, shoulders, grip and arm position, breathing in and out, checking his sight picture.

Magnified, the altar looked different than it had on first appearance. It had sharp angles on the south and east ends – almost forty-five degrees toward the ground, like a man-made table. He could not see the west edge, but the southern side was more graded, curving down like a small slide, sloping toward the cliff's edge, which dropped at least 70 meters to the canyon below. He checked his radio again, wishing feverishly that someone would hear his signal, dropping in to save Danny with a helicopter full of agents and firepower.

But his hopes were in vain. His message elicited no response from base camp. He was forced to wait, rechecking his position while trying in vain to relax his body, preparing for the task to come.

He didn't have to wait long. Victor was there, visible through the trees in short bursts, dragging Danny behind him.

At the edge of the clearing, Danny stumbled and fell, lying heartbreakingly still until Victor yanked him up again. Marius's stomach recoiled as he took in Danny's appearance – his expression bleak and closed down, his clothes stained, his face covered with dirt and blood. He took three more steps then stumbled again. This time Victor picked him up, throwing him over his shoulder as he limped into the clearing and toward the altar.

Marius dropped the binoculars and refocused through the rifle scope, going through each step of preparation again. He didn't know or care how long Victor planned to make his abominable ritual last. If he had a clear shot, he was going to take it. The sooner the better.

But he had not counted on Victor holding Danny so close, cradling his head in the crook of one arm with his knees bent over the other, creating a human shield with Rachel's son. It forced Marius into painful inactivity for several long minutes, the pad at the tip of his trigger finger holding, but itching to pull.

Behind the ridge, the sun was dipping below the horizon, bleeding red across the sky. Victor turned to watch. As the sky darkened with palpable evil, his body twitched. He threw back his head and swayed, his upturned lips moving as Danny lay limp in his arms, either unconscious or too afraid to move.

Victor lowered Danny to the mesa and curled over him. He pulled out his knife, holding it high above his head where it seemed to pulse against the sunset, sending an electric current through the air that jolted Marius from scalp to toe.

Stand up! Marius thought.

Though his cross hairs were trained on Victor's forehead, his chance of hitting Danny was too high to risk. Their heads were only inches apart. At this distance, even being off by one tenth of an inch could make him miss his target.

But soon twilight would make it impossible for him to risk it at all.

Waiting was torture. Acting too quickly would be worse. Marius had to rely on his training. He couldn't think about who or why, or what would happen if he failed.

Nothing exists but the target.

Just then, Victor turned sharply toward the south, his head low like an animal, his body still curled over Danny. Marius knew what he saw – someone breaking through the trees. It must be Rachel, her maternal strength propelling her to pass over the trails with speed and agility that belied human ability. But Marius couldn't afford to lift his eye from the scope to make sure. Victor was raising his knife again, pointing it toward Danny as he held out his other hand, warning Rachel to stay back. He yelled something incomprehensible, his eyes glazed as he prepared to strike.

Marius couldn't wait. He had to act now. Whatever words Rachel was using to plead for her son's life would not penetrate the feathered plumage Victor had donned in his mind, transmuting himself into a creature beyond reason.

He closed his eyes and opened them, bringing the front sight into focus with his dominant eye, aligning it with the crosshairs. He drew in his breath and let it out, waiting for a place between breaths so he would not shake and miss his target. He had one chance. He could not miss. Victor stretched up toward the sky, lifting the knife with both hands as he prepared to strike.

Marius squeezed the trigger.

In the second it took his bullet to travel from one ridge to the other, Rachel had leaped forward, crossing his sight line as she pushed Danny out of Victor's reach. Marius saw it all in slow motion – Danny tumbling over the side of the altar and rolling precariously close to the edge, Rachel's body flinching with impact, her blood like a burst of red smoke against the night, and Victor's head snapping back, his mouth open in a scream of rage as the bullet penetrated his heart. They both slumped to the ground. Marius could do nothing but watch in horror. And as the shot echoed against the canyon walls, he pushed back from his rifle blindly, rolled away and threw up.

44

PHOENIX CHILDREN'S HOSPITAL was a paradox. Its exterior was painted red and purple and crowned with a large childish handprint with a heart in its palm. On the sidewalks, colorful paw prints led from the parking garage to the lobby, giving anxious children a momentary distraction from the illnesses that waged war within. Doctors and nurses dressed in bright scrubs covered with cartoon characters – likely to embarrass adolescent patients as much as they delighted the younger ones – and were armed with sugar-free gum, knock-knock jokes and disappearing coin tricks alongside their stethoscopes, latex gloves and syringes.

But sun-colored walls and a toy-filled gift shop could not distract adults from the dismal purpose of such a place – to heal wounds that should never have been caused, illnesses that human reason said should be reserved for those who were old and wise enough for perspective or resignation. Soul-sick parents followed those bright paw prints more than anyone else, wishing away whatever had brought them through these sliding doors. Often convinced that injury or illness might have been prevented with more vigilance, they spent their darkest hours wakeful and besieged with guilt at the side of their child's bed.

Marius was a childless parent. Being in such a place must have reminded him of his own loss, all those years ago, but he had come anyway, walking past paw prints and through bright hallways to find his way to Danny's room on the third floor. He entered quietly, stopping just inside the door to study the figure occupying such a small part of his hospital bed.

Afternoon sunlight passed through the blinds, painting lines on the floor and climbing up Marius's body as he took another step into the room. His face was somber, his eyes glossy and red-rimmed. Danny flinched at the sound of his footstep, his eyes wide as he turned from the wall to stare at his visitor with open fear.

"Shhh. It's okay." Rachel rose from her chair in the corner, hoping to head off Danny's panic attack before it could begin. He reached for her fingers, squeezing them hard without taking his eyes off the stranger.

"It's okay. This is Marius, Danny." Rachel swallowed a knot. "He's my... He helped..."

She stopped and looked up helplessly. Just holding Marius's handsome gaze provoked a fresh batch of tears. He nodded, a sad smile tugging at his lips. She knew he understood. She didn't want to introduce him as a friend. That had been Victor's label too. And she couldn't tell Danny that this man had saved his life in the canyon. Right now Danny couldn't even hear words like *canyon*, *Mexico* or *rescue* without falling into complete panic or – worse – retreating into his own dark thoughts.

So, what could she say? Not the truth – that Marius was the love of her life, that her heart never felt whole until he walked in the room and that she could never, ever repay him for what he had done for Danny. These were the truths that beat with her pulse, but they were also tragically immaterial now that her son was within reach and needing every drop of energy she had to give. Danny was alive – breathing in and out, though broken, bruised and dehydrated. He had survived – and would continue to survive, she vowed, despite the trauma whirling like a hurricane inside his fragile mind.

But panic would not be deflected this time. Danny began to shake. His shadowed eyes wider still as he pushed himself back against the pillow, willing himself, it seemed, to fade against the white sheet – a smooth, blank camouflage that hands could not grasp or steal or hurt. His breath came out in short bursts, his small chest heaving, his skin beading up with sweat.

Marius looked stricken, gray as ashes. "I'll go."

"Can you wait outside for me?" Rachel lowered the bed rail and climbed up to draw Danny close. Her injured shoulder screamed in protest, but she bit back the pain. Marius nodded and left, quietly pulling the door closed behind him. Rachel began to rock and sing, praying that sleep would come soon to grant Danny at least a few hours of peace.

ଔ

MARIUS LEANED against the corridor wall, his heart pummeling his ribcage.

It's over, he kept telling himself last night. *It's over. It's over.*

After the torment of thinking he had killed Rachel, he had stumbled through the darkness, desperate for the radio signal that sidestepped him at every turn. Finally he heard the beautiful beat of helicopter blades against the black sky and then the sweetest sound – static-shrouded words through his radio. Danny and Rachel were being loaded onto the chopper – he with a broken arm and she with a clean bullet wound through the soft tissue of her shoulder.

It's over. Those two words had been Marius's grateful mantra ever since.

But it wasn't over.

Danny's reaction to his visit made him wonder if it ever would be.

He waited twenty minutes outside his door, hearing Rachel's soothing voice as she sang Danny song after song. Then she stopped and he held his breath, imagining her doing the same as she carefully climbed off his bed. He had seen the pain she was masking – the paleness of her face, the tightening of her lips as she moved – and was again flooded with guilt. He was responsible.

Heavy footsteps along the corridor made Marius turn. Craig was walking toward him. Recognition made him falter, then he picked up speed, coming at Marius with his arms raised, his eyes blazing.

"You shot my wife!"

Marius fended off the attack, pushing Craig back with more force than necessary. His voice was low, but a vein of hot rage pulsed against his temple. "You threw away the privilege of calling her that, don't you think?"

"You could have killed her," Craig said through gritted teeth. "You could have killed my son. It's a miracle you didn't."

Marius lowered his arms, losing the will to fight.

"I'll agree with you there," he muttered.

Craig continued, unabated. "As it is, she has nerve damage. Did you know that? She's only patched up temporarily. She needs surgery, but won't ever regain full range of motion."

"I'll gladly take responsibility wherever it's deserved." Marius moved closer, his voice lower still with fresh anger. "But it was you who lost Danny at the arena – and it was your friend who kidnapped him – someone Rachel would never have been forced to lean on, had you been the husband she deserved."

Craig curled his lip. "A man who turned out to be from *your* country, following some idiotic ancient Mexican religion—"

Rachel interrupted, emerging from Danny's room and closing the door behind her. "Would you keep your voice down?" She stepped between them, crossing her arms as she turned to face Craig. "Danny just fell asleep. Do you want to wake him again?"

He dropped his arms. "No."

"You honestly think you can lay Victor's crimes at the feet of *race*, Craig?" she asked sharply. "You think he wouldn't have found motivation wherever he wanted it – twisting folklore from Celtic or Egyptian or Greek history to make a god of himself?"

Craig scowled. "That doesn't…" He trailed off when a young nurse passed by, watching them with round eyes.

"Marius saved Danny's life," Rachel said. "Let's be clear on that point, because it's something I will never forget – something you should never forget."

"Rachel—"

"I'm to blame for getting in the way of his bullet." Her voice shook. Marius crossed his arms, resisting the impulse to reach for her. "I didn't know if he was in position or not. I saw that Victor was too far into his warped fantasy…" She took a controlled breath. "I knew he couldn't be stopped, so I ran. I didn't think. I pushed Danny out of the way and – by the grace of God – he didn't go over the edge. It would have been my fault if he did."

She swayed and Marius didn't stop himself this time. He pulled her against him, vowing that he would be her rock.

"We don't have to talk about that now." His voice was soft, but he focused on Craig, daring him to disagree. "You need to rest while Danny rests," he told Rachel. "Don't you think?"

Craig rubbed one hand over his stubbled chin. "He's right, Rach," he said. "I was out of line. I'm sorry." He reached out his hand. Marius shook it.

"I'll rest if you sit with Danny for a while." Rachel frowned. "I don't think he'll sleep for long."

"Can I drive you home for a few hours?" Marius asked.

She shook her head. "Melissa picked up clothes for me. She's getting a hotel room across the street. Would you take me there?"

She returned to Danny's room to retrieve her bag, carefully kissing his forehead before joining Marius in the hallway. Her pace grew slower as they walked the length of the corridor to the elevators. He suspected only extreme exhaustion and pain were making her leave Danny's side. She was a stubborn, amazing woman.

"Do you have prescriptions that need filling?" he asked.

"Melissa will have them."

The hotel was just west of the hospital. Melissa greeted them somberly as Marius helped Rachel through the door.

"If she doesn't rest, she'll end up back in the hospital," he told Melissa quietly. She nodded, reaching for the pain medicine. Marius waited in the hallway while she helped Rachel into bed. After ten minutes, she came out, motioning him back inside.

"She insists I go to the hospital to help Craig with Danny."

Marius frowned. "He can handle it. Doesn't she need you more right now?"

Melissa's smile was brief. "It's a mother thing. I'm sure I would do the same thing in her shoes." She tucked her purse under her arm. "Will you stay with her?"

"Of course."

Melissa nodded, heading toward the door. She stopped and turned back, her eyes wet.

"Thank you." Her voice was barely above a whisper. "For saving Danny. Thank you for saving them both."

He nodded, a familiar knot in his throat.

For the next two hours, Marius sat in the corner of the darkened hotel room, mostly content to watch Rachel sleep. The even rise and fall of her chest was more comforting than he would have thought possible. His thoughts wandered to the events of the night before.

Sometime after the helicopter carried Rachel and Danny to the hospital in Chihuahua, another arrived – searching out Marius's lonely position on one ridge and then turning to the other, where Victor's body still lay sprawled beside the altar. Agents poured out of the helicopter to preserve the scene, taping it off, positioning lights, snapping pictures.

Marius stood at the edge of it all. He didn't want to examine the crime scene. His eyes were instead focused on the black plateau below the ridge. Moonlight revealed a distinct T-shaped meadow. Its western tip was the site of Libby's grave. He had no doubt that Mary Ellen Potter and Jonas Flynn were buried there as well, probably at the northern and eastern ends. It was something he and Rachel couldn't see when they searched the area, the adjacent peak blocking their view of the ridge and the altar. But if they had known then about the grave in Paquime and the T-shaped ball court...

For a moment his mind whirled with the things they had learned too late and the things they had learned just in time. He began to shake more violently than he had all evening.

"I'm ready to leave," he told the helicopter pilot. Back at base camp, Marius and José were slapped on the back and asked to retell the evening's dramatic rescue. Marius had no qualms about disappointing them. Instead, he asked for permission to check on Agent Mueller and her son at the hospital. His request was declined. He spent the rest of the evening debriefing Graham and several higher-ups in the Federal Police. It was close to midnight by the time they released him with orders to avoid the rabid media in Creel, and to report to the FBI field office in Phoenix the following day for a more thorough debriefing. The plan suited him just fine when he arrived at the Chihuahua hospital Sunday morning only to learn that the Mueller family had already been flown back to the states.

"Marius."

He started, sitting up in his chair. "I'm here." He groped in the dark for Rachel's hand, realizing he must have dozed off.

"Come here," she said softly. Marius gladly shifted to the bed, where he carefully wrapped his arms around her. Peace washed over him, just by the weight of her head on his shoulder.

45

MARIUS STAYED in Phoenix for a week, dividing his time between the Bureau office and the hospital while Rachel steadily recovered from her gunshot wound. Though doctors urged her to have surgery as soon as possible, she insisted on waiting. They guaranteed nothing but the hope of greater range of motion and that wasn't something she was willing to trade for Danny's peace of mind. For now she was content to devote whatever energy she had to her son, who continued to struggle, the veil of post-traumatic stress covering both his waking and sleeping hours like a shroud.

His nightmares were especially bad, dragging him back to the canyon in painful detail. Rachel had learned early in the week that she alone could do little to comfort him when he woke from one. She had her own accident in the canyon, the psychiatrist explained, and Danny knew it. When he awoke and found her at his bedside, he was not always able to pull himself toward reality, instead drawing his fears for her safety into the waking nightmare, making them even more severe. They quickly learned that Craig's presence was the best remedy, his deep, familiar voice calming their son more quickly than anything else.

Craig surprised Rachel by adapting so well to whatever role the doctor suggested. Her heart warmed at the sight of Danny wrapped in his father's arms as he rocked him back and forth. It was something Craig hadn't done since the first weeks of his son's life. When he went a step further, taking a leave of absence from the firm for a few weeks, Rachel felt both gratitude and relief. They were united in this, at least – Danny's recovery was more important than anything else.

While nightmares plagued his nights, it was Danny's behavior during the day that concerned Rachel the most. Smiles were a thing of the past. His new somber countenance was sadly fixed in situations that once would have spurred laughter, embarrassment or even juvenile scorn. Rachel would have given anything to hear him whine or complain of boredom. He still didn't respond well to visitors either – not his grandfather, friends from school or even his cousins could rouse him to engage in play or conversation. Aside from Rachel and Craig, Melissa was the only one welcome in his room. But he showed special fear toward any dark-haired male. Whether a doctor, nurse or technician, his reaction was the same he had shown to Marius on Sunday. The doctor told Rachel and Craig this was also in keeping with PTSD – his devastated mind fearing people with features even vaguely similar to Victor's.

"It's all compounded by his initial trust of his kidnapper," she said. "They had a relationship. Danny thought he knew and understood him. After something like this, even adults will doubt their ability to distinguish true friends from false ones. In a child of eight, those feelings are immeasurably higher. Eventually we'll use cognitive behavior therapy, role-playing and relaxation techniques to help Danny move past these fears. For now, though, we simply reassign people who match that description away from his care. Emphasis needs to be placed on making Danny feel safe, free from outside stressors and secure in his environment – both at the hospital and at home."

Rachel had collided with Marius in the corridor after that conversation, lost in her tortured thoughts, intent only on finding a place where she could privately let loose tears of sorrow and rage.

"In here," Marius said. They entered a small family waiting room that was thankfully empty and Rachel spent the next fifteen minutes shaking in his arms, her tears coming in violent waves that made speech impossible. When she could, she repeated the doctor's words.

"Danny shouldn't be dealing with any of this," she said. "He should be playing video games, sneaking cookies – at worst, worrying about a strict teacher or a schoolyard bully."

Marius smoothed her hair from her face, listening.

"I failed him miserably. How could I have let that man into our home? Into our lives? I would have let him take Danny to that hockey game himself – I would have handed over my son to that monster with complete trust—"

"Rachel, you can't do this to yourself."

"Why? Why can't I?" She pulled away from his wet shirt front. "I'm his mother. I'm supposed to have instincts. I'm supposed to guard him from danger. Instead, I was so caught up in my own life that I welcomed it through the front door."

"That's not fair," he said. "You were going through a tough time and Victor knew it. He manipulated the situation to make himself seem like a safe shoulder to lean on. He was a master deceiver – patient and calculating. Using his charm as a weapon."

Rachel remembered those same descriptions used for Tezcatlipoca. He had been charming, a seducer of women, masterful at playing both sides of an issue and causing turmoil to his own benefit.

When Devlin visited her yesterday, she said agents had found pictures in Victor's home. Her picture and Craig's – from before they knew him.

"Your picture was labeled *Xochiquetzal*. Craig's was labeled *Tlaloc*. Do you know what that means?"

Rachel struggled to find her voice. "Tlaloc was the Aztec god of thunder, fertility. He was Tezcatlipoca's mortal enemy. Xochiquetzal was goddess of love, motherhood." She choked on the last word. It took her several minutes to continue. "Tezcatlipoca seduced her from Tlaloc."

Devlin reached out, uncharacteristically gentle as she squeezed Rachel's hand. "You were his target all along – the member of law enforcement he kept close."

Rachel nodded. Now she understood all his calls while she was in Mexico, why she caught him rattling her office door, every subtle attempt he made at getting her to talk about the case.

When she told Marius about Devlin's visit, he pulled her against his chest – the only place she felt the weight of her pain lessen. "He pulled all of you into his sick fantasy."

"But if he planned to take Danny all along, why the elaborate scheme – cancelling on the hockey game only to show up and take him anyway?"

Marius sighed. "He thought he wouldn't be caught. It was his alibi."

And I didn't see—"

He shook his head. "You'll understand in time, *querida*, just like you've seen it in mothers of other victims. Your guilt is false – one of a madman's most evil tricks. It can eat away at you if you don't put it in its place and accept what's even harder to face. It was out of your control. You were a victim too, helpless to stop this."

Rachel took a deep breath and thought about Samantha's mother, who wished she had kept her daughter from college, competition, experience – from life itself, just to ensure her safety.

"Danny would not have survived without you," Marius said. "You had a chance few victims have – to take action and be part of the rescue. It may not mean much now, but in time it will."

They sat together for five more minutes until responsibility forced Rachel to rise and wipe her face. She needed to get back to Danny's room.

"I brought him something." Marius handed over a small package bearing the logo of a nearby bookstore. Rachel reached inside, smiling as she pulled out a small book.

"*Danny the Champion of the World*," she read.

"I thought he could use some – reassurance." Marius's voice was hoarse. Rachel nodded, her own voice lost to emotion. She had read it as a child – the story of one boy's small victory over injustice.

"Thank you," she finally managed.

He walked her back to Danny's door.

"I need to run an errand." He squeezed her hand. Rachel knew it was an excuse. Danny wouldn't welcome him inside and he didn't want her to feel guilty over it.

"He'll know all you've done for him," she told him. "Someday, when he's able to understand."

ಞ

MARIUS FLEW back to Chihuahua on Saturday. As he walked through the airport, he was greeted steadily by strangers who recognized his face from the newspapers. He was a hero now, the man who had rescued the American boy, and everyone wanted to buy him a beer.

Danny was still in the hospital when he boarded the plane in Phoenix. The doctors looked at the possibility of release every day – his mental state a much greater concern than his physical now that dehydration was no longer an issue and his broken arm was healing. As much as Marius wanted to remain close to Rachel, he knew separation was inevitable. He had to face the real world. He had to report back to work. He saw little of her anyway and the possibility of Danny being comfortable with his presence seemed light years away.

Before even reaching his desk Monday morning, Marius received word that the U.S. government had dismissed charges against Agent Cruces, handing him back over to his own country – his own agency, specifically – with stern admonitions regarding his misconduct. His daughter had been placed in Arizona's foster care system pending their investigation of abuse charges – an issue complicated by her status as a member of the Apache nation. Johnny vowed to fight for custody, but for now was left with little to do but cool his heels on unpaid leave while the PFM decided what discipline was warranted.

Marius wasn't ready to face his old friend yet. He wondered if he ever would be. He was angry that Johnny had not confided in him and angry his prejudices had led him to take custody matters into his own hands. But most of all, he was angry that his personal agenda had interfered with the communication of vital evidence – information that would likely have led to Katseli's capture before he got his hands on Danny. It wasn't a decision he would easily forgive – and one that would irrevocably change their friendship.

It took a week for him to settle back into a routine, writing his report on the rescue, organizing a team to return to the canyon to look for the graves of Mary Ellen Potter and Jonas Flynn, and reviewing personnel files for Johnny's replacement. He also needed to find time for an agency psychiatric evaluation – mandatory whenever an agent shot and killed a suspect, and probably not unwarranted, he realized, considering what little interest he had in his job this week.

He and Rachel usually spoke once a day by phone, though the time varied and their conversations were inevitably brief. Danny had been released from the hospital on Wednesday and the results were not encouraging. His nightmares increased at home, his anxiety leading to repetitive rituals – checking locks, washing his hands over and over, vomiting. Rachel told him she had to box up all of Danny's action figures. He had been using them to recreate the altar scene again and again, his face rigid, his breath ragged after only a few minutes of these compulsive reenactments. Though the psychiatrist was not surprised by this behavior, it had clearly unsettled Rachel. He could hear the fatigue in her voice and wondered if she was getting any sleep – and how her body was supposed to heal under such duress.

"How has he been today?" Marius asked last night.

Rachel said nothing and Marius felt an acidic jolt in his stomach. A sixth sense. She was about to tell him something he didn't want to hear.

"What is it?"

Rachel cleared her throat.

"Craig's moving back in with us," she said. "Into the guest room next to Danny's," she added firmly, "just until things get better."

Marius swallowed a knot. He didn't know what to say – everything that came to mind was selfish.

"He has been here so much anyway," Rachel continued. "Danny begins to deteriorate as soon as he leaves and several times I've had to call him to come back, just about the time he reached the apartment. I haven't been able to sleep and…" She broke off.

Marius understood. She was always careful to not add to his guilt over her gunshot wound.

"Is Melissa still there?" he asked.

"She went home for a few days. She'll be back this weekend."

He wanted to ask – *How long?* How soon would Danny be better? Why couldn't they go to Cottonwood instead? But he knew what her answers would be. There were no timetables, only priorities and sacrifices to be made.

"He could improve within weeks." She tried, but failed to brighten her voice. "Maybe months, realistically. The doctor said it can take years to recover, but I don't think…" She cleared her throat again. "We're going to do whatever it takes to help him feel safe as soon as possible."

"*Raquel…*" He wished he could touch her, hold her. "Will Danny understand? Won't he think his father has moved back in for good?"

"I told him it was just until he was feeling better, but I don't know what penetrates lately."

"With Craig in the house, so recently wanting to reconcile…"

"Marius, you do understand, don't you? This is all about Danny. I can't be anything right now but a mother – not an agent, not a wife. Not a lover either – just Danny's mom."

"I'm not asking for anything from you, *querida*," he said, anguished. "I just… I just wish I was the one who could be there for you to lean on."

She was quiet for a moment. Marius shouldn't have voiced his fears.

"I do too," she said. "But we both know that's not possible right now."

The defeat in her voice scared him.

"I'm sorry," he said. "Just forget everything I said, okay? You can't look at the future right now, I understand that. Just focus on Danny. Do what you need to do. Everything else can wait for another day."

"I've never been good at that," she said. "I've always had to see what road I was facing. It was one of the hardest things about the divorce and now…" Her voice caught. "This is so much worse – so much darker."

He wanted to be her light – the bright place at the end of this nightmare. But he knew enough to hold his tongue. Rachel's love had never been needy – pulling, grasping or jealous. He would gladly expect nothing but the joy of watching her move to a safer, happier place. But he knew Rachel. She couldn't just take and not give back. He was afraid it would bleed her of who she was, twisting this beautiful thing between them into something choked with guilt and regret.

That was the night his own nightmares began to intensify, leaving him sweating and breathless in the dead of night, still convinced that Rachel and Danny were lost in the canyon.

"Post-traumatic stress is almost inevitable in your case," the agency therapist told him. "Fifty to seventy-five percent of people involved in disaster experience some level of PTS. As central as you were to this rescue, it was unlikely you would escape."

Marius half-heartedly promised to schedule a follow-up appointment with the therapist, hoping to at least report decreased symptoms by the time it rolled around. Meanwhile, he planned to return to Arizona within a couple of weeks. He needed to see Rachel and lay aside his growing fears.

But nothing had gone as planned. Five days after learning about Craig and Rachel's new living arrangements, Marius's father had a heart attack.

Waiting in the hospital lounge in Sonora, Marius felt numb but for the added weight of guilt. He had neglected and disappointed his father, always putting off the conversation about assuming management of the ranch. As he sat alone, hour after hour, his mind searched for solutions. He promised himself that if his father lived, he would find a way to make things right.

Marius's prayers were answered. Julian Suarez survived the attack and was well enough to go back to his beloved ranch two weeks later. But the cardiologist warned Marius that a drastic change in his father's lifestyle was vital. Julian was too weak to continue as he had.

Marius had only hesitated internally before accepting his filial duty. If not for commitments of the heart that drew him farther north than the

Sonoran ranch, he might have seen it as a sign, combined with his jaded attitude toward agency service, that ranch life was just what he needed. He asked to be placed on indefinite leave rather than for early retirement. His calls to Rachel became less regular. The isolated ranch had not kept up with communication technology. Phone service was spotty – something Marius hoped to remedy within his first few weeks.

Julian's health had not been the only thing deteriorating in Marius's absence. The ranch was in desperate need of physical and financial attention – perhaps from someone who could use the rigors of labor to help fight the pain lodged in his chest. As he set about putting the ranch back in order, he realized with no small measure of guilt that had his father not suffered the attack, he might have been too late to save it from bankruptcy.

He threw himself into the work at hand, finding strange comfort from knowing that each day presented more than could reasonably be accomplished. He watched days give way to weeks and then months. He hired new hands – some who had to be fired and replaced, others who surprised him with their work ethic. He spent his nights reworking the books, found new buyers and made a five-year plan for buying more cattle. He was thankful for Anna's hard work and the simple joy of watching her little boy play. This ranch was too isolated for them both, he thought, but he was glad they were here all the same, unable to imagine adding household chores and cooking to his list of chores.

His father continued to convalesce, spending much of his time in his rocking chair on the porch, his old Bible open in his lap. Marius's hope for improvement in his father's stamina slowly dissipated. Julian had given the ranch all he had. Now he would only watch it survive under his son's guidance. He accepted his diminished role, at least, and remained kind and gentle, giving thanks to God and Marius for his blessings.

"What would I do without you, *Mijo*?" he asked almost daily.

Whenever Marius called Rachel, he learned Danny was showing only small signs of improvement. As one problem tapered off, another surfaced. He had barely been able to finish the school year with a homebound tutoring program. Now she worried he would not make enough progress over the summer to rejoin his classmates in the fall.

"I think of you every moment," she told him quietly. Her voice broke through the lousy phone connection. It wasn't bad enough to disguise the growing resignation in her voice.

"I'll find a way to leave the ranch soon," he promised.

If just for a couple of days. He needed to see her again.

It didn't happen until early August. Rachel called before noon to tell him Danny was back in the hospital. He had an extreme panic attack, she said, his heart beating so fast and his level of agitation so high, Rachel had rushed him to the emergency room.

Marius had left his father in Anna's care and arrived at the hospital late that evening, his plane barely touching down at Sky Harbor before a violent monsoon blew into the valley. The rain fell in visible waves, riding on the wind as it tugged at the stronger trees and snapped the weaker. He splashed through ankle deep water to reach the hospital's entrance. When Rachel saw him coming down the corridor, she ran to greet him, hugging him tightly, mindless of his wet clothes.

"How is he?"

"Sleeping finally." She glanced behind her. "Craig's just gone to call his mother. He'll be back in a minute and we can find a place to talk."

It was surreal. Months had passed and yet they stood just where they had before. Nothing had changed. Danny was sick, Rachel was overwhelmed and Craig was lurking somewhere in the periphery.

And then there was Marius. What role did he play in this drama? The shoulder to cry on at irregular intervals? The stranger, too frightening to befriend this troubled little boy? Or the outsider, pushed or pulled like the trees in the storm, ready to bend or snap?

Resentment had no place in his heart, but he wondered if it threatened, standing in line behind fear and helplessness. He had no choice but to go back to the ranch tomorrow and yet Rachel was here. For the first time, Marius recognized that pure anger threatened more than anything else. It wasn't fair – not any of it.

Late that night while Danny slept with his father stretched out in a recliner by his side, Rachel found Marius in the family waiting room. She sat down beside him, looking exhausted and more life-weary than she ever had. He threaded his fingers through hers, kissing them. She was beautiful, in spite of it all. The desire to stay with her surged through him like a physical ache.

"How long can you do this, *querida*?" he asked softly.

"I don't know. As long as I have to."

His mind swirled with questions. What more could be done? Would different doctors have better ideas? What therapies had not yet been tried?

But he didn't ask them. It was his instinct to try to fix things, but Rachel would have already asked all of these questions – had likely stayed up at night going through each possibility with aching guilt. Patience had been pulled from her every pore, but she had remained strong – a maternal engine that would not be stopped.

"My best dreams are spent imagining moments like this," she said quietly. She stared at their intertwined fingers. "Dreams so simple, so beautiful – I hurt when I wake up. I ache, Marius. I can hardly stand it."

"Rachel—"

"Because no matter which way I twist things, this doesn't work in the real world. And when I come to that conclusion, I can't breathe, and I can't hold my breath either – and I know there's no other option."

He wanted to tell Rachel that they could find a way to make it work – a beautiful place between breaths. But he knew the truth. Any such place was fleeting. Over before it had begun.

"No. I don't accept that." His throat closed over his words. He leaned in, releasing her hands, mindless that his own shook as he pulled her toward him until their foreheads touched. "*Querida*," he whispered. "*Mi vida* – please don't do this."

She closed her eyes, breathing in deeply, memorizing his love. He didn't want her to – he wanted her to see it, to feel it every day.

"I'm not going to let go," he said. "Please don't ask me to. I did that once. I walked away when I should have stayed and fought for this."

Rachel pulled away, touching his face. "I understand very little, love. But I know there are times to hold on and times to let go."

He shook his head. "No. It's still too soon. Eventually you'll see. You deserve a life. You deserve some happiness."

"Please don't say that," she said. "Craig told me he deserved happiness when he had the affair. And even Victor…" She stopped a moment, struggling as if the air had momentarily left her lungs. "Before he died, Victor said that when his sacrifices were complete, we could find happiness too."

"Rachel, you are not Craig. And you're not Victor!"

"Maybe not, but I'll tell you what I am. I'm a woman who almost took Danny from his home for my own chance at happiness. If given the chance, I would have taken it – just to be closer to you."

Marius stilled for a moment, his heart twisting.

"El Paso?" he asked.

"Yes."

"I heard rumors, but didn't let myself believe them."

Rachel said nothing. It seemed like she was trying to hold her breath, just so she wouldn't fall apart.

"You've always put Danny first," he told her. "And that was before any of this – a time when a move like that would not have necessarily been a bad thing."

"For him it would," she said. "And I knew it, deep down. It's what Melissa and I argued about. I knew he wasn't ready for change like that – not so soon after the divorce. But I wanted it anyway – for you and me. I wanted my chance at happiness – just like Craig – just like Victor.

"And that's what we do, isn't it, Marius? We think our own happiness is some kind of God-given right, no matter the consequences, then we sacrifice our kids on that altar, justifying ourselves and leaving them to search through the broken pieces for their own worth."

"Rachel, that's not you," he said. "How can you think that? You love your son more than anyone. You almost died for him."

"Maybe I wasn't supposed to die for him." She looked at the storm beyond the window. "Maybe I'm supposed to live for him."

Marius suddenly wished himself back on the ranch, where the hope of Rachel stayed with him as he worked, ate and dreamed. To be here, watching her push him painfully away was too much to bear. He rose, ready to turn away, but she stopped him, pulling him gently back until she was against his chest, listening to his heart grasp for hers, broken, but still beating.

For the rest of the night they sat together. The storm dwindled outside, now weeping softly against the pane. Marius felt numb. His mind refused to offer any arguments that would stand up to reality.

As the unwelcome fingers of dawn threatened the dark horizon, Rachel rose, still holding his hand. Like him, afraid to let go.

"You need to catch your plane." She kissed him, her lips trembling, her fingers clinging to his skin. When she pulled away, her tears were on his face. "And I need to go check on my son."

As Marius walked away, he told himself it wasn't goodbye. Then later he thought perhaps it had been fitting – that her final words were not about him or their love, but about Danny. Over time, he learned to think of his own son, so tiny when he had died in Carmen's arms, and his heart ached, reminding him that he would give up anything to have him back, even if it meant missing his second chance with Rachel.

But his feelings refused to remain constant, turning this way and that on the lonely ranch. Sometimes beautiful, sometimes bitter. Eventually the hope that Marius promised himself would never fade did just that, pressed under by the responsibilities of life and the distortion of memories. It stayed in his heart, an ache that reared its head to ask, *What if?* He often reached for the phone to ask the question out loud, but always put it down again. Just looking around at the ranch and the growing number of people who depended on its survival made Marius finally acknowledge that Rachel's choices were not completely to blame for their separation. He might fantasize about walking away, but whenever his imagination took him toward his father's rocking chair for a last goodbye, it faded like the morning mist.

When a year had passed since Danny's rescue, Marius did not stop himself from picking up the phone. Still his hand shook as he dialed.

"Hello?" It was Craig.

Marius opened his mouth to speak, but the sound of laughter in the background stopped him. "Hold it down you two, will you?" Craig's voice was light with pleasure as he turned away and tried to muffle the phone. "I can't hear anything! I'm sorry... Hello? Hello?"

So Danny had learned to laugh again. And so had Rachel.

Marius hung up the phone. For a moment, he couldn't breathe. He leaned against the wall and reached for the closest thing, his father's Bible, which he gripped until the world righted itself again. Then he turned and headed back out to the ranch.

 C8

EPILOGUE

HE KNEW he would see her again someday. It was a truth logged in the marrow of his bones – something he had considered with alarm, but more often with a familiar yearning. During his darkest hours, he feared that the moment would be the kind most difficult to bear, beauty marred only by death – a casket the scene of their final goodbye.

Today, when he first spotted her through a veil of dripping flowers, her fingertips trailing languidly through a bubbling fountain, his heart stilled in wonder. Perhaps death had claimed them both. Maybe this was Heaven.

A moment passed while he considered the world around them, the people who passed by, the smog in the distance. This was no dream. So many years had passed between their first and second goodbye. Could it really be that almost as many had passed again?

It was sunny in London today. An early morning shower had come and gone and now the tourists were crowding the throughways, enjoying the afternoon. He had taken advantage too, heading out on foot to Regents Park.

But he wasn't fooled. He had been to London often enough to know another shower was looming. Still, he sent a quiet prayer up to a place beyond the sky, thanking God for the impulse that had directed him along this path – and for the sunlight that filtered through white clouds like a spotlight, focusing on the fountain where she sat.

He walked toward her slowly, his heart beating like the boy he had once been. He wondered what she would think when she looked up. Would she recognize his lined face? His hair, now more salt than pepper? With every step, her face grew clearer, though she was bent over a book. Her hair was cut to the level of her chin, but still curly, frosted with strands of silver. She crossed her legs, moving lithely as ever, making his throat contract.

"Rachel," he said softly.

She looked up, the crease of concentration on her brow passing through confusion until it settled into astonishment.

"Marius?"

She stood quickly, dumping her book as they embraced. For a moment, it all came back – the pain, the heartache, but mostly the joy. When Marius released her, he reached down and picked up her book.

"*Persuasion*." He smiled.

"I'm in England." She took it from him. "It seemed fitting."

They sat down together.

"Were you visiting Spain?" she asked.

"Yes." He could not explain what had drawn him to pause for a few days in London. Until this moment, the decision had perplexed him. Now it felt providential.

"Is your mother…?"

Marius rolled his eyes. "Still causing problems? Yes. Imagine being wakened by a transatlantic phone call from a nursing home administrator who warns you that if your mother doesn't stop harassing the handsome nurses and refusing care from the homely ones, she's going to have to find a new place to live."

Rachel laughed.

"How about you? What are you doing in London?"

She smiled. "I'm here to meet Danny's fiancé."

She explained that Danny had spent the past semester in London on an exchange program, where he had met and fallen in love with a pretty English girl. They were planning a wedding for the following summer after he graduated.

"A doctor?" Marius asked, impressed.

"Clinical pediatric psychiatry is his goal," Rachel said. "When the cloud of PTSD began to disappear for good during high school, he started talking about his desire to make a difference – to study new ways to treat the disorder with more lasting results."

"I'm glad to hear he has done so well. He wrote to me once. Did you know?"

Rachel's eyes widened and she shook her head.

"He wrote to you?" she repeated.

Marius nodded. "A few years ago – probably around the time he graduated from high school, I would think. He said you had taken a trip back to the Copper Canyon together and that he had been happy to create positive memories of such a beautiful place."

Rachel nodded. "That was just before he headed off to Stanford. I was worried when we booked the trip, but relieved once we were there – to see him smiling, able to stand on a trailhead and admire the wonder without fear or panic." She pressed her lips together, then continued. "He asked me about you then. I had told him many times about your role in his rescue, but I think it must have connected in that moment. I had no idea he did anything about it."

Marius nodded. "He seems like a fine young man," he said sincerely. "You must be very proud."

"We are," she said.

Marius held his smile. He had heard rumors in the years following Danny's abduction that the Mueller family had reunited for good. He had not bothered to confirm or deny them, trying to embrace the small measure of peace that was his.

"Where is Craig?" he asked.

Rachel tilted her head over her shoulder. "Back at the hotel."

Marius swallowed hard.

"He – remarried several years ago. His wife is expecting. She's young and a little high strung. This is their second." She shrugged. "Danny loves being a big brother."

Marius nodded, unable to speak for a moment. He saw details between her simple words and wondered which of them were true. He could imagine that she had tried at some point to make it work again with Craig – that Danny's full recovery had been the catalyst to a second and permanent separation. But he didn't know, and he wouldn't ask.

"How is Anna?"

His brow creased. "Anna? She's fine."

Rachel nodded and played with the edges of her book.

"I spoke to Agent Cruces about a year after Danny's abduction," she explained. "I was subpoenaed by the Apache Nation to testify in his guardianship hearing. He told me that you and Anna were planning to marry." She cleared her throat, her eyes meeting his before darting away. "Do you have kids?"

Johnny. Marius wanted to wring his worthless neck.

"No, I don't. Anna does – more than Manuel, I mean." Why couldn't he make sense? He took a steadying breath and hoped she didn't notice how foolish he was behaving. "Johnny was mistaken. We never married. She remarried some years after I took over the ranch."

He didn't tell Rachel he *had* proposed to Anna during one of his darkest hours, but that it hadn't happened until long after Johnny and his daughter were reunited for good. Luckily, Anna had been smarter than he was as they sat on the porch together, watching Manuel ride his small bike in circles.

"I could love you, Marius," she had answered quietly. "And maybe pride is not a good thing in a woman in my position, but I am proud – too proud to want a husband who will always love another."

Marius had kissed her cheek and walked away. After his father's death, he had hired a foreman who came to love Anna to the depth of his soul. They had four children now, including Manuel, who would be a sophomore in college this fall, and were permanent fixtures at the ranch, making it possible for Marius to leave without worry, knowing all was in good hands.

Rachel asked Marius more questions about ranch life – educated questions that made him suspect she had shown the subject more than passing curiosity through the years. He couldn't help smiling. How like her to stay passionate and curious.

"What do you do these days?" he asked.

"I teach. Spanish and history at Yavapai College," she said.

"Let me guess, you bought one of those enormous Victorian houses in Prescott," he said.

"Well it's not enormous," she said. "But it is old – practically falling apart when I bought it."

"And you've spent all your spare time fixing it up."

She smiled. "Yes I have."

Marius had run out of things to ask. The sunlight was ducking behind thickening clouds and they both watched in awkward silence as someone's lost umbrella cartwheeled across their path. Rachel shoved her book inside a large tote bag bearing the Union Flag.

"I have dinner with Danny and Kate tonight," she said, standing up.

Marius supposed that was his cue. He stood too.

"It was nice seeing you, Rachel," he said softly.

"If you're ever in Arizona," she said, "though I don't recommend Prescott on the Fourth of July."

He nodded. For a moment, they looked at each other in silence. Finally, Marius leaned forward and kissed her on the cheek, letting his fingers touch her face for just a moment before letting go.

Rain began to splatter the pavement as he turned and walked away.

"Marius?"

He turned around. She was still standing by the fountain, getting thoroughly soaked. He blinked his eyes against the rain, wondering why she wasn't running for cover like every other woman within sight.

"Yes?" He raised his voice above the din and walked back toward her.

"Have you ever noticed that we're always getting caught in the rain?"

He shook his head. She was right.

"Maybe we should have the good sense to run for cover," he said. His heart began to pound and it was as if half a lifetime passed away. "Do you have time for a cup of coffee?" He offered her his hand. "Or are you in a hurry to get back?"

"No. I mean yes." Rachel smiled and took his hand. "What I mean is – I'm totally free."

ACKNOWLEDGMENTS

If I didn't have wonderful family and friends supporting me, pushing me, giving me space and sometimes whacking me over the head, my stories would never reach the page. I owe them all my heartfelt thanks.

Christy Ford, my sister and this novel's first and most enthusiastic reader. What would I do without you? My sister, Michelle Britton, who is constant and so supportive, thank you both so much. Thanks also to my parents, who first taught me to love reading. I love you all.

My husband, Bryan, who works in the real world, allowing me to follow my dream. I love you. My beautiful children, Drew and Tara, who are and always will be, my most precious works of art – I love you more than I can say.

My reading group – the Pemberley Ladies: Jane Belcher, Judy Boyer, Michelle Britton, Rhonda Burks, Sarah K. Fleming, Linda Forbes, Christy Ford, Sendy Green, Hailey Hastings, Chelsie Phillips, Dawndi Phillips, Bailey Ross, Lara Russell, Martha Russell, Ann Sexton, Vicki Smay and Holly Wagner – thank you so much for your support.

Special thanks also to my nephews, Devon and Wesley, who are such supportive beta readers. Great eye on all those Aztec names, Wes!

Thank you to Tamara Forsyth, my extraordinary proofreader and editor. I really appreciate your eye for detail.

As always, I'm thankful to Josh Groban for keeping my ears and soul happy while I write.

For expertise on law enforcement, my heartfelt thanks to our friend, Sergeant Larry Kenyon, Arizona Department of Public Safety. God bless you.

For medical expertise, my thanks go to Dr. Douglas P. Lyle. Thanks also to Shayne Britton for excellent weapons advice.

For invaluable information about the Copper Canyon, many thanks to M. John Fayhee, author of *Mexico's Copper Canyon Country: A Hiking and Backpacking Guide*. For an amazingly helpful website on the *tonalpohuali* (www.azteccalendar.com), thank you, René Voorburg. Many thanks also to the librarians at the Star Branch of the Ada County Library for support and encouragement.

Most of all, thank you, Lord. I love Your Words best of all.

ABOUT THE AUTHOR

Before writing her debut novel, *Dream of Me,* Jennifer Froelich worked as a freelance writer, editor and ghost writer. A graduate of Arizona State University's Walter Cronkite School of Journalism, she now lives in Idaho with her husband and two children. Find out more at www.jenniferfroelich.com.

Made in the USA
San Bernardino, CA
28 December 2013